A Silken Thread

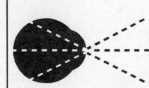

This Large Print Book carries the
Seal of Approval of N.A.V.H.

A Silken Thread

Kim Vogel Sawyer

THORNDIKE PRESS
A part of Gale, a Cengage Company

GALE
A Cengage Company

Farmington Hills, Mich • San Francisco • New York • Waterville, Maine
Meriden, Conn • Mason, Ohio • Chicago

LIBRARY OF CONGRESS CIP DATA ON FILE.
CATALOGUING IN PUBLICATION FOR THIS BOOK
IS AVAILABLE FROM THE LIBRARY OF CONGRESS

ISBN-13: 978-1-4328-6248-0 (hardcover alk. paper)

Published in 2019 by arrangement with WaterBrook, an imprint of Crown Publishing Group, a division of Penguin Random House LLC

Printed in the United States of America
1 2 3 4 5 6 7 23 22 21 20 19

For Connie and John
with appreciation for your southern
hospitality

As ye would that men should do to you,
do ye also to them likewise.

— LUKE 6:31

Dear Reader,
In 2015, my husband and I spent a week in Georgia with some friends. While there, we visited several museums, and in one I came upon a huge photograph with the heading *Atlanta Exposition 1895.* I immediately experienced "author tingles." Before I came home, I purchased a few books about the exposition, and a story began to take shape in my head.

I admit I was nervous about including a thread about racism, even though it was historically accurate for that time and place. It's so easy to offend, and I did not want to do so. I wanted to use the elements of story to show the injustice and unfairness of treating people differently based on differences in appearance.

Talking about racism isn't easy, but it's a topic that needs to be addressed. Racism — bigotry — is ugly. Treating people unkindly because of their skin color, their religious practices, or how much money they have (or don't have) is, simply put, wrong. It contradicts the biblical instruction in Luke 6:31, "As ye would that men should do to you, do ye also to them likewise."

While writing this story, and especially the part about Willie and Quincy's friendship, I couldn't help but think back to my childhood in Garden City, Kansas. My family lived in what we would call today an ethnically diverse neighborhood. All my brother and I knew then was that we had a lot of playmates. And play we did! Our favorite family was the Browns. Of the four children, the middle two — Chipper and Crystal — were just the right ages for Brad and me. We were in and out of each other's house, their aunt was our favorite babysitter, and their Grandma Jennings became like a surrogate grandmother to us.

I will never forget the day my mom, with my brother and me in the back seat of the car, drove past a playground where Chipper was engaged in a football game with several other boys. Brad gasped and exclaimed, "Mommy! Chipper's face is brack [black]!" Not until Brad saw Chipper in a group of white children did he realize his friend's skin color was different from his own.

Because in Brad's eyes, Chipper was just Chipper, his friend.

It may seem simplistic, but I think the key to overcoming bigotry is be-coming acquainted. When we take the time to get to know the *person* underneath the clothes or the skin or whatever else might seem different to us, we discover that most people have commonalities. We all have the same desire Laurel has in the story: to love and be loved, to belong, to matter. God values humanity. As His followers, should we not emulate Him?

I truly hope this story will provide you a few hours of entertainment, and — admittedly — I also hope it helps you view the world a little differently: through God's eyes of love and acceptance.

May God bless you muchly
as you journey with Him,
Kim

1

Sunday, September 1, 1895
Pine Hill neighborhood, Atlanta, Georgia
Laurel Millard

Laurel swung her feet from the armrest of the sofa to the floor and sat up. The book she'd been reading slid from her lap and landed with a soft thud on the faded square of carpet that formed an island in the middle of the scuffed hardwood floor. Ordinarily, retrieving a book — a precious thing to both her and Mama — would take precedence over all else, but the mutter of voices from the porch and the click of a key in the front door stole her attention. Which of her siblings had chosen to disturb Mama's afternoon nap?

The door creaked open, and her brother Alfred, the oldest of the Millard siblings, stepped over the threshold with his usual air of importance. Their sister Nell followed him in. Worry smote Laurel, and she bounded to her feet. There must be a family emergency if both pompous Alfred and strong-minded Nell, who couldn't even sit together on the Millard family pew in the Episcopal church without breaking into an argument midsermon, had come together.

"Alfred, Nell, what —" Laurel's jaw dropped. Eugene, Raymond, and Mayme trailed in behind Nell. Never before had all five of her siblings shown up at the same time, no spouses or children in tow, for a visit. Her knees gave way, and she plopped onto the sofa's center cushion, gaping in both confusion and apprehension.

Alfred fixed his unsmiling brown-eyed gaze on her. "Is Mama sleepin'?"

What else would Mama be doing at three thirty on a Sunday afternoon? Laurel kept the question to herself. Nineteen years her senior, Alfred tended to construe nearly everything she said as insolence. She nodded.

"Good." Alfred flicked his hand at the others, and they removed their light cloaks and hats and draped them on the hall tree beside the door. Nell pressed her finger against her pursed lips, her frown giving a warning, and then they all chose seats — Alfred in what Laurel always called Papa's chair, although she had no memory of her papa sitting in it,

14

Nell in Mama's rocker, Eugene on the round stool in front of Mama's loom, and Raymond and Mayme on either side of Laurel on the sofa.

Her stomach fluttered. Was this how a rabbit cornered by a pack of hungry coyotes felt? Needing to do something to calm her jumping nerves, she leaned forward and reached for the book.

Raymond clamped his hand over her knee and shook his head.

Laurel pointed at the book. "But I only wanted to —"

"Hush." Mayme retrieved the green-fabric-covered volume of Verne's *Cesar Cascabel,* smoothed the rumpled pages, and closed it, then placed it on the table next to the beautiful hand-painted oil lamp Papa had gifted Mama on their last wedding anniversary before his death over fifteen years ago.

The moment Mayme released the book, Alfred cleared his throat. As if it were a secret signal, everyone — Laurel included — folded their hands in their laps and turned their attention on him. He crossed his legs. "We've come about Mama."

Laurel's mouth went dry. "Is somethin' wrong? Is she ill?"

Of course Mama was fine. If she had been

stricken with some sort of disease, Laurel would have noticed. After all, she lived with Mama, worked with her side by side at the loom or on stitching projects, and sat with her in the parlor every evening, taking turns reading aloud from one of the books on their single, overstuffed shelf. It had been only the two of them since Mayme, the closest in age to Laurel, married and moved into her own home ten years ago, so Laurel would know better than anyone the state of Mama's health.

Nell made a sour face. "Of course not, Laurel. Don't be dramatic."

Did she mean more dramatic than all of them swooping in at once? "Then what?"

Alfred bounced his foot. Sunlight from the uncovered parlor windows flashed white on the toe of his highly polished boot. "Mama turns sixty next week."

Laurel wrinkled her nose. "Yes, I know. But she's already told me she doesn't want a party, so if y'all are here to help organize one, then —"

"She's getting up in years" — Alfred, probably viewing her comment as an interruption, gave her a severe look — "and shouldn't be left to take care of the house and yard on her own."

Nell pressed her lips together and tsk-

tsked. "Ideally, she would have a husband to help her." The room was stifling despite the open windows, but even so, Nell's icy stare sent a shiver down Laurel's spine. "Had you not chased off the only prospect, we wouldn't be havin' this conversation."

Would they never forgive her for crying every time Mr. Davis paid Mama a visit? Laurel held her hands wide. "I was barely three years old."

Nell rolled her eyes. "It doesn't matter. After your caterwauling, he abandoned the attempt at courtship, and Mama has been alone to this day."

Eugene, always the quietest of the group and Laurel's favorite of all her siblings, twisted back and forth on the stool. "At her age, it's not likely another chance for marriage will come along." He glanced at Alfred, as if questioning whether he'd gotten his lines right. "So that one chance she had with Mr. Davis . . ."

Laurel gritted her teeth. She couldn't even recall Mr. Davis, let alone her reason for bawling when he looked at her. If Mama hadn't confirmed the story, Laurel would suspect Mayme or Raymond had made it up to have another excuse to torment her.

She had come along late in Mama's life, following the loss of three babies in a row, and the others always accused her of being Mama's favorite. After all these years, she wouldn't change their opinion, so she didn't waste her breath by defending herself. But, oh, how hard to stay silent against the unfair accusation. She pinched a loose strand of hair falling from the nape of her neck and coiled it around her finger.

Eugene seemed to have run out of words, so Laurel turned to Alfred. "What is it you're trying to tell me?"

Alfred uncrossed his legs and leaned forward slightly, his dark brows descending. "Someone will need to care for Mama into her dotage, and we believe the rightful person is you."

Laurel's mouth fell open. She touched her fingertips to her bodice in silent query.

Nell nodded so hard the knot of dark hair atop her head lost a pin. "That's exactly right. Mama risked her life bringing you into this world. She nearly died along with your twin."

Sadness struck with such force that tears stung Laurel's eyes. How could she so deeply mourn someone she'd never met? She'd spent her life missing two important people — her papa and the twin her parents had named Lily.

Nell continued in a strident tone, unaware

of — or, perhaps more accurate, uncon-
cerned by — Laurel's inner pain. "Why, at
forty-two she should have been preparing to
spoil her first grandchildren, but instead she
was suckling you at her breast. You owe her
a debt of gratitude, Laurel, and you can
repay it by agreein' to remain here with
Mama until that day we lay her to rest next
to Papa."

Laurel released a disbelieving laugh. "You
can't mean that."

Mayme folded her arms over her chest
and peered down her nose at Laurel. "Oh,
she does. We all do."

"It only makes sense," Raymond said.
"The rest of us have our own homes."

"And our own families," Mayme added.

Raymond snorted. "You can't expect us
to ignore those responsibilities."

"You can't possibly be that selfish."
Mayme's voice turned wheedling. "Not
after everything you've already cost her."

Laurel looked back and forth from brother
to sister so rapidly her head began to swim.
She held up both hands and closed her eyes.
"Stop. Please . . . be quiet and let me think."

"There's nothing to think about."

She popped her eyes open and met Alfred's stern frown.

"We've given it much thought, discussed

it at length, and all agree this is the best way to ascertain Mama's needs will be met."

"But . . ." Laurel swallowed. What of her needs? Her wants? She'd largely stopped socializing with her girlfriends two years back when they all became so boy besotted it embarrassed her. But since the passage of her eighteenth birthday, she'd often contemplated the joy of becoming a wife and a mother. Why, Mama must be considering Laurel's future, because she'd allowed Patrick Brinkley to call on her. Twice!

Twirling the strand of hair around her finger again, she looked around the room and examined each of her siblings' faces by turn. Was there a hint of understanding in at least one pair of Millard coffee-brown eyes? She saw none, although she suspected if Eugene raised his head and met her gaze, she might witness sympathy from him.

She dropped the strand of hair and blinked back tears. "You really want me to give up on having my own family?"

"For a time, yes." Nell snapped the answer. "It's only right. You're the baby. She doted on you. Now it's her turn to be doted upon."

"And your turn," Mayme said, "to be the doter."

"So that's settled." Alfred slapped his

knees and stretched to his feet. Nell, Eugene, Raymond, and Mayme also stood and moved to the hall tree. While they retrieved their items, Alfred turned a somber look on Laurel. "I trust you to make sure Mama's final years are not spent in loneliness and want. You won't disappoint me, will you?"

Laurel remained seated, her muscles too quivery to support her weight. A part of her rebelled against her siblings' expectations, but Alfred had never vowed to trust her before. The grown-up big brother she'd always tried — and failed — to please now offered her a chance to redeem herself in his eyes.

The hopeful child residing deep inside her shook its head. "No, Alfred. I won't."

Peachtree Street, Atlanta
Langdon Rochester

"Langdon, I am sorely disappointed in you."

Langdon choked back a snort. When was Father not disappointed in him? He maintained his relaxed position on the sofa — head resting on a tufted pillow, feet crossed on the opposite armrest — but angled his face and followed his father's progress from the library's wide doorway to the wingback chairs in front of the cold fireplace. His mind tripped backward through the day's

21

happenings. Church with his parents, during which he'd stayed awake, followed by an insufferably long lunch, during which he'd engaged Mother in cheerful conversation. He'd even denied himself an afternoon cigar. For what reason had Harrison Faulk Rochester found fault with his son today?

His expression distorting into a grimace, Father held both hands toward Langdon. "Look at you. Twenty-three years old, a university graduate, and you have nothing better to do than lie about reading . . . reading . . ." He scowled at the magazine propped against Langdon's stomach. "What is that you've got?"

Langdon turned the *Harper's Weekly* cover toward his father. "It's an older issue — January of '93 — but the article about the International Monetary Conference in Brussels is quite interesting."

Father huffed. "At least you aren't filling your brain with drivel."

Langdon sat up and tossed the magazine aside. Father would have had a conniption if he'd come in while his son was caught up in the serial story about a soldier named Connors. Romantic drivel at its best. Or, as Father would term it, its worst. "If my reading magazines on a Sunday afternoon offends you, Father, I'll gladly choose a book instead." He rose and perused one of the twenty-four floor-to-ceiling bookcases.

Father dropped into one of the chairs and slapped the brocaded armrest. "It isn't your reading on a Sunday afternoon that offends me. Of course Sunday is a day of rest practiced by the religious and nonreligious alike. It's your lazy attitude the remainder of the week causing my indigestion and your mother's fretfulness."

Mother was fretful? Langdon faced his father and folded his arms over his chest. He had shed his suit jacket and unfastened the top buttons of his shirt after the church service. Here it was after four o'clock, and Father still wore every bit of his formal attire, down to the black-and-gray-striped silk tie fashioned in its crisp four-in-hand knot. The collar of his shirt, bound by the tie, bit into his neck and forced the flesh to mushroom above the band of white. So stodgy and stuffy he appeared. Had Father ever been young and blissfully unburdened? Likely not.

Langdon crossed to the second chair and seated himself, taking care to mimic his father's dignified pose. "I only finished with university two and a half months ago. I wasn't aware my enjoying a few weeks of relaxation was a source of angst to Mother."

He ran his hand through his hair, sweeping the thick strands away from his forehead. "What would she have me do instead?"

"Grow up." Father barked the words, then bowed his head and massaged his graying temples with his fingertips.

Langdon gritted his teeth and dug his fingers into the chair's carved handrests. Those weren't Mother's words. Gentle Mother never spoke abruptly. And Father never spoke anything but abruptly. As a matter of fact, it seemed the only time Father spoke to him was to deliver reprimands. While living in university housing, Langdon had decided that since he couldn't please his father, he may as well please himself. But if he truly was causing Mother heartache . . .

Father fixed Langdon with a weary yet firm look. "I tolerated you repeating several classes, which meant an additional year at the university. At your mother's insistence, I've held my tongue when you've come in late night after night, often disheveled and reeking of cigar smoke, and then stayed in bed until noon." He shook his head, his cheeks mottling crimson. "I admit, I am partially to blame. I allowed your mother to overindulge you because you are our only child. But those days are over. You're no longer a child to be pampered. You're a grown man, Langdon. You must behave like one."

"You're six years old, Langdon, old enough to buckle your own shoes."

"You're nine years old, Langdon, too old to cry over a skinned knee."

"You're fifteen years old, Langdon. You will remain at the dinner table and engage in intelligent conversation."

Expectation after expectation rolled through the back of his mind. He'd learned to buckle his shoes, had learned to control his tears, had learned to contribute to conversation around a dinner table. All without ever receiving a word of praise. He swallowed his resentment and forced a disinterested tone. "What is it you want from me, Father?"

The older man stood and glared down at Langdon. "I want assurance that the company I've worked so hard to build will be well cared for into the future." He drew a deep breath that expanded his midsection and strained the buttons of his vest. "Thus, beginning tomorrow, you will rise at six and accompany me to the factory."

"But tomorrow is Labor Day." Although the national holiday recognizing both union and nonunion workers was still relatively new, Father was a stickler for honoring presidential dictates.

Father pinched the bridge of his nose and closed his eyes for a moment. When he opened them, determination gleamed in his blue-gray irises. "Yes, tomorrow is Labor Day, but I will be in the office in the afternoon so my workers may collect their pay envelopes. Payday was already delayed, given the first of the month has fallen on a Sunday. I won't ask them to wait another full day."

"If you'll only be there in the afternoon, why must we rise at six?"

"Because you are sorely out of practice at finding your way to the breakfast table, and you need the opportunity to change your sleeping-late habit." Father sank into his chair. "Beginning tomorrow you will be my apprentice, for lack of a better word, and you will learn every aspect of managing the factory as well as overseeing my rental properties."

Narrowing his gaze, Langdon leaned back in the chair and cupped his chin with his hand. His studies at the university — engineering, accounting, and business management — had been chosen by Father to prepare him to assume ownership of the factory. Langdon had long known his life's course, and he'd accepted it, had even anticipated it. Being in charge of nearly a hundred workers? Having them heed his orders the way he'd always heeded Father's? His chest swelled as he considered the power he would possess.

Of course, he'd hoped for a few more months of holiday before assuming the reins of leadership. But he'd learned to bluff his way through poker games. Playing the dutiful son and dedicated trainee until the time Father released the business into his keeping shouldn't tax him overmuch. He gave a decisive nod. "Very well."

Father's brows pinched. "I'm not finished. Learning to manage my holdings is my expectation of you. Your mother expects something as well. She longs for a grandchild."

Langdon sat up straight. Father couldn't mean —

"Having a wife and children dependent upon you has a way of quickly maturing a man. Thus, I require you to court a young woman. By this time next year, you will be married."

Langdon shot to his feet. He would do most anything for Mother, but saddle him with a wife and squalling babies? Father had gone too far. "And if I choose not to?"

Father shrugged. "I can't force you. It's your decision."

Langdon blew out a relieved breath.

"But I've already put a proviso in my will. If you haven't proven yourself adept at handling the business and settled into family life by September first of next year, your mother's oldest nephew, Timothy, who has been my faithful floor supervisor for the past three years, will become my heir."

2

Workers' quarters on Factory Street, Atlanta
Willie Sharp

Willie carried two steaming bowls to the scarred square table in the corner of the small kitchen. Pa already waited in his chair, a cloth napkin tied around his neck, and a spoon held awkwardly in his left fist. Even after a full four months, his right-handed father didn't do too well using his left hand. Willie didn't mind that Pa scooped up food like a two-year-old, but he hated the napkin hanging across Pa's chest like a baby's bib. But if they didn't use it, Pa would stain up every shirt he owned. Which was worse — having to wear a bib, or always being stained up? He could never decide for sure, and he wouldn't ask Pa to choose.

He placed one bowl in front of his father and put the other at his spot. "No fatback in the beans tonight. I went by the butcher after I collected my pay, but he wasn't open.

Probably takin' advantage of Labor Day. I'll stop there tomorrow on the way home from work and get a pound or two of fatback. And some ham. I know you like ham with your eggs."

Willie talked to Pa even though Pa couldn't talk to him. At least not in understandable words. But sitting in silence was worse than doing all the talking. Besides, seemed like Pa enjoyed the sound of Willie's voice. His eyes always lit up, and most times he nodded or shook his head in response to questions. That was enough encouragement to keep Willie talking.

Willie slid onto his chair and put his hand over Pa's limp fingers. "Let's pray, huh?"

Pa's head bobbed — two short jerks.

Willie bowed his head. "Dear Lord, thank Thee for —"

A firm knock at the door intruded. Probably Mr. Rochester coming to collect the monthly rent, like he always did on payday. Some young fellows from the factory squandered their wages, but Willie always made sure to have the rent ready to hand over. He couldn't risk losing their home. What would happen to Pa then?

He rose and gave Pa's shoulder a gentle squeeze. "Go ahead and eat. God knows we're thankful. I'll see to the door an' be right back." He strode to the pie safe and picked up the stack of coins he'd set aside. He bounced them on his palm on the way to the door. Two gold half eagles and one Morgan silver dollar — eleven dollars in all, a third of his pay. Another third went to food, then half the remaining third to Mrs. Blaricum, the neighbor lady who looked after Pa while Willie was at the factory. It didn't leave much, but they got by, probably because Willie faithfully dropped a tenth of his wages into the offering plate every month, the way he'd been taught to.

"God blesses those who honor Him." Ma's voice echoed in Willie's thoughts. He sure missed her. Pa did, too.

He opened the front door. A young man dressed in a three-piece suit and brown bowler waited on the stoop. A salesman, probably, although peddlers didn't visit the factory-owned neighborhood much. Willie offered a weak smile. "I don't know what you're sellin', mister, but me an' my pa don't have extra to buy anything."

The man scowled. "I'm not peddling wares." He held up a small notepad and pointed at one of the lines. "Can you read this?"

Heat flamed in Willie's cheeks. They might not've been wealthy, but his folks had sent him to school. All the way through the eighth grade. "Sure I can."

"Well, then, you can see a name there — *Sharp.* Is that you?"

Willie nodded.

"And you see the amount right behind it?"

Willie nodded again.

The man jammed the pad into his jacket pocket and looked at Willie. "Well?"

Willie hunched his shoulders. "Well, what?"

The fellow sighed. "Do you have the rent money?"

"Oh! Right here." He dropped the coins into the man's outstretched hand.

The man counted them, then clinked them into a leather pouch exactly like the one Mr. Rochester always carried. He turned to leave.

Willie stepped out on the stoop. "Can I ask . . ." The man looked over his shoulder. "Did Mr. Rochester take sick?" He'd seemed fine three hours ago when Willie received his pay, but sickness could attack a man fairly quick, the way it had Pa.

"Why?"

" 'Cause he usually collects the rent. Just wondered if somethin' happened to him." If so, he'd say a prayer for his boss.

"He's fine, but I'll be the one collecting

the rent from now on." The man tugged his bowler a little lower on his forehead. "Or at least for a while."

"Oh. All right."

The fellow took a step.

"Somethin' else."

This time he turned clear around, glowering.

Willie pointed to the notepad sticking out of the man's pocket. "Mr. Rochester always has me put a mark behind the payment. Says it's his way of makin' sure I get credit for it."

With a huff, the man yanked the pad out and thrust it at Willie. "Make your mark, then."

Willie scratched his head. "He always lends me a pencil."

"For the love of . . ." The man scrounged in his pocket and pulled out a stubby pencil. "Here."

Willie carefully wrote "W. S." behind the amount. Then he returned the pad and pencil to the collector. "Thanks." The man pocketed both items and strode off, muttering.

Willie closed the door and returned to the table. Pa's bowl was empty, and beans lay scattered on the table and floor. Willie chuckled. The big orange tabby cat that had taken up residence under their small toolshed shortly before the illness struck Pa would have a good supper if he cleaned up all the beans from the floor. Sometimes Willie suspected Pa dropped food down his front on purpose, just so the scrounging cat would have extra to eat. Pa must've gotten quite a bit in his mouth, too, though. Sauce smears decorated his face.

Willie grabbed the cloth from the washbasin, wrung it out, and used it to gently clean Pa's lips, chin, and cheeks. Then he straightened and pointed at Pa's bowl. "You get enough, or do you want more?" He cringed. Pa couldn't answer a two-halved question. Especially one with opposite answers. "Sorry, Pa. You get enough?"

Pa nodded.

"You sure?"

Pa grunted.

Willie grinned. "All right, I'll quit pesterin' you. Just wanna make sure you don't wake up hungry in the middle of the night."

The left side of Pa's mouth lifted into his version of a smile. He shook his head.

"You won't get up an' prowl around the kitchen when we're s'posed to be sleepin'?"

Another shake that rocked his shoulders with it.

Willie unhooked the stained napkin, wadded it up, and set it aside. "You wanna go to your chair?"

Unblinking, Pa stared into Willie's eyes.

"You wanna stay with me while I eat?"

A nod.

Willie plopped into his chair. "Sounds good. I like havin' company." He ate his beans, pausing now and then to ask Pa simple yes-or-no questions. He sure missed the sound of his pa's deep, rumbling voice. The doctor'd told him the only way to bring Pa back to how he'd been before the attack of apoplexy was to put him in a special hospital where trained folks would work with him every day. Willie didn't have money to pay for a special hospital. So he relied on prayers. If God could raise Lazarus from the dead, then He could help Pa talk and use his right hand good again. So Willie would keep praying, and he'd keep talking to Pa, and he'd keep reminding Mrs. Blaricum to get him up and walking every hour or so. And he'd hold on to hope.

When he finished eating, he helped Pa to his chair. Ma'd saved her stitching-up-clothes money for a whole year to buy it. The seat cushion had a Pa-sized scoop in its middle, and the woven brown wool was worn down on the armrests, but even if one of the springs came clear through and poked him on the backside, Pa wouldn't get rid of the chair.

Pa flopped into the seat, releasing a sigh. He gave Willie one of his half smiles, and Willie patted his curled right hand.

"Lemme get these dishes washed, and then we'll read the paper together."

Pa's gaze shifted to the floor underneath the table. His head stayed still, but his eyes slid back and forth from the beans to Willie.

Willie laughed. "All right, I'll let ol' Rusty in so he can take care o' your mess."

Pa made some soft huffing noises — his means of chuckling.

Willie didn't even have to call for the cat. As soon as he opened the back door, the big orange tom sauntered in, fluffy tail straight up and its tip flicking back and forth. He brushed against Willie's pant leg on the way to the table, and by the time Willie'd finished their few dishes, the floor was as clean as if Ma had taken a scrub brush to it.

"All right, you, outside now." Willie reached for Rusty, but the cat darted for the sitting room. With a leap that made Willie think of a mountain lion bounding onto a boulder, Rusty flew through the air and landed on the back of Pa's chair. He hunkered low, gold eyes gleaming, his tail swishing like the pendulum on a clock. The tail brushed Pa's ear with every sweep.

Willie shook his head, crossing the floor slow so he wouldn't startle the cat into hopping onto Pa's head. "Now, Rusty, you know you're not s'posed to stay in here. Mr. Rochester would raise Cain for sure if he knew we had an animal in the house. You gotta go out."

A sigh heaved from Pa's parted lips. The disappointment in his father's sagging face brought Willie up short. Pa wanted the old cat's company. He had so few pleasures these days. Would it hurt to let Rusty stay for a while? The rent had been collected, so they didn't have to worry about being caught with a cat in the house.

Willie rubbed his stubbly chin with his knuckles. "Well . . . how 'bout I put him out after we've read the paper. Would that be better?"

A short nod and half smile gave the answer.

"All right, then." Willie sat on the faded sofa and picked up the newest *Atlanta Constitution* he'd bought from the dirty-faced boy who always positioned himself outside the factory on paydays. He perused the pages, looking for something Pa might find interesting. He read a story about an electric generator at Niagara Falls producing power. Electric power instead of steam, like came from the engines he helped put together at the factory.

Willie glanced at the tarnished brass lamp next to the sofa. What would it be like to have lamps that came on with a twist of a key instead of needing oil, a wick, and a match? Such things existed, but they cost dear. And a person had to live in a house with electric lines run to it. He doubted he'd ever be able to afford a luxury like an electric lamp, but it was fine to think about.

He shared some local news articles, and in between paragraphs, he glanced at Pa. By the middle of the third article, Pa's eyelids were drooping. Willie set the paper aside and helped his father to the outhouse.

Some of the fellows from the factory thought Willie ought to take Pa to one of the poorhouses. "Why waste your life takin' care o' somebody who can't do nothin' for himself or for you?" they asked. He didn't understand their kind of thinking. If you loved somebody, you did what needed doing. He loved Pa, so he'd take care of him, and that was that.

After he'd settled Pa in his bed, he lifted Rusty from the back of the chair. The cat dug in his claws, but Willie gave a little tug and Rusty melted into his arms. Willie chuckled. Carrying the cat was like carrying a hairy bag of sand. "You're fatter'n a tick on a hound dog, you big ol' brute. Pa should've named you Goliath." He set the cat outside and watched it hop-skip over the sparse grass for the hollowed space under the toolshed. Willie called good night, then closed and locked the door.

He headed for the lamp by the sofa, intending to turn down the wick, but since he hadn't done a lick of work worth mentioning on this Labor Day, he wasn't tired enough for bed. So he flopped onto the sofa and reached for the paper again. Ma always said that not being in a classroom wasn't an excuse to quit learning. So Willie grabbed every chance he got to read. He had a lot fewer chances since Pa fell sick, but tonight the house was quiet and Pa was tucked in.

He read every article on the front page, then turned it over. Most of the second page was taken up with information about the upcoming Cotton States and International Exposition. There'd already been an exposition in Atlanta, back in 1881 at Oglethorpe Park. Willie'd only been eight or nine at the time, but he remembered Pa and Ma talking about it and wishing they could go.

This one looked to be bigger than the last,

with brand-new buildings going up for exhibits and six states contributing displays. Willie used his finger to underline the words as he read, excitement quivering through him at the mention of speeches and bands and visits by celebrities, including Buffalo Bill Cody. Wouldn't it be something to see Buffalo Bill? Pa would smile for a week if he got to see the marksman in action.

Willie's spirits fell. Even though the exposition was scheduled to last more than three months, he probably wouldn't get to see even one day of it. Not while working at the factory six days a week. And he sure wouldn't be able to take Pa. Pa could shuffle short distances, but all over the park grounds? Nope, and he was too big for Willie to carry. If only Pa could go to one of the special hospitals where he'd get stronger again. Then if Atlanta hosted another exposition, they'd be able to go together.

He started to close the paper, but a small box at the bottom of the page caught his eye. He angled the page toward the light and read slowly.

HIRING laborers, security guards, silk weavers, and custodians to work grounds for duration of exposition (Sept. 18–Dec.

31). Monthly salaries range $54–$65.

Willie stared at the dollar amounts, his heart thudding like a bass drum. Even if he took one of the lowest-paying jobs, he'd be able to set aside ten or twelve dollars a month — money he could put toward a hospital stay. He read on.

Apply to Mr. Grover Sterling at First National Bank, Atlanta, Mondays through Saturdays, Sept. 3–12, between 10 a.m. and 6 p.m.

Willie rubbed his knuckles against his chin, thinking hard. If Mrs. Blaricum agreed to stay late tomorrow or on Wednesday, he could hurry to the bank after work and put in an application with Mr. Sterling. If he got hired, he'd have to quit his factory job, though. He'd counted the days until he turned fourteen, old enough to put in to work at the big factory that'd been rebuilt after Sherman came through and burned any business that might benefit the Confederacy. He loved his job. Loved putting parts together — almost like playing with pieces of a giant puzzle. Loved seeing steam blow from the whistle when all the parts went together right. Could he really give it up?

And if he quit, would Mr. Rochester make

him and Pa move out of factory housing? Harrison Rochester was a fair man. Willie'd worked for him now going on eight years, and Pa had worked for him more than twelve years before that. Mr. Rochester had always treated them good. He might let them stay if they kept up the rent and nobody else needed the house. But the exposition would last just a little over three months. Should he quit at the factory when he might not be able to hire back on when the event was done?

He looked again at the possible salaries. Dollar signs seemed to dance across the page. He closed his eyes and turned his focus to his heavenly Father. "God, I've been prayin' for some way to get Pa better. If this is the way, then will You let me get hired? But if it's not what You want, have Mr. Rochester or Mr. Sterling tell me no. I'll accept whatever You decide. But, God?" He licked his dry lips. "If You tell me no about the exposition, please at least say yes about Pa gettin' better some other way. He . . . he's a good man. He deserves to get better, don't You reckon?"

3

Laurel

The soft feather mattress and rumpled sheets beneath her offered a cozy nest. Only a hint of light from the gas lamp on the street corner sneaked past her lace curtains. The quiet, dove-gray shadowed room created an ideal place for reflection. Laurel drew up her knees and wrapped her arms around her legs.

Resting her cheek on her knee, she thought back over the day. She'd spent all of it, from breakfast time to bedtime, observing Mama. According to Webster's *American Dictionary of the English Language,* one of Mama's most prized possessions, *dotage* was defined as "feebleness or imbecility of understanding or mind, particularly in old age." How could her siblings believe such a thing about Mama?

Oh, threads of silver had nearly overtaken her once dark hair, and her face bore lines that spoke of years of smiles and frowns, but Mama was not feeble of mind or body. Alfred and the others expected Laurel to stay with her all the way through her dotage. Since Mama hadn't even entered it yet, they were speaking of years and years — perhaps decades and decades.

Her stomach hurt. How she loved Mama, the only parent she'd known. Of course she wanted to do what was best for her mother. She wanted to please her siblings, too. But did all that have to mean giving up her life? She didn't want to become an old maid like the church organist, Miss Sophoria Dewey, who hadn't smiled in at least six years. Mama said it was because Miss Dewey was bitter about being alone. Did loneliness turn one embittered? Laurel didn't want to experience it for herself. Nor did she want to leave Mama alone to become embittered or forlorn.

Her bedroom door eased open, and she straightened her legs, leaning into the pile of feather pillows propped against the tall walnut headboard. Mama peeked in, and when her gaze met Laurel's, a soft smile graced her face. "Oh, good, you're still awake. May I come in?"

"Of course." Laurel scooted over a few inches and patted the edge of her mattress.

Mama crossed the floor, her cotton night-gown and wrap skimming the carpet and making it seem she glided instead of walked. Such a beautiful, graceful woman was Adelia Smith Millard, even now. Dotage? Nowhere near her dotage.

She sat in the spot Laurel had patted and placed her hand on Laurel's gown-covered knee. "You've been so quiet today, dear one. Are you feelin' unwell?"

The ache in her middle had nothing to do with sickness, so Laurel shook her head. "Not at all, Mama. I'm sorry if I concerned you. I've only been . . . lost in thought."

"Would you like to talk about it? I'm willing to listen."

Laurel aimed her gaze at the lace-covered window, searching for a way to speak truthfully without divulging the ultimatum her siblings had given her. Although they hadn't sworn her to secrecy, she knew that they would not want her to tell Mama what they'd said. Otherwise they wouldn't have come during her Sunday nap.

She sighed and looked into her mother's attentive face. "About my future, I suppose."

A sweet smile curved Mama's lips. "Ah. My youngest girl is no longer a little girl. Of course she's contemplating the future . . .

45

and perhaps future beaux?"

Laurel shrugged, grinning sheepishly.

Mama squeezed Laurel's knee. "Patrick Brinkley is a nice-lookin' young man, and he was raised in the church. I wouldn't oppose him courting you, if that's what you want."

Laurel linked her hands on top of her head and huffed a noisy breath. "You're right that he's nice lookin'." Although not strikingly handsome. "And I'm sure he has faith." He and his family attended church every Sunday, but she had seen him dozing during at least one sermon. "But . . ." She gazed into her mother's blue eyes, an errant thought tripping through her brain. What if she married someone who was willing to let Mama live with them? Someone who had enough wealth to support a wife, children, and a mother-in-law? Would her siblings then accuse her of shirking her duty?

"Laurel?"

She'd left Mama waiting too long. She dropped her hands to her lap and forced a smile. "I'm not sure I want to be courted by Patrick Brinkley. I want to know what . . . who . . . else is available." She cringed. "Is that awful?"

Mama laughed. "No, my darling girl, there's nothing wrong with exploring. Why,

I entertained visits from three different young men before I chose your father."

Laurel gave a little jolt of surprise. "You did?"

"I did."

Laurel tilted her head, trying to imagine her quiet, gentle, always-proper mother as a young girl entertaining a host of beaux. The image refused to form.

Mama's expression turned pensive, as if she'd drifted away somewhere inside herself. "And when I met your papa and I discovered that bein' in his presence made my heart sing, then I knew I would never look at anyone except him for as long as I lived."

Laurel gave another start. Mayme and Raymond blamed her for scaring away Mama's only prospective beau after Papa's death, but had she just been the excuse Mama used to keep from replacing Papa? Her pulse pounded with the desire to ask, but before the question found its way from her dry throat, Mama took one of Laurel's hands between her warm, smooth palms.

"If you'd like to explore, I won't interfere or try to shame you. I only ask that you don't play the coquette." A frown pinched Mama's brow. "Men might seem tough and unemotional, but they can be hurt as easily as anyone else. There's never any reason to toy with a man's affection."

Laurel sat straight up. "I would never play such a hurtful game."

Mama squeezed Laurel's hand. "I'm glad to hear it. Some of the very pretty girls — and you are very pretty — use flirtation as a means of seeing how many hearts they can lure in and then toss aside, finding pleasure in the power they hold over someone else's feelings. But it's a dangerous game, one that can lead to regret and a ruined reputation. Even more important, I believe it grieves the Lord. The Bible advises us to treat others the way we want to be treated. I can't imagine anyone enjoying havin' their heart trampled for someone else's amusement."

Perhaps her siblings needed to take the biblical advice to heart. Had they considered Laurel's feelings at all before demanding she care single-handedly for Mama? But then, they hadn't said single-handedly, had they? Which meant she could pursue a husband . . . as long as she chose someone who was willing to accept Mama, too.

"You've fallen quiet again." Mama's soft singsong voice cut into Laurel's musings. "Where have your thoughts taken you now, dear one?"

Laurel took a firm grip on Mama's hands. "If I were to — as you put it — explore,

48

where would I find these men? I already know all the young men near my age at church and in our neighborhood. None of them, other than Patrick Brinkley, have shown any interest in me."

Mama released a little gasp, and then a sly grin dimpled her cheek. "I have an idea." She rose and pointed at Laurel. "Stay put. I'll be right back." She lifted the hem of her gown and hurried toward the door on bare feet.

"Mama?" Laurel leaned forward, confused and curious at the same time. "What are you doing?"

Mama sent a bright smile over her shoulder. "I'm getting the newspaper. I saw somethin' earlier, and I think it might be exactly what you need."

Willie

Willie sat on a straight-back chair outside a six-paneled office door, waiting his turn to interview with Mr. Sterling. When he'd arrived after work, four others were already lined up in the hallway — a man old enough to have deep lines carved into his forehead, two men closer to Willie's age, and a pretty young lady who kept wrapping and unwrapping a strand of brown hair around her finger. One at a time, the two younger fellows had entered the office and come out again. Now the girl was in there, most likely applying to be a silk weaver. He couldn't imagine someone so dainty and timid looking hiring on as a security guard or custodian.

Only one more ahead of him, and then it'd be Willie's turn. Seemed like at least a dozen frogs were jumping around in his stomach, and he considered pacing up and down the hallway, the same way the other man was doing. He compared his workman's trousers and shirt to the man's dark-gray three-piece suit, and he grimaced. Should he have gone home and gussied up in his church clothes? He'd look like a bum, coming in after the well-dressed fellow. At least he'd been sent with Mr. Rochester's blessing.

"Willie," his boss had said when Willie approached him yesterday during the lunch break and asked permission to apply for an exposition job, *"your father was a faithful employee and you've been one, too. I'm proud of you for trying so hard to take good care of Otto. You interview, and if you're hired, you and I will work things out about your job here."*

Willie'd been surprised to find the young man who'd collected rent on Monday in Mr. Rochester's office. Mr. Rochester introduced the man as his son, Langdon. The younger Rochester sat with his arms crossed and didn't say a thing the whole time Willie was in there, but he spoke plenty with his eyes. Willie suspected if the younger Rochester had been the one making the decision, Willie wouldn't be applying for an exposition job. But Mr. Rochester had obliged him, and Willie was grateful.

The office door opened, and the young woman stepped out. Willie jolted to his feet, the way his pa'd taught him to do when a lady was present. She glanced at him, and he gave a little nod of greeting. He couldn't doff his cap because he wasn't wearing it, but his hand automatically drifted to his forehead.

She bobbed her chin, her pale cheeks flushing pink. Then she scurried across the floor to the man in the gray suit. "All done." Her voice wheezed out on a sigh.

"Good. Let's get you home." He stuck out his elbow, and the girl took hold.

So the man wasn't applying for a job. He was escorting the girl. Willie nearly sagged in relief. He wouldn't have to worry about having his clothes compared to the other man's. The pair walked quickly up the hallway, the brown strand of hair the girl'd been twirling floating over her shoulder like a kite's tail.

"Next." The gruff invitation came from inside the office.

Willie sent up a hopeful prayer, crossed the threshold, and started across the polished oak floor. "Mr. Sterling? I'm —"

The skinny red-haired man behind the desk pointed to the door. "Close that, please."

"Yes, sir." Willie shut the door with a firm click, then moved to the opposite side of the desk and stuck out his hand. "I'm Willie — er, William Sharp, sir."

The man gave Willie's hand a single pump and let go. He lifted a clean sheet of paper from a tray on the corner of his desk. "Have a seat, Mr. Sharp."

Willie settled on the chair in front of the desk, cringing when the legs squeaked, and rested his palms on his thighs. He wished his stomach would stop hopping. He hadn't been this nervous when he applied to work at the factory. Of course, then Pa had already put in a good word for him. This time he was on his own, and Pa's recovery rested on him getting hired.

Mr. Sterling squinted toward the grandfather clock lurking in the corner. "Almost six. Is there anyone else waitin' to interview?"

Willie shook his head.

The older man sighed. "Good." He picked up a pen and dipped the nib in the inkwell. "All right, Mr. Sharp, for what position are you applyin'?"

Willie rubbed his chin. Stubble poked his knuckles. Why'd his beard have to grow so fast? He wished he'd had time to shave again before coming in. At least the whiskers were blond instead of black. Maybe Mr. Sterling wouldn't notice. "Well, sir, anything but silk weavin'. I don't know too much about that."

Mr. Sterling's red brows came down. "But you are experienced in the other areas — general custodial work, groundskeepin', and patrol?"

"Custodial — if that means cleanin' — I can do. And groundskeepin', sure." Mr. Sterling scratched the pen nib across the page, creating a line of squiggly words Willie couldn't decipher. "I did both of those things when I first started at the Rochester Steam-Powered Engines factory until I was old enough to work on the engines themselves."

The man shot a pointed look across the desk. "You've worked at Rochester's?"

Willie nodded, and pride puffed his chest. "More'n seven years now."

"He purchased a display booth at the exposition."

Willie nodded again. Mr. Rochester had mentioned it during their short conversation.

"Do you have any objection to me contacting him and askin' his opinion about hiring you?"

Willie chafed his chin with a knuckle. He couldn't imagine Mr. Rochester saying anything bad about him. He showed up to work on time and did his best on the job no matter what he was assigned. Must've always been good enough because Mr. Rochester had never criticized him or docked his pay. Willie clamped his hand over his knee again and shrugged. "I reckon not."

"Very well." Mr. Sterling scribbled something at the bottom of the page. "What about patrol? Are you proficient with a pistol?"

Willie swallowed. Would his honesty cost him a job? If so, it'd have to be. He wouldn't lie. "Well, sir, I've never shot a pistol. But I've gone deer and turkey huntin', and I'm a fair aim with a rifle. Generally hit what I point at."

"Mmm-hmm." The interviewer wrote a few more words and then set the pen and paper aside. He linked his fingers on the edge of the desk and met Willie's gaze. "Do you have any questions?"

Willie searched his mind for something intelligent to ask. "When'll work start over at the exposition grounds?"

"Monday the sixteenth —"

A full twelve days away.

"— with the gate opened to the public on the eighteenth." Awe broke across the man's face. "Grover Cleveland himself will flip the switch to turn on the electric lights in all the buildings, and one of the president's advisors, Booker T. Washington, is givin' the first speech of the exposition. The owner of First National Bank declared we'd close our doors and go as a full staff to the opening ceremony. It's bound to be an exhilaratin' day."

Excitement stirred in Willie's middle as he thought about seeing buildings lit up. Some of the engines he helped build powered electric lights in some places, but he never got to see it happen.

"If you're chosen to be part of the exposition work team, you will receive notification on Saturday the fourteenth. We assume by submittin' an application that you're giving your agreement to appear for duty according to the instructions in the notification."

"Yes, sir." Willie nodded hard. "I sure am."

Mr. Sterling rounded the desk and guided Willie to the door. "Thank you for comin' in, young man. And good luck."

4

Laurel

Eugene drew the carriage horse to a stop at the edge of the street. Laurel had climbed up on the driver's seat with him, hoping for a chat, but he hadn't said a word the entire drive from the bank to their family's house on Fowler Street, leaving her unsettled. She shifted on the leather-covered seat and gave him her brightest smile. "Thank you for taking me to the interview. Please thank Mr. Salisbury for letting you make use of his carriage. I'm not keen on taking the trolleys through the city."

Eugene wrapped the reins around the brake handle. "Mr. Salisbury agreed that you shouldn't take the trolley by yourself." He met Laurel's smile with a frown. "If you succeed in securin' a position as silk weaver, I intend to ask permission to carry you to and from the park grounds each day. He'll most likely say yes."

Alfred and Raymond both worked at Hobbes Security Bank — Alfred as a bookkeeper and Raymond as a clerk — but Mama often said Eugene was the most blessed to drive for such a kindhearted man. Laurel toyed with a loose strand of hair falling along her neck, hope rising in her chest. "Do you think there's a chance I'll be hired? Although`I'm very adept at weaving spun cotton and wool on Mama's loom, I've never worked with silk thread."

Eugene shrugged. "How many girls in Atlanta can claim to be accomplished silk weavers? I reckon your chance is as good as anyone else's."

His dismal tone stirred affection. She placed her hand on his arm. "You don't need to worry. If I'm hired, I'll be under the supervision of a woman named Miss Eloise Warner. Mr. Sterling told me she is quite responsible and will keep close watch over her weavers."

"Supervised on the park grounds doesn't mean supervised going to and from. It isn't decent for you to be traipsing about unescorted. Especially in early morning or late evening when it's dark."

Disappointing Alfred made her quiver in apprehension, but disappointing Eugene — the brother who'd brought her a black licorice whip every Saturday from the time Papa died in an awful stagecoach accident until the year he married Ethel Perry and moved across town — pierced her heart.

Laurel clasped her hands beneath her chin. "Please don't scold. Mama's the one who came up with this idea. She wants me to . . ." How had Mama phrased it last night at supper? Ah yes. Laurel swept her arms wide, grinning. "Sample new experiences while I'm still young and unencumbered."

Eugene pinched his lips so tight his lower lip sneaked beneath his mustache.

"And think of how helpful the wages will be. Mr. Sterling said each weaver will be paid two dollars and forty-five cents a day." She'd never imagined earning so much money on her own. This year's Christmas would be brighter than ever because she would be able to purchase toys for the youngest of her nieces and nephews and books or store-bought clothes for the older ones. For the family dinner, she'd choose the biggest goose available in the butcher shop. The thought nearly made her giddy.

Eugene shot a sharp look at her. "Do you need money? Are you and Mama havin' to do without? If so, maybe I —"

She held up both hands. "No, no, you and Alfred and Raymond are already generous enough.." Especially considering they had their own families to support. Guilt often attacked when Alfred deposited coins collected from his and her other brothers' pay envelopes into Mama's keeping, as if she were stealing food from the mouths of her nieces and nephews. "The fabric and rugs we make on the loom bring in an adequate amount of money each month. We aren't in want."

"Then why, Laurel?"

She examined his serious face. He'd always been kinder and more supportive than her other siblings. Could she trust him with the most pressing reason she wanted to work at the exposition? The bell from the steeple on the big church four blocks north began its seven o'clock toll. Laurel cringed. "It's late. I should help Mama put supper on the table."

Dusk had fallen, but the gaslight on the corner lit the path formed of large, flat stones leading to Laurel's front porch. She braced her hand on the low rail of the landau's driver's seat and stretched her foot toward the wheel hub.

"Wait. Let me help you."

Tears stung. Even though he was unhappy with her, he was still thoughtful. She waited until he hopped down, trotted around the back of the carriage, and assisted her from the seat. She managed a wobbly smile. "Thank you."

"You're welcome." He slipped her hand into the bend of his elbow. "Time to get you inside and for me to return Mr. Salisbury's carriage before he thinks I intend to keep it."

She stepped free of his light grasp. "It's fewer than ten yards to the house. I can walk that far by myself."

He caught her hand again. "No, I'll walk you in."

She couldn't hold back a soft laugh. "How is it you and the others trust me to take care of Mama, but you find me incapable of walkin' thirty feet to my own front porch?"

His fingers loosened their hold. He looked aside, dismay creasing his features. "Laurel, you . . . I . . ."

She'd meant to tease, not taunt. She cupped her hands around his elbow. "I'm sorry. I was only funning with you."

He nodded but didn't look at her. The lines marching across his forehead seemed deep in the faint glow from the gaslight. "What we asked of you . . ." He angled his gaze to peer into her eyes. "It isn't fair. Not to you."

Laurel experienced another prick of tears.

Grateful ones. His acknowledging the unfairness of her siblings' expectation lifted her heart in a way she couldn't explain.

"But what else to do? None of us have an extra room in our homes for Mama. We can't afford to hire a live-in caretaker or maid, so . . ." He hung his head. "I told Alfred and Nell you should have the same chance the rest of us had to marry and start a family, but their minds were made up. Raymond and Mayme won't fight against them. And that leaves me on my own. I . . ." He sighed. "I'm not strong enough on my own."

"I understand." She'd been bullied into compliance by Alfred and worn down by Nell countless times. Mama claimed the two felt responsible for everyone since they were the oldest and Papa was gone. Laurel tried to be understanding, but sometimes, such as now, she wished Alfred and Nell would tend to their own families and leave the rest of the Millards to tend to themselves.

"Come on." A half grin formed on Eugene's face, tenderness glowing in his Millard brown eyes. "You need to go in, and I need to get the carriage and horse put away. By now Ethel is probably wonderin' if I decided to spend the night in the Salisbury stable."

Laurel giggled, envisioning her tall brother curled in the hay next to one of the horses in Mr. Salisbury's monstrous stable. She watched the toes of her shoes peeping from beneath the hem of her best dress as Eugene escorted her to the spindled porch. She expected him to leave her at the door, but he came in and stayed long enough to tell Mama the stew smelled wonderful, give each woman a peck on the cheek, and make a promise to come by on Saturday with pecans his children had gathered from the Salisbury orchard. "The hired harvesters had already come and gone, so Mr. Salisbury said they could keep all they found. They scrounged like little squirrels until they filled their pails." Pride lit his narrow face. "They could've sold the pecans to the grocer, but they chose to share their bounty with Granny."

Tears winked in Mama's eyes. "I'll reward them with a batch of oatmeal cookies with lots of nuts." Mama walked Eugene to the door and gave him a goodbye hug. The moment she closed the door behind him, she whirled on Laurel. "Well? Were you hired?"

Mama's exuberance so contrasted with Eugene's concern that a delighted giggle trickled from Laurel's throat. "I won't know until the fourteenth. If I receive a notice, then I must report to the exposition grounds on the sixteenth for training in silk extraction and weaving."

"Oh." Mama's face fell. "Such a long time to wait."

Laurel looped arms with her mother, and they sauntered through the parlor toward the kitchen. "Yes, but Mr. Sterling seemed to think I stand a good chance because I already know how to turn thread into fabric."

"Then all our work together at the loom has been helpful." Mama spooned thick vegetable stew from a kettle on the stove into crockery bowls.

Laurel carried the bowls to the small round table in the center of the toasty kitchen. A basket of crusty rolls and a dish of home-churned butter were already waiting. She liked the quiet, cozy meals, only she and Mama at the little table. But lots of people and the noise around the big table in the dining room was nice, too. She wanted a big dining room, a big table, and lots of children seated around it someday.

Mama slid into the chair next to Laurel, and she held out her hand. "I'll ask the blessing, and then I want to hear all about your interview."

Langdon

Langdon, elbow on the table and cheek on his fist, pushed cubes of honeyed sweet potatoes from one side of his plate to the other with the back of his fork's tines. Only three days of being at the factory from opening to closing, and he was already weary of it. How did Father tolerate following the same routine day after day? The clangs and shouts, the odors of hot steel and grease, the monotony . . . He inwardly shuddered. Being in charge had lost its appeal. The moment Father handed the keys of ownership into his keeping, he would hire a full-time manager and visit only once or twice a year to be certain the factory hadn't blown up.

From the foot and head of the long table, Mother and Father engaged in their typical evening conversation — Mother sharing the details of her most recent philanthropic endeavors and Father outlining his day at the factory. Langdon listened with half an ear, flicking peeks at the clock on the fireplace mantel. When the clock hands showed eight o'clock, the supper hour would reach its end and he would be free to excuse himself. Wednesday evenings his buddies met for faro in Claude Jersey's father's smoking parlor, and he intended to

65

get in on the game.

The minute hand trembled and then clicked forward one increment. Seven fifty-six. Langdon sat up and wadded his napkin in his fist, ready to blot his lips and toss the square of linen over his unfinished dinner the moment the clock began its chime.

"Whom have you decided to send to the exposition?"

Mother's query caught Langdon's attention. He still couldn't believe Father had allowed one of his floor workers to apply for an exposition job. Father's words of praise to the common laborer still chafed, too. What if more workers requested a reprieve from factory work? Would Father grant all of them approval? If so, who would fill their vacated spots in the assembly lines? Surely Father wouldn't expect Langdon to step in. The assembly men always had grease under their fingernails, and several of them had smashed a finger or two between heavy iron parts. He couldn't risk having his fingers smashed. He needed them to keep a good grip on a hand of cards.

"I haven't quite made up my mind, but I've put together a list of possible workers." Father chewed and swallowed a chunk of potato, wiped his lips, and smiled at Mother. "Think of it — businessmen from as far away as Latin America perusing the exhibits. Why, it's possible that Rochester Steam-Powered Engines could one day operate equipment not only outside our fine state, but in foreign countries as well."

"Oh, Harrison, how exciting to contemplate." Mother briefly pressed her steepled fingers to her chin. "Your hard work deserves such recognition, my dear. I'm so proud of you."

Father chuckled. "Now, no overseas companies have ordered an engine. Yet." A slight scowl marred his brow. "I will need to exercise great care when selecting the representatives for the Rochester Steam-Powered Engines exhibit."

Langdon tossed his napkin aside. Why should mere factory employees have the privilege of a months-long lark on the park grounds? "Father, am I" — the clock began to chime, and he raised his voice above the echoing *bong-bong* — "on your list of possible factory representatives for the exposition?"

"No." Father also increased his volume, aiming a frown at the clock. "My list is made up of faithful long-term employees who are fully acquainted with the engine's operation, men who will be able to answer questions and enthusiastically tout the

Rochester engine as superior to other steam-powered engines available."

The clock reached its final chime and fell silent, but it still rang in Langdon's ears. He huffed a sigh. "Who better to encourage others to purchase one of our engines than the very person who will one day own and operate the Rochester Steam-Powered Engines factory?"

Father's frown fixed on Langdon. "You're being presumptuous, considering our recent conversation. Besides, you are no more familiar with the engine's unique features than any other newly hired worker. I want experienced men at the exposition." He picked up his fork.

If Langdon wanted to get in on the first faro game, he needed to leave, but unfairness held him in his seat. "Speaking of presumption, you presume that because I haven't spent years in the factory, I'm unable to speak positively of the engines. Have you forgotten I grew up in this house? I listened at this very dinner table to your explanations to Mother about the quality of the steel, about our engines' strength and durability, about the added safety features that make our engines less likely to explode and injure someone."

He searched his memory for other tidbits,

but none came to mind. No matter. He had Father's full attention now, a rarity. He folded his arms over his chest, gazing intently into Father's eyes. "I cannot imagine a hired employee speaking with greater eloquence about the superiority of the Rochester steam-powered engine than your own son."

Sternness remained etched in Father's features. "Eloquence is one thing, familiarity quite another."

"Oh, Harrison." Mother tsk-tsked, shaking her head. "Give Langdon a chance."

Father glared at Mother for a moment, then pointed at Langdon. "Before I agree to allow you to serve as a spokesman at the exposition, I will want to assure myself that you are able to answer questions accurately and confidently."

Cockiness easily masqueraded as confidence. But accuracy? He lowered his head and commanded himself not to grimace. He'd rather eat a cupful of worms, the pledge requirement that had changed his mind about joining Phi Delta Theta, Father's pick of fraternities, than study. But if a few hours of study meant earning a lengthy reprieve from the factory . . .

He met his father's gaze. "Give me until the fourteenth, Father, and then test me. If

I am able to answer your questions correctly, will you allow me to go?"

"If you fail to meet my expectations, will you graciously concede defeat?"

"Of course." He could learn material quickly when motivated. Enjoying over three months of free rein at the park grounds was strong motivation. He bounced a grin at his mother and headed for the doorway. "Excuse me, please. I have some reviewing to do." He'd have to skip the faro game, but he had a bigger bet to win.

5

Willie

Willie trudged up the grassless path carved by hundreds of treks back and forth from the street to the stoop of his little house. Tiredness tugged at him. He'd been working double hard since Mr. Rochester gave him permission to apply for an exposition job. Didn't want his boss to think he was slacking off because he was hankering for greener pastures ahead. Ten workdays in a row of being first through the door, working through breaks, and staying until everybody else cleared the floor was near about to frazzle him, though.

But rest was coming. Sunday — the Lord's day — tomorrow, and next week he'd either be back to normal at the factory or doing a different kind of work. His pulse gave a little double skip. No matter whether he got hired for the exposition or not, he had a treat waiting inside. Today was Saturday . . .

fried-ham-and-eggs day.

His stomach growled. The cheese sandwiches and raw carrots he'd eaten for lunch had seemed plenty filling at the time, but now emptiness gnawed at his belly. He sure appreciated Mrs. Blaricum putting supper on the table every Saturday night, even if she did put the same thing out week after week. The woman knew how to sear a ham steak and fry an egg all the way through, the same way Ma used to. Willie liked a runny yolk, but he ate his eggs over hard because that's how Ma had fixed 'em and how Pa liked 'em.

Even though he was hungry and tired, he paused on the stoop and stuck his hands in his pockets instead of reaching for the doorknob. After all these days of waiting and praying and hoping and wondering, as soon as he stepped into the house he'd know. He wanted an exposition job. Wanted it more than he'd ever wanted anything, even more than the painted tin flute he'd begged for at Christmastime when he was six. Pa'd carved him a whistle from a piece of hickory instead. It only played one note, but he'd found joy in making it sing.

He scrunched his brow and looked at the gray evening sky. Gray. A dull color. A sad color. But a few stringy-looking clouds with pink underbellies interrupted the gray. Pink. Ma's favorite color. A joyful color.

His chest pinched. Would he find a touch of joy if he didn't get a job at the Cotton Exposition? Hurt something awful to see Pa so weak. How would he ever be able to put him in the special hospital without extra money? He'd been taught to believe that God knew best. Even when Ma died of that awful fever, Pa said it was for the best because she wasn't hurting anymore.

Willie dug deep down inside himself and pushed words past his dry throat. "I told You I'd accept Your will. And I'll do it, the same way Pa's always done. No matter what, come Sunday mornin', Pa an' me will be in a church pew. We'll worship an' sing — well, I'll sing while Pa listens — and we'll praise Your name. 'Cause no matter what job I have, You'll always be there for Pa an' me."

Saying it all out loud took some weight off his chest. He pulled in a breath, whisked one more glance at the sky, then took hold of the doorknob.

"Willie! Willie!"

He jerked around so fast he almost fell off the stoop. His best boyhood friend, Quincy, ran up the street. Quincy's dark face was shining, and he waved a piece of paper. He panted to a stop at the base of the stoop and jammed the paper at Willie.

"Lookee here what I got! Notice come today. I been hired for grounds-keepin' at the exposition." Quincy held the paper toward Willie the way Willie used to show Ma his best essays from school.

Willie grinned at his pal. "Congratulations. I'm happy for you." If Willie got hired, the two of them could ride the trolleys back and forth every day together. Willie'd enjoy that a lot.

Quincy nodded hard. "I'm happy, too. Me an' Bunson both put in, but he didn' get chose."

Quincy's younger brother always tagged after Quincy. The sixteen-year-old was probably plenty disappointed. The same way Willie would be if he didn't get hired. "That's too bad."

Quincy sighed. "Pap's some sorry we didn' both make it. He was countin' on us bein' able to buy a new mule right quick since ol' Rosebud jus' can't pull Pap's junk wagon no mo'. I reckon Pap an' Bunson'll hafta keep pullin' the wagon until I save up enough. Gon' take longer with only one o' us at the fairgrounds, but Mam says we gotta thank God for provision."

Willie smiled. Quincy's ma was always finding reasons to thank God, same as

Willie's ma always had. Maybe that's why they'd been such good friends.

Quincy shook his head. "Bunson, he's most sad about not gettin' hired, 'cause Pap'd vowed to let 'im keep some pocket money. But I promised I'd take him on openin' day so he can hear the speakers. I can't hardly wait to hear what Booker T. Washington's gonna say. Whole family an' all our neighbors is real excited 'bout Mr. Washington speakin' to so many folks. Me an' Bunson's gonna hafta listen close so we can tell 'em what'n all he says."

Willie hoped he'd be there to hear Mr. Washington and all the other speakers for himself. He clapped Quincy on the shoulder. "I'm sure glad you got one of those jobs. It must feel real good to know you'll be helpin' your family."

"Uh-huh." Quincy squinted up at Willie, pressing the notice against the front of his striped shirt. "What about you? You get one, too?"

Willie swallowed. "Dunno yet. I'm hopin' so."

Quincy huffed and backed up two steps, waving the paper. "I can't wait to find out — Mam's got victuals on the table an' tell me not to dawdle. Lemme know after you know. It'd be real nice if we was both hired on." He turned and trotted off.

Nervousness rolled through Willie's middle. As much as he wanted to know, he stayed on the stoop a few more seconds. *Your will, God. Whatever it is, I'll accept Your will.* He stepped into the house and called, "Pa? Mrs. Blaricum? I'm home."

The woman peeked from around the kitchen doorway. "Supper's on the table. Your father's already eating."

"Did —" His voice cracked. He cleared his throat. "Did a notice get delivered here today?"

" 'Bout an hour ago. It's on the table by the sofa." She disappeared from view.

Willie bounded across the floor and snatched up the folded piece of paper. According to Mr. Sterling, only the ones being hired would receive a notice, so the paper itself told him yes. But would he be a groundskeeper like Quincy or something else? Biting down on his lower lip, he unfolded the page.

Mr. William Sharp, report to the Administration Building (at 14th St. entrance, east side of park) at 8:00 a.m. Monday the 16th of September for instructions and training as a security guard for the Cotton States and International Exposition.

There was more, but he'd read enough. He let out a whoop and threw the paper in the air.

Mrs. Blaricum bustled from the kitchen. "What are you doing?"

Willie laughed. "Thanking God, that's what."

She pursed her lips. "Well, He hears just fine without us hollerin' at Him. Come set yourself down. I'll fill your plate."

Willie tossed his jacket on the worn sofa and skedaddled through the front room to the warm kitchen. A sweet smell reached his nose. A pie was cooling on top of the pantry cupboard. Cherry, if his sniffer worked right. His favorite. He licked his lips. This evening was fixing to be a good one.

He plopped in a chair, giving Pa a smile. Mrs. Blaricum put a speckled tin plate in front of him. The slab of ham and two fried eggs looked so good his stomach sat up and begged. His fingers itched to grab up his fork and dig in, but first he thanked Mrs. Blaricum. Then he bowed his head and thanked God — quietly this time — for the food and for the new job. He reached for his fork.

"Headin' to my place now." Mrs. Blaricum whipped Ma's apron from her waist and hung it on the hook by the stove. "When you've finished eatin', come knock on my door. I need a few words with you."

Willie stopped the fork tines before they reached the food. She'd never made a request like that before. "Somethin' wrong?"

She glanced at Pa, who was giving the chopped pieces of ham on his plate clumsy jabs. "Might be. But we'll talk after you eat." She headed out the back door.

Willie's appetite escaped. He laid his fork on his plate and touched Pa's arm. "Will you be all right for a bit? Gonna go see what Mrs. Blaricum needs."

Pa gave a jerky nod.

Willie patted his arm, then followed after Mrs. Blaricum. She was already on her stoop, her hand on the back door's porcelain knob. Willie called her name, and she paused, frowning.

"Didn't I tell you to eat first?"

Willie stopped next to the stoop. "Yes, ma'am, but I don't think I'll be able to swallow a bite until I know what's on your mind. Did something happen with Pa?" Thank goodness he'd got this new job. The sooner he got Pa into the special hospital, the better it would be.

Her brow crinkled up, and she sent glances left and right. Then she hung her head. A strand of gray hair fell across her forehead and swayed in the light breeze. "No, no, nothing's changed with your pa."

Willie heaved a sigh so big his breath made a whooshing sound. It couldn't be something so bad, then.

"The thing is, I can't come over and stay with Otto anymore."

He'd been wrong. This was terrible. He pressed his gripped hands against his stomach. "Do you need more money? I can pay you more startin' next week." Paying her extra would take away from his hospital fund, but somehow he'd make do.

She shook her head. "It ain't the money. It's the time." Sadness sagged her wrinkled face. "Reckon you remember my youngest girl, Myrtle."

"Sure do." They'd played together when they were little, until she started seeing him as something more than a frog-catching buddy. He'd felt plenty bad about it, but he only liked her as a friend, so he quit meeting her at the pond. She'd married up with a fellow from across town over a year ago. He hadn't seen her much since.

"She an' Lambert had their first baby a couple months back — a little boy, Lambert Jr." No pride lit the woman's face, which left Willie unsettled. "Myrtle's had a hard time bouncin' back, an' she needs somebody to look in on her every day, help see to the baby 'n' all. They don't have extra money to pay somebody, so naturally they asked if I could help."

Mrs. Blaricum held out her hands in a helpless gesture. "I can't turn down my own kin, but unless I give up sittin' with your pa, the only hours I'll have to spare are evenin' hours. I don't see how that'll do Myrtle an' baby Lambert much good."

The older woman appeared forlorn in the heavy evening shadows. Willie figured he didn't look much happier. Worry gnawed at him, but he couldn't tell her to ignore her own daughter. "I understand."

Relief flooded her features. "Thank you, Willie." She made a *tsk-tsk* noise. "I am sorry, though. I'm fond of your pa. And you. Always have been. But you know how family comes first. After all, you've been keepin' your pa comp'ny, seein' to him ever since your ma passed. An' now with him ailin' . . ."

Willie started to tell her that taking care of Pa wasn't a burden because he loved Pa.

"If I can't go over every day, I guess you'll think on havin' him put somewhere. Maybe at a poor farm. Or a state asylum." She nodded, and her gaze drifted someplace beyond

Willie, like she'd forgot he was there. "It'll be better for you, bein' free to find yourself a girl an' settle down. Of course, it's too late to settle with Myrtle, but . . ."

Did she think keeping Pa company had kept him from marrying up with her daughter? There wasn't a good way to ask or a kind way to set her straight, so Willie edged backward. "I'll figure somethin' out, ma'am. Don't worry. You see to Myrtle an' her baby."

She jolted. "What? Oh. Yes, I will. Thank you, Willie. Good night, now." She hurried inside her house.

Willie turned and scuffed across the dried grass toward his own back stoop. He couldn't blame Mrs. Blaricum for wanting to tend to her daughter and grandson. He wasn't mad at her for leaving him in the lurch. Not even a little bit. But he was plenty worried. He couldn't take the exposition job — or even return to the factory — unless he found somebody to spend days with Pa.

Something brushed against his leg. Willie sidestepped and looked down. Rusty, the big old tomcat, leaned in for a second swipe against Willie's pant leg. He scooped the cat into his arms. "Glad to see you, Rusty. You might as well eat my ham an' eggs. I'm not hungry anymore."

He carried the cat to the house, grateful for the company. He wished Rusty was a person. As much as the old tom liked Pa, he'd be willing to stay every day at the house. But he couldn't leave Pa with a cat. How would he find someone trustworthy by early Monday morning?

6

Laurel

"Why, Laurel, what a pretty combination of colors."

Laurel paused with the shuttle in her hand and smiled at her mother. "Thank you." She ran her finger along the tightly woven threads of dyed wool. "I wasn't sure at first how it would look with the red and brown side by side. We usually alternate dark and light colors. But we had extra bales of red and brown, so I decided to experiment."

Laurel slid the shuttle through the shed, pulled the weft tight, and pumped the treadle, adding another row to the rug.

"Making the brown stripes narrower than the red keeps it from being too dark," Mama said. "Then the brown border keeps the red from overwhelming the brown. Very well balanced."

Laurel couldn't hold back a pleased grin. Mama had been baking while Laurel started

83

a new rug. The scent of fresh bread clung to her apron, and Mama's praise was even more pleasant than the aroma rising from the cotton cloth. They'd decided when they began selling rugs that they wanted them to be serviceable but also pretty. Laurel didn't have Mama's experience, and therefore her rugs weren't always as pleasing to the eye as the ones Mama designed.

Mama pinched her chin and seemed to frown at the two-feet-wide partial rug. "You've made a great deal of progress on it already, too — nearly twice as far as I'd expect, given the amount of time you've spent." Her gaze shifted to Laurel, and a touch of admonishment colored her expression. "I thought the treadle thuds seemed more rapid than usual. Haste can decrease quality or damage the loom."

Laurel grimaced. "I'm sorry. I've been trying to keep myself too occupied to think."

Mama tucked a strand of hair that had come loose from Laurel's braid behind her ear. The tender gesture assured Laurel she'd been forgiven for treating the loom recklessly. "Worrying about the exposition job?"

"Yes, ma'am." Laurel set the shuttle on the loom's breast beam, swiveled the stool, and peered up at her mother. "Everyone was to receive their notices today. Mr.

Sterling at the bank seemed certain I would be hired since I already know how to work a loom." She twirled the end of her braid around her finger and hung her head. "But no one's knocked at the door all day. So I guess . . ." She sighed.

"Laurel Adelaide Millard." Mama cupped Laurel's chin and lifted her face. "I wanted the exposition job for you as much as you did. Maybe even more. But God knows what is best for you. If He answered our prayer with a no, then He has a reason for it, and we will accept it without a moment of pouting or bemoaning."

Shame swept through her. Tears stung. Laurel blinked rapidly.

Mama's warm hand glided along Laurel's cheek, and a sympathetic half smile formed on her face. "Well, perhaps a moment of pouting is all right. After all, God surely understands how disappointment feels." Then she shook her finger. "But only a moment's worth. Then you get back to your rug weaving." She set her head at a determined angle. "And I'll go back to the kitchen. If we both stay busy, we won't think about our disappointment."

Langdon

Logs snapped in the small fireplace in

Father's study, sending out an uncomfortable amount of heat. But Langdon remained rooted on the plush carpet in front of the desk and met Father's stoic gaze. Not once in the twenty minutes since he'd entered the study and begun his presentation about the Rochester steam-powered engines had Father's expression changed, but he'd stared down poker faces before. An emotionless countenance did not necessarily indicate a lack of feeling beneath the surface.

Langdon pushed aside his jacket flaps and slipped his fingers into his trouser pockets, lifting his chin slightly. "In conclusion, the Rochester factory is the only steam engine factory in the state of Georgia currently moving toward the manufacture of steam turbines. Thus, you can depend upon Rochester to meet today's as well as tomorrow's developing and advancing needs to power your equipment, locomotive or ship, or the electrical lights in your home or place of business."

He fell silent. Did a flicker of admiration glint in Father's blue-gray irises? His lips twitched with the desire to grin, but he clenched his teeth and squelched it.

Father rose from his leather chair and rounded the desk, his steps slow and measured, his eyes seemingly fixed on the glowing log in the fireplace. He stopped within two feet of Langdon and slowly raised his head. He held out his hand, and Langdon clasped it. Father gave a formal handshake. A tight smile lifted the corners of his mustache.

"I told your mother you wouldn't be able to pass muster, but I can't fault a thing you said, nor can I add to it. You were accurate and complete. Perhaps you have been paying attention."

Langdon would never confess how many hours he'd spent quizzing his cousin Timothy and memorizing notes about steam engines. Several years' worth of information crammed into less than two weeks. But he'd accomplished his goal. He'd impressed Harrison Faulk Rochester. Oh, Father hadn't come straight out and expressed pride or approval, and for a moment Langdon's spirits sagged, but what did he want most — Father's spoken approval or the chance to attend the exposition? The truthful answer was something else he would never confess.

He cleared his throat. "Will you allow me to represent Rochester Steam-Powered Engines at the Cotton States and International Exposition?"

Father drew in a breath that expanded his vest. When his breath whooshed out, the cherry scent of his cigar tobacco filled Langdon's nostrils. He nearly groaned. How he'd missed smoking cigars with his buddies these past days. But freedom waited. If only Father would grant it.

"Yes."

Langdon jolted. "Yes?"

"Yes."

He socked the air and whooped.

Father pushed aside his jacket flaps and rested his hands on his hips. "You will attend with Girard Sanders, John Stevens, and Clyde Allday."

Another groan strained for release. All the men Father named were old — in their fifties already. He'd hoped his cousin might be assigned duty at the expo. Timothy would cover for Langdon whenever he wanted to sneak off for some fun. He couldn't imagine Sanders, Stevens, or Allday giving him free rein. He doubted they'd give him even an inch of rein.

Father guided Langdon to the pocket doors and slid the right one into its casing. He then turned a serious look on Langdon. "It's wise that you're taking my expectations about the business seriously. But I feel the need to remind you of your mother's desire."

Langdon's stomach knotted. "She wants grandchildren."

Father frowned. "She wants to see you settled into family life. That entails taking a —"

"I know. A wife."

"First."

Father needn't be so stern. Langdon wasn't foolish enough to sire a child outside of wedlock. A couple of his college buddies had gotten trapped into matrimony that way, and another would be paying blackmail money for the rest of his life to keep his parents from finding out what he'd done. "Of course, Father."

Father rocked on his heels. "Any of the young women who attend our church and any of the daughters of our friends and acquaintances who are of marriageable age are possible prospects. Your mother would know better than I the names of girls upon whom you could call."

An idea seemed to fall from the ceiling and bop Langdon on the head. Another shout of elation built in his chest, but he stifled it. "It's very likely I'll meet young women at the exposition." He pretended to adjust his cuff link, feigning nonchalance.

"That is, if I'm given a chance to roam the grounds a bit each day, visit the other exhibits, and mingle with the attendees." He flicked a glance at his father.

Father chewed his mustache, his brows low. "I suppose it's only fair to allow you to explore all options."

Langdon swallowed a chuckle. Maybe Father wasn't so stodgy after all.

"I will inform Stevens to give you the task of drumming up visitors to our booth. This should put you in contact with a number of families. Perhaps one of them will have a daughter who captures your attention."

Given the organizers' expectation of a million visitors, chances were good he'd find one young woman in the place who appealed to him. He ambled through the hallway and up the winding staircase leading to his suite, the plan solidifying in his mind. He'd choose a girl who was pretty enough to make his buddies jealous, maternal enough to win Mother's favor, and naive enough to believe he wanted to settle down.

Laurel

Sunday morning Laurel held the front window curtains aside and watched the street for Eugene's arrival. She and Mama didn't mind walking four blocks to church, but Eugene insisted on driving them. First, though, he had to deliver his employer's family to their church on the other side of Atlanta. Consequently, depending on how quickly Mr. and Mrs. Salisbury and their children readied themselves in the morning, they could never predict when Eugene would arrive. So Laurel stood sentry. She and Mama didn't want to keep Eugene waiting — especially when he was running late. How she disliked entering the church service after it had already begun.

"Is he here yet?"

Laurel glanced over her shoulder. Mama entered the parlor, adjusting her Sunday earrings. Laurel had asked to wear them once, and Mama had granted permission with a stern caution not to lose them. So Laurel twisted the little clamp an extra turn to keep them snug. Within an hour, her earlobes throbbed so badly she had no desire to ever wear them again. Yet Mama put on the little drop pearls every Sunday, and if her ears hurt, she never complained. Probably because the earrings had been a gift from Papa, and Mama cherished everything from Papa. The earrings, the hand-painted lamp, and the books. With every return from a sales trip, Papa had brought Mama a new book because he'd known how

91

much she loved them.

How Laurel wanted to marry someone who would love her as much as Papa had loved Mama, someone she could love as deeply as Mama still loved Papa.

Laurel swallowed. "Not yet."

Mama tugged at her collar. "Then I'm going to change this. I must have used too much starch. It's scratching me this morning." She turned and hurried up the hallway toward the bedrooms.

Laurel fixed her attention on the street again. Only a few seconds later, Mr. Salisbury's sorrel horse came around the corner. Laurel darted for the hall tree and took down her wrap. "Mama! Eugene is here."

Mama bustled across the parlor. "I didn't have time to fasten a new collar, so I'll have to do without."

"Your dress looks fine without it." Laurel handed Mama her wrap.

"It isn't for the dress that I wear a collar." Mama fussed with her wrap, shifting it on her shoulders. "It helps hide my double chin."

"I've never noticed your double chin."

"Because I usually wear a collar."

Laurel stifled a giggle. "You always look beautiful, Mama."

Mama released a little huff, but she smiled

as she opened the front door and gave the screen door a push. A piece of paper fluttered to the porch floor. Mama stepped over the threshold and sent a puzzled look toward the small folded page. "What . . ."

Laurel picked it up and handed it to Mama. "What is it?"

Mama unfolded the paper, and her eyes widened. "Laurel!"

"What?"

"You are hired."

"Hired?" Understanding dawned. Joy exploded through her chest. "For the exposition?" She grabbed the paper and read the short missive. She captured Mama in a hug, crushing the notice. "I'm hired!"

Mama rocked Laurel back and forth. "You must have been making too much noise with the treadle to hear the messenger at the door. I'm so glad we found the notice before wind carried it away or you never would have known to report to the fairgrounds."

"Mama? Laurel?" Eugene hollered from the carriage. "We need to go." A chorus of "come ons" and "hurry ups" came from inside the coach — Eugene's wife, Ethel, and their children voicing their impatience.

Laurel and Mama pulled back, smiled at each other, then embraced again, laughing through tears.

"Mama." Eugene strode to the edge of the porch, hands on his hips. "What are you doin'?"

Mama released Laurel and aimed a saucy grin at Eugene. "Celebrating."

He shook his head. "Can you do it later? Church will start in —"

The tower began its call-to-worship tolls.

Eugene groaned. "It's startin' now."

Mama looped arms with Laurel and propelled her across the yard. They climbed into the carriage, and Eugene prodded the horse, but the preacher had already given the opening prayer and parishioners were singing a hymn of praise when Laurel trailed Mama, Eugene, and his family into the sanctuary. Mama led them all to the Millard family pew, and Nell scowled at them as they filed in. But for the first time Laurel didn't care at all that they arrived late.

She'd been hired! God hadn't said no after all. Surely that meant she'd meet someone at the exposition who would make her heart sing, the way Papa had stirred Mama's heart. She could hardly wait.

7

Willie

" 'Bear ye one another's burdens, and so fulfil the law of Christ.' " Willie gave a little jolt. The preacher read on, but the second verse from Galatians 6 seemed to bounce off the wood-planked walls and echo in Willie's mind. He glanced at Pa, who slumped sideways in the chair at the end of the bench. Willie was grateful for the chair. Pa couldn't support himself good enough to sit on one of the backless benches, and Willie'd been plenty burdened about leaving Pa at home on Sunday mornings. So Preacher Estel Hines had brought the chair from his own dining room table. He'd told Willie, *"We'll do whatever we can for Otto. You just let me know what he needs."*

Willie zinged his attention to the kind-faced preacher who stood at the front of the sanctuary with his open Bible draped on his wide palm. *"We'll do whatever we can for*

Otto." Willie believed Preacher Hines meant it. So why hadn't Willie ever asked for the preacher's help? Because Willie didn't like asking for help. Pa was his responsibility, the same way Willie'd always been Pa's responsibility. They took care of each other. Even after Ma died, they'd managed on their own.

Oh, they didn't eat as good as they had when Ma did the cooking. And their clothes weren't ironed as neat. The house wasn't as clean, either. But Willie did his best, and even before the attack of apoplexy, Pa never complained. They'd always been content. But this burden — finding somebody responsible to stay with Pa all day — was one Willie couldn't carry on his own.

The sermon couldn't have come at a better time. He'd spent hours yesterday evening praying to find a way for him to take the exposition job. And there stood Preacher Hines, delivering a sermon about Christian brothers and sisters doing God's will when they took care of one another. He sat in a chapel full of people. One of them might be able to help carry his burden. He only needed to ask.

At the end of the service, as he always did, Preacher Hines stepped off the raised platform and stood on the floor at the front.

"Before we go our separate ways, let's share our praises and petitions."

A lady near the front shot from her seat. "My sister over in Winder had her baby boy last Thursday, and the baby's as healthy as can be. My sister's doin' good, too. My whole family's praisin' God for the safe arrival of little Jimmy." Folks called out congratulations and amens, and the woman sent a smile across the congregation before she sat.

Willie raised his hand, but so did the man sitting in front of him. Preacher Hines called on the other fellow.

"We need prayer for our middle girl. She's been sick now three days runnin'. The elixir the doc gave her doesn't seem to help much. She's needin' a touch from the Lord."

Preacher Hines gave a solemn nod. "We'll ask for that touch, Brother Gaines." He angled his head and caught Willie's eye. "Willie, did you have a request?"

"Yes, sir." Willie stood. "I need —" His mouth went dry. Everybody was looking at him. Men, women, even the children. If he said out loud how he needed a babysitter for Pa, would any of the kids laugh? If they did, they'd strip away what was left of Pa's pride. He swallowed his planned request. "I need to talk to you after the service."

The preacher nodded. "All right, Willie."

A few more folks asked for prayer, and then Preacher Hines prayed. After his amen, people got up and filed out, talking, laughing. Willie missed the days when he and Pa would talk and laugh with others on the way out of church. He stayed on the bench and waited until Preacher Hines told everybody goodbye. When they'd all gone, the preacher strode up the side aisle and stopped next to Pa's chair. He grabbed hold of Pa's limp hand and shook it, smiling into his face.

"So good to have you here with us, Otto."

"He likes being here." Willie didn't much like talking for Pa, but he knew Pa was happy to be in church. Was happy to get out of the house now and then. "The sermon was real good. Spoke to me where I needed it."

"I'm glad to know that." Pastor Hines's warm smile reminded Willie of how Pa used to smile before the apoplexy sagged his face. He hitched his black pant legs and sat facing Willie, then fixed Willie with another one of his warm smiles. "Now, what is it you needed to talk to me about?"

Willie put his hand on Pa's knee. It seemed the right thing to do. A way of making Pa part of the conversation even if he couldn't talk. Willie told the preacher about the exposition job, about Mr. Rochester giving him permission to apply for it, and how he wanted to use the extra money. He explained about Mrs. Blaricum needing to see to her daughter and grandson. Then, choosing his words careful — he didn't want to humiliate Pa — he admitted that he couldn't leave Pa by himself.

"So," Willie said, his breath whooshing out with the word, "I can't go to work tomorrow, not at the exposition or even at the factory, unless I find somebody real quick to spend the days with Pa. I . . ." His chest ached. "I need help."

Preacher Hines hadn't said a word the whole time Willie talked, but he'd nodded every so often, crunched his eyebrows or pinched his lips, like he was thinking deep. Now he leaned forward and put one hand over Willie's on Pa's knee. "I'm glad you told me about this, Willie." He turned and looked straight at Pa. "I've been prayin' for you to get better, an' stayin' at the convalescent hospital could do you a lot of good, Otto. You need more help than Willie can give you."

Willie appreciated Preacher Hines talking to Pa. Most people talked about him right in front of him.

Preacher Hines turned to Willie again. "If

workin' at the exposition will give you the money you need to pay for the convalescent hospital, then you've got to be at the fairgrounds tomorrow mornin'. I don't believe God would give you the job if He didn't mean for you to take it."

He stood. "I'd like to talk some more, but my family's probably sittin' around the table waitin' for me. Why don't you an' your pa come home with me, have dinner with Faye, our children, an' me? Faye put a fat goose in the oven early this mornin', more'n enough for all of us."

Willie's mouth watered, but he shook his head. He wouldn't make Pa eat in front of other folks. Especially not kids. They were the preacher's kids, who'd been taught right from wrong, so they probably wouldn't poke fun at Pa's napkin around his neck or the way he dropped food from his fork, but they would stare. They wouldn't be able to help it. And Willie wouldn't put Pa on display.

He stood and helped Pa to his feet. "Thank you, Preacher, but I've got dinner waitin' for us." Beans with fatback and onion.

"Then can I call on you later today? After I've had a chance to pray an' talk with my wife?"

Willie nodded. "You're welcome to come

by anytime you want. An' thank you for prayin'."

Willie guided Pa toward the front door. In the quiet room, the drag of Pa's right foot across the wood floor sounded loud. Sad. Pa'd been so strong, so able. Willie hated all the things the sickness had taken from his father. But hope followed him out the door of the chapel. Surely God would tell Preacher Hines who could stay with Pa, and God would answer a preacher right quick.

When they reached their house — only a three-block walk from the chapel — half an hour later, Quincy was sitting on the front stoop with a napkin-covered basket in his lap. Quincy settled the basket in the crook of his elbow and stood.

"Hey, Mr. Sharp, Willie. Been waitin' on ya."

The breeze carried a good smell across the yard, and Willie suspected the smell came from what was in Quincy's basket. Quincy's ma, Zenia, made some of the best fried chicken in Atlanta. One time Willie'd told her she should open a little café, but she said she had enough mouths around her table — why would she want to be feeding strangers, too? He was awfully glad she didn't consider him a stranger.

He grinned at Quincy. "Did you bring us

some fried chicken?"

"An' biscuits." Quincy moved to the other side of Pa. He grabbed Pa's right arm, and he and Willie hefted him up onto the stoop. Quincy kept hold while Willie unlocked the door. "Church musta run long today, huh?"

Willie opened the door and helped Pa over the threshold. "Nah. Me an' Pa stayed behind an' talked to the preacher." He took Pa to the kitchen and helped him into his chair.

Quincy put the basket on the table, then headed to the cupboard and fetched plates. "Preacher ask you to stay? You get yo'self in trouble durin' the service?"

Willie shook his head at his friend's teasing grin. "I gave up causin' trouble in services when I was six. Ma made sure it wasn't worth my time to get into mischief there." His ma had been a mild-mannered lady, generally quiet and gentle. Unless she thought Willie'd been disrespectful or disobedient. Then she wielded a switch. She hadn't needed to actually use it more than half a dozen times. Willie'd never been keen on displeasing his ma. And not because he was scared of the switch. He hadn't wanted to disappoint her. He didn't want to disappoint her now by not doing the best he could for Pa.

"Then whatcha need with 'im?"

Willie counted three plates at the table. "Guess I'll tell you after we all eat."

Willie said grace. Then they partook of Willie's beans and the fried chicken and biscuits from Quincy's basket. It might not've been a roasted goose, but it all tasted good, and by the time they were done, Willie's stomach was achingly full. He opened the back door, and as usual ol' Rusty came running. The cat went straight to the food scraps under the table and set to cleaning them up, the tip of his bushy tail twitching and his purr rumbling.

Willie helped Pa to his bed. Walking to church and back made him slap wore out worse than a full day at the factory used to. If Pa got help at the convalescent hospital, would he be able to work again? He'd always been so busy — gardening with Ma, carving wooden horses and dogs and baby rattles for neighborhood kids, lending a hand wherever it was needed. The only time he'd sat was to eat or read the paper. Now he couldn't do much more than sit. He wasn't able to say so, but he had to be frustrated with his uncooperative body. Willie wanted Pa whole again. For Pa's sake, not Willie's.

Willie draped the quilt over Pa. "Have a

good rest, now."

Pa's gaze went back and forth from the doorway to Willie. "Aaaa . . . Aaaa . . ."

Willie frowned. "What is it you want, Pa?" He searched his mind for things starting with the letter *a*. "Apple cider?" They still had some left in the jug. "An antacid?" Maybe he'd ate too much.

Pa shook his head. He made petting motions with his left hand.

Ah. So *a* wasn't the starting letter. "When he's done eatin', I'll bring Rusty in to you."

Pa rewarded Willie with one of his lopsided smiles. Then he closed his eyes. He was already snoring softly when Willie carried the cat into the room, but Willie put Rusty on the bed anyway. The yellow tom walked back and forth across the rumpled covers and then curled into a ball next to Pa's hip and closed his gold eyes. His purr matched Pa's snore for volume.

Chuckling, Willie returned to the kitchen.

Quincy still sat at the table with the dirty plates. "Get your pa settled?"

Willie nodded. He carried the plates and spoons to the dry sink and left them in the washbasin. He'd wash them later, after Quincy'd gone home. He sat in his chair and crossed his arms on the table. "Tell your ma thanks for the food. I know Pa gets tired of eating beans or scrambled eggs, but that's about as much as I know how to make."

"Mam worries about you'n Otto. Said if she didn't have Port, Stu, an' Sassy all underfoot ever' day, she'd come by to cook an' clean."

Willie couldn't imagine having eleven brothers and sisters, the way Quincy did. He used to envy Quincy, but now, with Ma gone and Pa so sick, he was glad God didn't see fit to give his folks a houseful of youngsters. He wouldn't be able to take care of Pa and all of them, too. "That's nice of her, but she doesn't need to worry about us. We're doin' all right."

Quincy's dark eyes narrowed to slits. "Part o' the reason Mam sent me by is to find out why you didn' come say if you got a exposition job."

Willie groaned. "Quincy, I'm sorry. Right after I found out I got a job —"

"You did?" Quincy sat straight up, his smile wide. He smacked Willie on the shoulder. "Good! Now you an' me c'n —"

"Hold up. Lemme finish." He hated stomping on Quincy's joy, but there wasn't any sense in getting him all excited. Not yet. "I got a notice sayin' I'd been chosen for security guard, but right afterward, Mrs.

Blaricum told me she couldn't stay days with Pa anymore. An' you know I can't leave him alone. Not all day."

Quincy slumped low in his chair. "What you gonna do?"

"I don't know. That's why I stayed an' talked to the preacher. He's gonna come by later an' talk to me some more." He remembered something Preacher Hines said, and a hint of happiness struck. "He said he didn't think God would let me get hired if I wasn't supposed to take the job."

A grin crept up Quincy's cheeks. "Then why're we sittin' here all glum an' gloomy? You got the job. You gonna get to do it." He shrugged. "I'd ruther you was doin' groundskeepin', same as me, but I'm mostly glad we'll be goin' ovuh togethuh. Mam, she was some worried 'bout me goin' by myself, what with the unsettledness between white an' black folk."

Willie couldn't understand why so many people had trouble looking past the color of somebody else's skin. He and Quincy had never cared that Quincy's hair was tight coils of coal black and Willie's was straight and the color of straw. Their families didn't care, either. Pa and Ma considered the Tates good friends, and Ruger and Zenia Tate felt the same way about Willie's folks. People

106

needed to be more like God, who looked on folks' hearts, like He did with the shepherd boy David in First Samuel. Every one of the Tates had a good heart. Even Quincy, who sometimes let his temper get the best of him.

Willie brushed crumbs from the table to the floor, wishing he could get rid of bigotry so easy. "Well, that's part of what the exposition is s'posed to do — settle things." It'd be fine to be involved in bringing an end to the unrest the War Between the States hadn't managed to erase.

Quincy pushed his chair away from the table and stood. "I reckon I oughta get on home. Mam'll be lookin' for me to help Bunson with choppin' wood into tomorrow's stove kindlin'. She go through firewood the way Stu an' Sassy go through molasses cookies. Them two was born with sweet tooths."

Willie stood, too, and handed Quincy the empty basket. "If you can wrestle some molasses cookies away from the twins, put 'em in here an' bring 'em over."

Quincy laughed. They turned toward the front door, and at the same time someone knocked on it. Quincy jolted. "Betcha that's the preacher, comin' like he said he would."

"Uh-huh." Willie gnawed at a piece of dry

skin on his lip. "S'pose God's already told him who can take care of Pa?"

"Ain't gonna know 'less you ask 'im."

Willie broke out in a sweat — mostly from eagerness, and a little from nervousness. God didn't always answer yes. Pa still being sickly and weak proved it. But Willie needed a yes, and quick. What would he do if the preacher didn't have any more ideas than Willie had?

Quincy nudged him. "Go on. Can't leave a preacher standin' on yo' stoop. Let 'im in." He inched in the direction of the back door. "I'll head on home. Come tell me later what he say. I'll tell Mam an' Pap what you's needin', an' they'll be prayin'." He slipped out.

Willie pulled in a breath and marched to the front door. He swung it wide. Preacher Hines waited on the other side of the threshold. His wife stood beside him.

The preacher removed his hat. "Willie, can we come in?"

Uncertain, Willie looked from one to the other. Besides Mrs. Blaricum, who didn't count because she was a helper instead of a guest, a woman hadn't visited since the day of Ma's funeral. All he could think about was the dirty dishes in the basin and the crumbs under the table. "Um . . ."

"We have some news to share."

Willie couldn't tell by the man's expression or voice if it was good news or bad. He wouldn't know until he let them in. He moved out of the way. "Yes. Come on in, Preacher Hines, Mrs. Hines." What would Ma say to guests? "Please have a seat."

8

Laurel

The loom in the corner of the Millards'
parlor sat idle. Sunday, Mama said, was the
day of rest. Mama was, at this very minute,
taking her customary nap. Ordinarily Laurel
read while Mama napped, but she couldn't
sit still. Too much excitement quivered
through her. So she removed the cover from
the loom, perched on the stool, and added
rows to the rug she'd begun the day before.

She operated the loom without conscious
thought, the actions as natural as breathing
— shuttle through the shed, pull the beater,
pump-pump on the treadles, send the
shuttle through again, repeat. While she
worked, she thought about the plans Mama
and Eugene had made during lunch for
transporting Laurel to and from the fairgrounds each day. Riding in the comfort of
Mr. Salisbury's fine carriage every morning
and evening would be a treat in itself. The

leather seat cradled her against any bump in the road, and the fold-up sides and top prevented the wind from tousling her hair. Why, she'd feel like a princess being carried to a ball each day! Would she ever have imagined such adventure?

Before Eugene and his family left for their own little cottage on the edge of the Salisbury property, she had thanked her brother profusely, but he hadn't so much as smiled in reply. It gave her no pleasure to worry him, but his somber countenance could not rob her of joy. Not even Nell's stern frown or Alfred's disapproving glare, tossed at her in tandem upon her late arrival to service that morning, had squashed her happy mood. If she came away from the fairgrounds each day smiling and unharmed, eventually Eugene would see there was no need to fret. Maybe she'd find a vendor and buy a licorice whip for him each payday. That should sweeten him up.

A giggle found its way from her throat, adding a lilting melody to the percussion of the loom's thumps and thuds. She paused and scanned the rows she'd added to the rug. The vertical stripes were perfectly aligned, the thread tension even. With a nod of satisfaction, she put the loom to work again, keeping a slow, steady rhythm, unwilling to awaken Mama or earn a scolding for carelessness.

Would the loom at the fairgrounds be as easy to operate as Mama's thirty-year-old floor loom? Silk must be far different than the bulky cotton and wool she and Mama used. What if her familiarity with this old loom made it difficult for her to learn how to thread and weave the silken strands on a different kind of loom?

Worry nibbled at her. But she gave the beater a firm yank, and the dull thunk sent the unwelcome emotion scuttling from her thoughts.

God had given her this job. Mama had approved it. All would be well.

Quincy

Real early Monday morning, even before the sun was full up, Quincy tromped across the dewy grass. His grin stretched his freshly shaved cheeks. Willie'd be going with him to the exposition after all.

Preacher Hines had sure fixed things up fine, finding church ladies who'd come stay with Mr. Sharp while Willie was working. The preacher even promised to get things arranged at the convalescent hospital so Mr. Sharp could move in there soon as Willie got his first pay envelope from the exposition.

Mam had sung praises for an hour after Willie come and shared the good news with all of Quincy's family. The white folks took care of their own almost as good as black folks did, Mam said. And that was saying something, 'cause them in his neighborhood never left a need untended. Mam always said there be three things in life he could depend on — his heavenly Father, his family, and his neighbors. Sure made Quincy happy to know all that was true for Willie, too.

Quincy stepped up on the Sharps' stoop and tapped his knuckles on the door. The door popped open right away, and Willie come out, all dressed up in his church clothes.

"Mornin,' Quincy. Ready to go?"

Quincy reared back and looked him up and down. "Hoo-ee, you all spit shined an' fancy. How come you's wearin' yo' go-to-meetin' suit?"

Willie shrugged and pulled at his shirt collar. "Mrs. Hines said I ought to. To make a good impression."

Quincy glanced at his patched britches and Pap's blue-striped hand-me-down shirt. Should he run home and change quick into something nicer? He didn't own no suit like Willie was wearing, but he had one pair of trousers and a shirt he saved for Sunday, so they didn't have no holes or patches. He scratched his cheek, worrying. If he started work this first day, he'd likely get dirty. Didn't matter he was twenty years old. Mam'd have his hide if he mussed his best clothes. He'd best stay in what he'd put on.

He stepped to the ground. "Miz Hines . . . She who seein' to yo' pa today?"

"Yep." Willie gave a little hop off the stoop, the way he and Quincy used to hop off felled logs by the creek when they was no taller'n Pap's waist. Sure looked funny, him doing that in his good suit. "She packed me a lunch, too."

"That be right nice."

"Yep." Willie peeked over his shoulder, like he feared somebody was listening in, and then leaned close to Quincy's ear. "That's mostly why I didn't argue about puttin' on my Sunday duds. Didn't wanna hurt her feelings." He straightened, poking his finger under his collar again. "We best get goin'. Don't wanna be late our first day."

Swinging their lunch pails, they loped across the yard and headed up the street. After only one block, Quincy's underarms started to prickle. Sun wasn't hardly peeking past the treetops and already the air was sticky. Might be they'd get some rain today. Good thing he was wearing work clothes. Wouldn't hurt them none to get wet. But Willie, he'd ruin his suit if he got caught in the rain.

He nudged Willie with his elbow. "I got a nickel in my pocket. If you got one, too, we c'n ketch a streetcar, ride in style to the fairgrounds. Atlanta Railway Comp'ny's got a line goin' right by Piedmont Park now."

Willie grinned. "I brought a dime so I could pay for the streetcar for both of us. We'll be plumb tuckered if we walk the whole way."

Quincy chuckled. "Good thinkin'."

Funny how him and Willie was so different on the outside but so alike on the inside. Mam said they should've been brothers, the way they liked the same things and got into so much mischief together. 'Course, all that mischief making was years back, when they was young and foolish. Willie hadn't piddled in foolishness for some years now. Six, at least. Since his ma passed on, for sure. Willie didn't have time for foolishness these days. Not with taking care of his pa.

Mam said Willie was earning jewels in his crown. Quincy doubted Willie cared much about jewels. He just wanted his pa to get

115

better. And who could blame him? Mam and Pap was praying for Mr. Sharp and Willie, and they'd keep praying until Mr. Sharp was up walking and talking and back to hisself again, even if they had to pray until doomsday.

The sun creeped up above the rooftops, and morning shadows stretched like they was working the kinks out of tired muscles. Quincy's and Willie's shadows slid side by side over the dirt road. Quincy stared at the pair of long dark shapes. Wasn't it something how shadows was all the same color? How would it be if folks only saw other folks' shadows and not their real selves? Everybody looking the same on the outside would make a heap of difference. Probably more folks'd end up being friends, the way him and Willie'd always been friends.

Quincy heaved out a sigh. Mam said the Good Lord done made people in all shapes, sizes, and colors so's the world would have variety, and she claimed He loved all them people the same. Still and all, Quincy wondered if God loved the white folks a little better. Sure seemed like things went easier for most whites than blacks.

He'd pondered it out loud one time when he was thirteen or fourteen, and Mam had sat him down and made him read John 3:16

seventy-seven times in a row, each time saying the *whosoever* a little louder until he
was plumb shouting at the end. Then she'd
told him, real firm but with her eyes all tear-
shiny like she was trying not to cry, "Son,
we can't be puttin' God's feelin's on people.
Always gon' be people who is hateful to ya.
Ain't nothin' we can do 'bout that. But God
— He loves you deep. Don't you fo'get it."
Next day, his voice was hoarse. He didn't
never say something like that again. But he
couldn't help wondering.

Mam and Pap put great stock in what
God's Book said. Mam liked John 3:16 real
good — said it gave her comfort. And Pap
liked reciting John 13:35. Pap told all his
youngsters, if a person loved God — and
every one of his children was expected to
love God — then he was naturally supposed
to love others.

Quincy scratched his cheek where the
razor had nipped him. Some folks was easier
to love than others, and that was a fact. Pap
had warned him that being at the fairgrounds every day, he'd likely come across
some who'd be hard to love. But Mam was
praying for him. And Willie'd be there in
case Quincy needed somebody to talk him
down. Between Mam's powerful prayers
and Willie being close by, he'd be able to

hold his temper if somebody got ugly.

He turned to Willie, ready to tell him how glad he was to be going together. He caught Willie pulling at his collar with one finger and making an awful face. Quincy burst out laughing. "You wishin' you'd left that collar at home?"

Willie bounced a sheepish grin at Quincy. "I'm not wearing it tomorrow, that's for sure." A streetcar bell's clang carried from a few blocks away. Willie broke into a trot. "Hurry. See if we can catch it."

Quincy rolled his eyes. The new steam-powered dummies pulled the streetcars faster'n a man could walk. He wanted to say so, but Willie was already a half block ahead. So he raced after him, the two of them pounding up the road like they'd used to run for the swimming hole. They reached the corner right before the streetcar did.

Willie thumped Quincy on the shoulder with the heel of his hand. "Made it, didn't we?"

Quincy, still winded from his run, didn't answer. He dug in his pocket for his nickel.

Willie shook his head. "Lemme get it today. You can pay tomorrow."

Quincy pocketed the coin and followed Willie to the paused streetcar. The huffing steam engine rattled the car. Back when

118

mules pulled the streetcars, there wasn't none of this shaking. Quincy grabbed the tarnished brass handrail and climbed aboard, grimacing at the vibration under his worn soles.

Willie dropped his dime in the tin cup and picked up two stubs, and they moved between the seats clear to the back. Willie could've took a bench closer to the front, but he shared a rear bench with Quincy. A few folks sent sour looks their way, but Willie didn't seem to notice, so Quincy pretended not to. But a fire raged in his belly.

The streetcar rocked and bounced its way along the route, stopping every block to let some folks off and others on. Willie kept checking the windup pocket watch he carried. The third time he pulled it out, Quincy peeked at it, too. The hands showed seven thirty-two. They was supposed to be at the fairgrounds in their appointed buildings by eight for instruction and training. Sweat tickled the back of his neck and sneaked down his temples. He swiped it away and stared out the window, inwardly pleading for the streetcar to get them to the fairgrounds on time.

Willie's watch showed seven fifty-one when the streetcar stopped where Fourteenth Street met Piedmont Avenue. Willie leaped off the back landing, and Quincy jumped down behind him. Then Quincy stood and stared. Was his eyes playing tricks? Where only grass had been the last time he'd been in this area, a tall building that reminded him of the castle drawings in a dime novel about King Arthur rose up in front of him.

He squeezed Willie's arm. "You seein' what I'm seein'?"

Willie nodded. "It's something, isn't it?" He gave Quincy a little push. "Get on inside."

Quincy's legs took to quivering the way they'd done when he was a youngster and he'd riled his pappy. But somehow he scuffed forward alongside Willie through an arched tunnel big enough for two carriages to pass side by side. On the other side of the tunnel, he stopped again. His mouth fell open.

"Hoo-ee . . ." Willie sounded plain awed. "Look at it."

Quincy shifted his gaze left and right, taking in buildings fancy and plain, paved roadways, and what looked like a queen's flower garden smack in the middle of it all. Shaking his head, he blew out a breath and laughed. "Don't hardly know what kinda groundskeepin' I gon' be doin'. The ground's all filled up!" It'd be a pleasure working on these grounds, everything looked so clean and new. Better, even, than the parts of town built over after ol' General Sherman's troops put a torch to buildings.

"Passage, please."

The polite call came from behind him. Willie grabbed Quincy's arm and pulled him to the edge of the paved roadway. A fancy carriage rolled past. The driver tipped his hat, and Quincy gave him a nod in reply.

Quincy whistled through his teeth and nudged Willie. "That's some carriage, ain't it? All glossy on the sides, an' that bonnet's gotta be real leather."

"Pretty fancy." Willie stared after the carriage. "Rich folks can afford such things."

Rich folks . . . Quincy'd be coming in contact with lots of rich folks here at the exposition. Rich folks, like ones who'd kept his mam and pap working in fields, not letting them learn to read or write, clear up until they was the same age as him now. The hot feeling he always got in his stomach when his temper was getting ready to flare hit hard. He gritted his teeth and told the feeling to scat. He wanted this job. He needed it. Pap an' Bunson couldn't be pulling that wagon forever.

Willie turned around and frowned at the castle. "This is where I'm supposed to go — the Administration Building. Where're you supposed to be?"

"The maint'nance shack. My note say behind the Gov'ment Buildin' on the north side o' the grounds." Now that he'd seen how big the place was, he'd best skedaddle. He started trotting backward, waving his lunch pail. "Bye, Willie. Meetcha here when we's all done today."

Quincy darted up the wide paved path. The soles of his boots slapped the ground, and the hard rock under his feet jarred him, but he didn't slow even when he had to weave around some men in suits nicer than Willie's. The men went on talking like they didn't even see him running by. More rich folks, probably.

A fist gripped his belly. Good thing Mam was praying. Good thing Willie was here. 'Cause even though he was supposed to love all other people the way God loved 'em, Quincy didn't hold much liking for rich folks like the ones who'd kept his mam and pap picking cotton till their fingers bled.

9

Laurel

With her fingers curled over the window sash, Laurel watched out the opening as the carriage rolled past several newly built structures. Fancy buildings. Impressive buildings. The clop of the horse's hooves on the cobblestone sounded loud in the otherwise quiet morning, but not loud enough to drown out the pound of her pulse in her temples. She couldn't recall the last time she'd been so nervous.

The carriage stopped, and Laurel gaped at the row of two-story-high pillars holding up the porch roof of a monstrous building that seemed to be covered in unpainted plaster. Several statues stood guard on top of the structure, and Laurel got the eerie feeling they were staring down at her.

The carriage door popped open, and she released a little squawk of surprise. Eugene gave her a puzzled look and held out his hand. With a self-conscious giggle, she grabbed hold. When her feet touched the ground, she knew she should let go, but she gripped his hand even harder. "W-will you walk me into the Women's Building?"

Sympathy glowed in his brown eyes, but he shook his head. "If you're old enough to take this job, you're old enough to walk yourself in."

Where was the brother who wouldn't let her walk across her own lawn to her front porch a couple of weeks ago? For that matter, where was the girl who'd wanted to walk across her lawn alone? She swallowed and slowly loosened her hold on his hand. "You're right." She clenched her hands at her waist. "I can take myself in." And she would, as soon as her pulse stopped galloping and she was able to draw a full breath.

Eugene gave her a pat on her shoulder. "I'll return at six o'clock for you."

Six o'clock. Ten hours here on her own. Her chest fluttered.

"I'll pull right up here to the building this evening to fetch you, but I'm not sure if I'll be able to come so close after the exposition is open to visitors. They might limit carriages to attendees."

She gulped. That meant she would have to walk through the crowds all the way to the gate to meet the carriage. Why hadn't she considered the crowds before applying for this job? She'd never liked being in places with lots of people. Especially people she didn't know. Mama said she'd been a friendly toddler but was taken to shyness after Papa died, yet Laurel couldn't recall ever being anything but nervous in groups. She wished she could remember. Then she'd know how to act now.

Eugene gazed at her, a worried scowl on his face. "Laurel, are you going in?"

"Yes. Yes, I am." She spoke staunchly, hoping her feet would choose to cooperate.

"Take your lunch pail."

Mama had packed a chicken sandwich, two pickles, and an oatmeal-pecan cookie, all of which had sounded so good half an hour ago. But now? Laurel was certain she wouldn't be able to hold down a bite. She pressed her hands more firmly against her jumping stomach. "Why don't you take it and enjoy it? As a thank-you for carrying me here."

Eugene chuckled, shaking his head the indulgent way he often reacted to his children's antics. "By lunchtime you will have settled in and will be hungry. Take it with you." He reached into the carriage and picked up the pail from the seat. He pressed the bent wire handle into her palm, and her fingers automatically closed around it. "Now, go on in before the clock chimes eight." He pointed to a huge round clock on the tower in front of the Fine Arts Building.

Laurel gasped. The hands showed only one minute before eight. She couldn't be late — not on the very first day. "Goodbye, Eugene. I'll see you this evening." She clambered up the stairs and darted for the double doors.

The first chime tolled in unison with the click of the door latch behind her. She'd made it. She sighed in relief and scurried to the middle of a room shaped like an octagon, then stopped and looked right and left. This area seemed to be a lobby, much like a hotel lobby, with beautiful pictures gracing the walls, potted plants standing proudly in corners, and groupings of chairs offering places to sit. Unlike at a hotel lobby, though, there wasn't a desk clerk. What should she do next?

Twin staircases with polished spindles curved upward on both sides, and several short hallways branched away from the main room. She twirled a loose strand of hair and bit the corner of her lower lip. Why hadn't the notice indicated where the Silk

Room was located? Laurel turned a slow circle, peering up each hallway by turn. When her gaze reached the fourth one, she gave a start. A tall dark-haired woman in a solid-gray dress stood framed in the opening. Were it not for her pale complexion and the cream-colored cameo pinned at her throat, she would have completely blended into the shadows.

"Miss Millard?" The woman's tone was as severe as her appearance.

Laurel gulped and nodded.

"Please follow me." She turned and disappeared from view.

Laurel followed on trembling legs. When she crossed the threshold of the doorway at the end of the hallway, the woman was already in the center of a large rectangular room. A brass chandelier with four light bulbs aimed downward hung from the ceiling above her head. The bulbs weren't lit, but a row of windows across the back of the room allowed in morning sunlight and illuminated the space as sufficiently as a dozen oil lamps.

Laurel's feet slowed of their own volition, and she let her gaze drift around the room where she would spend much of the next several months. Fairly large, cheerful, with walls painted yellow and beautiful tapestries hanging from gold tasseled ropes at each end. A pleasant space.

The woman crossed behind a long glass case that stretched across the west side, dividing the room not quite in half. She beckoned with her fingers. Laurel walked the length of the case, squinting at the large jars arranged inside on a bed of blue satin. Or was the fabric silk? With the sun bouncing off the glass, Laurel couldn't determine what was inside the jars, but it must be important to be housed in such a beautiful case on the sheeny, rich-colored fabric bed.

Behind the glass case, a huge loom filled half of the space. On the other half, a row of three chairs sat tucked beneath a tapestry of butterflies fluttering around a stem of salvia. Two of the chairs were already occupied by a pair of unsmiling girls who appeared close to Laurel's age. They'd been so quiet she hadn't realized they were there.

She offered each of them a shy smile as she placed her lunch pail on the floor and perched on the remaining chair. They glanced at her, but neither spoke or smiled in reply. Laurel folded her hands in her lap, the way the others were sitting. The same way she often sat when Alfred or Nell was speaking. The comparison did little to calm her jangled nerves.

The gray-dressed woman stood between them and the glass case and linked her hands at her waist. "Now that we are all here, please introduce yourselves." She nodded to the tall, thin blond-haired girl seated in the first chair.

The girl's face flushed bright pink. "Felicia Hill."

"Hello, Felicia." Laurel spoke without thinking and earned a frown from the dour-faced woman. She shrank back in her chair.

The woman shifted her gaze to the somewhat plump girl with frizzy red hair who was seated in the middle.

"I'm Berta Collinwood."

The woman turned to Laurel and arched a brow in silent query.

Nervousness made Laurel's mouth dry. She wished she could request a glass of water. Or maybe some Coca-Cola. Her oldest niece was partial to the fizzy drink. "Laurel Millard."

"Thank you." The woman straightened her shoulders and placed her fingertips against the unadorned bodice of her dress. "I am Miss Eloise Beatrice Warner. You may call me Miss Warner."

Berta and Felicia nodded, and Laurel imitated the action.

Apparently Miss Warner found the reaction pleasing, because a slight smile lifted the corners of her thin lips. "Over the next several weeks, we will become well acquainted, and I am sure we shall get along very well if you follow the simple rules I've established for you."

Miss Warner began listing her expectations. By the sixth rule — *Lunch break will last half an hour and will be taken on a rotating schedule* — Laurel wished she'd brought a pad of paper and a pencil. How would she remember everything?

The recitation of the "simple" rules continued, and when Miss Warner reached number ten, her expression turned stern. "There will be no fraternizing with guests to the exposition."

Berta gave a little jerk. "We can't talk to the people who come in to watch us make the silk?"

Laurel wouldn't have had the courage to ask the question, but she was very glad Berta had.

"Of course you'll answer the visitors' questions. But engaging in idle chitchat or otherwise frivolous conversation is strictly forbidden." Miss Warner placed her hands on her hips. "You are here to perform a duty, Miss Collinwood. A duty, I might add, for which you are being paid very well.

Extraction of silk from the cocoons is a delicate process, and each cocoon is precious. The owners will not tolerate damaged silk or cocoons. Consequently, if you cannot remain focused, you will be dismissed."

The girls exchanged a quick look, and Laurel read in their eyes the same uncertainty that held her captive. She'd come in the hopes of meeting the young man destined to make her heart sing. How would she know if he was the right one if she had no opportunity to speak with him?

Willie

Willie smoothed his hand down the front of his new security guard uniform as he strode toward a circle of benches near the man-made lake called Clara Meer, where the men had been directed to take their lunch break. His church suit was folded real neat and tucked into a square cubby in the small room in the basement of the Administration Building. His name — William Sharp — was etched on a tiny plate and tacked to the lower edge of his cubby.

All sixteen of the fellows hired for security had their own cubbies where they'd store their lunches each day. Willie liked the setup. At the factory, the workers put their lunches on a table in the break room.

Sometimes somebody picked up the wrong pail, and if he liked what was in it better than what he'd brought himself, he ate it instead of finding his own. Willie'd lost more than one dinner because of it. Nobody'd get confused about whose lunch was whose here.

Willie took a spot at the end of one of the benches and opened his pail, eager to taste the roast-beef-and-horseradish sandwiches Mrs. Hines had packed for him. The sun made him squint, but he welcomed the brightness after being cooped up in the windowless room where they'd received instruction all morning.

He glanced around the circle. Out in the sunshine it was easier to make out the men's faces. It sure looked like every other fellow had more years on him than Willie had. How'd he gotten so lucky to be hired? Young, no real experience, but here he sat. If Pa could talk sentences, he'd say God had made it happen, and Willie would say Pa was right. There wasn't no other explanation.

"Whaddaya think about them folks from Ohio settin' up a room for silk makin'?" A fellow named Briggs talked around a bite of his sandwich. "Don't it seem kinda strange, considerin' this is a cotton exposition?"

The man beside Willie leaned forward and looked around him at Briggs. "I reckon it's no stranger than the California people makin' orange juice or the barley people makin' beer."

Briggs huffed. "Are you dim-witted, Cooley? You don't use orange juice or beer to make cloth. It ain't the same."

Cooley's jaw muscles bulged. "You're the dim-witted one if you're thinkin' silk'll take the place of cotton."

Briggs started to say something else, but laughter blasted from somewhere on the grounds. Deep, throaty laughter. Willie blew out a breath of relief. The laughing interrupted what could've turned into a skirmish, and even better, he recognized Quincy's hearty chuckle in the mix. Willie'd never had any scuffles with Quincy. Their friendship ran too deep to let reasons for scuffles come between them. But Quincy was quick to pull up his fists and defend himself against insults, whether real or imagined. If Quincy was chuckling, he was having a good time.

Briggs jabbed his thumb over his shoulder. "That's the kind o' ruckus that'll probably come from the Negro Building when they get it all finished. They hired at least thirty of 'em to scrape horse dung off the streets

133

an' sweep the buildings an' so forth."

A fellow named Turner snorted. "As if it'd take thirty men to keep things up around here. Twenty could've done it easy."

Briggs nudged him. "Had to hire so many 'cause they're lazy. The whole lot of 'em."

Willie prickled. He'd heard such talk before. Some people still held grudges about the war, and for reasons he'd never understand, they blamed the ones who'd been emancipated instead of the ones who'd kept people enslaved. Pa was born and raised in the South, and he'd put on a Confederate uniform to please his daddy, but he came from a sharecropping family. Even if he'd been a plantation owner, Pa wouldn't've kept slaves. Pa said Jesus came to break the chains that bound a man, and that included the chains clamped on field workers' ankles. In Pa's opinion, one man didn't have any right to put chains on another man. But there were lots of folks who, even now, didn't hold with Pa's opinion.

"At least they're all on groundskeepin'," Turner said. "They've got their place an' we've got ours, so we won't have to work alongside 'em."

Haverman, the fellow sitting across from Willie, dropped his half-eaten sandwich into his lunch pail and flung his checked napkin in on top of it. "You fellas're gonna have to adjust your thinkin'. Times're changin'. In some places, colored fellas are being let into universities. Some of 'em are even gettin' into government."

Briggs shook his head. "Not *my* government."

"You're wrong on that. Openin' day, we'll be hearin' from one o' the president's advisors, a Negro man by the name of —"

Briggs swiped his hand through the air. "I know all about the plans for openin' day. You all wanna go listen, go ahead, but I won't be standin' close enough to hear him."

Haverman arched one bushy eyebrow. "You will if you're assigned a post in the Auditorium."

Briggs smirked. "No, I won't."

One of the other men leaned in. "If you don't do what you're told, you'll get fired. You'd really let yourself get fired just to keep from listenin' to a colored man's speech?"

"If I have to sacrifice my principles, then nobody'll need to fire me. I'll quit. Ain't no amount of money big enough to make me stand side by side with *them.*" Briggs wadded up the square of waxed paper that had held his sandwich and tossed it over his shoulder. He sent a grin around the circle. "Let one of the groundskeepers take care o' that. They're gettin' paid for it." He stood and sauntered toward the Administration Building, whistling.

The others — some muttering, some snickering — rose and followed. Willie went last. He passed the crumpled paper. Several of the men had stepped on it, smashing it almost flat. He shot a furtive glance at the men's backs. Nobody was looking. He stooped over, snatched up the paper, and stuck it in his lunch pail.

The supervisor had said they'd all be assigned a partner and would patrol in pairs. Willie stared at the flattened wad of paper and prayed he wouldn't get paired with Briggs. Or he might have to quit.

10

Laurel

At the end of the day, Laurel descended the porch steps with Berta and Felicia. Mr. Salisbury's landau already waited outside the building, and Eugene was poised beside the carriage door. She waved goodbye to the other girls, who set off in the direction of the footbridge that stretched across Clara Meer, and scampered across the ground to her brother.

"Hello, Eugene. I hope you haven't been waiting long."

"I arrived only a few minutes ago." He gave her a look that seemed half-worried, half-hopeful. "Did you have a good day?"

Laurel tipped her head, trying to choose an accurate answer. Berta and Felicia were nice enough. The three of them might become friends over time. Miss Warner was strict, but Laurel sensed she wasn't unkind. Laurel had enjoyed examining the contents of the jars inside the case, which showed the various phases of a silkworm's life from egg to worm to cocoon to moth. The elaborate staging inside each jar reminded her of the miniature replicas she and her classmates had constructed of Indian villages or British colonies.

She shrugged. "I think it was good."

Eugene smiled and grazed her shoulder with his fingers. "I'm glad."

"There's a lot to learn, but I think I'll be able to remember it."

"Of course you will."

His confidence gave her a happy lift. Such sweet words. Sweeter, even, than the candy he used to bring her. She beamed at him. "Thank you." Then she laughed lightly. "But tomorrow I'm bringing paper and a pencil so I can write down everything Miss Warner says. I had no idea there was so much to know about silkworms."

Eugene had opened the carriage door, but now he closed it with a snap. "Why don't you tell me about it on the drive home? It might help you to remember it all if you recite it for me."

Laurel agreed without a moment's pause. He assisted her onto the driver's seat and then climbed up beside her. He took the reins and turned a gentle smile on her.

"All right. I'm listening."

Her mind whirled with all the information she'd received about silkworms — their gestation, the percentage of cocoons harvested, and the percentage allowed to transition into moths to lay eggs for more worms. Where should she start? "Well, silkworms hatch from the eggs of the *Bombyx mori* moth and begin spinning cocoons after only thirty-two to thirty-eight days — hardly more than a month." He flicked the reins. The carriage lurched forward, and the horse broke into a steady clip-clop. "The cocoon is formed of a half-mile-long thread called a —"

Ahead, another carriage and a wagon stacked high with milled boards rolled from between buildings and took position in front of them. The rattle of the lengths of wood bouncing in the back of the wagon combined with the grind and *thunk-thunk* of several wheels on cobblestone proved too noisy for Laurel to continue without yelling. She held out her hands in a gesture of futility and fell silent.

From her high seat, she had a better view of the fairgrounds. The buildings were, as she'd noted in the morning, quite elaborate, but some didn't appear finished. The exposition started the day after tomorrow. Would the construction team be able to complete it all in time? For that matter, would one more day be long enough for her to learn everything about silk making? A shiver trembled through her.

Eugene bumped her with his elbow. "If you're chilly, I can stop and let you get inside the carriage."

"No, I'm fine." How silly to holler at each other when they sat side by side. She hoped the lumber-filled wagon would turn off soon. She needed all the practice she could get reciting the facts she would be expected to share with visitors to the Silk Room.

Willie

Willie waited for Quincy behind the Administration Building, close to the tunnel archway. He'd changed out of his uniform and into his suit, but he'd put the stiff collar in his jacket pocket instead of around his neck. He hoped Mrs. Hines wouldn't notice. All the other guards were already gone, and Willie was more glad of that than being free of his collar. When Quincy came, Willie wouldn't have to worry about Briggs or Turner or one of the others saying something that would stir Quincy's temper.

A carriage pulled by a pair of bays passed by, and a wagon loaded down by a pile of lumber rolled out behind it. The swaybacked horses attached to the wagon hung their heads low and they plodded, very different from the high-stepping bays. A second carriage followed the wagon, the same fancy carriage that had forced him and Quincy off the road that morning. The sorrel gelding hitched to the carriage was the prettiest thing Willie'd ever seen.

His family didn't have a stable, and they couldn't have afforded a horse if they did have a place to put it. But if he owned a horse, he'd want one like the sorrel. The animal's mane bounced against its sleek neck, and sunlight shimmered on its red-brown coat.

He started to wave to the driver, but then he froze with his hand in midair. The girl he'd seen in the bank — the one who'd twirled a strand of brown hair into a spring around her finger — was sitting beside the driver.

With a jerk, he raised his hand as high as his head and waved. The driver nodded, and the girl offered a shy smile and a little wave with her fingers. The tunnel swallowed the horse and carriage, hiding the driver and girl from his sight. So she'd gotten hired, too. His heart gave a happy flip. She'd seemed so nervous that day. The same way he'd felt. He was as happy for her as he was for himself, even though he wasn't sure why she needed a job if her family was wealthy enough to afford a fancy carriage and such a beautiful horse.

"Hey, Willie!" Quincy panted to a stop next to Willie, his dark face shining with perspiration. "Sorry I took so long. We all got assigned our own tools an' such, an' I wanted mine put away neat so's I could get to 'em quick an' easy tomorrow mornin'."

"*. . . they're lazy. The whole lot of 'em.*" Briggs's sneering comment echoed in Willie's mind. Would he say such a thing if he'd heard Quincy talk about taking good care of his tools? Willie grimaced. Probably. Men like Briggs had their minds made up and weren't likely to change, even if the truth looked them in the eye.

He slung his arm across Quincy's shoulders. "I didn't mind waitin'. Got to see some pretty horses." He also got to see a pretty girl, but for some reason he didn't want to share that with Quincy. He forced a chuckle and put his feet into motion. "Also saw a couple of nags. Betcha if there was a race, you an' me could beat those two tired ol' horses without breakin' a sweat."

Quincy grinned. "Not today I couldn', after the work I put in." He breathed a sigh heavy with satisfaction. "I was kinda hopin' they'd put me on the Negro Buildin'. It ain't finished yet, an' it would be mighty fine to have a hand in gettin' it done an' ready for visitors. But Supervisor say me an' a white-haired fella named Cass'll be takin' care o' the area aroun' the lake. Even get to loan out the rowboats to folks an' put 'em up at the end o' the day. Sure like bein' aroun' the watuh. Reminds me o' when we went fishin' an' frog catchin' at the crick down the hill, 'member?"

Good memories flooded Willie's mind of him and Quincy bringing strings of speckled trout home, Pa helping them clean them, and Ma frying them up. Hunger struck. For the fish, and for the bygone days. "I remember."

Quincy shook his head, wonder blooming on his face. "Ain't never had a chance to sit in a rowboat, but I might get to 'cause o' this job. Won't that be somethin'?"

"Sure will." Willie clapped Quincy's shoulder and dropped his hand to his pocket. "I got this morning's trolley stubs. Let's use 'em to get a ride close to home, huh?"

"That sound good to me. I's slap wore out."

Mrs. Hines had supper waiting — ham-and-potato hash and biscuits — when Willie came through the door. As much as he appreciated her kindness, he hoped the other ladies wouldn't treat him so good. He'd get used to it and have trouble seeing to his and Pa's meals when the church ladies didn't come anymore. Of course, if they didn't fix supper, him and Pa would be eating pretty late in the evening. Maybe it was better if the ladies did the supper cooking.

While Willie ate, Mrs. Hines told him about Pa's day, how they'd read the paper together, how she let the cat in to sit on Pa's lap, and how they made pictures with puzzle blocks because a nurse at the convalescent hospital had said it would be good for Pa to "practice his dexterity."

Willie glanced into the front room. Pa was sitting in his chair with his head back and his eyes closed. The man who'd carved detailed animals from a chunk of wood had willingly played with a child's toy? "Pa . . . do all right with that?"

"He had some trouble grippin' the blocks." Mrs. Hines sounded cheerful. A lot happier than Willie felt. "It took some time, but we made a tiger's face. We almost finished a lamb's face, too, but he seemed tired so we stopped."

Tired? Maybe. Pa did wear out quick

144

these days. But Willie suspected sometimes Pa used naps to escape the boring life he now lived.

"I'll leave the blocks here for Mrs. Bullard. She's comin' tomorrow. Maybe she and Otto will be able to finish the lamb's face."

Willie couldn't decide if he wanted that or not. He wanted Pa well again. Sure he did. But playing with children's toys? He stuffed the last bite of biscuit in his mouth so he wouldn't be able to say what he was thinking. No need to hurt the preacher's wife's feelings. She meant well, but making a lamb's face with blocks wasn't a very manly thing for Pa to do.

A sudden thought jarred him. He swallowed the lump of biscuit. "Ma'am? Playin' with blocks, practicin' " — what had she called it? — "dexterity, is that what Pa'll do at the hospital?"

"In part." She picked up his empty plate and fork and carried them to the washbasin. "The nurse also suggested havin' him string beads, draw lines or shapes with pastels, and turn the pages in a book."

Willie stifled a grunt. Was Pa going to a convalescent hospital or a nursery school? How would he keep his dignity if they made him play with toys?

"The nurse said it's important to get him usin' his right hand as much as possible. He said muscles . . ." Mrs. Hines scowled and tapped her chin. Then she brightened. "Atrophy. That's the word — atrophy. That means they waste away if they aren't used. Of course Otto wants to use his left hand because he has better control of it."

But not good control. The pieces of chopped ham and potatoes on the table and floor let Willie know Pa had dropped quite a bit of his supper.

"But the longer he allows his right hand to lie idle, the harder it'll be for him to regain full use of it again."

Willie leaned his elbows on the table and watched her wash and dry his plate and fork. When she put them on the shelf with the other dishes, he cleared his throat. "Ma'am?"

She returned to the table with a wet dishcloth and swished it over the tabletop. "Yes?"

He glanced at Pa again. Was he really asleep? Just in case he was playing possum, Willie lowered his voice to a raspy whisper. "Do you think stackin' blocks and stringin' beads will really help Pa get his right hand workin' again?"

"I think it can't hurt. At least he'll be usin'

it, and that's better than not usin' it, yes?"

Willie couldn't come up with an argument. Even more than he missed seeing his pa whittle or swing an ax or stride up the street to the factory every day, he missed hearing his voice. Stringing beads and such wouldn't help Pa talk again. Would the people at the hospital be able to make his tongue work like it had before?

Mrs. Hines headed for the front door. "Now, remember, tomorrow Mrs. Bullard'll be here. The names of the ladies for Wednesday through Saturday are on a piece of paper on top of your pie safe so you'll be able to tell Otto ahead of time who's comin'."

Willie slid his arm around Pa's shoulders. His bones poked out where muscle used to be. Willie swallowed a lump of sadness. "Thank you. It sure eases my mind to know there's folks willin' to see to Pa when I'm not here."

"The people in Estel's congregation are kindhearted souls. They were glad to help once they knew there was a need." She paused and stared at Pa for a few seconds, her brow all puckered. "Maybe I'll talk to Estel about usin' some of the church's benevolence funds so you can get Otto into the convalescent hospital right away."

147

"Ma'am, thank you, but —"

"It's already been . . . what? Four months since he fell ill?"

Willie gulped. "Comin' up on five."

"Then I should say the sooner he begins receivin' treatment, the better." She nodded, like she was agreeing with herself about something. "Goodbye, Willie an' Otto. Enjoy your evenin'."

Willie considered going after her, telling her there wasn't any need to dip into the special emergencies account, but Mrs. Hines was probably eager to get home to her family. She'd been here with Pa close to twelve hours now. He grimaced. He was expecting an awful lot from the ladies at church.

He sat on the armrest of the chair and patted Pa's shoulder. "Didja have a good day, Pa?"

One short nod.

Willie smiled. "Me, too. Wanna hear about it?"

Another nod.

"All right, then. Want I should let Rusty in for a while?"

A bigger nod.

Willie laughed. He crossed to the back door. The big tom was waiting, like he knew Willie planned to open the door. He bounded under the table and went to cleaning up the mess. The cat would come to Pa when he'd finished eating, so Willie returned to the sitting room and perched on the edge of the sofa. He told Pa about getting to wear a uniform and how nervous he felt about carrying a pistol on his hip like a real lawman. He described the buildings at the park and even told him about the horses he'd seen at the end of the day.

He talked until Pa's eyelids drooped and his shoulders sagged. Willie helped him to the outhouse and then to bed. As he closed Pa's door, sadness struck. He'd sure miss his company while he was at the convalescent hospital. Whether Pa was here or at the hospital, Willie wouldn't get to see him much, what with working the exposition every day except Sunday.

He scooped Rusty from Pa's chair and put him out. Then he readied himself for bed, but even though he was tired, he couldn't sleep. God gave him the job. Preacher Hines even said so. Willie'd been wanting to find a way to get Pa into the convalescent hospital for months, and now he could do it. But he sure didn't want to pay all that money just for Pa to play with blocks.

11

Quincy

In all his born days, Quincy wouldn't never have thought he'd get to hear somebody like Booker T. Washington make a speech. But here he was on the exposition's official opening day, standing at the back of the Auditorium with the other fellows hired for groundskeeping, listening in. Bunson was with him, too, all wide eyed and twitchy, acting like the little 'uns did on Christmas morning. Quincy understood his brother's excitement. His insides was jumping, and his cheeks hurt from smiling. Probably looked plumb foolish. But he couldn't help it. This was a *good* day.

Why, right after thanking them who put together the exposition, Mr. Washington talked straight to the black folks. The black folks! Praised them for being loyal in service to the whites. Told them how they had better opportunities in commerce and industry here in the South than they would in the North. Quincy couldn't help peeking at the white side of the audience. Was they listening, too? Mostly they was the ones owning the businesses, so they had the opportunities to give. They needed the nudge to notice the black folks and give 'em the chance for better jobs.

He liked one of Mr. Washington's phrases — "Cast down your bucket." He memorized it so he could repeat it to Mam and Pap. And he memorized what it meant. In part, make friends with people of all races. Tremors rattled Quincy's frame. Wouldn't it be fine if all the folks in this room did just that? Become friends together the way him and Willie had always been friends? He hoped all those white folks filling the seats on the other side of the room was paying attention.

The speech went on, now talking direct to the whites. Folks all over the Auditorium fanned themselves, and sweat dribbled down Quincy's temples. He shrugged away the moisture with his shirtsleeve and kept his gaze fixed on Mr. Washington. Seemed like fire blazed in the speaker's eyes. He stood so tall and proud, raising his arms like the preacher sometimes did during rowdy sermons.

Some of his words — *glorify, ornamental gewgaws, magnificent representation* — was too fancy for Quincy to grasp, but they sounded so pretty he couldn't stop listening. Mr. Washington dressed so fine, talked so proud. And everybody listened. Even the white folks. Like they all knowed he was somebody special. Quincy's chest went tight. How would it feel to have folks look at him the way they watched Mr. Washington, all respectful-like?

"In all things that are purely social we can be as separate as the fingers, yet one as the hand in all things essential to mutual progress."

Quincy held up his hand and stared at his callused fingers. He wiggled them one by one and then tightened them together in a fist. He scanned the audience, frowning, thinking hard. Could it be done? Could all these folks here — whites and blacks — work together to make the South strong?

". . . let us pray God will come, in a blotting out of sectional differences an' racial animosities an' suspicions . . ."

His heart pounding, Quincy gulped and stared at the speaker.

"This, coupled with our material prosperity, will bring into our beloved South a new heaven an' a new earth." Mr. Washington took a step away from the podium. His arms dropped to his sides. He bowed his head. He was done.

Such a stillness fell in the room that it gave Quincy chills. The stillness lasted a little while, maybe for the count of ten, and then folks on the black side of the Auditorium started clapping. The whites on the other side joined in. The applause was loud as thunder, and Quincy smacked his palms together so hard they stung, but he wanted to be part of that noise. It went on and on, white folks and black folks giving honor to the man who'd told them they could be "one as the hand."

Finally all that clapping came to an end, and folks milled up the aisles for the exit doors. Quincy grabbed Bunson's arm and pulled him along with the throng. Outside, he tugged Bunson off the walkway and gave his arm a squeeze.

"You gon' remember good enough to tell Mam an' Pap what'n all Mr. Washington say?"

Bunson's dark eyes shone. "I sho' am. Best speech I ever did hear."

Quincy chuckled. That was the only speech they'd ever heard. But he couldn't imagine one being any better. "Head on home, then, an' —"

"Quincy?" Bunson almost danced in place. "You reckon I could someday go to the college in Alabama that Mr. Washington started? I'd like to wear a fancy suit an' learn to speak fine like him, maybe study on how to keep books an' get a job in a bank or some big comp'ny."

Bunson always did like arithmetic. He'd probably be a right good bookkeeper. But where would Mam and Pap find the money to send him to Alabama? They barely had enough to pay for the little 'uns' shoes and the pencils and such they needed for school. Looking into his brother's hopeful eyes, Quincy couldn't find the heart to stomp on his dream.

He clapped Bunson on the shoulder. "You ask Mam an' Pap 'bout that. I gotta get to work now, so head on home."

Bunson shot off across the grass. Quincy turned and braced himself to break into a jog, but his body came up short. His eyes beheld a sea of folks spreading out across the grounds. Black folks and white folks, the ladies wearing everything from home-spun to bustled suits, white men in top hats and jackets with tails only feet away from black men in trousers and checked shirts. Nobody sneering at somebody else. Nobody shying away from somebody else. Everybody just . . . walking.

"*. . . a new heaven an' a new earth.*"

Quincy shook his head, wonderment warming him from head to toe. "I reckon I might be seein' what'n all that'd look like."

Laurel

Laurel, Felicia, and Berta followed Miss Warner on a weaving path through the crowd. She'd insisted they attend the opening speech, and Laurel was grateful for the opportunity. The exuberant applause echoed in her ears. She wished Mama could have heard the president's advisor. Mama and Mr. Washington seemed to agree on the importance of education. Laurel's heart still pounded in excitement, covering the sound of her soles pattering against the cobblestone walkway. She had to trot to keep up with her supervisor, whose stride nearly doubled hers.

Miss Warner glanced over her shoulder. "Hurry, girls. We need to be in the building before visitors begin arriving."

Berta huffed and muttered, "Then we should've left before the speech ended. Look at all these people! They got a head start on us."

"No fussing, Miss Collinwood." Miss Warner didn't slow her pace or glance back.

"Save your breath for answering questions."

Berta aimed a disbelieving look at Laurel and Felicia, but she didn't say anything. They reached the Women's Building and clattered up the steps. As Miss Warner had feared, exposition guests were already inside. She ushered the girls past them and into the Silk Room. Three women stood in front of a tapestry, their gazes rapt.

Miss Warner drew the girls to the back side of the glass counter. "Felicia, go welcome our visitors and ask if they'd like to know more about the dyeing process for the colored threads in the tapestries. Berta, remain here to answer questions about the silkworms and silk extraction. Laurel, you know what to do."

Laurel nodded. "Yes, ma'am." Her experience on Mama's loom had proved helpful, making learning to weave the silk threads an easy transition. Rather than try to teach Berta and Felicia to use the loom in such a short period of time, Miss Warner chose to give Laurel the responsibility of operating the loom. During quiet times, Laurel would instruct the other girls so they would be able to fill her spot when she took breaks.

She scurried to the loom and seated herself on the bench. Her pulse raced, in part from the brisk walk across the park grounds, but mostly from nervousness. Would she be able to remember all the steps when an audience observed? She positioned her trembling hands in readiness and prayed they would cooperate. Pulling in a deep breath, she picked up the shuttle and began.

Her breath eased out, and a smile pulled at her lips as her hands and feet fell into rhythm. The loom's gentle melody — the soft *thunk-thunk* of the treadles, *ker-thump* of the beater, and *whisper-whir* of the shuttle — lulled Laurel into a familiar dance. One so familiar she could perform it without conscious thought.

Dimly aware of the activity on the other side of the glass case barrier, she continued weaving the glistening yellow strands she'd threaded through the warp and heddle the day before. The progress seemed painstaking because the silk thread was so fine, but by noon a two-inch length of silk fabric shimmered on the cloth beam. Laurel couldn't resist stopping and running her fingers lightly over the woven threads. As smooth as ice and soft as down. So different from cotton.

Someone touched her shoulder, and she gave a start. Laughter filled her ear. She looked up into Felicia's amused face.

"I'm back from my lunch break. Miss

Warner says you should take yours now."

"Oh!" Laurel darted a glance around the room, seeking Miss Warner. Their supervisor was near the door, visiting with a woman who wore a hat overtaken by three enormous ostrich feathers. She heaved a sigh of relief. "I thought you were her, reminding me to keep weaving."

"Not this time."

Laurel rose from the bench and stretched. "Did you take your lunch to the bench by Clara Meer?" The three of them had enjoyed impromptu picnics by the lake the past two days.

Felicia nodded. "It's not as peaceful today as it's been, with so many people wandering around, but it's still nice to get out of this room for a little bit." She gave Laurel a nudge. "You better go if you want a break. You need to be back by half past twelve so Berta can take her turn."

Laurel retrieved her lunch pail and headed outside. She stifled a groan as she descended the steps to the street. Her muscles had stiffened up during her long time of sitting on the stool. She hoped there would be time for her to tutor Berta and Felicia so they could take turns weaving. Her body wasn't accustomed to operating the loom for such lengthy periods.

A band was playing at the fountain in the center of the square, and a crowd milled on the walkways. Laurel skirted around folks and angled her steps toward Clara Meer. The man-made lake that had been dug for the exposition had the most unique shape — like a sock. Yesterday she and the others had taken their lunch on a bench near the sock's ankle. By the time she reached the area, she'd used up five minutes of her break but had worked the stiffness from her legs and back. The bench was filled by visitors, but a sloping patch of grass near the bridge beckoned.

She crossed to the spot and sat, then placed her pail in her lap. Mama had packed a fried-egg-on-toast sandwich, an apple, and two applesauce cookies. Her stomach rumbled, but before she lifted anything from the pail, she bowed her head and asked a blessing for the food. She also thanked God for guiding her hands at the loom and requested strength for the remainder of the day.

Her prayer complete, she opened her eyes and reached into the pail, only to discover someone else's hand in the way. Her gaze collided with that of a boy perhaps seven or eight years old. She released a startled gasp, and he fell backward on his bottom, spilling her pail in the process. His feet flew in the air and he flipped, somersaulting toward the lake.

Laurel lunged for him, but he slipped past her reach. She scrambled up from all fours, hollering, "Help! Help!"

A man galloped past her and caught the boy by one arm. The little fellow's feet splashed into the water, but the man gave a yank and the boy landed upright on the grass two yards from the lake. Laurel rushed to him and took hold of his shoulders.

"Are you all right? Did you hurt yourself?" Grass littered his hair and clothes, but she didn't see blood anywhere.

He jerked loose and scowled at his wet shoes and stockings exposed by his knee-length knickers. "You made me get wet."

Laurel's mouth fell open. "I . . . made you . . ."

He squinted up at her. "You scared me."

Such an impertinent little imp! She plunked her fists on her hips. "You deserve to be scared. What were you doing with your hand in my lunch pail?"

"Wanted to see what you had." He blinked up at her, as innocent as could be, his thick lashes throwing a shadow on his apple cheeks.

"Rupert? Rupert, where are you?" The

worried screech came from behind Laurel and carried over the sound of the band.

The boy made a face. "That's my ma. I gotta go." He clambered up the rise, hollering, "Comin', Ma!"

Laurel stared after him. "Well!" She turned toward her spilled lunch and discovered the man who'd rescued the boy standing not three feet from her. She drew back in surprise. "Oh!"

He grimaced, his expression nearly matching the boy's when the mother had yelled. "I'm sorry. I didn't mean to scare you. I wanted to make sure you were all right. You almost went tumblin', tryin' to catch that little scalawag."

For the first time she noticed he wore the blue trousers, buttoned shirt, and billed cap of a security officer. She also thought he looked vaguely familiar. "Do I know you?"

A bashful smile curved his lips. "No. That is, we haven't met. But I saw you at the bank when you interviewed for a job here. An' you waved at me Monday when you were leavin' in your carriage."

Of course — the young man who'd been waiting his turn at the bank. She hadn't realized he was the same one who'd waved to her and Eugene. In her nervousness, she'd hardly looked at him at the bank, and

Monday the carriage had rolled past so fast, she only got a glimpse, but she was certain he hadn't been wearing a uniform then. How stately and gallant he appeared in the neat uniform. Standing this close, she couldn't help but take note of the friendly sparkle in his blue eyes and the shining strands of his blond hair, almost as yellow as the silk threads on the loom, peeping from beneath the brim of his cap.

She gave a slow nod. "Now I remember." She extended her hand. "I'm Laurel Millard."

He swiped his palm down his pant leg before shaking her hand. "Willie Sharp. It's nice to meet you, Miss Millard."

"You, too." She turned and scooped up her lunch pail. Her sandwich and cookies lay in the grass, ruined, but her apple must have rolled into the lake. She picked up each item by turn and dropped them into her pail. She aimed a scowl in the direction the boy had disappeared. "I hope that child is happy. He spoiled my lunch."

Officer Sharp's face pinched, but then he brightened. "There's a food shack right close to the Women's Building. Called the Creole Kitchen. They sell jambalaya. I had some with shrimp a little while ago, an' it was real tasty. If you want, I can —"

Laurel backed away, one hand raised. "Oh, I couldn't let you —"

"— show you where it is."

She blinked twice. "Sh-show me?"

"Uh-huh."

Fire seared her face. She'd presumed he meant to purchase her lunch. Something she would never allow a stranger to do. But she could let him walk her to the food shack. He was a security guard, after all. "Um, how much do they charge for a plate?"

"Five cents."

She had two nickels in the pocket of her dress. For emergencies, Mama had said. Her stomach growled. Perhaps it was only a small emergency, but she believed Mama would understand. She nodded. "Please show me where the Creole Kitchen is located."

"Lemme tell my partner what I'm doing." He jogged to the footbridge, where another guard seemed to monitor the activity from the bridge's highest point. The two spoke briefly, and then Officer Sharp returned. "All right. This way."

He led her up the rise, tempering his stride to match hers. Pink stained his clean-shaven cheeks. "I'd offer to buy your plate, but I spent most of my pocket money on the trolley this mornin'. They upped the price from five to twenty-five cents." His forehead furrowed. "That's gonna eat up a lot o' my salary."

Laurel sympathized with him, but she didn't know what to say, so she offered a sad smile.

" 'Course, God gave me two good legs. It won't hurt me to use 'em."

Two teenage boys darted past, and one of them bumped Laurel's shoulder. The push sent her sideways a step.

Officer Sharp pulled in a quick breath. "You all right?"

The worry on his face both pleased and embarrassed her. "Yes, no harm done." She glanced across the park. "I wonder if it will be this busy every day."

He linked his hands behind his back, and they set off again. "It's openin' day. Speeches, parades . . . All the schools let out, an' some businesses closed an' sent their whole staff. I reckon tomorrow'll be some quieter."

They eased around a woman cleaning something from a child's face and then paused so a group of men could pass. When they were able to proceed, Laurel said, "I'm not used to so much activity. This is even noisier than when all my brothers and sisters bring their children over for a family dinner."

"Big family?"

She laughed. "I'm the youngest of six. All my brothers and sisters are married and have two, three, or four children apiece. It's quite chaotic when they all come home, but my mama says it's happy chaos."

"That's nice." But he sounded sad. He pointed ahead. "There's the food shack — where those folks're standin' in line."

A spicy aroma drifted on the breeze, making her stomach pinch with hunger, but no less than a dozen people already waited to be served. The clock on the tower showed twenty-five past twelve. She wouldn't be able to purchase a plate, let alone eat, in only five minutes.

She sighed. "Thank you for taking me, but I have to be back in the Silk Room by twelve thirty. I'll have to skip lunch today."

He scratched his temple, sending his cap askew. "A person shouldn't ought to go without eatin'. Will you have another break?"

His concern touched her. "Yes, mid-afternoon we each get a ten-minute break." She inched in the direction of the Women's Building. "I'll run down and see if I can get

165

a plate then. Thank you again, Officer Sharp."

She turned to take a step and plowed into a solid chest. The wind left her lungs, but strong hands caught her upper arms and held her erect. When her vision cleared, she was looking into a pair of deep-blue eyes.

12

Langdon

When he'd told his father being at the exposition would be a good place to encounter women, Langdon hadn't expected one to fall into his arms. He grinned into the blushing face of a lovely girl. "Hello there."

She stared at him for the length of two heartbeats and then pulled loose. "I . . . have to go. Excuse me." She lifted the skirt of her green-and-white-striped dress a mere inch and darted in the direction of the Women's Building, as if chased by a cluster of bees. A shimmering brown strand of hair escaped the coil pinned high on her crown and waved goodbye.

Chuckling, Langdon watched her until she disappeared into the crowd. Then he fixed his gaze on the entry to the Women's Building and, moments later, witnessed her patter up the steps and into the building. Now he knew where to go if he wanted to bump into her again.

But not right now. He'd been away from his booth for over an hour. He needed to at least check in. Father might question the other men about his activities. Still chortling, he turned in the direction of the Georgia Manufacturers Building at the southeast corner of the fairgrounds. To his surprise, Willie Sharp, wearing a guard uniform complete with gun belt, stood in his pathway.

"I'm proud of you for trying so hard to take good care of Otto."

Father's praise rang in Langdon's mind and stole the chuckle from his throat. He looked Willie up and down, curling his lip. "Well, well, well . . . Security guard, hmm? I figured you as a groundskeeper or maintenance man. I had no idea you were qualified to be a guard." He started to step around Willie, but something occurred to him. He poked his thumb over his shoulder. "That girl . . . do you know her?"

"The one you ran into?"

Langdon gritted his teeth. Was the man addlebrained? "Yes. Her."

"Not much more'n her name."

The band on the square suddenly blasted out the newest Sousa piece, titled "King Cotton." So raucous. How could a person

168

even think? "So what is her name?"

Willie's brows dipped. "Why do you want to know?"

Langdon huffed. "Not that it's any of your business, but she ran off so quickly I didn't get a chance to ask if she'd hurt herself." He rubbed his chin where her forehead had struck. "I want to check on her. Make sure she's all right."

Suspicion was etched in the other man's features, but he took one step closer. "Millard. Laurel Millard."

Laurel . . . Pretty name for a pretty girl. Langdon shouted over the band's blare into Willie's ear, "And she works in the Women's Building?"

"The Silk Room."

Now he knew exactly where to find her after he'd checked in with Sanders, Stevens, and Allday. He raised one eyebrow and gave Willie another cap-to-shoes sweep. "Shouldn't you be patrolling or something?"

Willie strode off, his frame stiff. Langdon choked back a laugh and returned to the Georgia Manufacturers Building. Father's booth was central on the floor, only a few paces from the front doors — a prime location. No walls separated the booths, but Father had arranged the placement of a twenty-four-by-twenty-four-foot square of carpet. The carpet, a row of tall wood stools, a cloth-draped table covered with brochures and informational bulletins, and a large banner hanging from the ceiling behind the sample engine defined the Rochester Steam-Powered Engines space.

Clyde Allday was alone in the booth, near the table in the front corner. He gave Langdon a surprised look. "Did you hand out all the flyers already?"

Langdon raised his palms, surrender style. "Guilty." Some people hadn't seemed terribly keen on taking the invitations to visit the Rochester booth, but by using his most charming smile and persuasive speech, he'd disposed of all fifty of them. He tapped the stack of brochures. "Have you had much business?"

Allday snorted. "There's too much going on out at the square. Not many have wandered through here." Then he shrugged. "But it's only the first day. We can't judge success based on one day."

"True enough." Langdon perched on a stool and hooked the heel of his right boot on a low rung. "Have you had your lunch yet?"

Allday shook his head. "How about you?"

"I went to the restaurant on the roof of the Minerals and Forestry Building." The view from the roof had been enjoyable but the fish and chips only passable. He wouldn't order them again. Maybe he'd try something from the Mexican Village tomorrow. The spicy scents rising from the open cook fires promised something good. "If you want to go, I'll stay here, answer questions and hand out brochures."

The older man smoothed the tiny patch of salt-and-pepper whiskers growing on his chin with his thumb. "That's fine. I'll wait until Stevens and Sanders return."

Had Father told the men not to leave Langdon untended in the booth? He stifled a grunt and forced a smile instead. "Suit yourself." He remained on the stool and observed the few visitors who filed past the booth. He presumed most were curiosity seekers — not interested in making purchases but wanting to see the displays. He didn't mind. Purchasers would come later. Today was meant to be celebratory. From his spot he had a good view of the passersby, and he smiled and tipped his hat to every girl who appeared between the ages of seventeen and twenty-three.

Some simpered and fluttered their eyelashes. Some of them blushed, the way Laurel Millard from the Silk Room had gone pink in her cheeks. Others were hurried past by their parents. He liked the blushing ones best. Only shy girls blushed, and shy girls were usually chaste, which would please Mother. They were also unlikely to voice complaints — something he preferred. Of course, he wouldn't set his sights on one girl on the very first day. Over the course of the exposition, there would be lots of girls. He might as well have a little fun before he made his choice.

Sanders and Stevens ambled in a little after one, and Allday departed minutes later in a brisk stride. Two people in the booth was plenty, so Langdon grabbed another handful of flyers and rolled them into a tube.

He waved with the tube and headed for the door. "I'll try to send a few people this way." While he was wandering, he might as well wander to the Women's Building and see if he could raise another blush on Laurel Millard's pretty face.

Laurel

To Laurel's relief, Miss Warner allowed her to take the first break in the afternoon. She'd only have ten minutes, so she hoped the food shack where she could buy a plate of jambalaya for five cents was open and not busy. With one hand against her empty stomach, she hurried down the porch steps.

As she recalled, the shack was just a few feet north. She rounded the corner of the building and released a happy sigh. The front window was open, and not a soul waited in line. She double-stepped in that direction.

"Miss Millard? Miss Millard!"

She came to a halt and searched for the caller. The man whose chest had brought her up short at lunchtime trotted across the pavement toward her. She sent a longing look at the food shack, but she couldn't be rude and ignore him. Fidgeting in place, she waited for him to reach her.

"Miss Millard, I've been watching for you."

He had? How unsettling. And yet somehow flattering, as well. She pressed her palms to her stomach. "Why?"

He removed his bowler and ran his fingers through his dark hair, sweeping the thick locks into a wave from forehead to crown. "To ascertain our collision didn't cause you any harm." He seemed to search her face, then touched the center of her forehead with one finger. "Is that a bruise?"

Heat exploded in her face. She didn't carry a hand mirror, so she didn't know if she sported a bruise, but it wouldn't surprise her, given the tenderness of the spot he'd touched. She took a small step away from him. "I'm fine. Honestly." She took another step toward the food shack. "It's kind of you to inquire after me, Mr. — Mr. —"

He bowed. "Langdon Rochester."

His formality invited a response. She dipped a quick curtsy. "Mr. Rochester." Then she gave a start. "How do you know my name?"

He toyed with the brim of his hat, his grin turning sheepish. "I questioned one of the security guards."

The only security guard with whom she'd become acquainted was Officer Sharp. Why had he shared her name with a stranger? "Well, as you can see, I'm quite well, and I . . ." She took two more slow steps closer to the shack. An aproned man came out from behind the small structure. He unhooked the supports holding the window open and let it slap shut. Then he returned to the back again.

Laurel stomped her foot. "Oh! They closed."

Mr. Rochester shot a frown at the shack. "Is that where you were heading?"

She sighed. "Yes."

Contrition bloomed on his face. "You haven't had any lunch."

Not a question but a statement. A sympathetic one, at that. She twirled her strand of hair around her finger. "A small boy dumped the lunch I'd brought with me, and then I ran out of time to buy something. I'd hoped to purchase a plate of jambalaya on my break." As if on cue, her stomach growled. She cringed. "Please excuse me."

"No, please excuse me for interrupting you." He closed the distance between them, holding his hat against the buttoned front of his vest. His blue eyes shone with remorse. "If I hadn't stopped you, you could be eating by now. I'm truly sorry."

How could she resist such a sincere apology? She smiled and shook her head. "It's all right. You didn't know I hadn't eaten." She squinted at the tower clock. Eight past three. She'd have no time to search for something else. She edged toward the Women's Building with sideways steps. "My break time is over. I have to go."

"Already?" He looked so crestfallen that guilt struck her. He trailed after her. "Will you have another break?"

"No. But missing one meal won't hurt me." Her stomach growled again. Oh, so embarrassing. She pressed her hands hard against her midsection. "Thank you again for your concern, Mr. Rochester."

He slipped his hat over his hair, settling it at a roguish angle that somehow suited him. "Take care, Miss Millard. I hope our paths might . . . cross again." An impish smile curved the corners of his lips.

A giggle built in her throat. Mama's warning about coquetry squelched it. "Good day, Mr. Rochester." She scurried into the building and stepped into the Silk Room as the minute hand on the wall clock reached the two. Breathing a sigh of relief, she moved behind the counter.

Felicia shifted aside and allowed Laurel passage to the loom. Her fine brows dipped, and she caught Laurel's sleeve. "Are you all right?" she whispered.

Laurel sent her a puzzled look. "Yes. Why?"

"Your face is all red."

Laurel placed her cool palms over her cheeks. "The sun must be warmer than I realized."

"Mmm-hmm." Felicia's lips quirked. She leaned close. "I peeked out the window and saw you talking to a handsome gentleman."

Laurel glanced at Miss Warner, who sat at her small desk in the corner, busily writing something. Laurel gave Felicia a stern look. "He was only apologizing for bumping into me earlier today." She touched her forehead, where his fingertip had brushed her skin. Felicia had called him a handsome gentleman, an apt description. How courtly he appeared, and how solicitous his behavior.

Felicia shrugged, still grinning. "Whatever you say, Laurel." She flounced around the counter. "Miss Warner, I'm taking my break now."

The supervisor waved her hand in dismissal, and Laurel settled at the loom. She began the familiar push and pull of beam, warp, and treadles, hoping busyness would prevent her from thinking about her empty stomach.

What seemed only moments later, someone tapped her shoulder. She angled a quick look, her hands continuing to work the loom, and found Felicia smirking down at her. "What?"

Felicia held up a waxed-paper-wrapped square. "I've been instructed to give this to you."

Laurel stopped midpull on the beater. "From . . ."

"Your gentleman." Giggling, Felicia plunked the package into Laurel's idle hands. "He said to tell you he hopes goat cheese on rye with mustard is an acceptable replacement for jambalaya."

She'd never eaten goat cheese on rye, with

or without mustard. Her pulse skittered into rapid beats. She'd been appalled when she thought Officer Sharp meant to buy her a plate of rice, so should she accept this sandwich from Mr. Rochester? Uncertainty held her captive for several seconds. Her stomach growled.

Felicia patted her shoulder. "Go ahead and eat it."

Laurel's mouth watered, but she didn't unwrap the sandwich. "I already took my break."

"So many people are in the Auditorium listening to speakers that it's quiet in here."

"But Miss Warner —"

"I told Miss Warner about your lost lunch, and she said it was all right for you to take the time to eat the sandwich." She bent close to Laurel's ear. "I didn't tell her a gentleman gave it to me. She presumed I bought it." Felicia straightened and giggled again. "Eat the sandwich, silly. If you get mustard on your fingers, at least it won't show since the silk thread is dyed yellow."

13

Willie

Willie tucked his shirt into the waistband of his trousers and then slipped his suspenders into place. He looked down his length at his work shirt and trousers. How many men wearing pinstriped suits and bright-colored silk ties and top hats had he encountered today? He didn't envy them their fine clothes, but he wished he carried as many coins in his pocket as those fellows likely had.

"I didn't even have an extra nickel to buy Miss Millard's lunch." He made the embarrassed confession to his uniform, which he'd folded and put in his cubby.

"What's that you said, Sharp?" Ted Dunning, Willie's assigned partner, plopped onto the bench in front of the wall of cubbies and reached for his scuffed boots.

Willie shook his head. "Nothing important."

"Somethin' about buyin'. I heard that much." Dunning was at least ten years older than Willie. Not much taller, but paunchier. He grunted as he tugged the boot shank over his trouser leg. "I was plenty mad about the trolleys raisin' their prices. Carney" — he pointed with his chin to another of the guards — "says the herdics're only chargin' a dime for up to two passengers. They'll drop you off at the Transportation Building, an' some of 'em plan to hang around there all day so people can catch rides. They'll even cart you around the grounds if you want. Carney an' me are gonna try an' get one tomorrow mornin'. Nickel apiece. That'll save us lots of money."

Willie and Quincy could save more of their pay by taking a one-horse buggy instead of the trolley. Maybe it was good Dunning had overheard him.

Dunning stood and gave his waistband a pull. "See you tomorrow mornin', Sharp." He sauntered out of the room behind the other few stragglers.

Willie didn't need to hurry. It took Quincy a while to put away his tools and cross the grounds from the maintenance shack clear at the north end of the park. Tomorrow, though, if they made use of a herdic cab, they'd both take a long walk to meet up at the end of the day. They'd used the trolley to reach the west entrance since it was closest to their houses. But the Transportation Building sat at the east side, on the other side of Clara Meer. Willie didn't mind the extra walking at the end of the day. But he didn't want to walk the whole way home. He'd wear out his shoes before the exposition ended.

He left the building through the side door and moved around to the back, heading for the tunnel's opening to the park, him and Quincy's meeting spot. Somebody was already waiting there, leaning against the brick and peering up the tunnel, but it wasn't Quincy. Willie was as happy to see her as he would've been to see Quincy, though.

He loped the last few paces and stopped next to her. "Hello, Miss Millard."

She turned her head and met his gaze. Her brow puckered, like she wasn't sure she should talk to him.

He touched his chest with his fingers. "It's me — Willie Sharp. I showed you to the Creole Kitchen today."

Her expression cleared. "Oh, yes. I'm sorry. I didn't recognize you without your uniform."

"We don't wear 'em home. Just for here at

the expo." The Silk Room girls must not need uniforms. Her dress was as pretty as any worn by other lady visitors, except hers had a big bow at the base of her spine instead of a bustle. He wished he had the courage to tell her how nice she looked.

"Well, I'm glad to see you."

He gawked at her. "You are?"

She nodded, and that little strand of hair that never seemed to stay pinned in her fat doughnut of brown hair drifted across her cheek. She caught it with her fingers and twirled it. "I was very disconcerted earlier today when a man I'd never met knew my name. He said you'd given it to him."

Willie thought back. The only person who'd asked for her name was Langdon Rochester. Worry tightened his chest. "Did he . . . accost you?"

"No." She released the curl of hair and clasped her hands at her waist. "He only inquired after me. But, Officer Sharp, I hope you aren't in the habit of sharing personal information about others with complete strangers."

"But he isn't a stranger." Willie blurted the statement in self-defense, but he wished he could take it back. It'd sounded like he meant to argue. He cleared his throat. "I mean, yes, he was a stranger to you, but he isn't a stranger to me. I know him. He's my boss's son."

She tipped her head. "Oh?"

Willie licked his dry lips and nodded. "Langdon Rochester's pa owns the Rochester Steam-Powered Engines factory. I work for him. That is, I did before I hired on here as a security guard. But when the expo's done, I will again. So he — Langdon's pa — is my boss."

Her rosy lips curved into a small smile, and a little sigh eased out. "I see. Thank you for the explanation."

She wasn't mad. The weight of worry rolled off him. He shrugged. "It's no problem. An' you don't need to call me Officer. Just Willie'll do."

"Willie!" Quincy pounded up, sweaty and breathing hard. "I'm here. So let's —" He jolted and aimed his face at the ground. "S'cuse me, ma'am."

Miss Millard held out her hand to Quincy. "Hello."

Quincy didn't lift his head, but his eyes shifted. He barely touched Miss Millard's hand and then pulled back. "Hello."

She looked at Willie with her eyebrows raised. "Mr. Sharp" — hadn't he told her to call him Willie? — "would you please introduce your friend?"

Willie slung his arm across Quincy's shoulders. "This is Quincy Tate. You're right he's my friend. You could say he's my best friend."

Finally Quincy lifted his chin. His shoulders straightened some, too, like Willie's words had given him pride.

Willie gestured to Miss Millard. "Quincy, this is Miss Laurel Millard. She's one of the weavers in the Silk Room."

Her fine brows pinched, and he wondered if he'd given out personal information again.

"It's nice to meet you, Mr. Tate." So she called Quincy "mister," too.

Quincy made a funny half smile but didn't say anything. He must've still been nervous about talking to Miss Millard. Probably because she was white. Not that Willie could blame him. He'd heard about black men in other places getting themselves lynched for being so bold. But nothing like that would happen in Atlanta. Especially not after the speech Mr. Booker T. Washington gave about blacks and whites coming together for the common good.

Willie dropped his arm from Quincy's shoulders. "Are you lookin' for the trolley, Miss Millard?" He should tell her about the herdic cabs.

"No, I'm waiting for my —" The sorrel

Willie had admired trotted up the opposite end of the tunnel, pulling the fine carriage. She pointed. "That's my ride now. Please excuse me, Mr. Sharp and Mr. Tate." She scurried through the tunnel and met the driver outside the carriage. He helped her in, and Willie got a peek at her bright smile before the door closed. Moments later, the carriage rolled out of the gate.

Quincy sucked in a big breath and let it whoosh out. He must've had onions for lunch, because his breath smelled strong of them. "You's keepin' some fancy comp'ny, Willie."

Willie couldn't argue about Miss Millard being fancy. Her clothes, the carriage, the way she spoke. She wasn't working class like him. "I'm not keepin' company with her. I helped her with somethin' earlier today, an' we were only talkin' to fill time until her driver came." Saying it made him sadder than he wanted to admit.

"Wal, she gone now, so c'n we get on home?" Quincy nudged Willie into the tunnel. "The cheese-an'-onion san'wiches I et for lunch got worked slap out o' me near three hours ago."

Willie started up the tunnel, waving his hand in front of his face. "Hoo-ee, Quincy, I hope you'll bring somethin' different

185

tomorrow. Your breath's strong enough to knock a mule off its feet."

Quincy laughed, and the smell of onions filled Willie's nose. "Can't be that bad."

"It is." They exited the tunnel and crossed Piedmont Avenue. The maple trees lining Fourteenth Street threw shade over them, but there was enough sun coming through the almost bare branches to light their path. "Now I'm glad you didn't talk any when Miss Millard was with us. You might've scared her away."

Quincy shot him a sideways look. "An' that'd trouble you, huh?"

Willie forced a grin. "You never want to breathe onions on a lady, Quince. It's bad manners."

Quincy nodded, but the knowing gleam in his eyes didn't clear.

Willie shook his head. "No need to think that way. Like you said, she's fancy. Too fancy for me."

They reached the intersection where the trolley passed, and they sat on the curb to wait. After a quiet minute or two, Quincy sighed. "Too bad."

Willie frowned. "What's too bad?"

"That she be too fancy for you. She talk to me. Not talkin' down to me. Jus' talkin'." Quincy tipped his head and looked straight into Willie's face. "Ain't no fancy lady done that to me before."

The trolley's clang sent the alert. They stood and dug their stubs from the morning from their pockets. Willie'd forgotten to tell Quincy about the herdics, but he'd do that when they got off the trolley closer to their houses. They took a bench clear in the back. Quincy dozed with his mouth open, sharing his onion breath, but Willie couldn't stop thinking about what Quincy'd said about Miss Millard.

Quincy was right about fancy folks — ladies and men — talking to black folks different than they talked to each other. Of course, they talked to Willie different, too. He was white, but he wasn't fancy. He rubbed his palms on the worn knees of his trousers. Not even close to fancy. But Miss Millard had talked to him . . . just talked. Maybe scolded a little at first, but she'd softened real quick and been as friendly as could be.

He leaned his head back and closed his eyes. A fancy lady who didn't act fancy. Pretty on the outside — any fool could see that — and pretty on the inside, too. His eyes popped open and he stared out the window. Why was a fancy girl like her working at the exposition?

14

Laurel

Before Laurel went to bed, Mama sat her down at the kitchen table and massaged castor oil into the blisters on her fingers. The ministration was pleasant, but the aroma of the oil made Laurel want to gag.

"Mama, isn't there something you could use that smells better?" She wrinkled her nose. "If the others get a whiff of this stench on me, they'll all stay on the opposite side of the room."

"We'll wash your hands well with soap when we're finished. This should soften things up so calluses don't form." Mama glanced up and smiled. "A lady shouldn't have calluses on her fingers."

Laurel sighed and relaxed against the chair's ladder back. "By the end of the exposition, I will have very unladylike hands, then. Miss Warner wants the loom in operation at least three hours each morning

188

and four in the afternoon. She'd intended for us three girls to trade off, but neither Berta nor Felicia seems terribly inclined to learn to operate it. They're content readying the cocoons for dyeing and extractin' the silk."

Mama released Laurel's right hand and reached for her left. She dipped Laurel's fingers in the bowl of oil and began massaging. "Perhaps their tasks will become monotonous and they'll change their minds in a few days."

Laurel examined her fingers. The places where blisters had formed now looked puckered. It didn't seem much of an improvement, but she wouldn't tell Mama so. "Maybe it's better if they don't. It's kind of sad, Mama. In order to harvest the silk from the cocoons, you have to boil them. With the worms still inside." She shuddered. "I don't think I could deliberately kill the little creatures. Especially knowing that if they'd been left alone, they would develop into very pretty moths."

Mama raised one eyebrow. "Pretty moths?"

"Oh my, yes. They have both male and female *Bombyx mori* in jars in the Silk Room." Laurel laughed. "They're covered all over in white fuzz, and they have antennae that resemble drooping rabbit ears snipped into fringe." She held up her little finger and gazed at it in wonder. "The wingspan is no longer than my finger, Mama — barely two inches. They're like little fairy-tale creatures."

Mama laughed, too. "I must visit the Silk Room and see them for myself."

"I hope you will. In fact, there are some special days planned — days you might want to spend at the fairgrounds. Eugene intends to bring his children this coming Saturday to hear Governor McKinley from Ohio speak." Excitement stirred in Laurel's chest. Miss Warner had promised to close the Silk Room so they could hear the governor's talk. "They're calling it Blue and Gray Day, and they intend to honor all war veterans no matter what uniform they wore."

Mama's hands stilled. Tears swam in her eyes. "What a wonderful thing to do. Please tell Eugene I would like to accompany him and the children to celebrate Blue and Gray Day."

Laurel placed her hand over her mother's wrist. "Along one wall in the Auditorium, they're setting up tables all draped with colored bunting for people to display photographic images of their family members who fought in the War Between the States. You could take the daguerreotype of Papa and place it with the others, if you'd like."

How many times when she was a little girl had Laurel gazed upon the oval of silver-plated copper that bore her father's youthful image? She loved that she had his brown hair and eyes, as well as his narrow chin. Mama said of all the children, she resembled him the most. Yet she knew him the least.

A knot filled Laurel's throat. "Will you display Papa's picture?"

Mama seemed to stare at something beyond Laurel's shoulder, a faraway look in her blue eyes. Laurel had witnessed her mother drift off into her thoughts at other times, and although Mama never said so, Laurel always presumed she was remembering moments with Papa. She wouldn't intrude upon Mama's reflections now.

Laurel stood and leaned forward. She brushed a kiss on Mama's cheek, then went to the little washstand beside the back door and washed the oil from her hands. It took two scrubbings with soap to remove every bit of the sticky residue, and when she returned to the kitchen, Mama's chair was empty. The bowl and bottle of oil were still on the table, though. So uncharacteristic of Mama to leave the room untidy. Laurel

191

cleaned up the mess, extinguished the lamp, and felt her way to the dark hallway.

A thin band of light along the floor under Mama's door let her know Mama hadn't fallen asleep yet. Laurel moved quietly to the door and leaned close, knuckles raised to knock. But she froze in place when Mama's broken voice penetrated the thick door and reached Laurel's ears.

"Leland . . . My dear Leland, I miss you so very —" A harsh sob replaced whatever else Mama intended to say, and then the sound of muffled weeping twisted Laurel's heart into a knot.

Laurel stood in the hallway, uncertainty holding her captive. Should she go in? Try to comfort Mama? Or should she allow her to mourn in private? Tears stung Laurel's eyes. How much Mama had loved Papa to still miss him so desperately after fifteen years of separation. She remained at Mama's door for several more minutes, her heart pounding, tears threatening, fist upraised but still, a prayer for guidance repeating itself through her mind.

The band of light disappeared. The creak of mattress springs and a lengthy shuddering sigh sounded. Silence fell. Although it was still early — not quite half past eight — Mama had obviously turned in.

Laurel waited a few more seconds. Then she pressed her fist to her lips and hurriedly tiptoed up the hallway to her room. By the time she'd readied herself for bed, she'd furthered her determination to find a love as deep and enduring as her parents had shared. And not to leave Mama alone. Her spry, healthy mother didn't need anyone to meet her physical needs, but Mama might wither and die of loneliness if left by herself. As much as Laurel had initially resented her siblings' demand, she now accepted it without a moment's angst.

She knelt beside the bed for her nighttime prayers. Eyes closed, hands clasped, she bowed her head. "Guide me to the one who will love me the way Papa loved Mama, dear God, and let him love my mama, too. Bind us — the three of us — together in doing Your will. Amen."

Willie

Willie wished Pa could come to the fairgrounds today. Blue and Gray Day. Special speeches, special bands, a ceremony to honor attending veterans. All veterans, whether Union or Confederate. At least Pa's picture would be laid out with the others. He'd found it in the trunk in the corner of Pa's room, folded inside a bandana and hidden in the pocket of Pa's old army jacket. Now it was secure in Willie's pocket.

Pa hadn't given him permission to display it, and a tiny finger of guilt poked his conscience. He should've asked yesterday evening when he'd said farewell to Pa at the convalescent hospital. Him and Pastor Hines had delivered Pa together, and the preacher paid for the first two weeks of Pa's care with part of the church's benevolence fund. Willie hadn't slept much his first night in the house alone, and it comforted him to carry Pa's photograph.

Mrs. Powell, the church lady who'd stayed with Pa yesterday, must've spent half the day cooking and baking, because there were three loaves of bread, two cakes — one chocolate and one that smelled like pumpkin — and a cherry pie in the pie safe. The icebox held a plump roasted chicken and a pot of beef stew. He wouldn't have to eat beans for maybe a week. Everybody'd sure been good to him. It'd feel fine to drop extra in the offering plate when he started collecting his exposition pay.

"A ten percent tithe for sure," he said to his full lunch pail, "an' an offering to boot." He'd be able to afford it since he wouldn't need to buy as many groceries.

He hooked the handle of his lunch pail

with his fingers, patted the bulge from Pa's photograph in his jacket pocket, and tromped to the front door. The sky was still gray, only a touch of pink in the east. Strange to be out when everything was so quiet. Him and Quincy had to leave a half hour earlier to get to the fairgrounds on time by taking a herdic cab, but it was worth it. Thirty cents a week compared to twenty-five cents a day for transport? Easy decision.

He waited on the porch stoop, squinting up the road where Quincy should come running, and a plaintive mew caught his attention. He dropped to one knee, and Rusty leaped onto the stoop, put his front paws on Willie's thigh, and bumped his head against Willie's rib cage.

Willie chuckled. "Aw, poor guy. You're missin' your pal, aren't you?" He scratched the cat's chin, but no rumbling purr started. Yep, Rusty was lonely for Pa. Willie sighed. "Me, too. Yep. Me, too." He gently set the cat on the stoop and removed the cloth cover from his lunch pail. He pulled a little piece of meat from the chicken leg he'd packed for himself and offered it to the cat. "Here you go."

Rusty sniffed the meat, then drew back.

"You want me to put it down?" Willie put

the sliver on the stoop and tapped his finger next to it. "C'mon, Rusty. Come get it."

Rusty turned his back and began washing his paw.

Willie choked back a chortle. Stubborn critter. He must only want Pa's leftovers from under the table. Well, if Rusty didn't eat the bit of chicken, some other little creature would come along and dispose of it.

The pound of approaching boots against the ground — Quincy coming — startled Rusty. With a hiss of protest, the cat took off between houses, and Willie stepped from the stoop and met Quincy at the edge of the yard.

"Thought maybe you'd overslept."

"No maybe about it. You thunk right. Got to bed too late las' night." Quincy made a face and kept right on going.

Willie caught up to him. He'd gone to bed later than usual after taking Pa to the hospital. "Why were you up? Somebody sick?"

"Nah. Had to argue some with Pap 'bout puttin' his war pi'ture out, an' then Mam got in on my side, an' the argufyin' got plenty noisy an' long, but lookit here what I got." He pulled a faded square photograph from his pocket and showed it to Willie.

"Pap in his Confed'rate suit. He stood in for his master's oldest boy, y'know. He say it don't count 'cause he didn' sign up by choice an' he for sho' didn' like fightin' on the side o' keepin' slaves. But Mam say he risk his life for somebody else an' that be what counts."

Willie nodded. "I'm on your ma's side with this one."

"Me, too." Quincy grinned. "Me an' her slap wore him down, an' she gimme the pi'ture. What about you? Yo' pa say you could take his?"

Willie showed Quincy Pa's picture in its stamped tin frame. "Let's put their pictures next to each other since they're friends, huh?" Pa would like that.

Quincy's bright smile faded fast. "Can't do that, Willie. The organizers, they got sep'rate tables for whites an' blacks. I know 'cause I helped carry 'em in an' set 'em up all across one whole wall up next to the stage. Six tables for whites, then a space, then two tables for blacks. Gonna mix the Union an' Confed'rates, but the white faces'll be apart from the black ones." He shrugged. "Don't change nothin' 'tween us, though."

Willie growled under his breath. "After that fine speech by Booker T. Washington, all his talk about whites and blacks bein' fingers on one hand, how come they wanna split things up? When they were on the battlefield, they were close enough together."

Quincy shrugged again. He held up his hand and splayed his fingers. He wriggled them one by one. "Guess the organizers are thinkin' mostly 'bout fingers an' not the palm. The fingers, they c'n all work on they own without touchin' the others. Maybe them in charge o' the exposition're wantin' whites an' blacks to keep workin' on they own without touchin' each other."

"You think that's what Mr. Washington wants, too?"

Quincy laughed. "I can't say what he want. He black as me, but he sho' a fancy 'un. If Bunson get to go to that college in Alabama like he wants, when he comes home with his head full o' smartness, he might could answer that. But I sho' can't."

They flagged down a herdic cab and climbed in. Neither talked during the ride to the fairgrounds. Quincy dozed, and Willie stayed quiet and let him. Besides, he couldn't think of anything to say. Indignation burned in his chest, hot as the flame in his cookstove. The war thirty years ago was supposed to bring freedom. Unity. Brotherhood. Didn't the Declaration of Independence, penned by this country's founders, declare that all men were created equal? But they weren't equal.

Rich and poor, black and white, educated and unschooled . . . There were more chasms holding people apart than bridges bringing them together. And he didn't have any idea how to fix it. Except — Willie jolted and shifted to stare at Quincy's sleeping face. What had Ma told him when he came home from school upset because some boys threw rotten apples at an old black man riding a mule? He searched his memory for her exact words, and they flooded in, making his nose sting.

"Set the better example, Willie. Be kind an' acceptin'. Sometimes all people need is someone to show them another way to be."

Back then, even though he hadn't said as much to Ma, he'd thought it was too simple a solution and too hard to do. One person? How much good could one person do?

But why couldn't one person make a difference? After all, God Himself sent one person — His Son — to earth instead of a whole legion of sons. If one person helped one more see things different, and that person showed somebody else, and on and on, pretty soon there'd be lots of people changing for the good.

The burn in his chest cooled some. He held up his hand, the way Quincy had earlier, with his fingers all spread apart, and he slowly drew them together until they fit so tight a drop of water wouldn't slip between them. Maybe part of the reason him and Quincy both got hired on at the exposition was so they could set the example. And he knew just how to start.

15

Laurel

"Oh, my . . ." Laurel looked down the row of tables stretched all the way from the edge of the stage to the corner along the north side of the Auditorium's back wall. The electric wall sconces spaced every three feet illuminated the sea of photographs. "There must be a hundred people represented here."

"At least." Mama held Papa's daguerreotype against the bodice of her best dress. "Where should I put Leland's? I don't want to lose track of it."

Eugene placed his hand on Mama's spine and guided her to the spot where the two tables closest to the stage had been pushed together. He traced his finger along the line formed by the tablecloths. "Put it here on the seam. Remember it's where the red and blue tablecloths come together, and we'll easily find it again at the end of the day."

Laurel found Eugene's suggestion very sensible, but Mama still hesitated. Laurel leaned in and whispered into her mother's ear, "If you don't want to display it, you don't have to."

Mama blinked several times, her fingers convulsing on the little frame, but then she lowered her hands and laid Papa's picture on the table as gently as a mother might lay her baby in a cradle. She touched the edge of the frame with her fingertip. "He deserves the recognition, the same as all these others. So he should be here." She aimed a wobbly smile at Laurel, which Laurel returned with one of her own.

Eugene cleared his throat. "We'd better get to the seats Ethel is holding. The place is filling up. People might not be patient enough to leave those seats open for us." He guided Mama along the tables toward the side aisle. Laurel followed them, excusing herself when she bumped into others trying to get close to the tables.

A man's irritable utterance — "What? Who put this here?" — brought her to a stop. Curious, she peeked over her shoulder. A scowling man held up a picture of a black soldier to another man, who stood with downturned lips and lowered brows. "That was right here in the middle of our men."

"Put it on their table." The second man waved his arm toward the corner.

The man holding the image gave a stern nod. The image clenched in his fist, he brushed past Laurel without a word of apology. Then a third man, a young one in a security guard uniform, hurried over and stepped directly into the man's pathway.

"What're you doin' with that picture?"

Laurel's pulse sped at the authority in Officer Sharp's voice. The man holding the picture was at least twice his age. The man's clothes identified him as one of Atlanta's wealthy, and his thunderous expression made Laurel want to shrink away. Yet Officer Sharp stood tall and unflinching.

The man jabbed the photograph inches from Officer Sharp's face. "Are you blind? The man in this picture is black. It belongs on the other table."

Officer Sharp held out his hand. "Can I have it, please?"

With his lip curled into a sneer, the man slapped the photograph into the younger man's palm. "Put it where it belongs."

"Yes, sir. I intend to." Officer Sharp stepped around the man and placed the photograph on the table in the middle of several pictures of white veterans.

The man grabbed Officer Sharp's arm

and yanked, forcing the younger man to face him. "That photograph doesn't belong here. This table's for the white veterans."

Officer Sharp removed his arm from the man's grasp and pointed to two pictures side by side on the table. "The one you picked up is Ruger Tate. The one right next to him is Otto Sharp. They became friends the last few months of the war when Otto came down with a bad fever and Ruger helped take care of him at the infirmary. They're still friends. So don't you think they oughta be able to be here together on the table?"

"The black veterans go over there." The man pointed, his movement stiff. "If you want to keep them together, you can take the white one, too, and put it on the blacks' table, but that soldier's picture is not going to stay here with any of my kin. It's not seemly."

"What's unseemly, sir, is honorin' some more than others when the sacrifice was the same."

Officer Sharp spoke with such respect and kindness in the face of condemnation that tears stung Laurel's eyes. He'd called a black man his best friend — something she'd never heard another white man say about a black man — and now he was proving it by defending the relationship between the two men, who must be his and his friend's fathers.

"What is your name, young man?" The older man nearly growled the question.

Officer Sharp squared his shoulders. "Willie Sharp, sir."

The man poked his finger in the center of the guard's chest. "I'll be talking to your supervisor about your insolent behavior. You'll be lucky to still have employment by the end of this ceremony." He stormed off, arms swinging, face as red as ripe tomatoes. The second man followed him, giving Officer Sharp a withering glare as he passed.

Officer Sharp stood for a moment beside the table, unmoving. Then he smiled down at the pictures. Finally he moved to the far end of the tables and took a position in the corner, his attentive gaze scanning the crowded room.

Laurel couldn't resist inching forward and peeking at the photograph that had caused the verbal altercation. Nothing more than a young man, unsmiling, attired in the uniform worn by the Confederate soldiers. The same as many others on the table except for his dark skin. Yet to the two men who'd tried to move it, the skin color made all the difference.

She slid her finger around the periphery of the soldier Tate's image. If her father were alive, would he agree with the angry man or with Officer Sharp?

"Laurel." Eugene strode up to her and took hold of her elbow. "What are you doing?"

"Thinking." Eugene had been eighteen when Papa died — the same age Laurel was now. He would be able to tell her how Papa would feel about leaving Ruger Tate's photo there with the white soldiers. The question hovered on her lips.

"The speech is going to begin. Come, sit." Eugene herded her to the rear of the Auditorium, where Mama, Ethel, Laurel's nieces Mary and Anna, and her nephew Little Gene sat in a row. The other chairs had been filled, though, so she and Eugene stood along the back wall with many others who hadn't been able to find a seat.

The exposition master of ceremonies, Mr. Rufus Bullock, a former governor of Georgia, introduced the current governor, and then Governor McKinley of Ohio took the stage. Although Laurel tried hard to listen to the speech — after all, Miss Warner had dismissed the girls to hear him — her attention was stolen by a harsh reality that raised a rush of guilt she didn't completely understand.

The seats on the entire right-hand side of the Auditorium and those on the front half of the left side were filled with white attendees. Black attendees sat in the back rows on the left. There'd been no ushers directing people to seats. They'd chosen their own places, and look at how they'd positioned themselves. Whites together. Blacks together. No whites and blacks sharing a row. Clearly this was the common pattern.

Why had she never paid attention to the dissociation before today? And why was she now noticing it with such startling clarity? She rose up on tiptoes and gazed across the room to Officer Sharp, who stood sentry in the corner next to the tables holding all the black war veterans' photographs, save one. He was responsible for opening her sheltered eyes to the truth that a separation existed. Her heart pinched. He might very well have lost his position here at the exposition because of it.

The speech ended with rousing applause, and Laurel automatically clapped, too. People rose and filed toward the doors or crossed the Auditorium and began perusing the tables. Eugene said, "Let's come back

207

later and look at all the pictures when it isn't so crowded." He led the members of Laurel's family outside, and they stepped off the pathway onto the grass. He smiled at Mama. "What would you like to do now?"

Laurel caught his arm. "Come to the Silk Room. I want to show Mary, Anna, and Little Gene the cocoons and moths, and you can watch me weave."

Eight-year-old Mary crinkled her face. "We've seen you and Granny weave lots of times."

Laurel tapped Mary on the end of her freckled nose. "Yes, but this is a different loom, strung with threads that come straight from a worm's cocoon. Besides, you've never seen a *Bombyx mori* moth. It's like a tiny bunny with fuzzy wings."

The child's eyes widened, and her younger sister bounced in place. Anna pulled at Eugene's jacket tail. "Let's go see the tiny bunny, Papa!"

Eugene chuckled. "All right, to the Silk Room we go." He scooped three-year-old Little Gene onto his arm. "Lead the way, Laurel."

Thursday and Friday had been fairly quiet, but today's crowd was as great or greater than the opening day's. It took a little time to weave their way across the park to the Women's Building, in part because of the groups of other attendees slowing their progress, and in part by the children wanting to stop and examine the fountains or walk tightrope style on the short brick wall surrounding the square.

Miss Warner, Berta, and Felicia were already in the Silk Room when Laurel and her family arrived, and Laurel introduced each of them by turn to Mama, Eugene, and the others. Miss Warner told Mama what a good worker Laurel was, and Laurel's face flamed with both embarrassment and pleasure. She wouldn't have thought her supervisor held such an opinion, based on her stoic treatment. The praise encouraged her and gave her the courage to make a special request.

Laurel put her hands on her nieces' narrow shoulders and offered Miss Warner a hopeful look. "I'd like to show the girls how the loom works. May I take them behind the counter for a close-up examination?"

Miss Warner's lips pursed, and she seemed to study each child's upturned face. Then she leaned down slightly. "Can you be trusted not to touch the loom or any of the threads?"

Mary and Anna both nodded solemnly, and Anna said, "We can't touch Granny's loom, either, 'cause it might pinch our fingers."

Miss Warner straightened, and the closest thing to a warm smile Laurel had seen on the woman's face appeared. "Then you may take a close look." She shifted her gaze to Laurel, and her expression turned stern. "If other visitors come in, you'll need to end your examination. I don't want others thinking the area behind the counter is open for exploration."

Laurel hurried the little girls to the loom, and Mama, Eugene, and Ethel stood on the other side of the counter and watched while Laurel slowly showed the girls the steps needed to add another row to the length of shimmery yellow silk fabric. Twice Anna's fingers stretched toward the cloth, and both times Mary pushed her sister's hand down, hissing, "Don't touch!" Laurel understood Anna's temptation. The beautiful cloth begged to be stroked.

Laurel turned on the stool and smiled at the girls. "By the end of the exposition, I should have a piece of cloth as long or longer than the pretty blue one in the case. Long enough to make a pair of dresses just the right size for the two of you."

Anna's eyes shone. "I like the pretty yellow. When you're all done, will you take the cloth home and make us dresses, Aunt Laurel?"

Mary rolled her eyes. "It's not Aunt Laurel's cloth, silly. She can't take it." Then she turned a longing look at the fabric. "Wish she could, though. It is awful pretty."

Eugene tweaked his fingers. "Come over here now, girls, and let Aunt Laurel work."

Laurel walked the girls around the counter to their parents. She wanted to show them the glass jars and tell them all about the *Bombyx mori* moth and the worms, but Berta had been given that duty for the day. So she left her family in Berta's care with the promise to meet them on the porch of the Women's Building at noon for lunch, and she returned to the loom.

She'd learned over the past few days to focus on her task regardless of distractions in the other part of the room. Dividing her attention could mean missing a step in the process, and she didn't want to ruin an entire length of fabric by creating a flaw in one row. Setting aside her internal pondering about the verbal altercation she'd witnessed earlier proved more difficult than blocking out the quiet conversations and activity of her coworkers and the exposition attendees. But eventually she became so absorbed in weaving she was startled by

211

Berta's interruption.

"Why are you still sitting there? Felicia told you five minutes ago to take your lunch break."

Laurel glanced at the round clock and gasped. Her family would think she'd changed her mind about meeting them. She locked the beater in place and scurried out to the front porch. To her relief, Eugene was waiting on a bench set in the shade at the back corner of the large covered area. A second man sat on the opposite end of the bench. They both rose when she approached.

"Laurel," Eugene said.

"Miss Millard," the man said at the same time.

The two men looked at each other with identical quizzical expressions. Laurel released a soft giggle. They both stared at her. She covered her mouth lest a second trickle of laughter escape. Their perfectly choreographed speech and actions reminded her of a puppet play she'd seen when she was a little girl.

She turned her puzzled gaze on the second man. "May I help you with something?"

He removed his bowler and placed it against his chest. The motion more than anything else stirred her memory to life, and she stated his name — "Langdon Rochester" — as he stated it at the same time. Perhaps they were all participants in the puppet show.

He chuckled. "Please forgive my intrusion. I didn't realize you'd made lunch plans." He glanced at Eugene, who was frowning at Mr. Rochester. "I thought I might treat you to the jambalaya I prevented you from enjoying earlier this week."

Eugene's frown deepened. He curled his hand around Laurel's elbow. "Yes, she has made plans, so excuse us." He guided Laurel toward the steps.

Laurel wriggled. "Eugene! Aren't we being rude?"

Eugene didn't slow his pace. When they reached the bottom of the steps, he shifted his hand to the small of her back and propelled her forward. "Mama and the others went to the Hotel Aragon's restaurant atop the Minerals and Forestry Building. I thought it best for them to place an order since your break time is short. As it is, you might not have time to eat." He glanced over his shoulder, as if to ascertain they weren't being followed, and set his lips in a grim line. "What was that all about — you being kept from enjoying jambalaya?"

Laurel explained the events of last

Wednesday, and by the time they reached the stairway leading to the rooftop restaurant, a sheepish look replaced Eugene's scowl.

"He must be a gentleman after all, then. I'm sorry if I overreacted." He cupped his hand over her shoulder. "I was struck with a sense of protectiveness when a man I'd never met addressed you by name."

Laurel smiled. "It's all right. I don't mind you being protective." She'd witnessed similar behavior toward her friends by their fathers. She'd never know the protection of a father, but at least she had one older brother who cared enough to look out for her. "But you needn't worry about Langdon Rochester. His father owns the Rochester Steam-Powered Engines factory, so he comes from a very respectable family." She hoped she would encounter him again. She still hadn't thanked him for the sandwich he'd sent with Felicia.

They climbed the steps and found Mama, Ethel, and the children already sharing a plate of chicken sandwiches and bowls of fruit salad. She and Eugene sat and partook as well. The others visited about the buildings and displays they'd viewed during their morning, but Laurel used her few minutes of time to eat. After missing lunch one day,

214

she didn't care to spend another day with a growling stomach.

When they'd finished eating, Eugene offered to walk her back to the Women's Building, which warmed Laurel, but she shook her head. "A marching band will perform in the square at one. You'll want to get there early to be in front or the children won't be able to see. I'll be fine. Thank you for lunch." She kissed Mama, hugged Eugene and Ethel, and waved to the children. Then she darted past the Mexican Village and followed the path between Clara Meer and the square, the shortest route to the Women's Building.

As she passed the small structure housing Colonial relics, the midway point between the restaurant and the Women's Building, Officer Sharp and his partner ambled up the rise from the lake. She released a happy gasp. Apparently the unpleasant gentleman who'd threatened to have Officer Sharp discharged for not moving the black soldier's photograph had been unsuccessful, because there the young man came, attired in his uniform.

A smile grew on her face without effort, and she raised her hand in a wild wave. "Officer Sharp! Oh, Officer Sharp, I'm so relieved to see you."

215

16

Willie

Willie stopped so fast his feet slid on the grass. Dunning stopped, too, and snickered real quiet. Willie wanted to elbow the man, but Miss Millard was hurrying toward them with a big smile on her face. The last time she'd said she was glad to see him, she'd scolded him about sharing her name with Mr. Rochester's son. But her smile . . . He swallowed. He didn't expect her to fuss at him about something this time.

She stopped a few feet in front of him and beamed at him the way his ma used to when he'd taken a bath without prompting. "You're wearing your uniform."

Dunning's eyebrows rose. He looked Willie up and down and shrugged.

Willie lifted his cap a little and scratched his head. "Um, shouldn't I be?"

Her cheeks went all pink and she dipped her chin. "I'm sorry, how silly that must have sounded."

Dunning snorted under his breath. Willie wanted to elbow him good.

"You see . . ." She lifted her face and met his gaze. "I overheard the gentleman in the Auditorium this morning threaten to have you discharged."

Dunning's jaw dropped. "What'd you do, Sharp?"

Willie ignored his partner and gave Miss Millard his full attention. "I wasn't tryin' to be contrary. I just wanted him to know how I felt."

"Felt about what?" Dunning shifted his foot against the ground, as impatient as a kid on a playground wanting his turn at bat. "What'd you do?"

Willie blew out a breath and stepped closer to Miss Millard. He hoped Dunning wouldn't stick his nose into their conversation. "I'm sorry you heard all that. But I'm not sorry I said what I did."

"You didn't say anything wrong, and I'm so glad you didn't lose your job." Her brown eyes glowed, giving Willie a warm feeling that went all the way from his head to his toes. "I —" The Chimes Tower began to play its short twelve-thirty melody. She jolted and took two stumbling steps backward. "I'm late for work. I have to go. Good day, Officer Sharp." She took off running before Willie could tell her goodbye.

Dunning grabbed his arm. "What was that all about? Who's wantin' to get you fired?"

Willie sighed. "A man at the governor's speech. He told me to take a black soldier's picture off the table with the white soldiers. I didn't want to do it 'cause the picture was next to a friend o' his. Seemed like since they were friends, the two oughta be together, even if one's black and one's white."

Dunning stared at him with his mouth slightly open for several seconds. Then he huffed a laugh. "You're funnin' me."

Willie shook his head. "No. That's what he got upset about."

"No, I meant you gotta be jokin' about leavin' those two pictures together. A black soldier's picture shouldn'ta been on the whites' table. You shoulda done what he said."

Willie's chest tightened, making it hard for him to suck in a full breath. "But —"

Dunning thrust his hand in the air. "Look, Sharp, you're young, too young to know how that war tore everything apart. Lots o' folks — me included — still have deep feelin's about what shoulda been left alone. I ain't gonna fault you for bein' young an' stupid, but don't expect me to back you if

218

you stick up for them over your own. Partners or not, I'll side against you."

Then, just as quick as he'd gotten stony, he broke into a smile and clapped Willie on the shoulder. "C'mon, we was headin' to get somethin' from the Mexican Village when that little gal stopped us. Let's go."

Willie didn't think he'd be able to choke down tortilla-wrapped spicy beans and beef. He kept his feet planted. "Tell you what, one of us should probably stay on patrol. I'll make another swing around the lake, keep an eye on things, while you get your tortilla."

Dunning's forehead crunched into an uncertain scowl. "You sure?"

"I'm sure. Go ahead."

His partner hesitated for a few more seconds, then nodded. "All right. I'll bring you one." He grinned. "Unless I get too hungry on the walk back. Then I might eat it."

Willie gave the expected laugh, and Dunning strode off, whistling. The owner of the little coffee shack set up near the lake had offered free coffee to the security guards. Willie wasn't any thirstier than he was hungry, and he'd never been much of a coffee drinker, but he needed something to occupy himself. So he walked to the shack and requested a cup of hearty Colombian coffee.

The good smell rising from the speckled pots on the roaring stove inside the shack cleared a little bit of the unpleasantness he carried from his brief exchange with Dunning. The owner's buxom, smiling wife gave Willie a steaming mug. He held it two handed and walked slow and careful across the grass to the edge of the lake.

All three rowboats were out on the water. Two of them carried teenage boys who hooted and tried to splash each other with their oars. Quincy was at the front of the third one, rowing a young couple around the lake. He spotted Willie and nodded, grinning big. Willie managed a smile and nod in reply. The man and woman snuggled close, making sheep's eyes at each other, while Quincy did all the work for them. A heaviness settled in Willie's stomach. Quincy was good enough to tote them on the water, but he bet they wouldn't invite him to have a meal at their table.

He lifted the cup to his lips and took a sip. Hot. Strong. It smelled a lot better than it tasted, but he wouldn't waste it. He was draining the last of it when Dunning clomped up beside him. His partner smelled like garlic and tomatoes, and he wasn't carrying a tortilla. So he either ate the one he'd planned to bring for Willie or he didn't get it at all. Willie didn't much care.

Dunning trailed Willie to the coffee shack. Willie returned the mug, and then the two of them set off across the footbridge to the other side of the lake. Neither of them talked. Dunning wasn't much of a talker, which suited Willie fine. They hadn't been hired to spend the day talking. They were supposed to keep watch over the fairgrounds. Besides, he was used to holding his talk during the day.

At the factory, signs warning men to pay attention hung on every wall. One of them read, "Idle talk brings work to a halt," and another stated, "Inattention = Accidents." Willie doubted getting caught up in chatter here at the exposition would make somebody lose a finger or otherwise get hurt, the way it could at the factory, but he was drawing a good wage to pay attention. So that's what he did. Even if the other guards didn't.

Raucous laughter exploded, so loud it could've been right next to Willie's ear, but it came from the other side of the lake. Years ago Pa had explained how the water made voices sound louder, which was why Jesus could teach a whole crowd from the middle of a lake. Willie hadn't understood it, but he'd believed it because Pa said it. He believed it especially now, with that laughter sounding even louder than the band playing in the square. Somebody was cutting up and having a good time.

He squinted against the splashes of sunlight on the water and peered across Clara Meer. Quincy was pulling a rowboat up onto the grass. Briggs and Turner were close by, pestering him. Willie's chest went tight. Why were the two of them by the lake? They'd been assigned the north end of the fairgrounds, the area around the Government Building.

Willie set off at a trot for the footbridge. Dunning called his name, but he didn't slow his pace, and his partner came pounding up alongside him. They crossed the bridge together, but at the other side Dunning fell back. Willie charged up to Briggs and Turner and stepped in front of Quincy.

"What're you fellows doin' over here? This isn't your area." Willie kept his voice low, friendly even, but underneath he was plenty worried. The bulging muscles in Quincy's jaw spoke of his temper building. When Quincy got riled, he didn't always use good sense. He hoped his pal would stay quiet and let Willie handle things.

Turner nudged Briggs with his elbow.

"Lookee here, Sharp's gone all territorial on us. Acts like he owns the lake."

Briggs smirked. "Or maybe he thinks he owns the —"

Quincy lunged. Willie grabbed him around the middle and hissed in his ear, "See to the rowboat."

Quincy quivered from head to toe, straining against Willie's grip.

"I mean it, Quince. You're gonna get yourself fired."

The threat must've pushed past Quincy's anger to his sensibility. He jerked loose of Willie and stomped to the edge of the lake. He crouched and fiddled with the oarlock.

Willie edged sideways and put himself between Quincy and the two guards, who were both grinning like they'd won a contest. He sent up a prayer for God's calm to fall on all of them and settled himself in a relaxed pose he didn't really feel. "Mr. Felton told us to stay in our assigned areas so no parts of the park are unprotected. Me an' Dunning have this part covered. So why're you here?"

"Takin' a break, Sharp." Briggs imitated Willie's stance, resting his weight on one hip and slipping one hand into his trouser pocket. "Felton might be a tough supervisor, but he lets us take breaks."

Willie glanced across the grounds to the huge clock on the Chimes Tower. The hands showed five minutes past one. "Kinda early, isn't it?"

Turner snorted. "Actually, it's kinda late. We're just now takin' our lunch. Had to 'help' a couple fellas off the fairgrounds who'd been drinkin' somethin' a little stronger'n root beer." He and Briggs shared a laugh. "They weren't any too happy to go, so it took some doing."

"We were headin' to the Mexican Village for stone-cooked tortillas an' beans." Briggs pointed past Willie to Quincy. "Saw this boy fightin' to pull the rowboat out o' the lake an' offered to give 'im a hand. But he didn't take it so well."

Based on their talk in the past, Willie could imagine what they'd offered. He had no authority over Briggs and Turner, but he couldn't stay quiet and let them torment Quincy. He looked over his shoulder to Dunning, who stood about ten paces away with his hands jammed in his pockets.

"Ted, you went after tortillas at the Mexican Village a little while ago, but you didn't bring any back. Are they out?"

Dunning harrumphed and shifted in place. "They was makin' more when I was there, but a whole lot o' folks were waitin' for some. Might be out by now."

Willie turned back to Turner and Briggs. "I ate at the Japanese Village yesterday. Had rice with vegetables an' fish, an' it was real tasty. Kinda fun to eat with chopsticks, too. You might wanna give it a try." He pointed to the colorful village set up near the lake, between the Women's Building and the Manufacturers and Liberal Arts Building. If they went to the Japanese Village, they'd be heading toward their assigned patrol area instead of away from it. Which meant they wouldn't cross Quincy's path again.

Briggs made a sound low in his throat — half growl, half chuckle — and took a step in the direction Willie wanted him to go. "All right, Sharp, I'm too hungry to argue, so we'll go get us some rice an' fish. Could be, though, before long you'll wish we were in your territory. You might need a little extra help to handle the trouble that's comin'."

Chills rolled through Willie. He glanced at Dunning. His partner seemed to examine the few clouds dotting the sky. He likely hadn't heard Briggs's last comment. Willie turned back to Briggs, a question ready to leave his tongue.

"C'mon, Simon. Let's git." The pair tromped by Willie without saying anything, but the fury in Briggs's eyes spoke plenty.

Dunning watched the pair go. Then he hustled to Willie. "If you aren't about the biggest fool I've ever seen. First you tell some expo guest you won't put a picture where he wants it, an' now you're accostin' two o' the men you're s'posed to work alongside. You're fixin' to get yourself booted right off these grounds. That what you want?"

Willie's chest pinched. " 'Course not. But when I said I'd patrol this area, keep trouble from breakin' out, I meant it. Those two" — he swung his arm in the direction Briggs and Turner had gone — "were causin' trouble. Causin' it on purpose. Am I supposed to ignore it just 'cause they're wearin' a uniform like mine?"

Dunning nodded hard, making his cap slip low on his forehead. He settled it back in place. "Yeah, that's exactly what you're s'posed to do. These uniforms put us all on the same side, same as the Confederate an' Union uniforms put all those soldiers on the same side."

A sad smile tugged at Willie's cheek. " 'Cept it didn't, did it?"

Dunning frowned. "Didn't what?"

"Put 'em all on the same side. They might've worn the same clothes on the outside, but the color of the man under-neath kept some apart."

Dunning lifted his gaze to the sky and drew both hands down his cheeks, pulling the skin into jowls. He looked at Willie again. "You aren't gettin' it through your thick head, are you? I'm gonna say this once more, an' then I'm done. The organizers of this exposition can shout from the stage how it's showin' the way blacks an' whites are workin' together in harmony, but the only way there'll be harmony is if they stay in their place an' we stay in ours. Look in a mirror when you get home today, Sharp. You're white. Start actin' like it, or —" He clamped his lips tight.

Willie waited a full thirty seconds before he braved the question. "Or . . . what?"

Dunning puffed his cheeks and blew out the air. "Never mind. I don't wanna threaten you." He folded his arms over his chest and gave Willie a mournful look. "Truth is, I like you, Willie. You seem like an honest, hard-workin' fellow. So lemme give you some advice, the same kind I'd give my own son if I had one. Just 'cause you believe somethin' doesn't mean you have to tell everybody about it. You'll be better off if you keep your comin'-together talk to yourself, because there's a lot who won't

227

listen to it as calm as I do. Understand?"

Willie glanced at Quincy. He must've fixed whatever needed fixing, because he was sitting on the bank with his knees pulled up and his arms draped over them. He looked more sad than mad. Willie understood what Dunning wanted him to do. But how could he do it without betraying his very best friend?

17

Langdon

Langdon leaned against the back of the cold steam engine and checked his pocket watch again. If the workers in the Silk Room followed their usual schedule, pretty little Laurel Millard would exit the Women's Building promptly at three. He would intercept her this time, ahead of that long-legged, sour-faced man who'd hurried her off at noon.

He slipped his watch into the little pocket of his vest and tapped his finger against the hard circle beneath the layer of silk. In only four days of the exposition, he'd enjoyed encounters with a dozen young women — three only a few words in passing, two only a flirtatious look, and the remaining seven at least a conversation similar in length to the one he'd had near the food shack with Miss Millard. He'd had what his buddies would call a sampling of women. He suspected a couple of the girls would be willing to delve deeper into a relationship with him, based on their simpering expressions and ridiculous giggles, but the one he found the most appealing was the one who didn't giggle, didn't simper, and didn't turn petulant even when denied a plate of food.

In truth, he wasn't willing to settle on any one girl. Not yet. But Miss Millard intrigued him enough that he desired more time with her. And he would have it in — he checked his watch — three more minutes. He strolled from behind the engine and gave Clyde Allday a light clap on the shoulder.

"Will you be all right for a bit, Clyde? I've got a hankering for one of those meat pies from the Costa Rica booth."

Clyde's watery eyes lit. "I've heard those are good." He dug in his pocket, withdrew a dime, and offered it to Langdon. "Would you buy one for me, too?"

Langdon stifled a groan. He'd only used the meat pie as a ruse to leave the building. Stevens and Sanders were at the Auditorium listening to war veterans share stories. A number of former Confederate and Union soldiers were expected to speak, which meant the two men could be gone for hours. He shouldn't leave Clyde alone in the booth too long — Father had been quite firm about that — but how could he have a decent conversation with Miss Millard and still go across the grounds to purchase a meat pie?

He held up his hand. "There's no guarantee they'll have meat pies for sale. It's been a pretty busy day here, so they could be sold out. If they have some, I'll buy one for you and you can pay me back. But this way I don't risk losing your dime on the way to their booth."

Clyde smiled and pocketed the coin. "That sounds fine, Langdon. Go ahead."

Langdon shot out the front doors, across the bridge, past the small fountain to the southeast corner of the Women's Building. Then he stopped. Using a window as a mirror, he straightened his tie, smoothed his hair into place with his fingers, and adjusted his lapels. Presentable, he locked his hands behind his back and sauntered around the corner, as nonchalant as could be.

He reached the bottom of the porch steps and placed his foot on the first riser. The front doors opened and Miss Laurel Millard scurried onto the porch. Langdon remained at the base of the steps and rested his palm on his upraised knee. Miss Millard came down two steps, and her gaze landed on his. He smiled. How shy and innocent

231

she seemed with the delightful blush stealing across her cheeks.

"Mr. Rochester." She glanced around, as if afraid of being caught. "H-how good to see you."

He surmised she made the statement to be polite, but he intended to entice her to utter it sincerely in the future. He held out his hand, she took hold, and he guided her to the base of the steps. "Pardon my intrusion on your break, but I'm not sure how else to speak with you. I presume you aren't allowed to socialize while you're on duty."

A rueful sigh escaped her lips. "You're right. Our supervisor is quite strict about personal visitors." Then her expression changed to curiosity. "Why did you want to speak with me?"

"Well . . ." He chuckled, pushing back his jacket and sliding his thumbs into his trouser pockets. "I wondered what you thought of the goat-cheese-on-rye sandwich. Assuming, of course, you had time to eat it."

She clasped her hands at her waist like a child reciting a poem. "Please forgive me. I've been remiss in thanking you. The sandwich was very good . . . different, but very good. In fact . . ." A delicate laugh trickled from her throat. "I told my mother

232

we need to purchase a jar of mustard the next time we visit the market."

He grinned. "Ah, a convert!" He leaned close and winked. "A pot of mustard sits in the middle of my family's dining room table. My mother turns up her nose at it, but both my father and I partake of it liberally at every meal." He'd done so for years, even though he wasn't particularly fond of the taste.

Her blush increased. "I hope you'll forgive my lapse in manners. My mother did teach me to offer appreciation for gifts."

He waved his hand. "No apology necessary."

She fell silent, fidgeting in place and averting her gaze. An uneasy feeling gripped him.

"Am I preventing you from going somewhere . . . again?"

She sent him a wide-eyed look. "No, I . . ."

He angled his head. "Are you sure? After all, you were escorted away by a gentleman earlier today. Perhaps you're meeting him?"

She shook her head and toyed with a loose strand of brown hair. "No. He left, along with Mama and my sister-in-law, nieces, and nephew. The little ones were getting restless, so they all went home."

Awareness dawned, carried on a tide of relief. "The man was your father?"

She burst out laughing and then stifled the sound with her fingers. She swallowed twice and linked her hands together again. "I'm so sorry. No, Eugene is my brother. He is fifteen years my senior, so I understand why you might presume what you did, but he isn't my father. Nor is he" — the blush returned — "a suitor."

"If I might be so bold, I'm very pleased to hear it."

She held her hands wide and shrugged. "I planned to walk to the fountain for my break. After sitting at the loom for hours at a time, I enjoy moving around a bit." She paused, appearing to hold her breath. "You're welcome to accompany me, if you'd like."

"Why, Miss Millard, I've never received a sweeter invitation." He offered his elbow. She slipped her fingers through the bend of his arm and, to her credit, did not giggle either nervously or flirtatiously. "If there's time, perhaps you'd enjoy walking across the footbridge to the other side of Clara Meer."

"I have to be back by three ten."

He bit back a huff of displeasure. So few minutes. But he could still make the most of them. "Only the fountain, then, but" — he guided her forward, his hand curved over her fingers on his arm — "while we walk, tell me all about yourself."

"What would you like to know?"

He gazed at her through lowered lids, a look he'd used to flatter many a young woman. "Everything, Miss Millard. I want to know everything."

Laurel

Laurel peeked at the wall clock, and a rush of impatience swept through her. Why couldn't the hands move faster? Would three o'clock never come?

After the Blue and Gray Day meeting at the base of the Women's Building porch steps, Langdon Rochester developed the habit of meeting Laurel for her mid-afternoon break and taking her on a short stroll around the small fountain or a walk across the footbridge and back. They had only ten minutes together. So few. Yet during those minutes, they talked incessantly, and by the end of the month she believed she was falling in love with him.

The rhythmic clunks, swishes, and thuds of the silk loom seemed to drift far away as she allowed herself to daydream about the one she secretly called her beloved. How could she not fall headlong in love with Langdon Rochester? He was so rakishly handsome with his thick, wavy dark hair sweeping away from his high forehead and his broad shoulders filling his fine tailored jackets. He had such impeccable manners — the kind storybook authors would describe as courtly. When he smiled at her in that low-lidded way he had, as if she were the only thing in the world worthy of his attention, her stomach went trembly and she longed to bask in the pools of his ocean-blue eyes for hours.

When she'd read the phrase "bask in the pools of his ocean-blue eyes" in a romance serial, she'd thought it melodramatic and even bordering on ridiculous. But now? She could only hope Langdon had similar feelings when he stared into her eyes, although, being such a dull brown, they could never be described as ocean-blue pools.

During their frustratingly short minutes together, she'd learned he had horses and loved to ride on Sunday afternoons after church. His favorite fruit was the peach, his favorite vegetable the artichoke, and his favorite animal the giraffe. He'd divulged he was given a stuffed giraffe for his third birthday and had it still, twenty years later, tucked away on a shelf in his closet. Thinking of little Langdon cuddling a stuffed giraffe nearly made Laurel swoon.

Best of all, Langdon loved books as much as she did. He must, because he'd told her his home had a full library. Not a single shelf like she and Mama had, but an entire room lined with shelves, and every shelf filled with books. He said she was welcome to visit and borrow as many as she wanted, but she hadn't asked Mama for permission to visit the Rochesters' estate. It was too soon. Too presumptuous. Too . . . telling.

If she asked permission to visit his home, she wouldn't be able to keep him hidden in the secret recesses of her heart. She wanted to hold these wonderfully exciting feelings about Langdon to herself a little longer. To savor them, treasure them. When she was ready to share, she'd be sure Mama was the first to know she'd found her own Leland Millard. What song might her heart sing if Langdon placed his lips against hers?

"Laurel, it's time for your break. You —"

Laurel leaped from the stool and darted past Felicia so quickly it seemed her feet had sprouted wings. She wove between the ladies visiting the Women's Building and dashed to the porch. She came to a panting halt at the top of the steps and automatically shifted her gaze to the left-hand side of the lowest riser, and there he was, as she'd known he would be, with his bowler against his chest and with sunshine shimmering on his dark hair and illuminating his ocean-blue eyes.

A smile dimpled his cheeks, a silent invitation. She pattered down the stairs and accepted his outstretched hand. He gave a gentle tug, guiding her away from the building. "Come quickly, Miss Millard. I've arranged a surprise for you."

"A surprise?" She had to trot to keep up with him, and her breath came out in little puffs. "What kind of surprise?"

"If I told you, it wouldn't be a surprise, now would it?"

His teasing tone made her laugh, and she held further questions inside while he escorted her to the very place she'd sat her first day at the exposition, when the little boy had toppled her lunch. A rowboat was pulled up on the bank, and the young black man Officer Sharp introduced as his best friend — what was his name? — stood next to it, as if keeping guard.

Langdon drew her directly to the rowboat and swung his arm toward the seat with a flourish. "Here you are, my dear. It's hardly a yacht, but then again this isn't even a real lake." He laughed, chasing away the slight derision in his tone. "Climb in and we'll take a short ride across Clara Meer."

Laurel twirled her hair around her finger. "Is there time?"

"There is if we hurry."

She hurried. The boat rocked with her weight, and she couldn't hold back a squeal. Langdon caught her hand, and Quincy — that was his name — steadied the boat. She settled on the wooden plank seat and curled her fingers over the edge while Langdon climbed in. Quincy gave the boat a push, and they glided into the water. Another squeal left her throat, but this one of pleasure rather than fear.

"It's like being a swan!"

"Oh?" Langdon plunged the oars into the water and pulled, sending them farther from the bank. "What would you know about being a swan?"

"Very little, except that they are lovely and graceful as they float on the water."

"Then you know enough, but in truth, dear Miss Millard, you are more lovely and graceful than any creature, including the swan."

She lowered her head. "Mr. Rochester . . ." She peeked at him and caught his knowing grin. She hadn't fooled him with her mild reprimand, so she lifted her face to the breeze and breathed in the scent of the water while he rowed them slowly around the metal pipe jutting up from the center of the larger half of the lake.

Langdon tapped the pipe with the end of an oar and released a snort. "This ride would be much more pleasurable if the fountain worked. They claim it will shoot water over a hundred feet in the air and will make pictures with colored lights. I'm beginning to think it will never happen. Divers have gone underwater every day to work on the connections, but they've been complete failures at making the fountain operational."

Laurel touched his wrist. "I don't need a fountain shooting water or making pictures to enjoy this time. Being with you" — should she say it? — "is enough." She searched his face for signs of displeasure.

A relaxed smile curved his lips, and his eyelids slipped low into the familiar contented, sated look she'd come to know. "You're easily satisfied, Miss Millard. Are you always so accepting?"

She considered his question. A truthful answer might seem boastful, but she wanted to be honest with him. "I've learned to appreciate what I have rather than yearning for more. Those who strive for more and more seem to always be dissatisfied. I'd rather not live that way."

He winked. "You're a wise girl. And our time is up. Let's get back to the bank."

Quincy was waiting, and he pulled the nose of the rowboat onto the grass. Langdon helped Laurel alight, and then he leaped out. He dug a coin from his pocket and tossed it to Quincy. "I'll want a boat again tomorrow, at lunchtime. Hold it for me." He offered Laurel his elbow and escorted her to the Women's Building. When they reached the step, he said, "Meet me by the lake for your lunch break tomorrow. Bring a basket lunch and we'll take a picnic on the water."

Something niggled in the back of Laurel's mind — a slight discomfort she couldn't quite identify. But then he lifted her hand to his lips and brushed a kiss onto her knuckles, and every conscious thought scuttled away. She smiled. "That sounds lovely. Tomorrow."

18

Willie

What was that? Willie shot from his chair and reached the back door in two quick strides. He swung the door open and looked out, seeking the source of the rustle he'd heard. "Rusty?" A large bird swooped from one of the trees behind the shed, but no big orange tomcat came running. With a sigh, he closed the door.

"God, where is he? Let him be all right, please." Maybe it was foolish to pray for a cat, but he couldn't help himself. The house was lonely without Pa's quiet presence, and now the yard was lonely, too. Only two days after Willie and Preacher Hines took Pa to the convalescent hospital, Rusty disappeared. Willie had searched the neighborhood and the woody area behind his house, had called the cat's name until his throat was hoarse, but Rusty never came. So Willie was completely alone. He missed his pa, and he missed the big orange cat.

Heels dragging, he carried his single plate, spoon, and cup to the washstand. Sunday's supper dishes still sat in the basin. He should wash them. Ma had never left dishes in the basin overnight. She said it would invite mice. With Rusty gone, he shouldn't risk it. But he scuffed out of the kitchen, right past the stove's water reservoir, to the front room. He flopped onto the sofa and stared across the dark room.

Only eight — too early for bed. Sleep beckoned anyway. Sleep was a good escape, he'd discovered. An escape from his loneliness for Pa. An escape from worrying about what'd happened to Rusty. An escape from the scornful way the other security guards treated him during the day.

Pa used to tease Ma about how women liked to talk, but men talked, too. Briggs and Turner did, for sure. They must've told all the security guards how Willie came to Quincy's defense, and maybe Dunning'd told them how Willie wanted to keep those two pictures together, because one by one the guards had started snubbing him. Now the crew ignored him in the changing room. Out on the grounds, if he waved at one of them, they pretended they didn't see, even though he knew they did. The only time they looked at him — really looked at him — was when he was with Quincy. Then he felt their eyes following him, searching for . . . what? Why did his friendship with Quincy matter to them so much?

Here in his neighborhood nobody cared about black or white. Sure, the black families worshipped in one church and the white families in another, and the children went to different schools. But all up and down the block, the grown-ups looked out for each other's children. The children — all the children — came together to play stickball or kick the can or hide-and-seek.

Him and Quincy had banged in and out of each other's house their whole lives long, and neither of their mas had ever said, "You shouldn't be with that boy 'cause he's not your same color." Quincy's ma teased or scolded or handed out cookies to Willie, and Willie's ma did the same for Quincy without so much as blinking an eye. Willie never thought of Quincy as his black friend. Quincy was just . . . his friend.

Young and stupid. That's what Dunning had called Willie. Willie felt it, too. Mostly stupid. Stupid for not knowing that the world outside his neighborhood thought so different than he did, and stupid for not knowing how to fix it. The things he'd tried

— putting Pa's and Ruger Tate's photographs together, stopping Briggs and Turner from bothering Quincy, stopping Quincy from starting a fight with the two guards, telling two older boys who were pointing and laughing at the little black children sitting on the porch of the rebuilt slave cabin in the Old Plantation attraction on the midway that if they couldn't be respectful they should move on — had only made things worse.

His supervisor's warning, delivered after all the other guards had left for the evening, stung in remembrance. *"Sharp, the black folks don't need you stickin' up for them, an' the white folks don't want your advice. You're hired to do a simple job, an' you're gettin' good money for it. So put your personal ideas in your pocket an' leave 'em there, or you can turn in your uniform. I won't put up with you stirrin' conflict."*

He was holding on to his job at the exposition by a thread. He didn't dare let it get snipped. But he sure didn't know how he'd do what his boss said and be able to live with his conscience.

He sighed and glanced at the clock. Half past eight. Still early. But he'd go to bed anyway. When he was little and had a problem, Ma always told him things looked brighter in the morning. There was even a verse that talked about God's mercies being new every morning. He pushed himself from the sofa and headed for his bedroom. He sure hoped some new mercies would wake up with him tomorrow morning.

"Sharp, Dunning, in my office."

Willie gulped. Being called into Felton's office first thing in the morning made his knees quake. At least Dunning was going in, too. He caught a glimpse of Turner elbowing Briggs, both of them smirking, before Mr. Felton snapped the door to his small office shut and pointed to a pair of chairs.

"We've got a problem."

The man's dire tone chilled Willie, even though the little room was uncomfortably warm. He sat on the edge of a chair and clamped his hands over his knees. "What is it?"

Dunning plopped into the other chair and folded his arms over his chest. "I don't know what anybody's told you, but I —"

"Last night, somebody came onto the fairgrounds an' damaged some property."

The pair of boys who'd taunted the little black children popped into Willie's mind. Had they come back to get revenge on him?

He imagined the slave cabin torn up or the Negro Building damaged. Quincy was so proud of the building going up for black artists to display their paintings and sculptures. He'd be awful upset if it'd been ruined.

"Which . . . which property?" His mouth was so dry it was hard to form words.

"One o' the rooms in the Women's Building."

Dunning sat straight up and bounced his fist on his knee. "It was the Silk Room, wasn't it?"

Felton nodded, and Willie gaped at his partner. "How'd you know?"

"There's been some fussin' about that room."

And he'd never said anything to Willie. Were they partners or not?

Dunning shook his head. "I only took it as talk — you know, cotton growers wantin' to say their product's better'n anything some little worm could make. A way of keepin' folks away from the Silk Room so the owners would maybe close it up. People talk all the time. I sure didn't expect anybody to act on the words."

Felton leaned on the edge of his desk and crossed his ankles. "No one else expected it, either, or we would've locked everything

247

up at night. We thought it was enough to put a couple of night watchmen on the property." He shook his head, scowling. "They swore they didn't see anything out o' the ordinary, nobody on the grounds who shouldn't be. But somehow intruders got past 'em, and the exposition organizers want to make sure it doesn't happen again."

Willie lifted his hand. "Sir, how bad is it?"

"There's a mess to clean up — broken glass an' such. Miss Warner, the lady in charge of the room, says she'll see to the mess. I don't think she wants anybody else in there pickin' up an' maybe throwin' away somethin' she thinks can be salvaged. When the cleanup's done, I'm gonna make sure all the buildings are locked up tight after closing time. For an extra safeguard, just in case somebody goes in during operation hours an' harasses Miss Warner, I'll put somebody at the Women's Building full time." His frown settled on Willie. "It'll likely be you, Sharp. I figure that'll solve two problems at once — keep riffraff out o' the buildin' an' keep you out o' trouble elsewhere on the grounds."

Heat rolled through Willie's chest. He didn't mind being put on duty at the Women's Building. Somebody needed to look out for those in the Silk Room. But it shamed him to have Dunning hear Mr. Felton talk about Willie getting into trouble.

"What about me?" Dunning sent a scowl in Willie's direction and then turned it on their boss. "Am I gonna be left on my own patrollin' the lake an' the buildings around it? That's a big piece of the fairgrounds."

"The exposition president an' me are meetin' this mornin'." Mr. Felton clumped around to the back of his desk and yanked a pad of paper from a drawer. He slapped it on the desk and plunked an inkpot and pen on top of it. "Mr. Collier says we're gonna map out a new patrol schedule, maybe even make a rotatin' schedule so folks don't get too familiar with one set o' guards an' think they can sneak past 'em to make mischief. All that'll be explained at the end o' the day. In the meantime . . ."

He rounded the desk again and stood in front of Willie and Dunning. "None o' this is to be talked about outside o' my office. The other guards'll know soon enough, but Mr. Collier was real firm that everybody stays quiet to let him figure out the best way to give information to the public. They're tryin' to build this exposition up. Word that one o' the displays was tromped all to pieces could shed poor light on the whole event. It might make some o' the other businesses displayin' their wares wanna pack up an' go home. So no talkin'."

Willie nodded. "Yes, sir."

Dunning released a soft snort. "You might be able to keep us from talkin', but how're you gonna silence all the folks who visit here every day? You think they won't notice how one o' the rooms got tore up?"

Mr. Felton's bushy eyebrows crunched together into a thick V. "You worry about controllin' your mouth, Dunning, an' let me an' Mr. Collier worry about everybody else's." Then he shrugged. "Collier's got a plan. With any luck, it'll work real fine."

Laurel

Laurel battled the urge to twirl across the tile floor to the hallway leading to the Silk Room. Such happiness propelled her that her feet wanted to dance instead of walk.

Mama's smallest shopping basket hung over her arm. She'd made two sandwiches — ham from the smoker in Alfred's backyard sliced thick and placed between two slices of Mama's homemade bread, which was slathered with mustard purchased on their most recent trip to the grocer. She also had a quart jar of ginger-flavored water and four pickled eggs. Enough to fill their stomachs but not so much it couldn't be consumed during a half-hour break. Noon couldn't come quickly enough to suit her.

She entered the hallway and then came to a stop. The door to the Silk Room was closed. How unusual. Not once since she'd begun her job as a weaver had Miss Warner not arrived ahead of the girls. She liked to open all the shades, adjust the draperies, and make a list of necessary tasks for each day. Worry for the tall, serious woman raised gooseflesh on Laurel's arms.

Laurel started to return to the foyer to wait for Miss Warner, but something caught her eye. Someone had fastened a paper to one of the door's upper panels. A note about Miss Warner? Or perhaps a note from her. The electric lights, which were controlled by a switch in the mechanical building, hadn't been illuminated yet, making the writing on the paper difficult to see. With a frown, she leaned close and read the words.

Silk Room closed for reorganizing. Please return Wednesday, October 2, at 9:00 a.m.

Reorganizing? Miss Warner hadn't said a word about wanting to rearrange the room's contents. She shifted the basket to her other arm and reached for the doorknob. Before her fingers connected with it, someone wrenched it from the other side. The door swung wide, and Miss Warner stood framed in the opening.

Laurel lifted a smile to her. "Good morning. I —" Her elation faded. Were tears pooling in Miss Warner's eyes? Worry struck hard, and Laurel placed her hand on her supervisor's arm. "Miss Warner, are you ill?"

"I'm fine." Her voice wavered, belying the staunch reply. "Please come in." The woman stepped aside, away from Laurel's hand.

Nervous but unsure why, Laurel crossed the threshold. Only one step into the room and she froze in place. Her arms went limp. The lunch basket slid over her wrist and landed on the floor. The crack of glass breaking might have been a rifle shot from the way Miss Warner winced. Liquid seeped from between the basket's woven strips and created a puddle between the two women's feet.

Laurel reached out blindly and gripped Miss Warner's icy fingers, staring in horror at the sight in front of her. "What . . ." She gulped. "What happened?"

19

"Isn't it obvious?" Felicia snatched a crumpled tapestry from the floor. Her green eyes sparked with fury, a stark contrast to the sorrow in Miss Warner's expression. "Someone broke in and tore the place apart."

Of course Laurel recognized what had taken place. But for what purpose?

Berta kicked at a crumpled lace panel that had once graced a tall window. "Somebody ought to be downright ashamed. Wish we could catch 'em and make 'em clean up after themselves."

Felicia flopped the tapestry over her arm and scowled at Miss Warner. "Why can't some of the maintenance workers clean the room? That's why they were hired."

Miss Warner shook her head. "No. This is our room, girls, and we will see to the mess. Instead of talking, let's get busy. We must have everything in order again by tomorrow morning."

Felicia draped the tapestry across a low tufted bench that had somehow escaped the onslaught. "We're going to need brooms and dustpans. I'll fetch some from the maintenance shack." She flounced out the door.

Miss Warner sent her forlorn gaze around the room. "Berta, go after Felicia. Ask her to also find some empty crates. We'll need something to hold the broken glass."

Berta scurried out.

Laurel held her hands outward. "Miss Warner, what would you like me to do?" With such a mess around her, she didn't know where to begin.

The older woman sighed. "Please gather the former contents of our display case. I am hopeful some bits and pieces might still be usable."

"Yes, ma'am."

"Be careful. Don't cut yourself."

"Yes, ma'am." Laurel lifted the hem of her skirt and moved on tiptoe around shards of broken glass. The display case now seemed a skeleton, only the wood frame standing. The lovely length of blue cloth that had supported the intricate dioramas lay wadded on the floor. Dirty bootprints marred its once sleek finish.

Laurel crouched and began to gather up the cloth. Something small and fluffy fell from the folds and floated onto her lap. A broken wing from the *Bombyx mori* moth. She stroked the fuzzy white scrap with one finger. Her nieces' excitement about seeing the tiny bunny filled her memory. Tears flooded her eyes, making her vision swim.

She turned her watery gaze on Miss Warner. "Why would someone destroy things that were so beautiful? I don't understand . . ."

Miss Warner's lips pinched into a firm line, and she stood for several seconds without speaking. Then she sighed. "I suppose it happened, Laurel, because some people don't see the beauty of a thing. They only see a threat. And in their ignorance, they seek to destroy it." She righted a toppled chair and then sank onto its seat, her shoulders bowed and head low.

Laurel set the delicate wing inside the broken case, alongside a dried mulberry leaf and a cocoon, the only parts remaining of one of the display jars. Rising with the rumpled, damaged cloth in her arms, she looked across the case to the loom. Pain stabbed her chest, and fresh tears filled her eyes. A moan built in her throat and emerged in a strangled sob.

She staggered forward, deposited the blue silk on the case's display shelf, and continued to the loom. The loom itself seemed intact, but someone had slashed the golden threads of silk. Only one strand remained in its heddle, and that single silken thread held the cloth Laurel had so slowly and painstakingly woven. She touched the fabric, which slumped over the breast beam much the way Miss Warner now slumped in her chair. Her finger slipped through a tattered hole, and sorrow nearly doubled her in half. Whoever slashed the threads had also stabbed holes in the fabric. Ruined. All of it was ruined. Her knees gave way, and she fell onto the stool. She felt as if she'd been personally attacked, personally battered, personally ravaged. If whoever did this had understood how many tiny silkworms had spun their cocoons, how the worms had died so the cocoons could be harvested, the time and effort it took to dye and then unravel the strand that formed the cocoon, would they have reconsidered their decision to destroy the cloth?

Felicia and Berta clattered into the room, and Laurel and Miss Warner rose at the same time. Felicia carried a broom over her shoulder. Berta balanced three empty crates in her arms. They both dropped their loads, and as they did so Officer Sharp strode in, carrying a mop and bucket.

Miss Warner crossed to the young security guard. "Thank you for assisting Miss Hill and Miss Collinwood. I'll take those now."

He released the items to her, then rocked on his heels, his sad gaze scanning the room. "They really did muck things up in here. I'm sure sorry, ma'am."

Miss Warner nodded, the motion brisk and even desperate. "Thank you. Now, if you'd kindly depart and close the door behind you, we'll be able to restore the room to order."

He crossed to the door and closed it with a snap. Then he faced Miss Warner again. "I'm here to help you restore order. Then I'll be stayin', keepin' an eye on things, makin' sure something like this doesn't happen again."

Laurel stifled a gasp. The exposition leaders found it necessary to post a guard in the Silk Room? She crept from behind the case, carefully stepping around the broken glass. "Should we be concerned about someone coming in during the day and . . . and . . . harming us?"

He looked at her. Compassion glowed in his blue eyes. He removed his cap and held it against his thigh. "There's no need to worry about that, Miss Millard. Even if somebody tried, I'd stop 'em. But I'm thinkin' whoever did this wasn't out to hurt you or the other ladies. They wanted to scare off the silk maker."

For the past couple of weeks, she had been the silk maker. Laurel folded her arms over her rib cage and hugged herself. "Whether they intended it or not, they certainly did hurt us." She fixed her gaze on the battered cloth caught in the loom by a thread. "I feel as though someone slashed my heart."

Miss Warner released a soft huff. "We needn't become maudlin, Miss Millard." She clapped her palms together and straightened her shoulders. "Standing here ruminating won't reverse what's done, and it won't bring restoration. So, everyone, let's get busy. Miss Collinwood, please sweep all the broken glass into a pile. Mr. Sharp, if you would assist her in transferring the broken glass into a crate, I would be most appreciative. Miss Hill, gather up the curtains and examine them. It could be they aren't damaged but only rumpled. If so, we will rehang them."

With each directive, her voice grew stronger. When she turned to Laurel, determination had erased all vestiges of defeat in her expression. "Miss Millard, it appears from here the cabinet behind the loom is un-scathed. If so, spools of silk should still be inside. Choose a color and thread the loom. When you're finished, sit down and weave. When we open the door to visitors again tomorrow morning, they will see a length of cloth in process." She paused and angled her head high. "The hoodlums who sought to thwart us will not have the victory."

With Miss Warner leading the charge, Laurel and the others attacked the mess. No one took their regular midmorning break. They each slipped out as needed to visit the little structure intended for public comfort and then quickly returned. At lunchtime Miss Warner fetched bowls of spicy sausage and crawdad jambalaya from the Creole Kitchen. They sat in a circle on the freshly swept floor and ate the rice dish in silence, too weary and upset to engage in idle conversation.

Although Laurel had never been particu-larly fond of spicy foods in general and crawdad in particular, she ate every bite. She didn't want to offend her supervisor, and she'd worked up an appetite, given the morning's activity. As she placed the spoon in her empty bowl, she suddenly remem-bered the lunch she'd packed and why she'd packed it. She sat up and gasped. "Miss

Warner, I was supposed to meet a gentleman today for a picnic." She gestured helplessly to the water-stained basket near the door. "He's probably waiting for me and wondering why I haven't come."

Sympathy pursed the supervisor's face, but she shook her head. "I'm sorry, but I can't allow you to deliver a message. Mr. Collier was very firm about keeping the incident private."

Officer Sharp set his bowl aside. "My boss, Mr. Felton, told me an' my partner the same thing. About keepin' things private. We aren't s'posed to let anybody know what happened in here. It could" — he scrunched his brow — "shed poor light on the whole exposition." He shrugged, smiling sadly at Laurel. "Sure hope your fellow won't be too upset."

Laurel bowed her head and sighed. "Me, too."

Langdon

Langdon paced back and forth at the edge of the lake, shooting frowns at the place on the rise where he expected Laurel to appear. He checked his watch, growled under his breath, and paced again.

A couple strolled past him arm in arm and approached the only rowboat that wasn't already on the water. He'd instructed Quincy Tate to hold the boat for him, and if the man had any sense, he'd do it. Langdon slowed his gait and observed the black man shrug, gesture to Langdon, and shrug again. The couple glanced Langdon's way, and he sent them a scathing glare. The two moved toward the bridge. Langdon nodded in satisfaction and took up his pacing again.

Where was she? It was twenty-five past the hour already. He'd told her to meet him at the lake so he could secure a rowboat, and she'd vowed to bring lunch. Had she gotten confused and was waiting for him at the porch? If so, he'd need to have a talk with her about paying attention to instructions. Not that he intended to bark at her. He wouldn't need to. He knew how to choose his words and temper his tone and thereby elicit guilt without being harsh. He'd learned the tactic from the best — his own father. If she were to become Mrs. Langdon Rochester, she must be made to understand that he expected her to be where he wanted her, when he wanted her. And right now he wanted her with him, full picnic lunch in hand.

He waited until the Chimes Tower announced the one o'clock hour. Time for him to return to Father's booth and check in with Stevens, who'd been left on his own while Langdon took a lunch break. He blew out a breath and stomped to the rowboat.

"Tate."

The black man jerked to attention. "Yes, suh?"

"When Miss Millard comes seeking me, advise her that I had to return to work. Without the benefit of lunch." He scowled. "Do you understand the message?"

Tate nodded, almost bowing at the waist. "Yes, suh. I's to tell her you hadda go an' you didn' have no dinner."

"Precisely. She will likely give you a message for me in return. I will come by here midafternoon to collect it." He jabbed his finger at Tate. "Don't you leave this spot."

The man drew back, scrunching his face into a grimace. "I got work to do. I can't jus' —"

"Your most pressing duty is to deliver my message to Miss Millard." Langdon affected his fiercest glower. Tate's eyes narrowed a bit, defiance flashing in his black pupils, but he didn't offer another argument. He must be smarter than Langdon originally surmised. "When I retrieve my message, I will give you a tip. But if you aren't here . . ."

Tate pooched his lips. "I gon' be here."

"Good." He crested the rise and joined

the flow of people moving along the walkway, intending to return to the Georgia Manufacturers Building. After only a few strides he changed his mind. Laurel might be waiting at the Women's Building. Seeing his displeasure face to face would be more effective than receiving a message from Tate.

He eased off the walkway and trotted the short distance to the Women's Building. Several ladies were standing in little groups on the porch, as noisy as a gaggle of geese. He climbed the steps slowly, searching for Laurel's familiar puffy coil of dark hair and its loose strands falling along her slender neck. He didn't find her.

Swallowing a grunt of aggravation, he turned to leave. He reached the base of the stairs, and then over the noise of the jabbering women, a voice called his name. He spun around, prepared to drench Laurel in a shower of guilt, but another girl from the Silk Room, the one who'd delivered a sandwich to Laurel for him, descended the steps balancing a teetering stack of bowls in her hands.

"Mr. Rochester, were you the one meeting Laurel today for a picnic?"

He stuffed his hands in his jacket pockets. "I was. But she didn't come."

The girl's face puckered into a pout. "I

know. She didn't leave the Silk Room."

"Why not?"

Red streaked her neck. "We . . . um . . . she couldn't."

Langdon huffed. "Again, why not?"

She chewed the corner of her lip and peered at him sheepishly over the stack of bowls. "I have to take these to the Creole Kitchen. Good day, Mr. Rochester." She scurried off.

Langdon scowled after her. The girl was hiding something. He jerked his gaze to the doors of the Women's Building. He'd never visited the building. Had certainly not entered the Silk Room. But curiosity combined with irritation propelled him up the steps. He edged between two gatherings of women, opened the door, and stepped inside.

At least four hallways branched from the main room, two of them tucked behind winding staircases. Why hadn't he asked Laurel whether the Silk Room was on the first or second floor? He had no desire to traipse through the entire building filled with feminine bric-a-brac. Perhaps he'd stick with his original plan and allow Tate to deliver a message to Laurel. He angled himself for the door. At that moment, security guard Willie Sharp clomped from behind the south staircase. He moved past Langdon without glancing right or left and headed out the front door.

Langdon charged after him. The groups of women had shifted, and he was forced to scoot around their periphery. By the time he reached the steps, Sharp was nowhere in sight. Langdon swallowed a curse and stomped down the stairs. He reached the bottom as the worker from the Silk Room rounded the corner of the building.

He put out his hand and waylaid her. "Has Officer Sharp been in the Silk Room?"

Her eyes widened. She blinked rapidly. It was answer enough.

"And he had lunch with Miss Millard." Not a question but a statement of fact.

She gulped. "Yes, but — That is, he — We —" She closed her mouth so abruptly her teeth clacked.

She hadn't given a full sentence, but he received full disclosure anyway. The factory worker turned security guard had already created conflict between Langdon and his father. Langdon would not allow Sharp to interfere in another of his relationships. Balling his hands into fists, he set off in search of Willie Sharp.

20

Willie

Willie headed across the fairgrounds to the Administration Building with his longest stride. A security guard running across the grounds would likely make people think there was an emergency somewhere. But walking fast he could do without scaring anybody.

All the busted glass and the frame for the display case needed to come out of the Silk Room. Willie was willing to carry it all out, but he didn't know where to take it. Mr. Felton had said, *"Help 'em get that room in order so a new display case can be set up in there."* But he hadn't given Willie any idea what to do with the old one. He hoped his boss was in his office and would have an idea on how to swap out the old for the new without giving folks a clue that something bad had happened in the Silk Room.

"Sharp! You, Sharp!"

Willie skidded to a stop and turned around. He expected to see one of the other security guards hollering for him, but instead it was Langdon Rochester. He fidgeted in place, wanting to finish his errand but not wanting to be rude to his boss's son.

The man charged up to Willie. His red face was all dotted with sweat. "I need a word with you."

Willie pointed to a white oak growing on the edge of the fairgrounds. "Let's get in the shade, then. Looks like you've been in the sun too long."

The man muttered but he followed Willie. They ducked beneath low-hanging branches, and Willie propped his hand against the tree's rough trunk. It felt good to stand still for a minute in the shade from the oak tree's red leaves. He took off his cap and swiped his forehead with the inside of his wrist, then plopped the cap in place again.

"Whatcha need with me?" Whatever it was, Willie hoped it wouldn't take long. There was still lots of work to be done in the Silk Room.

They were in the shade, but Rochester's face hadn't changed from beet red. He yanked off his bowler and slapped it against his leg — *whap, whap, whap.* "Did you eat lunch with Miss Millard today?"

That's what he needed to know? Willie shoved off from the tree. "I did. Had jambalaya from the Creole Kitchen. It's pretty good if you wanna give it a try sometime." He pushed aside a straggling branch. "If that's all, I —" He recalled what Miss Millard said about taking a picnic with a gentleman. All at once he understood. He swallowed. "She didn't meet up with you."

"So she told you we had made plans?"

Willie nodded.

"And yet she didn't come." The man glared at Willie. "Because she was with you."

How could he talk himself out of this without sharing things he wasn't supposed to share? Willie scratched his temple. "That's true enough, but not only with me. With me an' her boss, Miss Warner, an' the two other girls who work in the Silk Room. We all had lunch together."

"Even though she knew she was to meet me."

He held up both hands and hoped Rochester would see it as surrender. "You're gonna need to talk to Miss Millard about it. Right now I got work to do." He took a step.

"You won't have a lick of work to do if you don't stay away from Laurel Millard."

Willie stopped and shot Rochester a scowl. "What do you mean?"

The man's lip curled into a sneer. "I've decided to court Miss Millard. She's exactly the kind of wife I've been searching for — pretty, respectable . . . easily pleased."

Willie didn't know for sure what Rochester meant, but he didn't like the way it sounded. "What does that have to do with me?"

"She had lunch with you when she was supposed to picnic with me. You won't let that happen again."

Rochester spoke friendly enough, but the spark in his eyes gave a warning. A senseless one because Willie hadn't done a thing to keep Miss Millard away from Rochester. Although, the way the fellow was acting, he hoped Miss Millard would decide on her own to stay away from him.

Willie blew out a breath. "I don't have anything to say about what Miss Millard does." If he did, he'd tell her to be careful. "I can't promise I'll stay away from her, either." He'd been assigned to guard the room she worked in — they were going to be together whether Rochester liked it or not. "An' now I gotta go talk to my boss. Bye." He set off across the grass.

"I'm telling you, Sharp, keep your distance from Miss Millard. I possess the ability to

269

have your position terminated both here and at the factory. You don't want to put my words to the test."

Willie pretended not to hear Rochester's threats. The man was mad. Folks didn't think straight when they were mad. That's why Quincy got himself in trouble sometimes — he let his anger get out of control and the whole rest of him followed. In time the truth about the damage to the Silk Room would spread around. Mr. Collier, Mr. Felton, and Miss Warner didn't want it to, and Willie wouldn't be the one to spread it, but somehow, some way, it'd get told. Things like that always did. And then Rochester would understand all his blustering was wasted.

Willie shook his head. He didn't know Miss Millard. Not hardly at all. He knew she didn't turn up her nose at folks, because she'd talked nice to Quincy. He knew she came from a well-to-do family, because a driver carried her to and from the fairgrounds every day. And he knew she felt real strong about folks destroying somebody else's belongings — she'd been teary eyed most of the morning, sniffling the whole time she strung purple-colored thread into the loom. So no, he didn't know much, but what he did know made him think she could do a whole lot better than matching up with his boss's high-and-mighty son.

But Ma would say that wasn't any of his business, and Ma would be right. So he pushed aside thoughts of Langdon Rochester and Miss Millard and hurried on to Mr. Felton's office. He found his boss alone, bent over some sort of chart on his desk. Willie explained the problem about all the debris needing to come out of the Silk Room, and Mr. Felton scowled deeply, drumming his fingers on the chart.

"Mr. Collier's already got a new case waitin' to go in there. He saw to that even before he came an' met with me. But if we go carryin' things in an' out now, folks'll notice an' wonder about it."

"That's what I thought, too." Willie stood beside the desk and fiddled with his cap. Mr. Felton likely didn't need his advice, but he couldn't stop his thoughts from finding their way out of his mouth. "If we wait until dark an' let the night watchmen swap things out, nobody'll see, but it'll make it awful hard for Miss Warner an' her girls to get everything set up again before the doors open tomorrow."

Mr. Felton pushed back his chair and rounded the desk. "Guess it's best for me to talk to Miss Warner. C'mon."

The men climbed the basement steps, Willie behind his boss, and then the two of them headed through the center of the square. At the fountain, Mr. Felton stopped and plunked his fists on his hips.

Willie stopped, too. "Somethin' wrong?"

"Thinkin'." He tapped his foot. People walked around them, and he didn't even seem to notice them. He dropped his arms and huffed a short breath. "Mr. Collier's arranged to have a couple o' policemen start walkin' the grounds at night. Even so, I don't wanna put the night watchmen to work cartin' things out o' the Women's Buildin' an' settin' up the new display case in there. We had two" — he held up two fingers to Willie — "fellows on duty, an' somebody still sneaked into that buildin' an' caused a mess. I need those men doin' their job."

He paused, working his jaw back and forth and staring hard at the fountain. Willie had an idea that seemed to make good sense. He couldn't throw it at his boss without being asked, though. He'd already got himself in trouble for talking out of turn. Maybe this wasn't on the same subject, but he didn't want to risk aggravating Mr. Felton.

Finally Mr. Felton jerked into motion. Willie trotted after him. They went into the

272

Women's Building and straight to the Silk Room. Miss Millard was at the loom, where she'd been when he left, and the other two girls were standing on a bench, hanging curtains. Miss Warner seemed to be sorting through things in one of the crates. She looked up when Willie closed the door.

"Mr. Felton." She stood and crossed the floor with her hand out. Mr. Felton shook it. "I didn't expect you to come and assist Officer Sharp in discarding our rubble."

"We ain't here to clear it out. At least not yet." Mr. Felton folded his arms over his chest. "Fastest way to let our cat out o' the bag is to parade this stuff through the middle o' the grounds right under everybody's noses."

The woman made a face. "Of course. It would certainly invite questions." She shook her head, releasing a heavy sigh. "I should have realized it myself. I'm . . . not thinking clearly today."

Mr. Felton made a clicking sound with his tongue. "You're bound to be a little muddled, considerin' all this." He swung his arm toward the crates and pile of wood from the dismantled display case. "If we can't haul stuff out durin' the daytime, then it goes to follow we have to haul it out at night. I can have the supervisor of the

273

maintenance men ask a couple o' his workers to stay until sundown. They'll take all
the broken stuff out an' carry in the new
display case an' whatever else you need.
Then you an' your girls" — all three of the
Silk Room workers peeked in Mr. Felton's
direction — "can get ever'thing set up again
tomorrow."

"Absolutely not." Miss Warner lifted her
chin. "I cannot allow my employers to lose
another day of showcasing their product."

Mr. Felton gaped at her. "You all fixin' to
stay here all night?"

"Of course not. I will release my girls at
their regular quitting time." The woman
looked as puffed up as a mama cat defending her kittens against a neighbor dog. "I,
however, will stay as long as necessary to
make this room presentable for guests by
morning."

Mr. Felton puffed up, too. "I ain't lettin'
you stay here at night all by yourself."

She pinched her lips tight and crossed her
arms. Willie knew there wasn't one thing
funny, but it tickled him to see such a mild-
mannered lady fixing to butt heads with his
whisker-faced, gravel-voiced boss.

The idea he'd hatched out by the fountain
rolled in his head. It needed saying before
Miss Warner's face got any redder. He

274

tapped his boss on the arm. "Mr. Felton? I agree it's not safe to let Miss Warner stay here all alone" — her frown grew fierce — "but keepin' the room closed up for another day'll likely make folks wonder what's goin' on in here."

Both Miss Warner and Mr. Felton were frowning at him now. He swallowed. "If someone stays with Miss Warner until everything gets put to right in here, then she can get done before tomorrow, an' you won't hafta worry about her bein' alone."

Mr. Felton pinched his jaw between his finger and thumb. "Hmm . . . I reckon I could ask Mr. Collier to —"

"I'll stay."

His boss gave a jolt. "Why you?"

Willie glanced at Miss Warner. Ordinarily he wouldn't share something so personal with a stranger, but he couldn't ignore Mr. Felton's question. " 'Cause there's nobody lookin' for me to come home. It won't matter if I stay late."

Mr. Felton stared at Willie for another few seconds. Then he turned to Miss Warner. "Are you comfortable stayin' here by yourself with Officer Sharp? If you want me to get somebody else, too, or even somebody else altogether, I'll do it."

Miss Warner eyed Willie. Her face

drooped, real sad looking. "Have you no family at all, Mr. Sharp?"

He raised his shoulders in a slow shrug. "I've got a pa, but he's in the convalescent hospital, tryin' to get better. So for now, I got nobody waitin' for me." Not even a cat. He straightened his spine and looked her full in the face. "I'd be pleased to stay an' help you make the room nice again an' then escort you home. Truth is . . ." He couldn't stop a grin from lifting the corners of his mouth. "If my pa heard I did anything less, he'd skin me good."

To his surprise, she laughed. When she did, her hazel eyes lit up and her cheeks went rosy. She appeared ten years younger and a whole lot prettier. "Very well, Mr. Sharp. For one so young, you're very gallant. I will accept your kind offer." She shifted her attention to Mr. Felton. "Please arrange for a pair of strong, dependable men to assist me this evening. Then Mr. Sharp and I will ascertain the Silk Room can be open for visitors tomorrow morning."

Laurel

Laurel wanted to find Langdon at the end of the day and beg his forgiveness for not picnicking with him as they'd planned, but she couldn't delay meeting Eugene without alarming him. So with reluctance she trudged through the center of the square to the Administration Building's tunnel, frequently casting searching looks over her shoulder with the hope of spotting Langdon on the grounds. But she reached the tunnel without receiving so much as a glimpse of him.

Eugene was waiting beside Mr. Salisbury's carriage on the other side of the tunnel. For a moment she considered asking him to take her to the Georgia Manufacturers Building, but sensibility reigned. She couldn't ask without explaining why she needed to see Langdon. Eugene had been so protective the day Langdon approached her at the

Women's Building. Although he'd apologized for his reaction, he would certainly express curiosity if she insisted on seeking out the man before returning home. So she climbed into the carriage, hoping she would have a chance to speak with Langdon the next day.

Over supper, Laurel told Mama, who could be trusted not to speak of it elsewhere, about the damage done to the Silk Room. She pushed the last green pea back and forth across her plate with her fork, shaking her head in sad confusion. "So many things ruined, Mama, and so senseless! The hours I spent weaving that beautiful yellow cloth, only to have it destroyed by an intruder . . . I had planned to ask Miss Warner if I could purchase the length at the end of the exposition and sew dresses for Anna and Mary. They were so taken by the shimmering gold. Wouldn't the two of them, with their dark hair and brown eyes, be beautiful in yellow silk dresses?" She sighed. "That can't happen now."

"No, but maybe . . ." Mama tapped her chin with her finger. "Was the entire piece destroyed?"

Laurel envisioned the damaged strip of fabric. "It had holes poked in it here and there, and of course the whole end frayed where the threads were cut. There were a few sections, perhaps six to eight inches square, left unharmed."

"Was it discarded, or did Miss Warner choose to salvage it?"

None of the garbage had been carried out yet when Laurel left, and she couldn't remember if the poor battered yellow silk was in the toss-away or the keep box. She shrugged. "I'm not sure. I'll know tomorrow morning, I suppose."

A secretive smile formed on Mama's face. "If it's still there, ask to bring it home. If you can't sew dresses from the cloth, you might be able to fashion hair bows. They could even be displayed at the exposition as a sample project, the way the tapestries were on display."

Laurel gasped. "Oh, what a wonderful idea! A way to make something beautiful from the ashes of destruction. I'll look for it tomorrow, if the maintenance men didn't put it in the rubbish barrel."

An odd question flitted through her mind. Had Miss Warner and Officer Sharp eaten supper? They'd vowed to stay until the Silk Room was ready for visitors again. The five of them had accomplished much during the day — rehanging curtains and tapestries, fixing a broken chair, sweeping up all the broken glass, and even creating new dioramas from materials found in the cabinet. They weren't as nice as the original ones, but at least there was something ready to put in the new display case. She hoped the officer and her supervisor were able to finish quickly and go home for a good meal.

"But who would have fixed Officer Sharp's supper?"

Mama sent her a querying look. "What?"

Laurel hadn't realized she'd spoken out loud. She released a self-conscious laugh. "I'm sorry, I was thinking. The security guard who has been assigned to watch over the Silk Room made mention today he lives alone because his father is in the convalescent hospital. He and Miss Warner stayed late to finish the room, so they were probably very hungry when they were able to leave. I hope they had a chance to eat."

"I hope so, too." Mama picked up the dishes and carried them to the washbasin. "Why is Officer Sharp's father in the hospital?"

Laurel retrieved the dipper from its hook and ladled hot water from the reservoir into the basin. "He didn't say. But isn't the convalescent hospital a place for someone to recover from an illness?"

Mama scraped bits of lye soap into the

steaming water. "Yes, or from an injury." She paused and smiled at Laurel. "Perhaps we should pray for Officer Sharp's father to come home quickly. Then Officer Sharp won't be alone."

"That's a good idea. And we should pray for Officer Sharp." She told Mama about his dispute with the man on Blue and Gray Day and the man's threat to have him discharged from his position. "With his father in the hospital, he shouldn't need to worry about losing his job, too. Especially when he didn't do anything wrong."

Mama sighed and lowered the dishes into the water. "In many people's minds, he did a grave wrong by putting those pictures together." She swished a rag over a plate, sending up the scent of lye with the steam.

Laurel's nose stung, and she rubbed it. "But you don't think so, do you, Mama?"

"No, I don't."

Laurel sagged with relief.

"But my family wasn't as deeply affected by the war and the change of life many were forced to take. Those who had large land holdings and relied on slaves to harvest their crops lost the most. Of course they'd still be bitter even these thirty years later." She held up the dripping dish.

Laurel took it and rubbed it dry with a

281

length of toweling. The question she'd wanted to ask Eugene on Blue and Gray Day found its way from her lips. "Would Papa have minded having his daguerreotype next to a black soldier's picture on the table?"

Mama paused with her hands in the water. She kept her head down, her brow furrowed and lips pinched into a firm line. Finally she sighed and resumed applying the rag to a plate. "I honestly don't know. Although his family lived in town and didn't even have a house servant, Leland was eager to support the Confederate cause, claiming no Yankee should have the right to tell us how to live."

A knot formed in Laurel's throat.

"But he learned the attitude from his father, whose closest friends owned a plantation outside of Atlanta. Had it not been for his father's rigid beliefs, Leland might very well have had a different opinion. After the war, when it was clear the South would never return to the way it had been prior to Lincoln's Emancipation Proclamation, he didn't speak of it. I think, in a way, he wished to forget the war and the toll it took on our nation."

Mama lifted her hand from the water and placed it over Laurel's arm. "But it doesn't really matter what your father thought. You don't have to emulate his ideologies, or even mine, for that matter. You are free to form your own opinions, guided by God's Word and your tender conscience."

She removed her hand and continued washing their dishes, but a wet blotch remained on Laurel's sleeve. Just as a troubling thought about the papa she hadn't known remained in the back of her mind.

Quincy

Quincy took hold of his half of the long glass case, counted "One, two, three, up," and lifted. Cass at the other end lifted, too. He swallowed a grunt. Mercy, what'd this thing weigh? His muscles quivered and the veins in his temples started to pound, but he held tight and shuffled backward from the wagon toward the Women's Building.

If he'd been a tom turkey, his tail feathers would be spread all out like a fan and he'd be gobbling loud and proud. All 'cause he got picked for extra work. Who would've thunk it? The supervisor picked him and Cass to stay around after closing time and wait for dark to fall so they could sneak a big glass case into the Silk Room. Mr. Johnson said he picked them 'cause he could trust them to keep quiet about it.

He'd never been picked special for anything before. Quincy didn't know why toting in a new display case was such a secret, but he vowed not to break his boss's trust.

Cass grunted about every six steps or so. But even when they went up the porch stairs, which jarred Quincy something awful, he gritted his teeth and held his grunts inside. Didn't want Mr. Johnson to think he'd chose wrongly. Quincy's hands grew slick from sweat, and he gripped the underside of the case so hard his fingers ached worse'n the toothache he'd got when he was six and ate a whole bag of jelly beans. Still, he didn't let go.

He inched across the tiled floor of the Women's Building's foyer, his heels wanting to slide on the slick tile, taking little baby steps like Sassy did when she'd just woke up from a nap. Moving backward, Quincy couldn't see where he was going, but Mr. Johnson followed Cass and called out "little bit left" or "little bit right," and somehow Quincy made it up a hall and through a doorway without bumping a thing.

Inside the room, the lady who run the Silk Room scuttled out of the way and pointed to a spot in the middle of the floor. Quincy lowered his side of the case as gentle as a

284

butterfly coming to light on Mam's spirea bushes.

He let go and went a little dizzy with the sense of floating. He planted his palms on the case's top and closed his eyes, waiting for the feeling to pass. Only took a few seconds, and then he popped his eyes open and arched his back, same way Cass was. Felt mighty good to stretch.

Mr. Johnson clapped Cass on the shoulder and nodded in Quincy's direction. "I got my wagon waitin' behind the maintenance shack. Come on with me now an' I'll drive you boys home."

Cass followed the supervisor, but Quincy stayed put. "Nah."

"You sure?" Mr. Johnson paused, his face puckered up.

Quincy nodded. He'd go with Willie, same as he always did.

The man shrugged. "Suit yourself. C'mon, Cass." The two of them strode out.

Quincy grinned at Willie. "You ready?"

Willie scrunched his face, all sorrowful like. "I'm gonna stay, Quince, an' help Miss Warner put everything away, then see her home."

"Ah." Quincy rolled his shoulders. A joint popped and he rubbed the spot. "Then I'll stay an' help y'all."

Miss Warner's eyebrows pinched. Then she quick turned her back. Quincy stared hard at her. Like a clock's pendulum, he swung from pride to shame. A red-hot coal formed in his gut. He'd thought she scooted across the floor to get out of the way of the case. But she'd just been . . . getting away.

Willie came close, looking real sheepish, and put his hand on Quincy's arm. "You go on. Me an' Miss Warner, we'll get things done all right."

The coal burst into flame. Quincy jerked away from his friend and stomped out. He got to the bottom of the porch stairs and then plopped onto the second step. He propped his elbows on his knees and buried his face in his hands. The cold from the concrete seeped through his worn britches and chilled him, but he didn't move. The wary look on Miss Warner's face appeared behind his closed lids.

She'd looked, then turned around, like he wasn't even worth seeing.

She didn't bother him none, though. Fancy white women — most of 'em wouldn't look straight at him. He was used to it. But Willie . . . Willie should ought to know better. He should've told that woman Quincy was his friend, was trustworthy. But instead he'd told Quincy to go. Every day they'd come together and they'd gone home together. Until tonight. Because Willie'd let that fancy white woman's feelings trickle over on him.

The fire in Quincy's middle spread until his fingers and toes tingled. He ought to go home. Mam'd be wondering after him by now. But he couldn't go until he gave Willie what for. Maybe even a clop on the jaw. He bounced up, fists ready, and braced his boot sole on the first riser.

"You there."

The husky voice seemed to blast from nowhere. Quincy spun around, his flesh prickly. Two men in policeman uniforms stood a few yards away. The taller of the pair pointed at Quincy with his billy club. "What're you doin'?"

"Nothin'." Quincy's answer came out sharp, the mad making his throat tight.

The two advanced on him. The shorter one eased off to Quincy's side, and the tall one stopped in front of him, his frown fierce. "That ain't much of an answer."

Quincy swallowed, fear climbing above the coals of anger. "Sorry, suh. Ain't got no other 'un. 'Cause I ain't doin' nothin'."

Quick as Stu snatching the last cookie from a plate, the short one grabbed hold of Quincy's arm. "If you ain't doin' nothin',

287

it's only 'cause we caught you before you could do somethin'."

Quincy knew better than to try to twist free. The man's club would come down on his head. But he had to make them understand. "I work here. I tend the grounds aroun' the lake. I ain't doin' nothin' wrong by bein' here."

The tall one grabbed hold of Quincy's other arm. "Park closed more'n an hour ago." He looked up at the building, and his eyes went squinty. "Say, this is the buildin' where somebody broke in an' tore up one o' the rooms. You comin' back to do more mischief?"

"No, suh!" Quincy clenched his fists and quivered from head to toe. Panic made his ears ring. He looked at one officer and then the other. "I was workin'. Helpin'. I'm s'posed to be here."

"Only ones s'posed to be here are that woman workin' on the Silk Room, the night watchmen, an' us." The short one's fingers bit into Quincy's arm. He nodded at his partner. "We better take 'im in."

"Yep."

The two yanked Quincy forward so hard his feet left the ground. He scrambled to regain his footing, twisting like a wild animal caught in a trap. "Please, lemme go!

I didn' do —"
The taller one raised his billy club. And Quincy didn't say nothing more.

22

When Laurel, followed by Felicia and Berta, entered the Silk Room on Wednesday morning, she stared as openly as she had the day before. Yesterday, carnage had greeted her. Today, it appeared nothing had ever happened. Were it not for the purple-dyed strands of silk threaded in the loom's heddles, she might have believed she'd imagined the mess.

Miss Warner rose from her little desk in the corner and crossed to the girls. Her eyes bore dark circles, but she smiled — a warm, welcoming smile very different from the one with which she'd greeted them on previous days. "Good morning. Did you enjoy a good night's rest?"

"Yes, ma'am," Berta and Felicia said at the same time.

Laurel gazed at her supervisor, confused yet pleased by her change in demeanor.

"Did you rest well last night?"

"Surprisingly well, although morning seemed to come far too quickly." She covered a yawn with her hand. "You girls may need to poke me now and then to keep me awake today." A short laugh escaped her lips, and the three girls exchanged hesitant smiles.

Miss Warner strode to the new, intricately carved display case, beckoning the girls with her fingers. "Come and look. I scrunched the length of blue silk and placed the jars just so and succeeded in hiding all the footprints."

Berta bent down and pressed her fingertips to the glass, peering up and down the case. "I can't believe it. I shook out the cloth yesterday. It had at least a dozen bootprints on it." She grimaced over her shoulder at the others. "It looked like someone stood on one foot and hopped from one end to the other, the way a child would play hopscotch." She straightened and stepped back, hands on her hips. "I don't like the way we put those jars together, though. They're not nearly as nice as the other ones."

"You had very little time and limited resources." Miss Warner slipped her arm around Berta's shoulders. "The others were fashioned by a professional artist hired by the owners of the silkworm farm. Mr. Collier informed me more have been commissioned and these will eventually be replaced, but they will suit their purpose for now. Especially with you and Felicia providing such accurate commentary about each stage of the silkworm's life."

Berta gawked at Miss Warner, her mouth slightly ajar.

The older woman gave Berta's shoulder a pat and then turned to face Laurel and Felicia. "Laurel, are you ready to put the loom to work?"

Still stunned by their supervisor's overt friendliness, Laurel managed a jerky nod.

"Then please take your place. I believe the purple cloth will be even lovelier than the yellow was."

Laurel gasped. "Oh! Miss Warner, did the yellow cloth go to the rubbish barrel?"

The woman moved behind the display case and crossed to the tall cabinet filling the back corner of the room. She opened the door and pulled out the basket in which Laurel had toted yesterday's picnic lunch. She carried the basket to Laurel and placed it in her arms. "Although the fabric was in tatters, it represented a significant amount of work. I felt you should decide what to do with it."

Laurel gazed down at the fabric, which was folded into a neat square. "Thank you, ma'am."

Miss Warner brushed Laurel's arm with her fingers. "I hope you don't mind that Officer Sharp and I partook of the basket's contents for supper last night when we discovered the sandwiches hadn't been spoiled by the spilled water." She laughed, the same soft, almost rusty laugh she'd released earlier. "You wrapped them very well with waxed paper. But even so, we presumed they wouldn't be nice by morning. I'd be happy to purchase sandwiches for you to share with your gentleman friend today, if you'd like."

"That isn't necessary." Laurel set the basket on the floor near the loom. "Receiving the cloth is more than enough payment for two sandwiches."

"And four pickled eggs." She raised her eyebrows and held a finger aloft. "You mustn't forget the pickled eggs."

Felicia giggled. Berta started to laugh, sucked in her lips and stifled the sound, but then snorted through her nose, which sent Felicia into gales of laughter. Laurel tried to control herself, but their merriment was contagious. She laughed with them. Miss Warner didn't join, but she smiled at them

293

and shook her head, the gesture indulgent rather than disapproving.

At last the laughter faded, and Berta wheezed out a big sigh. "Oh, my. That felt good." She tipped her head, frowning at Felicia. "What was so funny about pickled eggs?"

Miss Warner pursed her lips. "Absolutely nothing. But yesterday was a very stressful day, and laughter is good medicine, don't you agree?"

"It must be," Felicia said. "I feel scads better."

"Good." Miss Warner turned and marched to her desk, her frame erect and chin high. "Then let's prepare to receive visitors." She slid into her chair but then sent a puzzled look toward the open doorway. "I wonder what's keeping Officer Sharp."

Willie

Willie rolled over and opened his eyes. Sunlight hit him full in the face. He squeezed his eyes shut and flopped his arm across them. He should've pulled his window shade last night. It would've kept out the sunlight. Then he jolted. Sunlight? He threw aside the covers and bounded out of bed in one movement. He dashed to the window and peeked out. The sun was full up, all the way above the neighbor's roof-tops. Must be nine o'clock or after.

Groaning, he scrambled out of his night-shirt and into the clothes he'd dropped at the end of his bed when he got in last night. His bare toes caught in the pant leg, and he hopped in a circle, trying to free himself without falling over. His foot popped through. He grabbed up his shirt and jammed his arms into the sleeves, heading for the back door, where he'd left his boots and socks.

He screeched out a kitchen chair, sat, and wrestled his socks and boots into place. His pulse pounded like a hammer on a nail. How'd he slept so long? Sure, he'd got in late — well past eleven. But that wasn't an excuse. He should've woke up. Why hadn't Quincy banged on the door when he wasn't out front to meet up with him? Maybe he had and Willie'd slept through it, although he couldn't imagine sleeping through that sound. Since Pa went to the hospital, Willie'd woke up at every coyote howl or limb crack.

He stood and buttoned up his wrinkled shirt. His fingers shook so bad he had a hard time sticking the buttons through the holes. Maybe Quincy hadn't come by be-cause he was sick. Or mad. He'd wanted

Quincy to stay last night and help in the Silk Room, but Willie could tell Miss Warner was uneasy about it. So he'd sent Quincy on without him. Maybe Quincy was sore about it and decided to go on to work by himself.

Willie fastened the last button and tucked in his tails, buttoned his trousers, and slipped his suspenders into place. No time for breakfast, to shave, or even to comb his hair. He needed to scat. Not until he was out the door and halfway down the block did another thought slam through his sleep-muddled mind. He'd sent Quincy to find his way home after dark all by himself. Had he come upon some mischief makers? Maybe got roughed up? Willie didn't like thinking such things, but it could've happened. It'd happened before with other black men out at night by themselves. Maybe Quincy hadn't made it home.

Willie came to a stop, two worries pulling him in opposite directions. He needed to get to work, but he also needed to make sure his friend was all right. He lifted his face to the sky and moaned out, "Lord? What should I do?"

No answer boomed from beyond the clouds, but it didn't matter. He was already late. He'd have to be later, because he needed to ask Quincy's ma if her oldest son had made it home all right.

Quincy
Quincy shook the iron bars that trapped him in the square cement-block room until they rattled. Waited. Shook them some more and then thumped his fists on a crossbeam — *wham! wham! wham!* That iron, it sang a high hum. Still nobody come running. He gathered up his breath and let loose. "Somebody! Hey! Somebody!"

Mutters and curses came from men in some of the other cells, but Quincy didn't pay them no mind. He pressed his face between bars and hollered again. "Hey! Hey!"

The door at the end of the hallway between the cells popped open, and a scowling man stomped up the concrete floor to Quincy's cell. He shook his billy club. "You better quiet yourself down."

Quincy'd been quiet all the night long, waiting for somebody to get him out of this place. Being quiet hadn't fixed nothing. So now he'd be noisy. "When you gon' let me outta here? I done tol' those p'licemen who brung me in to ask Mr. Johnson at the exposition how come I was at the fairgrounds so late. 'Cause he gon' tell you I wasn't doin' nothin' wrong. Has you ask 'im?"

The officer snarled, fierce as a rabid dog. "You think we got time to chase down folks just 'cause somebody who got caught doin' wrong says we should?"

"Then did somebody let my mam an' pap know where I is? They gon' worry theyselves sick 'cause I didn' come home." Mad as he was at Willie and the fool officers, he was even madder about his folks being scared. "I tol' that p'liceman where I live, tol' him to tell my folks. He at least do that?"

"Two officers went to your house last night. Your folks know you've been arrested for trespassin'. All they have to do is come an' pay five dollars an' you can be let go until your court hearin'. But they ain't brung in five dollars yet."

Quincy slammed his palm on the bar. Pain shot all the way up his arm. Wincing, he cradled his hand against his ribs. " 'Course they ain't brung five dollars. We don't got money like that jus' sittin' aroun'. Who you think we is, the Rockefellers?"

All up and down the hallway, other men started popping up at the bars to their cells. Some of 'em laughed. Some more of 'em taunted. Some taunted Quincy, and some taunted the policeman.

"Don't get smart with me, boy." The officer's fuzzy eyebrows went down and his voice growled low. He bounced his billy club. "You keep givin' me trouble an' I'll come in there an' teach you better." He whirled and waved the club at the other men. "All o' you, settle down unless you wanna feel this upside your head."

The others mumbled and backed away. The policeman faced Quincy again. " 'Less your folks come in with bail money, you're gonna stay here until the judge can hear your case. So you might as well sit down an' shut up." He strutted off. The iron door slammed behind him.

Quincy lurched away from the wall of iron bars and threw himself on the smelly, lumpy cot. His hand hurt like fury. His chest burned. He hadn't hardly slept a wink last night, worrying so much about Mam. His family didn't have no five dollars to spare. He didn't know nobody with that kind of money.

He buried his face in the stained pillow and groaned. He didn't do one single thing wrong, but no judge would take his word over a white policeman's. He wasn't never getting out of here.

23

Willie

"So I'm askin' to take Mr. Johnson to the jail. He can tell the police chief that Quincy wasn't trespassin' on the exposition grounds last night." Willie finally ran out of words. He stayed on his feet in front of Mr. Felton's desk, praying his boss'd let him help Quincy. Mrs. Tate's anguished wails — *"He's gon' rot in that jail!"* — still rang in his ears. Pained him something awful to see her so upset.

Mr. Felton leaned back in his chair, making the springs squeak, and fixed a frown on Willie. "I can excuse you for bein' late this mornin'. Miss Warner told me how you stayed an' helped her until past ten o'clock, then saw her home safe. That was gentlemanly of you. Those hours last night make up for the ones you missed this mornin'. But goin' to the jail . . . I don't know about excusin' you for that. Not durin' workin' hours."

Willie swallowed a protest and chose his words careful. "The reason I should go is 'cause I can tell the officers how Quincy was with me up until he left. I can be his . . ." What was the right word? "His witness. An' Mr. Johnson can tell 'em Quincy's been workin' here. Between the two of us, we oughta be able to get him out of the jail an' home again, where he belongs."

Mr. Felton frowned and rocked in his chair.

Willie hung his head. "It's my fault he got arrested. He wanted to stay an' help last night, then go with me when I left, but I said no, go on home. If I'd let him stay, if he'd been with me, the officers wouldn't've took him."

Mr. Felton sat up so quick the chair popped. "It could've happened anyway. Might be you both'd been arrested. There's too many young men — black an' white both — roamin' the streets at night, no jobs, lookin' for trouble. The officers was doin' their job. They didn't do anything wrong."

"A fellow could say the same thing about Quincy." Willie said it so quiet he wasn't sure if he'd spoke it out loud or only thought it.

A flicker of anger in his boss's eyes let Willie know the words had come out. "Listen, Sharp, durin' the war there was some folks we called Negro sympathizers. They took the side o' blacks over their own, looked out for 'em more'n their own. They wasn't respected by most Southerners." His boss talked quiet, too, but his tone was hard. So hard Willie wanted to cringe. "Do you want folks to respect you?"

To Pa — and Ma, too — respectable was high on what they wanted Willie to be. They wanted him to be proud of himself and to do the right things so people could trust him. They told him over and over, *"Remember who you are and whose you are."* They wanted him to represent their family well, but mostly they wanted him to represent God well. He wished Pa was here now to help him know how to answer Mr. Felton.

Finally he sighed. "Yessir, of course I wanna be respected."

"Then stop worryin'. Do the job you've been hired to do." Mr. Felton pointed to the door. "Go on."

Willie hesitated. "Can . . . can I least let Mr. Johnson know where Quincy is? So he doesn't think bad of him?"

Mr. Felton snorted. "Gettin' himself arrested doesn't look too good, but all right.

302

If it'll ease your conscience, tell Johnson where his missin' worker's at. Then it's up to him if he wants to try to get him out or not."

Willie left the office. His feet dragged, weighted by guilt for the choice he'd made last night, by the pain Mr. and Mrs. Tate were suffering, by worry about his friend. Quincy'd be plenty worked up. Would he do something foolish and get himself clubbed? If what Mrs. Tate said came true and Quincy ended up jailed for the rest of his days, Willie wouldn't be able to live with himself.

"Lord, don't let him get hurt in there. Please." He whispered the prayer, but he wanted to shout it. To make sure it carried past the noise of the exposition and reached God's ears.

He found Quincy's supervisor in the maintenance shack and told him why Quincy hadn't shown up for work. Mr. Johnson listened and even seemed concerned, but when Willie asked if he'd go to the jail and explain things to the officers, he shook his head.

"I can't do that. Not now."

Willie stifled a groan. "Why? Not to be quarrelsome, sir, but seems like you'd want to help him since he was here doin' what you asked him to do last night."

The gray-haired man made a sour face. "I got nearly three dozen men to manage. It's a sad fact, but some of 'em aren't dependable. If I'm not watchin' 'em, they don't do what they're paid to do. So I got to think about what's most important — the whole group or the one."

Seemed to Willie that the shepherd went hunting the one out of a hundred. Mr. Johnson probably didn't consider himself the workers' shepherd, though. Willie blew out a breath. "What about after work? Would you go then? Let the officers know Quincy wasn't trespassin' since he's hired on here?"

Mr. Johnson clamped his hand over Willie's shoulder. "After work I'll go an' see what I can do. Good enough?"

It wasn't good enough. Not nearly good enough. But Willie'd done all he could. Except for one thing. "I'll come by here at the end o' the day an' go with you." He prayed Quincy would last that long without creating a ruckus.

Langdon
Although he'd intended to avoid Laurel for an entire day, which would certainly make her worry she'd spoiled her chance for a

304

courtship with him, by midmorning on Wednesday Langdon had changed his mind. By her own admission she was easily pleased. What if, in her feminine, foolish mind, she chose someone else? Say, Willie Sharp? He shouldn't give her the opportunity to set her sights elsewhere. Not until he knew for sure whether he wanted her to fulfill the condition his mother had given.

He snatched a handful of informational flyers from the corner of the table and flapped them at Stevens. "I haven't handed any of these around yet this week. Since it's been fairly quiet in here, I'll try to send some visitors our way."

The older man gave a nod of approval, and Langdon set out, whapping his thigh with the papers as he went. No band played in the square today, but there was still plenty of music. Several of the smaller exhibits along the terrace utilized traditional instruments to lure visitors to their displays. Between the German Village's tubas, the Chinese Village's odd flutes and stringed lap harp, and the Indian Village's drums and recorder-type whistles, his ears suffered an onslaught of disharmonious melodies.

Above the various tunes rang hammers pounding on nails. A team of workers swarmed the California State Building. He curled his lip in disdain. Such poor planning. Why hadn't the construction been completed before the exposition was opened to the public? Crews were still working on several buildings. Between the unfinished structures, the small crowds on all but special days such as Blue and Gray Day, and the much-lauded but nonfunctioning fountain in the man-made lake, Langdon sometimes wondered if his father had invested unwisely when purchasing booth space. Would foreign or out-of-state business owners truly flock to the Cotton States and International Exposition and, as Mother predicted, purchase one of the Rochester steam-powered engines? Langdon would bet against it if given the opportunity. But the exposition did offer him an escape from the drudgery of the factory, so he kept his doubts to himself.

He meandered through the square, pressing flyers into the hands of all the gentlemen he encountered, even if they didn't seem particularly interested. He reached the Women's Building as the tower's clock hands showed straight-up twelve. Positioning himself a few feet from the steps, he assumed a somber countenance and waited. In less than a minute, the door opened and Laurel stepped out. She reached the edge of the porch, and her gaze met his. She seemed to freeze in place. Color flooded her cheeks.

Langdon didn't move. Didn't blink. Didn't smile, although it took great effort not to. How guilty she looked standing there with a little lunch pail held at her waist and her face sporting the rosy blush. After a few seconds, he took one small pace forward, and she pattered down the steps and ran directly to him.

"Mr. Rochester, I am so very sorry for missing our picnic yesterday." Her brown eyes took on a sheen. Unshed tears? "I hope you purchased a lunch for yourself and didn't go hungry."

He crunched his brows. She'd apologized very sweetly, but what was her explanation for lunching with others? "I waited by our reserved boat until well past one, certain you would honor your promise to meet me. But you didn't come, and by then my time away from the booth was spent and I had to return to work. So, yes, I did suffer hunger throughout the afternoon."

His feigned hurt had the desired effect. How pitiful she looked wringing her hands on the pail's handle and blinking back tears. Easily pleased and also easily manipulated. What a gem.

"Miss Millard, as much as it pains me to

say this, you betrayed my trust yesterday. A simple apology can't erase that." He allowed her several seconds to consider the grave harm she'd done, and then he sighed. "Perhaps if I understood why you chose to disregard our arranged picnic . . ."

She angled her gaze away from him and twirled a loose strand of hair.

Langdon shifted sideways a few inches and put himself in her view. "Miss Millard?"

Her brown irises slid to the corners of her eyes and peered sadly at him. "I . . . was working."

"All through the lunch break?"

She bit her lip. She blinked three times — a sure sign of nervousness.

He leaned in. "You had no lunch, either?"

"Yes, I ate. In the Silk Room."

She'd been truthful. Good for her. If she'd fibbed, no matter how pretty or easily manipulated she was, he would move on to another girl. He wouldn't marry someone guileful. "Then I truly do not understand. If you had time to take a lunch in the Silk Room, surely you had time to meet me. Yet you didn't." He placed his hand on his chest. "Miss Millard, if you've decided you don't want to spend time with me, then —"

"No!" She brought up her hand and almost touched his arm. "I do want time with you. I . . . I savor our minutes together. I am sorry about yesterday, so please give me the opportunity to make it up to you. I'll bring a picnic lunch for us tomorrow. I'll meet you at the lake."

Langdon gazed down at her for several seconds. He waited in silence while she wrapped the strand of hair around her finger so tightly the tip of her finger turned scarlet. Then he sighed. "All right. I can forgive one lapse of judgment. I will meet you tomorrow."

Relief flooded her features. She untangled the hair from her finger and grasped the handle on her lunch pail as if it were the rope preventing her from plunging off a cliff.

"But when we meet, I will expect an explanation. I need to know why you ate in the Silk Room . . . and with whom."

She lowered her head.

He slipped his finger under her chin and lifted her face. "Will you tell me?" Oh, those big eyes of hers. She held a secret. Would she divulge it to him?

"Yes. Yes, I will explain . . . tomorrow."

"Good girl." He pointed to her pail with his stack of paper. "Eat your lunch now. I have work to do. We'll chat tomorrow." He turned and strode toward the square, chuckling to himself. He needn't look any further for the future Mrs. Rochester. This girl would suit his purposes perfectly.

Laurel

After speaking with Langdon and seeing for herself how much her absence yesterday pained him, Laurel had no appetite. She returned to the Silk Room and trudged past Officer Sharp, who stood sentry at the door, to the loom. Weaving would provide a fine distraction from her gloomy thoughts.

Few visitors came to the room, leaving Berta and Felicia free to observe Laurel at the loom. Miss Warner encouraged them to watch carefully and learn to add rows to the silk fabric. If someone came in while Laurel was on break and wanted to see the loom in action, the other girls should be able to give a demonstration.

Laurel slowed her movements, explaining each of the steps as she performed them. She discovered that tossing the shuttle through the shed, pulling the beater, pumping the treadles, and pulling the beater again was simpler to do than to explain. She stumbled over her words. Mama had trained to be a schoolteacher before she married Papa, but apparently Laurel hadn't inherited her mother's ability to instruct. Or perhaps her exchange with Langdon had left her too upset to think clearly.

A worry rolled in the back of her mind. She'd willingly tell him with whom she'd eaten lunch yesterday. Why should she hide that she'd eaten with her supervisor, her coworkers, and Officer Sharp? But how would she explain why she hadn't left the room without divulging information Miss Warner had told them must be kept secret?

She pulled the beater to tighten the last row, pushed it back into its resting position, and stood. "All right, Berta, your turn."

Berta held up her hands and drew back. "I'll make a mess of it."

Laurel laughed. "No, you won't. I'm right here. I'll stop you from making a mess."

Her eyes wide, Berta slipped onto the stool. Her hands trembled, but she picked up the shuttle and gave it a little push through the shed. She looked at Laurel. "Pull it tight?"

Laurel nodded. "But not too tight. Snug enough to avoid a loop at the end, but not so snug it pulls the fabric inward."

Berta let out a high-pitched, nervous giggle and gave the thread a little tug.

Laurel smiled. "Perfect."

Miss Warner left her desk, and Officer Sharp followed her to the counter. They leaned on the opposite side and watched

Berta pull the beam forward in one smooth, deliberate movement. Then she reached for the shuttle.

"Nuh-uh." Officer Sharp pointed. "You gotta pump those things with your feet first. Right?"

Laurel raised her brows. "That's right." Had he been watching her instead of watching for possible vandals?

His forehead pinched. "Why is that?"

She sent him a puzzled look. "Why is what?"

"Why do you push those . . . those . . ." He gestured.

"The treadles?"

"If that's the floor things, yes. The treadles. Why do you pump 'em?"

He seemed so intrigued it tickled her. Her brothers had never shown any interest in Mama's loom. In fact, Alfred often complained about the money Mama spent to buy it. He didn't mind that Mama made money selling rugs, though.

She sought a simple answer to the officer's question. "Well, when you pump the treadle, it raises and lowers the harness."

He drew back. "Huh?"

"Um . . . it opens and closes the shed."

He stared at her, open mouthed.

She held out her hands and shrugged. "It

separates the warps."

He scratched his jaw, which, Laurel noticed for the first time, bore blond stubble. "Maybe it's better if you do it instead of talkin' about it."

Miss Warner laughed and shook her head at Officer Sharp. "Oh, Willie, you are a card."

Laurel swallowed a gasp. Had their proper supervisor done something as improper as addressing the security guard by his given name?

Miss Warner turned her warm smile on the girls. "This young man has a delightful sense of humor. I was so weary and burdened yesterday, but he lightened my mood considerably with his positive presence. And then he took the time to see me safely to my apartment before retiring to his own home last night." She smiled at him the way Mama smiled at her grandbabies. "I cannot thank you enough for your kindness and consideration, Willie."

The guard blushed pink. He ducked his head, as bashful as Laurel had ever seen anyone. "Thank you, ma'am, but it wasn't so much. Just doin' my job."

Miss Warner's expression sobered. "Willie, may I share your father's situation with the girls? I believe they would be happy to pray

313

for him."

His face still glowed pink, and he wouldn't look at any of them. "I reckon it's all right."

Berta turned sideways on the stool, and she, Laurel, and Felicia gave Miss Warner the same attention they offered when she delivered instructions.

"Willie's father suffered an attack of apoplexy several months ago. Up until recently, Willie has been his sole caretaker."

Laurel flicked a look at Officer Sharp — at Willie. The stubble on his chin and cheeks gave evidence of manhood, but he didn't seem much older than her. Such a responsibility he carried. He must love his father very much. The way she loved Mama.

"The position here at the exposition has given him the financial freedom to have his father placed into the convalescent hospital. I ask each of you to pray for Willie's father to experience a full recovery, and also pray for Willie." She slid her arm across his shoulders and gave him several pats. "With his mother gone on to glory, he's quite lonely."

"And pray he isn't discharged."

The others, including Willie, gaped at Laurel. Miss Warner placed her hands on her hips. "Why on earth would Willie be given a discharge from his position here?"

314

Laurel hadn't meant to blurt the thought that tripped through her brain. She couldn't shame him by sharing how the man in the Auditorium had berated him. The other girls or Miss Warner might feel the same way the angry man did about mixing blacks and whites together. Her face heated, and she fanned herself with both hands. "I only meant it's very important for his father to remain at the hospital. If it's the exposition pay keeping him there, then we want Will — Officer Sharp — to continue working here until the very end."

"Ah. Very well." Miss Warner relaxed her pose. "Yes, that's a fine idea."

Laurel offered him an apologetic smile, and he returned it with a slight nod. A silent thank-you glowed in his blue eyes. Laurel found it difficult to look away. How much she'd learned about him from Miss Warner in only a few minutes. Their commonalities — both having lost a parent, both being responsible for the surviving parent — gave her a feeling of kinship with him. He, too, seemed transfixed, his gaze unwavering.

A pair of middle-aged women and a toddler boy entered the room, and Willie lurched toward the door. Laurel replaced Berta at the loom, and Miss Warner invited the visitors to examine the diorama jars.

315

"Felicia, would you like to explain the life cycle of the silkworm to our guests?"

Laurel listened to Felicia's memorized monologue while she worked. Between pulls on the beater or pushes on the treadle, she sent glances at Officer Sharp. And for reasons she couldn't understand, no matter how closely she examined herself, she was suddenly reluctant to tell Langdon that Willie Sharp had been with her during lunch yesterday.

24

Quincy

Quincy stared at the tiny window way up high on the wall. The sunlight was near faded away. That meant the whole day'd gone by and nobody'd come for him. A couple other fellows had got let go. He'd watched them march past his cell, grinning all smug because somebody had five dollars to pay their bail.

A cramp attacked his middle. A hunger pang. The plate they'd brung him for lunch sat on the edge of his cot. He hadn't touched the scoop of beans dotted with chunks of fat and gristle. He couldn't make himself eat something that looked so awful. He'd considered eating the square of mealy corn bread. There wasn't no sorghum to pour on it like he would at home, but least it didn't have gristle in it. Then the fellow in the cell next to his said he found a little worm in his corn bread. So Quincy'd tossed his bread on top of the beans. He'd vowed he wouldn't never be hungry enough to put wormy corn bread in his mouth.

That's what he'd thunk at noontime. Now with evening coming on, he stared at those dried, crusty beans and broken chunks of hard corn bread. If he swallowed them down, would they stay down? The rumble in his belly was sure demanding something.

The click of the lock echoed against the cement walls. Somebody was coming. Bringing them a decent supper? He bounded up and took two steps. Didn't need more than two steps to make it to the wall of iron bars. He pressed his face to the cold metal, trying to see if whoever was coming pushed a squeaky cart with plates on it, like they'd done for lunch. No squeaky cart holding plates of food, but something better. Willie and Mr. Johnson came up the hallway with one of the officers. Quincy almost yelled a hallelujah.

Willie got to him first and reached through and took his hand. "You all right, Quince?"

Quincy looked Willie up and down. Rumpled clothes. Little yellow whiskers poking out all over his cheeks and chin. Hair standing on end. "Good as you, I reckon. You come to bail me out?"

Mr. Johnson stepped up close to Willie.

"No need for bail, Tate. I told the chief what you were doin' on the exposition grounds, an' he's droppin' the trespassin' charge."

This time Quincy didn't hold back. "Hallelujah!" The policeman stuck a key in the lock on the cell door and turned it. He bolted through the opening. "Let's get out o' here."

Out on the sidewalk, he sucked in a big breath of humid air. Then he laughed. "Sure am glad you foun' out where I was. Thank you, Mr. Johnson, for gettin' me out. Thank you, too, Willie."

Mr. Johnson took a couple of backward steps. "Get yourself home safe now, you hear?"

"Yes, suh. I will."

"An' don't be late to work tomorrow. You got some makin' up to do for missin' today."

"Yes, suh!"

Mr. Johnson set off up the street, and Willie squeezed Quincy's upper arm. "I couldn't hardly believe it this mornin' when your ma told me you'd been took in."

A funny feeling struck Quincy. "You talk to Mam this mornin'?"

Willie nodded. "When you didn't come meet me for work, I got worried you might be sick or hurt, so I went to your house to check on you. That's when I found out."

319

"This mornin'." Anger started boiling in Quincy's gut. More powerful than the hunger already in there. "An' you didn' come 'splain to them first thing? You left me sittin' in there all day? I ain't never had a mo' mis'able day'n this 'un, stuck in that li'l room, smellin' the stink from all the fellas who stay in there before me. Spent all last night an' the whole day thinkin' I wouldn' never get out."

"I'm sorry, Quince." Willie still had hold of Quincy's arm. He squeezed it again, but Quincy jerked loose.

"You can't be feelin' any sorrier'n I been, knowin' I didn' do nothin' to get took in for." Everything that happened yesterday evening — the policemen nabbing him and all that come before — rolled through his mind. He snorted. "An' don't be thinkin' I don't know why you wouldn' lemme stay an' help last night. I seen how that prissy white lady look at me an' Cass when we carry in the big case. She take our help but she watch us, all distrustful like."

Quincy tapped Willie in the middle of his chest with his finger. "She trust you fine, though, an' you know me real good. You coulda said, 'Quincy here's my friend. You don't hafta worry none 'bout him.' Then she prob'ly woulda said, 'That jus' fine,

320

Officer Sharp. He can stay an' help.' But you didn' say nothin'. You jus' send me on. An' then you wait the whole livelong day to come get me."

Willie stood there, mouth turned down all sad. He didn't say Quincy was right, that he could've done things different, but Quincy didn't need to hear it said to know it was true.

Quincy flipped his hand and turned away. "It ain't dark yet. I don't need you takin' me home." He took two steps, then turned back. "An' don't be worryin' 'bout me come mornin', neither. I'll take myself to work from now on. Not like you an' me're to-gethuh on the fairgrounds no how, you in yo' uniform an' me grubbin' in the dirt."

All of a sudden Willie seemed to wake up. He stomped up close to Quincy. "The only reason I didn't come here first thing in the mornin' is because Mr. Felton wouldn't let me. I asked him. I tried. But he said I couldn't or —"

Quincy cocked his head. "Or what?"

Willie kicked at the sidewalk and kept his head down.

"He say he fire you if you go?" Quincy would feel kindlier if Willie got threatened. Willie needed the job same as Quincy did. Maybe more. Quincy might could understand if Willie had to choose between helping his friend or helping his pa.

Willie growled in his throat. "Never mind what he said. It doesn't matter." He looked at Quincy again. "You're right. I should've told Miss Warner she could trust you. I made a mistake. I'm sorry. But like you said, I know you, an' you know me. We been friends our whole lives, Quince. You really wanna hold on to your mad an' not be friends anymore?"

Quincy stood for a long time, staring hard at Willie, his heart pounding like one of them big drums from the band at the fairgrounds. He couldn't remember a time when him and Willie wasn't friends. He'd thought for sure they'd be friends until they was old and gray headed. But what Willie'd done, letting that white lady think he wasn't worthy of staying and lending a hand . . . He bit the inside of his lip until he tasted blood.

"Stayin' mad . . . is that what you want, Quincy?"

Quincy sucked a breath through his nose, making his nostrils flare. "What I want is to feel like we's friends. Like I matter to you. The way I used to. But I don't. An' I'm thinkin' I never will again." He turned and stamped off before Willie could see tears popping into his eyes.

Willie

Willie stared at Quincy's retreating back. He should follow him. Make sure he got home all right. Quincy's clenched fists and stiff shoulders would tell everybody who crossed his path that he was toting a mighty rage. Could be someone would needle him, make him let all the mad out. Quincy could end up in a jail cell again. But his feet didn't move.

"*. . . you didn' say nothin'.*" The accusation stung. Mostly because it was right. Why hadn't he told Miss Warner she could trust Quincy? If he had it to do over, he'd speak up, tell her how he and Quince'd been friends their whole lives and he was a decent fellow. If he ran after Quincy and promised to do better next time, would his friend forgive him?

"Quincy'd probably tell me to go away anyhow." Crushed his heart to think of his good friend not wanting him around, but Quincy didn't think straight when he was all caught up in being angry. When Quincy's mad wore out, he'd change his mind. Until then, hard as it would be, Willie'd stay away from him. But there was somebody Willie wanted to see. He needed his pa something fierce.

Preacher Hines visited Pa almost every evening, since Willie could only go on Sundays. The preacher'd said the hospital let in visitors from four in the afternoon until eight at night. It wasn't quite seven yet. Could he make it to the hospital in time to at least look in on Pa, maybe unburden himself? Pa couldn't talk out loud, but he could still think clear. Which meant he could pray. Willie needed his pa's prayers.

He glanced up and down the street, trying to get his bearings. He'd never been in this part of Atlanta because he'd never needed to go to the jailhouse. Mr. Johnson had led the way, so Willie hadn't paid close attention, but it seemed like they'd taken the Piedmont and Magnolia trolley lines to get here. The Georgia line would carry him to where Pa was. He fingered the ticket stub in his pocket. Might as well get his full twenty-five cents' worth. He took off for the closest trolley stop.

His pocket watch showed ten 'til eight when Willie opened the doors to the convalescent hospital. He wrinkled his nose. Quincy'd spoke of the jail's stink. Was it worse than all the smells in this hospital? The people were nice. Willie'd set aside his worries about how they'd see to Pa. But he wished they could do something to make it smell less like an outhouse dipped in lye soap.

Willie followed the winding hallways to Pa's room, the last one on the first floor. The door stood open, so Willie went on in without knocking. Pa's bed was at the far end of the row of iron beds, in front of the windows. The other patients were lying flat, but Pa sat propped up in bed by three plump pillows. An older lady as plump as one of the pillows stood close by with her back to the door. She wore a blue apron and matching scarf over her hair, so she wasn't a visitor but a hospital worker. She was laughing. Laughing at Pa? Willie hurried over to see, then drew back in surprise.

Flopped on Pa's lap like he owned the whole bed was a huge fluffy orange cat. Willie's mouth fell open. "Rusty?"

The woman gave a start. "Who are you?"

"I'm Willie."

She looked at him the way someone might look at a bank robber. Kind of the way Miss Warner had looked at Quincy last night. "Willie who?"

"Willie Sharp." He pointed to Pa. "I'm his son."

Pa's face lit up with a big half smile. He

325

stretched his left hand to Willie, and Willie took hold.

The woman's scowl faded. "Oh. I'm Mrs. Bonebreaker."

Willie swallowed a chortle. What a funny name for someone who worked in a hospital. "Nice to meet you."

"You, too. Now, what did you say when you came in?"

"Rusty. That's what Pa named this big ol' brute." Willie stroked the cat from the top of his head to the middle of his back. Rusty rolled sideways, exposing his furry white belly. Willie laughed and gave it a rub, too. "What's he doing here?"

"Well, up until this minute, I thought he was a stray." She ran her fingers through the cat's thick coat. "He showed up at the kitchen door three or four days ago, yowlin' worse'n a whole pack of cats. The cook felt sorry for him an' put out a little dish of scraps, but this scoundrel darted inside, through the kitchen, an' up the hallway. Three workers went after him. You should've seen the chase!"

Willie grinned, imagining it.

"He slid into this room, jumped up on Mr. Sharp's bed, an' gave everybody such a glare they were afraid to touch him." Her expression went tender. "Except for your pa here. The way he took to the cat . . . Mr. Sharp's a hard worker. Tries to do everything we ask of him. But since this fellow" — she scratched Rusty's ears, and the cat closed his eyes and purred — "showed up, your pa's been a lot happier. The doctor said bein' in good spirits will help him mend, so even though we've never let an animal in before, Doc Blake declared the cat part o' your pa's therapy."

A knot formed in Willie's throat. He tried to swallow it, but it wouldn't budge. He talked around it, his voice coming out gruff. "Ma'am, we live north of the reservoir, a good eight miles from here. I can't think how Rusty found his way all by himself."

"Has your pa had him for a long time?"

"No. He meowed at our back door shortly before Pa took sick. He's stuck around ever since." Willie shrugged. "Well, up until just after Pa came here. I figured he'd wandered in an' now he'd wandered on, an' I felt pretty sad about it." He gazed at the purring cat, and his vision blurred. He sniffed and blinked before the tears fell down his cheeks and embarrassed him. "But he must've gone lookin' for Pa."

"I'm glad he found him." The woman patted Pa's arm. "So is Mr. Sharp, I think, yes?"

Pa nodded. "Caaaa . . . Ruuu-eeee . . ."

Willie's jaw dropped. "Pa! Did you say *cat*? An' *Rusty*?"

"He sure did." The woman beamed as bright as if she was personally responsible for Pa's words. "Isn't he doin' good? He lost his consonants when he had the attack. It's pretty hard to have a conversation with somebody when you only use vowels."

Willie wasn't sure what she meant, but she seemed so happy about it he nodded anyway.

"So the nurses've been workin' on gettin' his consonants. All the letters that come from the back of your tongue — *c, g, h, k,* and *r* — he can do now. We're all so proud of him. He only started saying the *kuh* sound yesterday. I think he's been wantin' to say *cat*."

Pa nodded again, smiling big. "Caaa. Caaa." He put his right hand on top of Rusty's head and slid it across the cat's neck. One slow, clumsy pet. But he'd done it all by himself.

Tears blinded Willie again. He swiped his eyes with the back of his hand. "You're doin' good, Pa. You're doin' so good." He coughed out a half laugh, half sob. "I'm startin' to think angels sent that cat to Pa."

Willie'd meant to joke, but Mrs. Bone-breaker nodded real slow and serious. "You could be right. You said the cat came to your house right before your pa had his attack. As soon as your pa came here, the cat came huntin' him." She turned her wide-eyed gaze on Rusty. "He might even be an angel cat." She shrugged, smiling a little sheepishly. "He's an unusual one, that's for sure. An' now" — she scooped Rusty from the bed — "visitin' time is done, so I'll put him out in the little house one o' the cook's helpers made for him. It's only a potato crate with some old torn towels stuffed in the bottom, but he seems to like it."

A crate with towels in it was better than a hole under a garden shed. Willie might put a bed like that together for Rusty when Pa came home.

"And you, young man, need to leave, too."

Willie shook his head. "But I didn't get to —"

"If you want your pa to get better, he needs his rest. I let you stay a little over since you come in so late, but now I gotta make you leave. Sleep is real important for healin'."

As much as Willie wanted to talk to Pa, to unload these worries, he wouldn't do anything to keep him from getting better. He kissed Pa goodbye and followed the woman out of the room.

She shifted Rusty to one arm, struggling some because the cat wriggled, and closed the door. "Good night, young man." She hurried off, wrestling with Rusty.

Willie scuffed up the hallway, head low and hands shoved in his pockets. He left the hospital. The air smelled better, so he breathed deep, the way Quincy had outside the jail. Willie's heart hurt as he recalled Quincy's fury. He could come back on Sunday with Preacher Hines, same as he'd done last Sunday and the Sunday before, but Sunday was still days away. Three more full days of carrying his worries all by himself.

Then shame smacked him. He didn't have to carry any worry by himself. Hadn't Pa and Ma taught him to take his cares to Jesus? Maybe it was best he hadn't got to talk to Pa about Quincy. It'd only upset him.

Willie yawned. Pa needed his rest, and Willie did, too. He aimed himself for the trolley that would carry him home.

25

Laurel

Butterflies danced in Laurel's stomach. She climbed into Mr. Salisbury's carriage on the morning of October ninth and scooted over to make room for Mama. Ethel, Anna, and Mary shared the seat across from Laurel and Mama. The children wriggled, excited about their day off from school in the middle of the week — a rare treat.

Little Gene rode with his papa on the driver's seat, and as the carriage rolled over the cobblestone streets, the little boy's chortles carried through the windows, making Ethel and Mama smile.

Laurel wanted to smile. She wanted to squirm in excitement like Anna and Mary. Liberty Bell Day at the exposition promised much fun and celebration. Since the trolleys had waived children's fares, all her siblings intended to bring their children to see the actual Liberty Bell from Philadelphia, Pennsylvania. She'd never imagined she would have the chance to see the bell for herself or be close enough to trace the crack from a cannonball and read the inscription. She knew the words by heart — "Proclaim LIBERTY Throughout all the Land unto all the Inhabitants Thereof" — from one of the history books on Mama's shelf.

Mama was eager to see the bell, but she claimed her main reason for attending was to watch her primary-school-age grandchildren participate in a children's choir on the square. Eugene teased that his girls had been practicing for a week already and he wasn't sure he could bear listening to it sung one more time, even if it was part of a special ceremony. As if privy to Laurel's thoughts, Mary began humming the tune "America."

Laurel propped her arm on the window case and rested her chin on her wrist, staring unseeingly at the city and its busyness. Why did something that seemed such a good idea yesterday now plague her with doubts? She envisioned Langdon's fervent expression during their brief ride yesterday on Clara Meer in one of the rowboats. He'd instructed Quincy Tate to command the oars, and he joined her on the bench at the back of the small boat. When the boat went beneath the bridge's shadow, he took her hands in his and leaned close. She thought he might steal a kiss, but he only voiced a request.

"Miss Millard, when your family attends the exposition tomorrow, introduce me to them."

Of course she'd agreed. How could she resist when he gazed at her so adoringly? Especially since he'd forgiven her for lunching with Willie Sharp instead of meeting him like she'd promised. He'd even accepted her simple explanation that Miss Warner had forbidden the girls to leave the Silk Room that day. How kind and understanding he'd been about her failing to meet him. How tender and attentive he'd been each day since. Even so, she should have begged a delay in his meeting Mama and the others.

Laurel pressed a palm to her churning stomach. Only three weeks had passed since the day she accidentally slammed against his frame and bruised her forehead on his chin. Nell and Mayme would probably gasp in shock at her audacity in bringing him to Mama after only such a short period of time. They, as well as Alfred and Raymond, would be furious that she'd been spending time with a man at all. Even Eugene might lower his brows in disapproval when he discovered how many times she and Langdon had met by the fountain or at the lake without a chaperone. It wouldn't matter that dozens of other people were always nearby. She had ignored propriety. If Eugene didn't scold, Mama or one of Laurel's other siblings certainly would. If they did so in Langdon's presence, she might die of mortification.

The carriage stopped. The familiar tunnel loomed outside the window. Laurel swallowed. They'd reached the fairgrounds. Already. Mama gave her a little nudge. "Hop out, Laurel."

She might have been wearing a suit of armor, such effort it took to lift herself from the seat and step from the carriage. Mama, Ethel, and the girls followed her out, and Eugene swung Little Gene over the edge. Ethel captured the giggling boy in her arms.

"Go on inside." Eugene took up the reins. "I'll park the carriage and catch up with you."

Laurel led her family through the tunnel and pointed to a spot beneath an oak tree off the sidewalk. "I need to go to work, but Miss Warner is closing the Silk Room for the ceremony to honor the bell, so I'll meet you in the square at eleven."

Mary shook her finger at Laurel. "Don't

be late, Aunt Laurel."

The gesture reminded her so much of Nell that resentment prickled. She tamped down a sharp retort and forced a smile. "Don't worry. I wouldn't miss hearing you and Anna sing." She turned and darted off, weaving her way through the throng of families pouring onto the grounds. At the Women's Building, she clattered up the steps and reached for the ornate door handle, but a hand shot out and caught it before she did. She turned and found Willie Sharp beside her.

"Where did you come from?" She clapped her hand over her mouth. What an ungracious greeting. She lowered her hand and offered an apologetic grimace. "I meant to say thank you. I didn't see you."

He followed her inside, chuckling. "Sorry if I startled you. I've been right behind you the whole way through the square. With so many folks around, no wonder you didn't notice." He glanced back, as if searching for something. "It's gonna be a busy day. Lots of people here even before the buildings open up."

"Well, it is Liberty Bell Day." Laurel crossed to the Silk Room hallway, aware of him close on her heels. "I would imagine nearly every family in Atlanta will try to bring their children to see the Liberty Bell. Such an important piece of American history."

"Is your family comin'?" He opened the Silk Room door for her and pushed the little piece of wood used to hold it against the wall into place.

"Yes." Laurel's stomach knotted again. "Mama, Alfred, Nell, Eugene, Raymond, Mayme, plus all the husbands, wives, and children — twenty-six in all." A hysterical giggle built in her throat, and she swallowed twice to control it. "They'll all be here to . . . see." As soon as they set their eyes on Langdon, no one would pay attention to the Liberty Bell.

Officer Sharp grinned. "That's real nice for you. I sure wish my pa could come see the bell." His face clouded. "It'd mean a lot to him."

How could she have forgotten about his father? She'd vowed to pray for Mr. Sharp, but in her worry over Langdon, the ailing man had slipped her mind. Guilt poked her. How could she be so self-centered? She longed to appease her conscience, but what could she do?

An idea struck. "A photographer is setting up a booth near the Liberty Bell today. Miss Warner said he would sell images for twenty-five cents. Perhaps you could have your picture taken beside the bell."

Officer Sharp nodded, a slow grin climbing his cheeks, which, she noticed, were pink from a fresh shave. "That's a fine idea, Miss Millard. Except . . ." His countenance fell again. He slipped his hand into his pocket and withdrew a few coins. "I gave the herdic driver ten cents for my ride this mornin'. Only have fifteen cents left. Even if I skip lunch, I won't have enough to have a picture made."

His crestfallen expression pierced her. She wished she could cheer him again. Langdon carried a pocketful of coins each day. He would be able to pay for a dozen images, and he would purchase a photograph for her, no doubt, but he surely wouldn't offer to help Officer Sharp. On impulse, she dug in her pocket for the coins she carried every day and held them out to him. "Here."

He stared at her open palm as if she'd produced a scorpion. "W-what?"

"Take it." She stretched her arm, bringing her hand a few inches closer to him, and smiled into his stunned face. "Mama sends me with ten cents each day. 'In case of emergencies,' she says. I won't need it today. With my whole family here, if I have an emergency they'll help with it. So I don't need the nickels, but you do. Take them and have your photograph made for your father."

He lifted his gaze to hers, his mouth slightly ajar and disbelief etched into his features.

"Please. Isn't it important to keep his spirits up? You said yourself seeing the bell would mean a lot to him. So let him see it. Let him see his son with it." She held her breath, inwardly begging him to lay aside his pride and take the two five-cent pieces.

Oh, such indecision on his face. He sighed. His shoulders slumped. Finally he pinched the coins from her palm and gave her a wobbly grin. "Thank you, Miss Millard. I . . . I'll get that photograph taken for my pa." He straightened his frame, and resolve flooded his face. "But I'm only borrowing this. I'll pay it back."

"That will be just fine. But" — she waggled her finger at him, more playfully than Mary had a little earlier — "you still need lunch. So please join my family and me. My sisters, Nell and Mayme, are bringing a large basket of sandwiches. They always make more than we need. Let us share with you."

A titter reached Laurel's ears. She shot a startled look over her shoulder. Berta and Felicia, as well as Miss Warner, stood a few feet behind her. All wearing teasing grins. Had they observed her and listened to everything she'd said to Officer Sharp?

She slid her hand to her neck and searched for a loose strand of hair. She didn't find one, so she tugged a piece free of her bun and twirled it. "He has to eat." The defensive comment sounded ridiculous even to her ears, but why did she feel defensive? She'd only offered a kindness. Even so, a cloak of embarrassment enveloped her.

She faced the security guard and stiffened her frame. "Officer Sharp, my family intends to picnic beside Clara Meer after the children sing on the square. Feel free to join us." Then she marched to the loom, flinging a silencing look at the trio of grinning women. "I think we'd all better get to work."

Langdon
"'. . . *From every mountainside, let freedom ring . . .'*"

The childish voices rang across the grounds. Langdon stood to the rear of the crowd. He had no youngsters to observe, so he hadn't bothered to press close. From his position, he couldn't even see the bell that had brought so many people to the exposition today, but he didn't mind. Why such a fuss over an old, cracked bell? However, he did want to locate Laurel. Eight of her fifteen nieces and nephews were part of the choir, so she was surely at the front.

He worked his way through the assembled listeners, ignoring the grunts and scowls of those he bumped. " *'Let music swell the breeze . . .'* " As the children began the third verse of the song penned in the 1830s by a reverend, he finally spotted her at the very edge of the crowd. The tall man who'd whisked her away from him stood behind her with his hand resting on the shoulder of an older woman who was most likely the matriarch of the family. Those clustered around them were probably her relatives.

His gaze drifted across the group, silently counting. Five siblings. Five spouses of siblings. Children . . . so many children. He shuddered. Laurel had mentioned her desire for a big family more than once during their brief meetings. Each time, he managed to squelch his true feelings, but he also dropped hints about the benefits of raising only one child — less of a financial burden, the ability to shower the child with undivided attention, the quietness of a home not overrun with squalling brats. Well, of course he hadn't said "squalling brats" to her, but it was what he meant. Mother deserved to be a doting grandmother, and he intended to grant her the desire, but she would be satisfied with one grandchild. Given time, the easily pleased Laurel would bow to his preference.

"'. . . *Author of liberty* . . .' "

If he remembered "America" correctly, the children were on the last stanza of the song. If he didn't reach Laurel before the choir finished, he might lose her in the crowd. He worked his way to the back, trotted around to the side, and came to a stop next to Laurel's group just as the children sang, "'. . . *great God our King!*' "

Langdon applauded along with the others, inching closer to Laurel with every smack of his palms. The overprotective brother noticed him first. He didn't smile, but neither did he frown. He stopped clapping and tapped Laurel's shoulder. Still patting her hands together, she lifted her face to her brother. He nodded in Langdon's direction, and she jerked her gaze.

Those warm brown eyes met his. Her applause slowed and stopped. Pink decorated her cheeks. She eased away from the group and stopped in front of him, hands linked, expression uncertain.

Trepidation attacked Langdon. "Is something wrong?"

She glanced over her shoulder. He looked,

too, and discovered both the older woman and the brother observing them. She turned back, biting her lip. "No, nothing's wrong. I only . . . well . . ." A nervous giggle erupted. "I neglected to tell my family about you."

He barely heard her over the chatter of the crowd, which meant he'd need to shout to be heard. He preferred a private exchange. He caught her elbow and guided her several yards away to the outer edge of the square. "Now, please repeat what you said." Not because he hadn't heard, but because he wanted her to reconsider her words.

"I . . ." She swallowed, wringing her hands. "There's something I haven't told you. About my family."

He crunched his brows and dipped his head toward her. "All right. I'm listening."

"You see, they . . ." She licked her lips. "That is, I'm the youngest."

"Yes." He already knew this.

"And as the youngest, my brothers and sisters feel that . . ." She swallowed. "They want me to take care of Mama."

He folded his arms over his chest. "Miss Millard, you're speaking in riddles. I'm an intelligent man, but I'm unable to discern the clues you're giving me. Would you please speak plainly?"

She closed her eyes for a moment, as if gathering strength, then fixed her gaze on him and said in a rush, "They told me I couldn't marry until Mama has gone to her reward with Papa. So if I'm to become someone's wife, it must be with the understanding that my mother accompanies me to my new home."

Her expression changed from distraught to desperate. "If I introduce you to my siblings, they will immediately assume you are courting me. If . . . if you are truly courting me, you must assure them Mama will be cared for, too. I know you have the financial means to do so. Do you possess the willingness?"

26

Langdon

"Of all the —" Langdon bit down on the tip of his tongue and stopped himself from expressing his true thoughts. He counted silently to three, took a deep breath, and curled his hand gently around her upper arm. "— things a person can do, caring for a loved one is the most important."

Hopefulness glittered in her eyes. "Then you'd take Mama in?"

The sun would have to turn green as a frog's belly and drop from the sky before he'd open his home to a mother-in-law who would question his every move and be a constant interloper in every conversation. He smiled. "Of course." He didn't have to admit where he'd take her. Not until the nuptials were over.

"Oh, Langdon . . ." She covered her blushing cheeks with her palms and gaped at him. "I-I mean Mr. Rochester."

Her blunder told him more about how smitten she'd become than anything else she could have said. He gave her arm a soft squeeze and slipped his hand into his trouser pocket. "Now, now, Miss Millard, no need to hide in embarrassment." He waited until she drew her hands from her face. "Truth be told, it gave me a lift to hear my given name flow so easily from your tongue."

He looked past her shoulder. The group of adults and children, with the woman he'd identified as Laurel's mother at the forefront, clustered near the square's fountain. He smiled and lifted his chin in a brief acknowledgment, then returned his attention to Laurel.

"It seems your family is waiting for you. Would you like me to escort you to them? Then you can make the introductions."

She held up one slender hand. "Before we go . . . my mother doesn't know the condition my brothers and sisters gave me. So we mustn't speak of it."

He frowned. "Then how am I to assure them your mother's future needs will be met?"

She sent a quick, frantic look over her shoulder. "See my brother Alfred? He's the one with the balding head and muttonchop whiskers."

Langdon picked the man from the group. "The one who seems to have been chewing on a sour pickle?"

She cringed. "Yes. He often scowls that way. Mama says it's because he's the oldest and feels accountable for all of us."

Then he should be the one to take in Mama. Langdon cleared his throat. "What about him?"

"If you could take him aside, explain to him that you aren't trying to squire me away from my duty to Mama, then it should ease his worries."

He considered her suggestion. If he refused, he would have to start over on his search for a suitable girl. In some ways it might be easier, but would he find a girl who fit all three of the stipulations he'd established for his future wife? He gazed into her upturned, besotted face and smiled. "Of course I can do that." He lowered his voice to a whisper and said, "Laurel."

The blush he'd come to expect brightened her cheeks. He chuckled and offered his elbow.

"Miss Millard, it's time for your family to become acquainted with me."

Willie

Willie stood in line for an hour to have his picture taken beside the Liberty Bell. While he waited, he constantly scanned the grounds. If any sort of altercation broke out, he'd leave his spot and return to duty. To his relief, even though people swarmed the grounds like ants on a honey spill, the high spirits never changed to orneriness.

He paid the twenty-five cents, smiling as he handed over Miss Millard's nickels along with his nickel and dime. What a nice person. He didn't intend to eat one of the sandwiches her family brought for their picnic, but he'd find her, thank her again, and tell her mother she'd raised a very nice girl. He recalled a lady at church telling his ma something like that about him when he was a boy, and Ma glowed like a full moon for days. Made him feel good, too, to have somebody notice when he did good. Most times folks were inclined to notice the bad things kids did.

Now with an empty pocket, he followed the walkway to Clara Meer, where Miss Millard said her family planned to take their lunch. Since she had a big family, he searched for a big group. He didn't see one on the east side of the lake, so he crossed the bridge to the other side. There, near the

Southern Railway exhibit, he found them. He couldn't hold back a smile. A pair of little boys chased each other in circles around the group, and a little girl squealed every time they raced past her. One of the women, probably their ma, grabbed at the boys and missed. But when one of the men snapped his fingers, the boys dropped to their bottoms on the grass. Like him and Quincy used to do when Pa or Mr. Tate let them know it was time to settle down.

Sadness stabbed — he missed Quincy — and envy bloomed on top of it. Quincy had a big family. He probably didn't miss Willie near as much as Willie missed him. What would it be like to be part of such a big family? No matter how hard he tried, he couldn't imagine it.

Miss Millard sat with her back to him. He stopped a foot or two behind her and cleared his throat. She didn't turn, so he coughed into his hand. This time she and the lady sitting next to her glanced over their shoulders. Miss Millard broke into a smile. "Officer Sharp." She patted the lady's arm. "Mama, this is Officer Sharp."

Mrs. Millard shielded her eyes with one hand and held the other one to him. "Officer Sharp, I'm Adelia Millard, Laurel's mother. It's very nice to meet you."

He yanked off his cap and leaned over to shake her hand. "Likewise, ma'am."

She gestured to the spot beside her. "Please join us."

He shifted in place, twisting his cap into a pretzel. "That's real nice of you, but I only came to let Miss Millard know I got that photograph done at the Liberty Bell and now I —" Seemed every person in the circle was looking at him.

And the man sitting on the other side of Miss Millard wasn't one of her brothers. Why was Langdon Rochester taking a picnic with the Millards?

"I, um, I have to get back on duty. Just wanted her — you, Miss Millard — not to worry if I didn't come. So thank you, ma'am — all of you — an' . . ."

Miss Millard rose. "Even if you can't stay, at least take a sandwich with you." She pointed to the large basket in the middle of the group. "Would you rather have chicken and sweet relish or beeftongue and cheese?"

They both sounded so good his mouth watered. But he shook his head and backed up a couple of steps. "That's all right. Helpin' me get my photograph took is more'n enough. You" — he took one more backward step — "enjoy yourselves." He turned, slapped his cap on his head, and took off, as eager to escape as he'd been the day a neighbor's dog tried to bite his leg.

Langdon Rochester's snide voice reached Willie's ears. "You kind people will have to excuse Officer Sharp. He lacks decorum. His upbringing, you know."

Willie's face blazed. He wanted to march back and plow his fist into the man's arrogant face. But he'd lectured Quincy too many times about giving in to his temper to act on the thought.

He stomped across the bridge, stinging himself by repeating Rochester's statement in his mind. On the other side of the bridge, he glanced right and left, trying to find the quickest route through the groups, and he saw Quincy snapping the canopy over one of the rowboats. The breeze caught the fabric and tossed it back at him. He heard Quincy's grunt from a dozen paces away.

Without thinking, he trotted over. "Here. Lemme help."

"Thanks. I —" Quincy looked full at Willie, and his grateful expression went hard. He yanked the canopy close. "I can get it."

Willie huffed. "When're you gonna stop bein' so mule stubborn? Been a full week. Ain't you over your mad yet?"

Quincy's jaw muscles bulged. He snapped

the canopy again. The breeze pushed it sideways. He muttered something under his breath that Willie didn't catch, but he was pretty sure some cuss words were in it.

Willie raised one eyebrow. "Your ma hears that kind o' talk, she'll wash out your mouth with soap, the way she did the two of us when she caught us practicin' our swearin' behind the barn when you were ten. Remember?"

Quincy draped the canopy over his shoulder, stepped inside the rowboat, and attached one corner of the canopy to a post. He whistled, fussing with that rectangle of striped cloth like Willie wasn't even there.

Willie put his hands on his knees and peeked under the canopy. "I know you hear me."

Quincy aimed a scowl at Willie. "Don't you got work to do?"

Sighing, Willie straightened. "Reckon I do." He started to leave, but then he turned back. "You been to the square to see the Liberty Bell? It's real pretty. Big, too. The train'll take it to Philadelphia tomorrow, so if you wanna see it, you'll hafta go today."

Quincy lurched out of the boat. The canopy slipped from its pole, and one corner dipped in the water. "No, I ain't seen it. Ain't intendin' to, neither."

Willie thought about the things the speaker said before the children's choir sang. "But that bell represents freedom, Quince. Freedom from tyranny, from bein' held down by a government that doesn't care about you near as much as it cares about itself. You don't wanna see the symbol of American liberty?"

"Nope."

"Why not?"

" 'Cause that bell, it got nothin' to do with me."

Willie shook his head. He must've heard wrong. "Sure it does."

"Why?"

" 'Cause you're an American."

Quincy stood there without saying a word. Without changing his expression. Almost, it looked like, without life. Then he snorted. "Listen to what you jus' said, but listen to it from my ears. From the ears o' folks like me. Me an' mine, we live in this country, but is we Americans like you?" He waved his arm in the direction of the square. "I heard them children singin'. Was they any black children in the choir? The crowd gath'rin' 'round. How they all stand? White folks here, black folks there?" He pointed right and then left, the movements jerky and stiff.

Shame smacked Willie. He'd known Quincy his whole life, but he'd never stopped to think about how life looked through Quincy's eyes. Now he saw, and the sight pained him. He held out his hands, helpless. "Quince, I . . ."

"You white folks, you talk a good talk, but none o' what you say makes a bit o' diff'rence for the likes o' me." A sneer curled his lips. "We ain't li'l boys, runnin' barefoot up an' down the crick. Time for us to face facts. We's diff'rent. Always gon' be diff'rent. You stick with yo' kind, Willie, an' I'll stick with mine. We both be happier that way. Now, you get on outta here."

He clomped to the boat, yanked the dripping corner from the lake, and flopped the canopy onto the seat. Then he stood with his arms folded tight over his chest and his head down.

Willie wanted to say something — anything — to prove Quincy wrong. But he couldn't. Because all of what Quincy'd said was true. Except for one thing. "Quince, you say we'll be happier stickin' to our own kind. I don't see how we can be. My folks, your folks, we're all tangled together. Have been even since before we were born. Different? Sure. Ain't two people anywhere that're exactly the same. But the differences between us'll only matter when we let 'em. So I guess what I'm askin' is, are you an' me gonna let 'em?"

Quincy

Quincy couldn't turn around. Wouldn't turn around. Why couldn't Willie leave him alone? Bad enough to have Mam chewing on him — *"That boy was near worked up as me 'bout you bein' in jail. You need to forgive an' forget."* — without Willie coming around, trying to act like nothing had changed when he knew good as Quincy that everything had changed.

If Pap wasn't needing the money from this job coming in, he'd quit right now and go home. He'd pick peaches at picking time and dig potatoes at digging time and crack pecans until his fingers bled. None of those jobs hardly paid piddly, but at least back then he didn't know how Willie'd take the side of a snooty white woman over his so-called best friend.

He turned around to tell him so, but Willie'd gone on. Which was exactly what Quincy'd told him to do. So why'd it make him so mad that he'd done it?

He grabbed a corner of the red-and-white-striped canopy and hooked it over the pole. He tied it in place, then stopped with his

354

hands on the strings. He couldn't help seeing his hands. They was right there in front
of his face. Leathery already even though he
was still shy of his twenty-first year. Every
finger wore at least one callus. Mam, she
told him all the time to rub duck fat on
them hard spots and they'd soften up. But
they didn't never go all the way gone. Hands
dark on the backs and pink on the palms.
Funny how white folks' hands was the same
color front and back, but most every black
person he knew had pinkish palms.

When Booker T. Washington held up his
hands that first day of the exposition,
Quincy'd seen his pink palms. How fancy
that man talked, using words as pretty as
any rich white man. Dressed like a rich
white man, too. Maybe that's why all them
white folks crowded in the Auditorium to
hear him speak. 'Cause his fine words and
fine clothes made them look at Mr. Washington the way they'd look at a white man.

Quincy gazed down his length. At his
hand-me-down shirt, patched britches, and
boots with toes so scuffed no amount of
shining could ever make them decent. He
brushed off the knees of his pants, watching
his black hands swish back and forth, sending all the dust away.

There wasn't one thing he could do to

change the color of his skin. But there might could be something that'd help folks see more'n his black face when they looked at him. But Mam and Pap would have to say yes.

27

Laurel

The tower chimed its song announcing the arrival of one o'clock. Laurel wadded the waxed-paper wrap from her sandwich and tossed it into the basket. "Thank you for lunch, Nell and Mayme. I have to go."

Langdon stood and offered her his hands. With a self-conscious glance at her siblings, she took hold and allowed him to assist her to her feet. He gave Mama the same gentlemanly treatment. Mama smiled and thanked him and then wrapped Laurel in a hug.

"Please thank your supervisor for allowing you the extra time to watch your nieces and nephews participate in the choir. It means so much to them to have their whole family in attendance."

"I will, Mama. I'll see you at home." Laurel bid farewell to her family with a wave, and then Langdon offered his arm. She slipped her hand into the bend of his elbow, but he didn't take a forward step.

Langdon bowed slightly to Mama. "Mrs. Millard, it was a pleasure to meet all of you. You have a lovely family."

At that moment, Mayme's boys, Lester and Luther, chose to dive on each other and roll around like puppies. Mayme aimed swats at their rears and missed, but their father, Russell, caught them each by the collar and plopped them down. Hard. They both wailed. Laurel wanted to cover her face and hide. Her nephews might frighten Langdon from wanting children at all.

Langdon laughed. "Lovely and high spirited."

Laurel gave him a smile she hoped conveyed both an apology and a thank-you.

"Since I've had the privilege of meeting all of you, I would very much like permission to introduce Laurel to my family."

Laurel's heart pounded so hard she feared she might faint. She tightened her grip on Langdon's elbow.

"I would collect her this coming Saturday evening in our family carriage at six o'clock sharp and carry her to my family's estate for predinner conversation followed by dining at seven with my parents, Harrison and Marinda Rochester. I assure you she will be home again, safe and sound, no later than ten."

Laurel didn't check, but she sensed her siblings' gazes on her. She gave Mama a pleading look. "May I go?"

Mama turned aside. "Alfred, would you come here, please?"

Laurel bit back a groan. If it were left to Alfred, she wouldn't visit the Rochester estate and meet Langdon's parents. Her brother strode around the group and stopped beside Mama. He folded his arms over his chest. "Yes? What is it?"

Mama repeated the details of Langdon's invitation. "What do you think? His parents will be there, so they'll be chaperoned."

Alfred glowered at Langdon. "Are you aware she is only eighteen years old, hardly more than a child?"

Should she remind him that he'd begun courting his Clara when he was only nineteen and she seventeen? And Mayme married Russell shortly after her eighteenth birthday. Why, Raymond's wife, Violet, was barely sixteen when they exchanged vows. Alfred wasn't at all concerned about her age. He wanted to scare Langdon away.

"She told me her age. And I told her mine — which is twenty-three, if you need to know."

Laurel couldn't be certain because he wore such a friendly expression, but was Langdon baiting Alfred? She pressed her fingers against his arm and met her brother's stormy gaze. "It's only a dinner, Alfred. I would enjoy meeting Mr. and Mrs. Rochester."

Eugene unfolded his tall frame from the grass and approached them. He glanced at Mama, then at Laurel. She glimpsed a hint of hesitance in his eyes, but then he drew a deep breath and faced Alfred.

"Let her have dinner with the Rochesters. We" — he gestured to their siblings — "had the pleasure of evenings out, and some of us accepted such invitations when we were younger than Laurel is now."

Laurel gazed at Eugene in amazement. Where had he found the courage to contradict Alfred? She returned her attention to her oldest brother, whose face had gone blotchy. Eugene would certainly pay for his stance when Alfred had him alone, and she would make up for it by giving Eugene the most heartfelt thank-you she could express.

"If Mama doesn't object, then I won't stand in the way." Alfred stomped back to his wife and sat nearly as abruptly as Russell had seated his errant sons.

Eugene winked at her — winked! — and

rejoined Ethel and his children.

Mama turned to Langdon and smiled. "Yes, Mr. Rochester, you and your driver may call for Laurel this Saturday evening. Do you need our address?"

"I will have Laurel write it for me when I return her to the Silk Room." He tugged his gold watch from the little pocket in his vest and frowned at it. "Which I had better do quickly. She's quite tardy. Good day, everyone." He guided Laurel forward, his strides long.

She scurried alongside him, hindered by her full skirts. She hoped she wouldn't catch the toe of her shoe in her hem and trip herself. They crossed the bridge with her at a near jog, and when they reached the opposite side, Laurel tugged at his sleeve. "Please slow down. I don't care to take a tumble."

He looked at her as if surprised to find her still clinging to his arm. "I hurried you because I wanted a short word with you away from your family's listening ears before you returned to work."

Puzzled by his serous expression, she tipped her head. "What is it?"

"I'm curious what Willie Sharp meant when he thanked you for your help getting his photograph taken at the Liberty Bell."

She quickly explained her morning exchange with Officer Sharp and then shrugged. "I thought it the kind thing to do."

His frown remained intact. "Kind, yes, but have you considered you could be giving him the wrong impression? You really need to exercise caution when it comes to making arrangements with strange men."

His concern was so misplaced she couldn't hold back a soft laugh. "Why, Officer Sharp isn't a strange man. I've come to know him very well over the past week."

"Oh?" With one short word, he conveyed much disapproval.

Eager to return to his good graces, she nodded. "He spends every day in the Silk Room, standing guard in case someone attempts to make mischief."

"To my knowledge, no other buildings on the grounds are given their own guard. Not even the Negro Building. If mischief were to occur, that would be the most likely place."

She wanted to question his reasoning, but she shouldn't spend any more time away from the Silk Room. She also needed to change the subject. She'd inadvertently divulged more than she should have. She pulled on his arm, drawing him toward the

Women's Building. "Come inside and let me write my address for you. Then I must return to the loom."

He remained rooted in place for several seconds, staring at her with his forehead creased. Finally he jerked into motion. "Very well. Let's go." He escorted her to the building using a more sedate pace, slowed by others meandering on the walkway. They climbed the steps side by side, and he pressed his hand over her fingers. "Miss Millard, we will speak again about Sharp. You're keeping company with me. I don't share. Not my toys when I was a child, and not my sweetheart now."

Her heart lurched. He'd stated his intentions toward her. Aloud! This educated, handsome, wealthy man wanted her — Laurel Adelaide Millard — to be his sweetheart. She nodded, one slow bob of her head, while gazing with wonder into his ocean-blue eyes. When would her heart begin to sing?

He offered his charming smile and bowed over her hand. He brushed a kiss on her knuckles, straightened, and gave her a little nudge toward the door. "It's late. Go on in. I'll come by at the end of the day for your address. I trust you'll have it ready for me."

■ ■ ■ ■

Eugene opened the carriage door for Laurel, but she stopped a few feet away with her arms folded. "I want to ride on the driver's seat with you."

His rare chuckle rolled. "You look as young as Anna in that stubborn pose."

She laughed and swung her arms at her sides, swishing her skirts with every sweep. "I feel as unfettered as a six-year-old right now, and I want to ride high on that seat with the wind in my face."

He glanced skyward. "Are you sure? Clouds are gathering. We might get rained on."

Not even a hurricane could dampen her spirits today. "I don't care. Not one bit."

He chuckled again and gestured to the front of the carriage. "All right, then. Let's go."

Once on the seat and with the carriage rolling out of the fairgrounds, Laurel hugged Eugene's arm. "Thank you, dear brother, for speaking on my behalf to Alfred today. I was so grateful. And so proud! I hope he didn't treat you unkindly after Mr. Rochester and I left."

He shrugged, his expression sheepish. "He

delivered a few unpleasant words. No worse than some I've heard in the past. But I meant what I said to him. Especially if they all expect you to stay with Mama and tend to her needs, you deserve a bit of frivolity. Enjoyin' an occasional dinner with a gentleman, especially in a well-chaperoned situation such as the one Mr. Rochester presented, won't harm you."

He pressed his arm against his ribs, squeezing her fingers against his coat in the process, and smiled. "So long as you remember it's only a dinner."

Her hands began to tremble. She released his arm and linked her fingers in her lap to control the slight quiver. "What do you mean?"

His eyebrows shot up. "Laurel, you have to know what I mean. The Rochesters are one of the wealthiest families in Atlanta. It appears their son is somewhat taken with you, thus the invitation, but nothing more than a casual friendship can grow between you."

The joy that had carried her through the afternoon after Langdon declared her his sweetheart dimmed. "But why?"

Eugene pulled the reins, and the sorrel turned left. Laurel gripped the side bar on the seat and held tight until the carriage was aimed straight ahead again. They'd left the brick-paved streets for ones of hard-packed earth. The carriage bounced through ruts, creating a more jarring ride, but the wheels no longer clattered against brick, making it easier to converse.

She tapped his arm. "You didn't answer me."

His lips pressed into a grim line. "I didn't realize you needed an explanation. You're an intelligent girl. You know as well as I that the social classes don't mix." He shot a somewhat embarrassed look her way. "Mr. Salisbury provides a cottage for my family. He gives me use of his carriage when it isn't needed for his business. He treats me with kindness, asks about my children, even inquires after you and the rest of the family. But not once in the fifteen years of my employment as his driver has he invited me to dine at the table with him and his family." He shrugged. "He is wealthy, and I am not. That difference puts a separation between us."

Laurel sniffed. "But that's silly. What did we hear today at the Liberty Bell celebratory speech? Our forefathers organized a country meant to offer liberty to all because all were created in God's image. All, Eugene! God doesn't put separations between people based on how much money they have. So why should we? Do we know more than God about a man's value?"

Eugene rolled his eyes. "Of course we don't. But men don't see as God sees. We understand those who are most like us, so we socialize and form friendships with those who are most like us. Trying to mix the different social classes only leads to confusion and discontentment. Haven't we seen evidence of it when leaders try to force whites to invite blacks into their work and social circles?" He shook his head. "It can't be done. Not comfortably."

"But it can." She shifted slightly on the seat and gazed intently at her brother's profile. "The guard from the Silk Room — remember Willie Sharp? — and a black man are best friends. Officer Sharp said so, and I've witnessed the ease with which they relate to each other. So it can be done."

His forehead furrowed. "From what social class is Officer Sharp?"

She shrugged. "He was a worker at the Rochester factory before he took the position of security guard at the exposition."

"So working class."

"I suppose so."

He flicked a look at her again, but sympathy now marred his expression. "Did you hear what Mr. Rochester said about the officer at lunch? The comment about his 'upbringing'?"

Laurel cringed, just as she'd wanted to when Langdon criticized Officer Sharp. "Yes, I heard him."

"Then you've also witnessed disparity between those of different backgrounds."

She flipped her hand, dismissing his statement. "But he only said such a thing because he's jealous of Officer Sharp."

The first raindrops fell from the graying sky, large and cold. Eugene tugged on the reins, guiding the horse to the side of the street, then drawing it to a stop. He set the brake, hopped down, and trotted around the back of the carriage to Laurel's side. "Come, Laurel."

She took his hands and allowed him to assist her to the ground. He hurried her into the carriage and, to her surprise, climbed in behind her. He snapped the door closed, sat on the seat across from her, and folded his arms over his chest. In the deeply shadowed space, his expression seemed particularly forbidding.

"Now, explain yourself, young lady."

Had she not known better, she would have thought she faced Alfred instead of her beloved Eugene. But it was Eugene, and she trusted him to support her just as he had at lunchtime. "I believe Mr. Rochester is jealous, because he's expressed displeasure in the past about my casual relationship with Officer Sharp." Heat filled her face, but the gloom of the carriage's interior would hide her blush. "And today Mr. Rochester called me his sweetheart. He said he wouldn't share his sweetheart with another man. So you see, Eugene? He isn't worrying about our different social classes. He is seeing me for myself, and he likes me for who I am on the inside."

Eugene snorted. "I'm sure he's also taken with your wrapping. No man can ignore a pretty face."

She ducked her head for a moment, both pleased and embarrassed by his statement. Then she met his gaze. "I'm well aware of Mr. Rochester's wealth. He's exactly the kind of man I'd hoped would choose to court me, because he will have the financial means to support me . . . and to support Mama."

Lightning flashed, briefly illuminating the astounded expression on Eugene's face. Thunder boomed, rattling the carriage. When the echo rolled away, she reached across the short space between the seats and took his cold hands. "I promised you and the others I would care for Mama until she joined Papa in heaven. If I marry Langdon Rochester, he will take in Mama as well. So don't you see, Eugene? I can have my own family *and* honor my promise. It's the perfect solution, don't you think?"

28

Laurel

Rain pattered on the roof of the carriage. Thunder rolled in the distance. And Eugene didn't say a word. Laurel squeezed his hands. "What are you thinking?"

He barked a short laugh. "I should ask you the same thing. What do you mean by taking up courtship with a man because of his financial standing?"

Stung, she released his hands and sat back. "I'm not."

"Did you not say he was the kind of man you were seeking because he would have the means to afford to take Mama into his home?"

She slipped her fingers around a coil of hair and twisted it. "Well, yes, but —"

"Then you're using him."

She jerked her hand downward so quickly she yanked a few hairs with it. Wincing, she shook her head. "I am not!"

"It certainly sounds that way to me." He glowered at her. "What if the security guard — what was his name again?"

"Willie Sharp." She snapped the name.

"What if Willie Sharp indicated a desire to court you? Would you accept?"

The question flustered her, but she didn't know why. "I . . . I don't know."

"Based on the stipulations you stated earlier, you would refuse him because he isn't a wealthy man."

Laurel huffed. "You aren't being fair. You haven't even asked me if I like Langdon Rochester."

"All right, then. Do you like Langdon Rochester?"

"Yes! In fact, I —" She wouldn't say she loved Langdon. Not to Eugene. The first time she made the admission, it should be to Langdon himself. She folded her arms over her chest and slumped into the supple leather seat, battling the urge to cry. Had she truly thought nothing would dampen her day?

Eugene rested his elbows on his knees and hung his head. "I'm sorry, Laurel." He spoke so softly the rain nearly drowned out his voice. "I didn't intend to upset you, but I would do you a grave disservice if I didn't warn you to be careful. Marriage is not something to be entered lightly. And in these times . . ."

He kept his bowed pose but raised his head, gazing at her with sadness. "Even if you and Mr. Rochester fall deeply in love, you'll still face many challenges because of the differences in your backgrounds. His friends will disdain you. He will likely disdain yours, the way he did Willie Sharp today. People like to say that love is enough, but to be perfectly honest, sometimes it isn't. I don't want to see you hurt. Do you understand?"

She sighed and sat up, taking his hands again. "I understand that you care about me and want what's best for me. What is best is for me to have a husband and a family of my own. Yet, like you and the others, I don't want to leave Mama all alone. I want to take care of her for the remainder of her years. So it only makes sense for me to marry someone who can give me everything I want."

"And you believe Langdon Rochester is the one who can do so?"

"Yes."

He sat very still for several seconds, seeming to search her face for signs of untruthfulness. Then he sighed and straightened, slipping his hands free of hers. "All right.

You're my baby sister, but you aren't a child anymore. You should be able to make your own decisions concerning your future. But, Laurel, I beg one thing of you."

Relieved to see his ire melt away, she nodded. "Of course."

"Seek God's will."

A chill wiggled down her spine. She hugged herself.

"You told me your plan," he continued. "Remember God has a plan for you, too. Please don't run headlong into a courtship without taking time to pray and ascertain this is what God would choose for you."

A band seemed to wrap around her chest, hindering her ability to draw a breath. She hadn't prayed about a courtship with Langdon. Not specifically. But surely God's plan must be for her to marry Langdon. Why else would He have brought them together?

"Do you promise to pray, Laurel?"

A knot formed in her throat. The loose strand of hair tickled her neck, and she began twirling it around her finger without conscious thought.

"Laurel?"

She nodded, loosening the knot. "Yes. Yes, of course I'll pray."

Finally a soft smile creased his face. He glanced out the isinglass window. "It appears the rain has slowed. Let me get you home."

Langdon

Langdon snapped the slicker over his shoulders, plopped his hat on his head, and stepped from the carriage into the curtain of rain. He scowled heavenward. When would this foul downpour cease? He hop-skipped over puddles on the rock pathway leading to the unpretentious bungalow that matched the address Laurel had given him.

After three days of rain, the ground was so soaked his shoes sank with every step. Dirty water oozed up around his feet. A pair of flowering bushes stood sentry on either side of the porch stairs. Their branches drooped low, their blossoms seeming to stare at the ground. Not even the plants appreciated this onslaught of water.

He stepped up on the porch and removed his slicker. A swing hung idle at one end of the long porch, and he draped the slicker over the white painted wood and then knocked on the door. It opened promptly, making him wonder if Laurel had been watching for him. The thought brightened his spirits enough to bring a genuine smile to his face.

Instead of Laurel, her mother stood on

the other side of the doorjamb. But she smiled warmly and invited him inside.

He shook his head and gestured to his muddy shoes. "No, ma'am. I don't want to dirty your floors. I'll wait here for Miss Millard."

At that moment Laurel hurried from a back hallway and stopped beside her mother. Her cheeks bore a pink flush the same color as the dress she'd chosen to wear. "Good evening, Mr. Rochester."

He made a half bow and smiled at her as he straightened. "You look lovely, Miss Millard." She did, despite the unembellished frock. Mother would fall instantly in love with Laurel's guilelessness. He hoped his father would focus on Laurel's delicate face and ignore the obviously homemade costume. "Are you ready?"

"Yes." She kissed her mother on the cheek and said her goodbye, then retrieved a cloak — brown, the color of her hair and eyes — from a standing rack next to the door. He plucked it from her hands.

"Allow me." He draped her cloak over her shoulders, swallowing a smile when the color in her cheeks increased. He bid Mrs. Millard a good evening. She said good night and closed the door, but she remained on the other side of the lace-draped glass, observing them.

Langdon fetched his slicker and started to put it on, but then he looked at Laurel's cloak. It seemed to be woven of wool. It would absorb the rain and take hours to dry. He couldn't allow her to catch a chill. "Here." He wrapped the slicker around her and pulled up the hood to cover her hair. "Now, let's hurry, hmm? Stay close."

If her mother hadn't been present, he would catch her around the waist and propel her across the yard. The sooner he reached the carriage, the less the rain would soak him. But he could only offer his arm and hope her skirts wouldn't trip her.

He escorted her to the edge of the porch, and she came to a stop and gasped, her gaze aimed ahead. Langdon's lips twitched with the desire to grin. She'd probably never seen a carriage as grand as the one he'd brought tonight. Chariot style, crafted of highly polished cherry that glistened like a jewel, complete with a velvet-covered driver's seat, brass gas lanterns, and an attached shelf on the back for a footman to ride standing up, it was his favorite of Father's three conveyances. Mostly because it seated only two in the enclosed cab.

"It's a lovely carriage, isn't it? I chose it because the cab is attached to elliptical springs. Even if the wheels fall into a deep rut or bump over a large stone, the ride inside is as smooth as if we were drifting on Clara Meer in a rowboat."

She turned a worried look on him. "But why is that man standing out in the rain? He should at least have a slicker."

He'd instructed one of the stable workers to don the footman's jacket, breeches, and stockings kept on hand for special events. The man obediently waited beside the carriage door, hand braced on the brass latch, with rain dripping down his stoic face.

Langdon patted her gloved fingers, which curled around his forearm. "Please set your concerns aside. Andrew is accustomed to providing service no matter the circumstances. I assure you, he will not complain." Not if he wanted to keep his job.

Laurel's worried expression didn't clear, but she descended the stairs and crossed the yard with him, holding to his arm with one hand and lifting her skirts a mere inch with the other. At the carriage, she offered Andrew a small smile before entering the cab. She slid on the tufted leather seat to the far side, and Langdon climbed in behind her. He sat and released a sigh of relief to be out of the wet. He leaned forward and tapped the window at the front of the cab, and at once the driver flipped the reins. The carriage rolled forward.

Laurel pushed the slicker's hood from her head, and droplets of water spattered the side of Langdon's face. He swiped his cheek with his palm, and she cringed. "I'm sorry."

He forced a chuckle. "No harm done. It's only water. And you needn't worry about suffering another drenching when we reach my home. The driver will pull the carriage beneath the covered portico, and we'll be able to enter the house without a single raindrop reaching us."

She smiled timidly and then seemed to stare out the window at the driver for the remainder of the ride.

Langdon observed Laurel's astounded face when the carriage pulled onto the long winding drive lined with gas lamps that led to the French Renaissance Revival–style house his family called home. Apparently Father had decided to make use of every electric lamp and chandelier in the house, because light glowed behind all twenty windows, even the ones on the third floor, where the household staff resided. The light cast a soft yellow glow beneath and above the windows on the painted white stucco and brought the black shutters into prominence. When compared to the small clapboard dwelling she called home, his house must seem like a palace.

He leaned in a bit, brushing her shoulder with his upper arm, and whispered, "You'll be the most lovely thing on the Rochester estate grounds this evening."

She cast a shy smile at him and toyed with a strand of damp hair.

The carriage halted, and Andrew opened the door. Langdon stepped out, then offered his hand to Laurel. Her gaze roved in every direction as she alighted, wonder shimmering in her eyes.

Andrew darted to the side door of the house and held it open for them. As they passed through the doorway, Laurel gave the young man a smile and thanked him.

Andrew shot Langdon a wide-eyed glance and made an awkward bow. Langdon scowled at him and jabbed his thumb over his shoulder, a silent message to depart. Andrew departed.

Inside the house, Langdon placed his hat on a shelf. He removed the slicker and Laurel's cloak from her shoulders and passed both items to one of their house servants, Damaris. Then he shrugged out of his damp suit jacket and flopped it into Damaris's arms. "I need a dry coat. Select a black one from my wardrobe. My shoes are muddy, so I need a pair of boots as well. I'll be in the front parlor."

"Yes, suh."

He kicked off his shoes and left them on a mat beside the door. "Tell Odie I need these shoes cleaned by Monday morning."

"Yes, suh, Mistuh Langdon." The girl scurried off, the ties of her apron fluttering behind her.

He turned to Laurel and found her staring after Damaris. He touched her back, and she jumped. He held his hand to the hallway. "Shall we go to the parlor? I'm sure Mother and Father are there waiting for us."

"Of course." But she didn't shift her gaze from the opening of the staircase where Damaris had disappeared.

He chuckled. "Damaris is very responsible. She'll see to my needs."

Laurel looked up at him, puzzlement pinching her features. "I don't question that. She seemed very capable. But . . ."

Ah, that sweet face of hers turned upward was tempting. He shoved his hands into his trouser pockets to prevent drawing her near and tasting her lips. "But what, Miss Millard? What's troubling you?"

She gazed intently into his eyes for several seconds, unblinking. Then she sighed. "You were rather harsh with her, don't you think?

381

And with the — what did you call him? — the footman, too."

"How was I harsh?"

"You didn't ask if she would fetch you a fresh coat and shoes. You . . . commanded. And you didn't thank her or the footman for their service."

He might regret it later, but he couldn't resist blasting a short laugh. "Let me ascertain I understand. You found my treatment harsh because I gave explicit directions and then neglected to express appreciation to those who performed a service for which they are being paid?"

Laurel's cheeks flooded with color, but she lifted her pert little chin. "Yes."

He chuckled, shaking his head. "My dear Miss Millard, you are quite" — he shouldn't call her ignorant, although the description fit — "unfamiliar with the appropriate means of dealing with servants. It's kind of you to be concerned, but I can assure you, neither Damaris nor Andrew is the least bit offended. One must speak directly to them. It's all their simple minds understand."

She still appeared uncertain. Langdon stifled a sigh. He grazed her cheek with his knuckles, giving her one of his low-lidded smiles. "Please believe me, dear Miss Millard. They accept their positions of servitude, they appreciate the wage they receive, and they willingly perform the duties necessary to earn the wage." He took hold of her shoulders and gently turned her in the direction of the parlor. "Now, my parents are probably wondering what we're doing here in the back hall. So let's go join them, hmm?"

The pocket doors had been pushed into their casings. Father turned his head at their approach from the hallway, set aside his book, and rose when they entered the guest parlor. Mother remained in her wingback chair near the fireplace. Langdon guided Laurel across the plush carpet to Father. In his peripheral vision, he witnessed Mother giving Laurel a slow head-to-toes examination.

"Father, may I introduce Miss Laurel Millard. Miss Millard, this is my father, Harrison Rochester."

Laurel dipped a pretty curtsy. "It's very nice to meet you, sir."

"And you as well, Miss Millard." He held his hand to Mother. "Miss Millard, my wife, Marinda."

Laurel made a second curtsy. "Hello, Mrs. Rochester. Thank you for inviting me to your home." Her brown-eyed gaze flitted from the high recessed ceiling to the velvet draperies to the marble fireplace to the grand piano standing proud and silent in the corner and finally back to Mother. "It's very beautiful." Wonderment filled her tone and expression.

Mother swished her hand in a humble gesture. "It's a mere replica of a grand estate Harrison and I visited when we spent a spring in Paris before Langdon was born. We so enjoyed our time there that we named our son in honor of Langdon Estate." She gave the room a quick perusal and then pinned a warm smile on Laurel. "Thank you for your kind words."

"You're welcome."

Mother clicked her tongue on her teeth and frowned at Langdon. "My, so disheveled. Why are you in your stocking feet, and where is your coat?"

Langdon leaned down and placed a kiss on his mother's cheek. "It's still raining and I got wet. Damaris is bringing me fresh items."

"Well, I hope she hurries. You can't enter the dining room like that."

Father gestured to the settee. "Please sit down, Miss Millard."

"Thank you, sir." Laurel whisked an uncertain look in Langdon's direction, but she sat on the edge of the settee where

Father had indicated. Langdon sat next to her and stretched his arm across the arched back.

Father settled into his chair and linked his hands on his stomach. "So tell me, Miss Millard, what does your father do?"

Langdon cleared his throat. "Miss Millard's father is deceased. But he was a salesman for a pharmaceutical company, isn't that right, Miss Millard?"

She folded her hands in her lap. "Yes. He died in a stagecoach accident when I was very young, so I don't remember him, but I have my mother and several older brothers and sisters. I'm very fortunate."

Langdon glanced at Mother. A sympathetic pout pursed her lips. A good sign. "Mother, Miss Millard is a very talented weaver. She and her mother make fabric and rugs on a loom in their home, and Miss Millard is using her skill to weave fabric from silk at the exposition. It's a fascinating process. You should visit the Silk Room. There are many displays in the Women's Building that you might find of interest."

"Perhaps I will."

Damaris stepped into the wide doorway holding a pair of Langdon's boots in one hand and a suit jacket by its hanger in the other. "E'scuse me, but I got Mistuh Langdon's things for him."

Langdon rose and crossed the floor. He took the items and examined them. He would have preferred his jacket with the silk lapels, but this one would do. "Where is my damp jacket?"

"I hung it ovuh the dressin' chair in yo' room, Mistuh Langdon. I go move it if you want."

"No, that's fine." He dropped the boots beside the door and slipped his arms into the jacket.

"Is they anythin' else?"

"No." Laurel was watching him, her lower lip caught between her teeth. He added for her benefit, "Thank you, Damaris."

The girl's eyes widened, and she bobbed a curtsy. "You welcome, suh." Then she leaned sideways a bit and peeked at Mother. "Cook say dinner's ready when you wanna eat."

"Very well. Tell her fifteen minutes."

"Yes'm." Damaris darted off.

Mother rose and held her hand to Laurel. "Come along, dear. I'll give you a quick tour of the main floor while Langdon puts on his shoes." She guided Laurel to the hallway, sending a half-chastising, half-amused smirk over her shoulder as she passed him. "Langdon informs us you have a fondness for books. I believe you'll find the library of particular interest."

29

Willie

First thing Monday morning, Mr. Felton called the guards' names one by one and slapped a brown pay envelope into their waiting hands.

Willie accepted his with a thank-you and stepped out of the way for Turner, who nearly knocked other fellows over in his rush. The man waved the pay packet over his head and bellowed, "Woo-hoo!" His voice echoed off the concrete walls, and the others laughed.

Ted Dunning smacked Turner on the back. "You got big plans for your pay, Simon?"

"I sure do." Turner plopped onto the bench in front of the cubbies and stuck both feet in the air. "Got my grandpa's boots when he passed, an' I been wearin' 'em for the past ten years. I'm gonna buy me some new ones. The right-and-left kind with soles meant to fit a fellow's feet."

Briggs pointed at Turner's soles and burst out laughing. "Lookit those things! Haven't seen a pair like that since I was no taller'n a picket fence. I plumb forgot they used to make 'em all the same an' a man hadda shape 'em to his right or left foot by wearin' 'em."

Turner dropped his worn heels to the floor and shifted his toes back and forth. "Gotta say, though, for bein' put together so long ago, they've held out better'n some you can buy in the store. Still in all, won't sadden me much to give 'em a toss." He grinned and waggled his eyebrows. "Been lookin' in the Montgomery Ward catalog an' picked out a pair of fine-lookin' boots. They're called a river driving boot. Dunno what that means, but it sounds pretty fancy to me. A whole four dollars an' two bits to buy 'em, but" — he waved the packet again — "I can afford it."

The others laughed and nudged each other, proclaiming what they planned to buy with the extra money in their packets. Willie had plans for his, too, but he kept them to himself.

Mr. Felton held up his hands. "All right, all right, enough horsin' around. Put your envelopes in your cubbies an' head out.

Earn that pay."

Still chuckling and whacking each other on the shoulders, the men jammed their envelopes under their clothes in their cubbies and filed out. Willie started to put his envelope in his cubby, but he remembered he owed Miss Millard ten cents. There wasn't time to dig through his envelope in search of a dime now, but if he kept the envelope with him, he could do it during his break. He opened one button, slid the packet inside his shirt, then buttoned up again.

Mr. Felton watched him. "You plannin' to carry that with you all day?"

Willie nodded.

The man whistled through his teeth. "Well, you watch yourself. After that break-in at the Women's Buildin', I've decided anything could happen. So be extra cautious. Carryin' a wad o' money is an open invitation for somebody to try an' take it from you."

Willie swallowed a grin. The man looked so serious. But who would even know he had a wad of money under his shirt? "I'll be cautious, sir. Thanks for the warnin'."

He climbed the narrow concrete stairs leading to the outside entrance and stepped from the building into full sunshine. He squinted as he strode across the square, but he wouldn't begrudge the sun shining down. The clouds had finally run out of wet yesterday afternoon, and now the sun had some work to do drying everything out.

Would folks mostly stay home since the ground was all muddy and the air made a person feel like he was fighting through a wet wool blanket? The rainy days had sure stretched long with so few visitors to the grounds. He couldn't help worrying that if folks didn't come, the organizers might decide to shut things down early. That'd mean no extra pay.

He patted the thick envelope resting against his rib cage. It'd feel good to repay Preacher Hines for the money collected by the church for Pa's care. He'd sort through the envelope tonight and make his pay stacks for rent, food, and coal oil, like he always did. Only this time it'd be different because there'd be a fourth stack — for Pa.

Thank You, God, for this job. Thank You, God, that Pa's gettin' better. He'd prayed that thank-you prayer about Pa at least ten times since his visit to the hospital yesterday afternoon. Seemed like Pa's right hand was getting better every day, and he had more sounds now, too. Pa'd greeted him with his name — *Wiii-eee* — when he came through the door, and it'd brought tears to his eyes. Brought 'em again now, thinking about it.

He stopped and cleared his eyes with the heels of his hands. It wouldn't do for the ladies in the Silk Room to see him all teary eyed. He sniffed hard, swiped his palms down his pant legs, and set off again. The patter of footsteps came from behind him, and Mr. Felton's warning rang in his mind. He whirled around, prepared to defend himself against an assault, but it was only Miss Millard, swinging her lunch pail in one hand and holding her skirts above her toes with the other. Her feet were moving fast, though, almost running.

The sight tickled him. She was generally so ladylike. But here she came, as reckless as a schoolkid let out for recess. He grinned when she came to a halt next to him. Little dots of perspiration decorated her forehead, and her cheeks glowed bright red. He chuckled. "Did you run the whole way from the Administration Buildin'?"

She nodded, her breath coming in puffs. "I don't want to arrive late to the Silk Room. Especially not on payday. But Eugene was late coming to get me. He said the muddy roads slowed the carriage."

He scratched his temple. "Doesn't your driver live right close by on your grounds?"

She gawked at him, open mouthed, for a few seconds, and then she laughed. "I don't have grounds. And Eugene isn't my driver. He's my brother."

Now Willie gawked. "Your brother? But . . . I thought . . ." He shook his head hard enough to rattle his brain. "Ain't you rich?"

Her laughter spilled again, so merry he couldn't take offense. "Mama would say we are rich in love and blessings, but no, we're not rich in money." She crinkled her nose. "You really thought I was rich?"

He shrugged, embarrassed. "The carriage, the way you talk . . ."

"The carriage belongs to my brother's employer, Mr. Salisbury, who kindly shares it with our family. As for my speech, Mama and I read together every day." She touched his sleeve. "I'm sorry if I misled you. It wasn't intentional."

He stared at her slender hand resting on his jacket sleeve. He swallowed. "No, no, you didn't do anything wrong. I got confused, that's all." He lowered his arm, and her hand slipped away. He gestured to the clock on the Chimes Tower. "An' all that runnin' put you in good stead. The clock won't chime eight for another three minutes."

"Whew!" She patted her forehead and grinned at him. "Then I'll walk the rest of the way."

Funny how it made his chest go light, walking with Miss Millard. He had to shorten up his stride some to match hers, and even that gave him pleasure. Knowing she wasn't rich seemed to crumble a barricade between them, and he gave the admiration he'd felt from the first time he'd seen her in the bank hallway the freedom to come out of hiding.

They reached the Women's Building at the same time as Miss Hill and Miss Collinwood. The other girls swooped in on either side of Miss Millard like vultures on a dead possum, bumping him out of the way. The three moved up the steps side by side, and he trailed them.

Miss Hill curled her arm around Miss Millard's waist. "Was his house beautiful?"

Miss Collinwood leaned close. "What did you eat for supper, somethin' exotic like duck à l'orange or steak tartare?"

Miss Millard giggled.

Willie darted around the girls and opened the door for them. They entered the building without so much as a glance at him. All the way to the Silk Room, they peppered Miss Millard with questions about her visit to the Rochester estate. He followed, listening close so he'd hear Miss Millard's answers. If she ever answered. So far all she'd done was giggle.

Miss Warner stood up from her desk and frowned when they burst through the Silk Room door and put their lunch pails behind the counter. "Gracious, girls, you're as noisy as a pack of baying hounds."

Miss Hill hunched her shoulders. "But, Miss Warner, me an' Berta haven't ever visited a fancy estate. An' Laurel isn't telling us anything. Don't you think she ought to, seein' as how she told us she'd be goin' to the Rochester estate with Langdon Rochester?"

Miss Warner sat on the edge of her desk and folded her arms. "A lady does not divulge the details of her courtship."

Willie blinked twice. Courtship? Was Miss Millard in a courtship with Mr. Rochester's son? A rock seemed to fall on his stomach.

Miss Collinwood huffed. "Laurel's hardly a *lady*. She's still a girl, like us. An' bein' asked to dinner one time doesn't mean she's bein' courted."

Miss Millard hung her head and pressed her lips into a thin line.

"If one of us got invited to the Rochester estate, we'd sure tell her all about it."

Miss Hill bumped Miss Millard with her elbow. "Please, Laurel? You don't have to tell us if he kissed you —"

Miss Millard's face turned bright red.

"— but at least tell us about the house an' what you ate an' . . . an' everything else."

Miss Millard lifted her head and peeked at Miss Warner. She didn't say anything, but her expression asked permission.

Miss Warner sighed. "It's your decision, Laurel, if you care to tell about the evening or keep the details to yourself."

Miss Millard twirled a strand of her hair, her brown eyes shifting back and forth from Miss Collinwood to Miss Hill. Finally she threw her arms wide. "All right. I'll tell you about the carriage that came for me, the house, and what we ate for dinner, but . . ." Her forehead pinched into a frown.

Miss Hill stamped her foot. "But what?"

To Willie's surprise, Miss Millard turned to him. "Officer Sharp, would you please join our conversation? I have some questions . . . about the way the Rochesters think . . . and I'm not sure how I feel about it. I believe you'll be able to help."

Laurel

Laurel waited for Officer Sharp to decide. He stood quietly, his shoulders stiff and his hand on his stomach. She hoped she hadn't broken a rule of etiquette by inviting him to take part in what her friends would call a girls-only talk, but his lifelong friendship with Quincy Tate gave him experience neither she nor the other women possessed.

He gave a little jerk, as if someone had pricked him with a pin, and took one step toward them. "I . . . reckon I can listen. If there's somethin' I can say that'll help, I'm willin', but . . ." He chuckled and scratched his head. "I don't know much about courtship, Miss Millard."

She smiled, an attempt to put him at ease. "My questions have nothing to do with courtship and everything to do with friendship."

Relief flooded his features. "Oh. All right. I know somethin' about that."

Miss Warner sent a stern look across the girls. "The only reason we're taking the time for chitchat is because I suspect you will be unable to focus on work until you've satisfied your curiosities. But if visitors come, the conversation will immediately cease and you will assume your assigned duties."

"Yes, ma'am." Laurel spoke first, and the other two girls echoed her agreement.

Miss Warner returned to her desk chair. Felicia and Berta pulled the tufted bench closer to the desk and sat side by side, as attentive as a pair of sparrows. Officer Sharp retrieved the stool from in front of the loom for Laurel and then perched on the corner of Miss Warner's desk.

Laurel described the driver's and footman's fine suits, the carriage, and its smooth ride. She shared her amazement at her first view of the house with all its windows aglow. Berta and Felicia sat slack jawed, their eyes wide, while Laurel recounted details about the furnishings and draperies, the floor's marble tile and thick carpets, and the beautiful china dishes and shining silver cutlery she used when partaking of french onion soup, roasted beef with sautéed onions and mushrooms, and a rum torte with sugared pecans.

"But the best part" — she closed her eyes for a moment, viewing the scene in her mind's eye — "was the library. Shelves built from dark-stained walnut and reaching from the floor to the ceiling all the way around the room, even above the doors and windows. Were it not for the fireplace's monstrous mantel with carved lion heads on either side of the marble inset, not an inch of wall space would have been wasted."

She placed her hands over her heart, remembering how her pulse had pounded.

"Mrs. Rochester gave me permission to borrow any books I wanted. I wanted to borrow an entire stack, but I was polite. I only took one — *The Marble Faun,* by Nathaniel Hawthorne. Mama and I started reading it yesterday afternoon and oh" — she sighed — "it's divine."

Felicia and Berta nudged each other and giggled. Felicia said, "Trust Laurel the bookworm to be most impressed by the library. I would have fainted dead away if a carriage with a driver and footman called for me."

Berta licked her lips. "A rum torte? I've never heard of such a thing, let alone tasted one." She grinned at Laurel. "Couldn't you have sneaked some in your pocket to share with us? Or" — her blue eyes sparkled — "asked to take an entire piece? They have servants, don't they? If you had asked, the servant would've got it for you. I hear servants have to do everything they're told. You lost your chance, Laurel."

Felicia covered her mouth and giggled. "But if Langdon Rochester does decide to court Laurel and she decides to marry him, she'll have other chances to order servants about. Maybe then she'll invite us to dinner and we'll be able to ask to take home a piece of rum torte." She and Berta laughed together, as if sharing the best joke in the world.

Laurel couldn't laugh, though. Langdon had claimed that the servants were grateful for their jobs. But she hadn't seen gratitude as much as resignation on the faces of the black men who'd brought the carriage or the black women who had served their meal. Even the youngest of the servants she'd met, Damaris, appeared perpetually nervous, old already when she couldn't have been any older than Laurel's oldest niece, Millie, who'd turned fourteen last summer.

She couldn't set aside Langdon's reaction when she questioned his lack of courtesy toward Andrew and Damaris. His attitude troubled her. He claimed he and his parents were churchgoers, but somehow he hadn't learned the biblical admonition from the sixth chapter of Luke, "As ye would that men should do to you, do ye also to them likewise." Langdon certainly wouldn't appreciate being ordered about without a please or thank-you.

Laurel turned her attention on Officer Sharp, whose gaze had never wavered from her face the entire time she spoke. How intently he'd listened. "Officer Sharp, I wondered —"

A mutter of feminine voices carried from

the reception room. Miss Warner rose abruptly. "Put things back where they belong and hasten to your posts. Visitors are in the building."

Laurel picked up the stool and scurried to the loom. Regret weighted her. How she needed to share these unsettling feelings. If she were to marry Langdon — and oh, to bring Mama into such a fine house and have access to that marvelous room full of books! — she would want to somehow make friends with the servants. Only Officer Sharp could advise her.

She perched on the stool, cranked the motion handle, and made a vow to herself. The moment all fell quiet in the building again, she would question Officer Sharp.

30

Willie

Willie stood guard at the door, wishing he could lean against the doorjamb. Two ladies who looked like they'd passed the age of seventy a few years back listened to Felicia explain the life cycle of the *Bombyx mori.* By now he could give the presentation, he'd heard it so many times. He stifled a yawn.

When would Mr. Felton decide the Silk Room didn't need a guard anymore? The break-in was two weeks past. The only visitors to the room were ladies and children, and he couldn't imagine any of them causing a ruckus. Well, except for toddlers throwing tantrums, but their mamas didn't need his help handling that. He slowly scanned the room, assuring himself all was in order, and he paused when he reached the corner with the loom. But he didn't watch the loom. He watched the weaver.

What had she wanted to ask him? No crowds had visited during the morning, but enough folks wandered through that he and Laurel didn't have a long enough quiet time for a chat. There'd barely been time to slip the dime he owed her into her hand. He'd hoped to talk to her during the lunch break, but Langdon Rochester had come to the door and escorted her away. Then Rochester returned for her afternoon break. Now the day was nearly gone, and the question still rolled unanswered in the back of his mind.

The two old ladies toddled out the door, and a middle-aged one entered. Willie nodded to the newcomer and then aimed his gaze at Miss Millard again. But something else caught his eye. Where was the length of blue silk? Had it been laid out under the jars that morning? Hard as he tried, he couldn't recall.

Irked with himself for being so absent-minded, he crossed the floor to Miss Warner's desk. "Ma'am?" He kept his voice low. No sense in distracting Berta from telling their guest about the tapestries.

She glanced up. "Yes, Willie, what is it?"

He liked how she called him Willie when nobody else was listening in. He wished all the girls would call him Willie and that he could call them Felicia, Berta, and — he

403

gulped — Laurel. "I'm sorry, but I just now noticed the blue silk ain't in the case."

She didn't even look that way. "I know. I took it home over the weekend. I'd hoped to remove the bootprints our intruder left behind, but the dirt was too deeply ground into the fabric. Then this morning I neglected to bring it with me." She tapped a paper on her desk. "I've made a note to remind myself to do so tomorrow."

Willie blew out a breath of relief. "That's good. I thought maybe it'd got stolen."

"No, merely ruined for all but very rudimentary purposes. Perhaps I'll give it to Laurel and have her make more hair bows, as she did with the yellow scraps." She shook her head. "Berta was absolutely right about the prints. It appeared someone laid the cloth out on the floor and played hopscotch — hopping first one direction and then the other, but so haphazardly. Whoever did it must be very nimble to hop side to side on one foot."

Willie scratched his head. "Maybe a child did it."

Miss Warner huffed. "The size of the prints point to a grown man."

He couldn't imagine a grown man hopping on a piece of fabric. But then, he couldn't imagine anyone being mean enough to come in and bust the place up, either. Some people didn't use good sense. Sure puzzled him why the night watchmen hadn't noticed somebody lurking on the grounds that night. The fellow must be a sneaky one.

Willie shrugged. "Sure am glad nobody's bothered the place again."

"Having a posted guard has undoubtedly discouraged the perpetrator from returning." She smiled at him, her eyes warm. "Thank you for your willingness to keep watch, Willie."

"That's no trouble, ma'am." He glanced over his shoulder. The lady was at the counter now, and Miss Millard was making her presentation about threading the loom and weaving the cloth. They'd be a while. He scooted to the side of the desk and braced his palms on the solid wood. "Ma'am, there's somethin' I've been meanin' to say to you ever since the break-in."

She laid her pen on the desk and looked up at him. "Yes, what is it?"

"It's about Quincy. You know, the man who helped carry in the new case an' then asked to stay around an' help some more?"

Her eyebrows scrunched together, making two little ridges form between her eyes.

"What about him?"

"He's a good friend of mine." Or at least, he had been. Quincy still wasn't talking to Willie, but maybe saying what he should've said that night would help. "He woulda been real helpful, an' I feel bad about not tellin' you so. I sent him on 'cause you seemed a mite suspicious of him. But if he comes around again, I hope you'll —"

She stood so fast her chair slid backward and hit the wall. It thudded pretty good, and the girls and the visitor all looked at him and Miss Warner. Then they kept looking while Miss Warner gave them something to see. Her whole body shook, and her face got all splotchy. "If your so-called friend enters this room again, I shall send him out so quickly he'll feel as if a hurricane chased him."

He stared at her angry face, his heart thudding against his ribs. A hundred questions paraded through his mind, but only one word came out. "M-ma'am . . . ?"

"Would you like to know why I am *Miss* Warner? I should be Mrs. Thaddeus Petrie. I would be had it not been for the War Between the States. My fiancé, although not a slave owner himself, felt it his beholden duty to defend his neighbors' way of life. So he joined the Confederate army, and he wrote letters to me every week from the battlefields, letters filled with his dreams for our life together when he and his fellow soldiers defeated the Union and he came home. The last letter arrived December 12, 1862, a full week after he was shot by an escaped slave who took up a gun and fought on the side of the Union."

Thirty-three years had gone by, but Willie saw as much pain in her eyes as if her loved one had died yesterday. He swallowed a lump in his throat. "I'm sorry, ma'am."

" 'Sorry' doesn't bring Thaddeus back to me. 'Sorry' doesn't erase the loneliness I've endured. My life was irrevocably shattered by a dark-skinned man."

Willie said what popped into his head. "But it wasn't Quincy who shot your fiancé. So why're you mad at him?"

Her eyes snapping, she leaned toward him. "I do not need a reminder of that . . . that murderer . . . in this room. You will tell your friend to keep his distance from me."

He nodded. "Yes, ma'am."

She stood up straight and lifted her chin. Then she swept around Willie like the hurricane she'd talked about was pushing her. "I'm going home. Secure the lock at the end of the day, Officer Sharp." The lady visitor scuttled out behind Miss Warner.

Willie's ears rang. Not from Miss Warner's rant. From the dead silence that came after it. He looked across the room. The three girls stared back at him, standing as still as the statues on top of the Women's Building. Except statues didn't cry. Tears were rolling down Miss Millard's pale cheeks.

He pulled his handkerchief from his pocket and crossed to her. He held out the square of white cotton. "Here."

She blinked several times and then squinted at it.

"Don't worry. It's clean."

She sniffed. "I couldn't see well enough to know what you had." She took it and wiped her eyes, then gave him a weak, wobbly smile. "Thank you."

"You're welcome." He wished he could take care of Miss Warner's hurt so easily.

She wadded his handkerchief in her fists and turned to Berta and Felicia. "Now I understand why she smiles so infrequently. She's full of bitterness."

Miss Collinwood crossed her arms. "I would be, too, if my fiancé got killed that way. It must be awful for her to come here every day, see the black men workin' in the flower beds, hear the singin' from the Negro Buildin'."

Miss Hill clapped her hands to her round

cheeks. "Do you reckon she means to go home for good?"

Willie shook his head, but before he could answer, Miss Millard said, "Miss Warner is too conscientious to abandon her responsibility to the owners of the silkworm farm. She'll be here tomorrow. I'm sure of it."

Miss Hill sighed. "I hope you're right. She left before she gave us our pay envelopes. I was sure hopin' to get paid today, but . . ." She scuffed toward the little broom closet. "Guess I'll sweep up. Berta, pull all the shades and close the curtains. Laurel, cover the loom. When Miss Warner comes in tomorrow, we don't want her thinkin' we shirked our duties."

Willie sat in Miss Warner's desk chair and waited until the girls finished their cleanup chores. They finished a few minutes before six, but most likely nobody else'd be coming, so he walked them out. Miss Hill and Miss Collinwood left right away, but Miss Millard stayed while he used the key Mr. Felton had given him and secured the door. He dropped the key into his pocket and turned to face her.

Her eyes were still all watery. He wished he could give her a hug. Seemed like she could use one. "You gonna be all right?"

"Yes." The look on her face didn't match

the answer. She pointed to his handkerchief in her lunch pail. "I'll wash this tonight and bring it to you tomorrow."

"No hurry. I've got more at home." He risked a smile, hoping to cheer her. "My preacher's wife has been doin' up my laundry for me since Pa went to the hospital. I've got a whole stack of clean handkerchiefs in my drawer, even more'n I had before. She must've sneaked some of the preacher's in there, too."

She laughed softly. It did his heart a lot of good. "I'll bring it back tomorrow anyway." Her face clouded. "Officer Sharp, I've been meaning to ask you all day . . . how is it that you —"

"Well, well, well. What's this? A tête-à-tête?"

Willie looked past Miss Millard. Langdon Rochester stood at the other end of the short hall with his feet set wide and his arms folded over his chest.

Miss Millard darted to him. "Is it six? I didn't hear the chimes."

He glared at Willie. "Perhaps because you were too caught up in . . . whatever it was you were doing."

"Talkin'." Willie marched up close so he could look Rochester straight in the eyes. "That's all we was doin'."

Rochester squinted like a snake getting ready to strike. "That better be all you *was doin'.*"

Miss Millard laughed. A nervous laugh. "Langdon, it's all right. Officer Sharp is correct. We were only talking. And he's always a perfect gentleman. You needn't worry."

Willie wasn't sure what bothered him most — her using Rochester's first name, or her trying so hard to make peace with the man.

Rochester slipped his arm around Miss Millard's waist, but he didn't look away from Willie. "Of course I must worry about you, my dear. Someone as young and unsophisticated as yourself is easy prey for men harboring nefarious intent."

Willie didn't know what *nefarious* meant, but he knew manipulation when he saw it. Miss Millard was young. And innocent. She could get taken in awful easy. He blurted, "What's your intent with her, Rochester?"

The man bristled. His free hand formed a fist. "My intent, right now, is to walk her safely to her waiting carriage." He spoke through gritted teeth. "My intent, later, could involve someone other than Miss Millard. Someone who is dangerously teetering on the brink of expulsion from these grounds."

411

Miss Millard placed her hand on Rochester's chest. "My brother will be waiting. Let's go, please?"

Rochester gave Willie one more glower before escorting Miss Millard across the floor and out the front doors. Willie watched after them, hoping she might change her mind about going with the arrogant man, but she didn't even glance back. Which bothered him. Bothered him a lot. He came close to following them, looking out for her. But he wasn't Miss Millard's keeper. He wasn't even sure she would call him a friend. But he wished she would.

With a sigh, he left the building, dragging his heels, and followed the walkway through the center of the square. To his left, steam rose from Clara Meer. Such an odd sight. Hot water from the buildings emptied into the lake. The cool evening air created the steam. It looked like a horde of spiders had spun their webs over the water. He shivered.

He opened the basement door of the Administration Room, and laughter filtered from downstairs. At least somebody was in a good mood. He clumped down the stairs and rounded the corner to the guards' changing room. Only five men were there — Dunning, Briggs, Turner, Carney, and Elkins — but they were making enough noise for a full dozen.

Willie needed a laugh. He ambled up to the circle. "What's so funny?"

Carney threw his arm across Willie's shoulders and chortled, pointing at Turner. "He — He —" His breath smelled like beer.

Willie'd rather smell Quincy's onions. He waved his hand in front of his face and stepped away from the man. "He what?" Turner, as wide eyed and innocent as Miss Millard, sat on the bench. "Why're they laughin' at you?"

Bart Elkins bent over and grabbed one of Turner's feet. He raised it in the air, nearly toppling backward. "This's how he says he's goin' home. In these!"

Only holey socks covered Turner's feet. His big toe stuck out of one hole, and he wriggled it, grinning. "Yessir, I'm done as done with my grandpappy's ol' boots. Not wearin' 'em one more hour, nuh-uh." He wobbled back and forth, grinning like he didn't have sense. Then his face twisted into a scowl. "Lemme go, wouldja, Elkins? I can't get up with you holdin' on to my foot that way."

Elkins roared and let go. Turner's foot hit the floor and he came close to following it. Fresh laughter blasted.

Willie shook his head. Grown men acting

like a bunch of little kids. "How many visits did y'all make to the brewery?"

"Aw, now, Sharp . . ." Carney grabbed him. "It's payday. A fellow's free to have a little fun on payday." He raised one eyebrow and pointed at Willie, swaying to and fro. "Wouldn't do you no harm to have a glass or two o' beer. Might jus' loosen you up some. Young feller like you always bein' so serious. Ain't natural."

Turner lurched to his feet and stumbled forward two steps. He poked Willie twice in the chest with his finger. "Carney's right. You come with us. We'll show you a good time. Better'n you c'n have with that boy you used to come with. 'Course" — he grinned, nodding — "ain't seen you with 'im in a while." He patted Willie's cheek. Hard. "Could be you already wised up, huh?"

Nothing about this was funny. Willie ducked from Carney's arm and moved out of reach of both him and Turner. "Y'all are drunk. You better go home before you get yourselves in trouble."

They all laughed and pounded each other on the back, then grabbed up their jackets and lunch pails and staggered up the stairs. The door slammed behind them. Silence fell. A silence almost as heavy as the one in

414

the Silk Room after Miss Warner left.

Willie hung his head for a moment, loneliness weighting his chest. He'd run off Miss Warner. He didn't have Quincy anymore. Miss Millard seemed all caught up with Langdon Rochester. The other guards didn't want anything to do with him. There wasn't even a cat waiting for him at home. But he should go there anyway. He changed out of his uniform and into his regular clothes. He put his pay envelope in the waistband of his britches and buttoned his shirt over it. At least he had one good thing from the day — his wages.

"Thank You, God."

Finding a reason to be thankful lifted his spirits a little bit. He turned toward the stairs and stumbled over something. He caught his balance and searched for what had tripped him. Turner's boots. He bent over and picked them up, then went to set them against the wall where nobody else would fall over them. But halfway across the floor he stopped. He flipped the boots sole side up. Hopscotch . . . or something else?

He tucked the boots under his arm and took the steps two at a time. Miss Warner needed to see this.

31

"Mam, this here, this's the one I'm wantin'."

Mam peered over Quincy's shoulder at the battered catalog laid open on the table. She puckered her lips out like she did when she was thinking. "Mmm-hmm . . ."

"Lemme read it." Quincy bent over the page. "Men's sack-style suit, black background with small blue pincheck. Do-mestic worsted goods." He scratched his ear. "What's 'worsted'?"

"Wool."

"Oh."

Mam took up the rag and went to scrubbing the table. "An' how much that one cos'?"

"Four dollars an' twenty-five cents." He flipped several pages and jammed his finger on a small drawing. "I'm wantin' this vest, too. It be eighty-five cents. You c'n get it in dark-blue cotton. That'll go real good with the suit I pick, won't it?"

"I s'pose it would look real fine."

Quincy breathed out a big sigh. One of pure contentment. Pap and the children from Bunson all the way down to Stu and Sassy was already in bed. Everything was quiet. Just him and Mam in the kitchen, lamplight low, stove still warm from cooking supper. Cozy. Made him feel all growed up.

He outlined the picture of the vest with his finger. "Be good to have new shoes, too. Black an' shiny ones. But I don't want a black suit. Not all the way black. With them blue checks an' the blue vest an' my white go-to-meetin' shirt an' maybe a gold-colored bow tie — bow ties, they only twenty cents — that suit'll look good as any the fancy men struttin' 'round the fairgrounds been wearin'."

Mam swished the rag up and down in the basin, splashing little waterdrops over the edge. "What is it you's wantin' to look good — the suit or the man wearin' it?"

"You know what I's wantin'." Quincy slapped the catalog shut and propped his chin in his hand.

"Reckon I do." Mam wrung the cloth real good, then hung it over a string tied to nails.

She carried the basin to the back door and flung the water in the yard. Humming some tune she must've made up in her head, 'cause Quincy didn't know it at all, she clanked the basin on the dry sink and came to the table. She eased down on the bench beside Quincy and slid the catalog in front of her. "Show me again."

He'd memorized the page, and he turned right to it. He pointed. "That'n."

Mam looked at it a long time. "It's a heap o' money, Quincy."

"Not as much as some. Look, this'n cost seven dollars, an' they's one over here cost twelve. So, considerin', four ain't so bad."

"Mmm-hmm."

" 'Course now, addin' in the vest an' bow tie, we's up to five dollars an' thirty cents. Still an' all, there be over forty-eight dollars left o' my pay. 'Nough for Pap to give a earnest payment to the mule seller — 'nough that maybe the seller let Pap take the mule on home right away. I'll be gettin' mo' next month an' the month after that. So when you think o' things that way, that five dollars an' some don't seem so bad." Quincy ran his hand back and forth over the page. "If Bunson end up goin' to Booker T. Washington's school like he's dreamin' o' doin', or even if he go to the one here in Atlanta — the one called Morris Brown that Bishop Gaines help start — he could take this suit an' wear it to classes. So way I reckon, that suit, it's a real good idea."

Mam put her warm hand over Quincy's on the catalog. Covered the suit. Covered near half the page. "Lemme ask you somethin', Son. You gone twenty years without havin' a suit, an' you ain't never seemed to care. Why all o' sudden you thinkin' you need to dress fancy?"

Quincy yanked his hand free. He took hold of the edge of the bench seat and squeezed. Squeezed so hard his fingers ached. "You don't know what it's like, Mam, bein' 'round all them fancy folks. Some of 'em, they look at me like I's nothin'. Some of 'em, they don't look at me at all, like I ain't even there. 'Cause to them, I just another black face."

His belly went all fiery hot. Made it hard to take a good breath. But he still had things needed saying. "Them same folks look straight at Booker T. Washington. They don't look past 'im. 'Cause he all dressin' fine an' fancy. He not just another black face in a whole crowd o' black faces. He somebody special." Quincy thumped his chest with his fist. "That's what I want,

419

Mam. I wanna be somebody special."

"An' you think changin' yo' clothes'll make you special?"

Quincy groaned and put his face in his hands. "Don't be tellin' me it won't work. 'Cause they ain't nothin' else I c'n change."

Mam grabbed his wrist and pulled his hand down. "They's a whole lotta things you c'n change got nothin' to do with suits an' bow ties. They's one big thing needs changin', an' you already know it."

Quincy pressed his palms on the table and lifted his rump from the bench. "I'm goin' to bed."

"No, you ain't." Mam clamped her hand over his shoulder and pushed. He sat down real quick. She shook her finger in his face. "You already know it, but I gon' say it anyway. Quincy Donan Tate, you gotta get a grip on yo' temper an' never let go."

The fire in his stomach climbed up until his whole head was burning. He growled, "I can't."

"You mean you won't."

A fellow shouldn't get so mad at his mam that he wanted to holler, but Quincy was close. "You think I like feelin' this way?" He clutched his gut. "Or maybe you think I got no reason to get mad at folks."

Mam snorted. " 'Course you got reasons.

420

We all got reasons. We all got choices, too."

"What choices? Is I s'posed to smile when they's rude to me? Or say, 'That's all right, suh, I don't got feelin's like you.' Maybe I oughta preten' that it don't matter if my best friend lets some white lady think I can't be trusted."

Mam shook her head real slow. Real sad. "Son, you listenin' to yo'self? Listenin' to all the ugly comin' out o' you? You's full o' pus, like a sore that can't heal 'cause the one who has it keeps a-pickin' at it."

She was right. Except it wasn't him picking at the sore. It was white folks picking, picking, picking. He angled his head and squinted at Mam. "How come *you* ain't mad? You been held down by white folk. You an' Pap both, you been slaves. I ain't no slave, but I still bein' held down by white folk who ain't gon' let me be nothin' more'n they wanna see."

"You's wrong, Quincy. You is a slave."

Quincy reared back and gaped. "Me? How's that?"

"Fetch my Bible."

He didn't move.

She snapped her fingers. "I said fetch my Bible."

Twenty years old or not, when Mam talked like that, he did as she said. If her

Bible wasn't in her hands, it was on the little table beside the settee. He picked it up careful. The leather cover had mouse chews at all the corners, and some of the pages were loose. But Mam called it the Word o' God, and every one of her children respected it or felt the sting of a switch.

He laid it on the table in front of her.

"Now sit."

Swallowing a grunt, he sat.

Real gentle, like she was putting a robin's egg back in its nest, she turned the thin pages, her lips puckering out. Seemed like she turned pages for hours, and Quincy tried not to fidget. Finally she nodded and sucked her lips back in.

"Here it be. Matthew 6:24. Now you listen close. 'No man . . . can serve two masters . . .' " Her brow was pinched up tight. She'd learned to read when Quincy learned, but it didn't come easy for her. It didn't keep her from trying, though. " '. . . for either he will hate the one, an' love the other; or else . . . he will hold . . . to the one . . . an' des— des—' "

" 'Despise,' Mam."

She glared at him. "I know." She leaned over the Bible again. " 'Despise the other. Ye cannot serve God an' mammon.' " She sat up and nodded, looking all proud.

"Mammon. That be money, but truth be tol', it's anythin' we put before God. It be a sin we hold on to 'stead o' relyin' on the Maker." She pointed at him. "Yo' temper is yo' mammon. It's the sin you won't let go."

"Mam, I —"

"Hush. You listen to me." She took hold of Quincy's chin and made him look her square in the face. Fire blazed in her eyes. "You say you ain't a slave, but you's wrong. If you's owned, you a slave. Ever'body who's born got two choices — be owned by God or be owned by sin. Me, I was a slave to a man, but now I choose to be a slave to God. 'Cause He bought me with a price — the life o' His own Son. He pay that price for you, too."

Tears made her eyes shine even brighter. A feeling like he got when he ate too many sweets attacked his middle, and he wanted to leave — leave Mam and leave the feeling — but he didn't try to pull away.

"You already know that good as me. You heard it in church, an' you heard it from me an' yo' pap. But somehow, Quincy, you ain't took hold o' God. An' you need to take hold o' God. Until you do, you gon' be owned by that temper you pull out any time somethin' don't go like you's wantin'."

She let go of his chin and cupped his

cheek with her hand. "Whatever control you, that what owns you. You got to choose, Quincy. You gon' serve God, or you gon' serve yo' mammon? Lemme tell you, no fancy suit gon' make a bit o' diff'rence, 'cause what needs fixin' is on yo' insides, not yo' out. Now you think on that."

Quincy nodded.

Mam yawned real big. "Ooo, been a long day. Gon' turn in now." She tugged his face close and kissed him noisy on the cheek. "Blow out that lamp when you done thinkin'."

"I will, Mam."

She pulled herself off the bench, groaning some. She shuffled to the door to her and Pap's room and closed herself inside.

Quincy looked at the verse in Mam's Bible. Then he looked at the suit in the catalog. Back and forth. Verse and suit, verse and suit. Took him a while, but he made his choice.

32

Willie

Willie helped Miss Warner spread the blue silk across the concrete floor in front of Mr. Felton's desk. She pointed to Turner's boots, which he'd laid off to the side. "Position them, please, the way you did in my parlor yesterday evening."

Mr. Felton's eyebrows shot high. Whatever he was thinking, he kept it to himself, but that didn't make Willie any less nervous. If he was looking at this wrong, he'd be setting up an innocent man for condemnation. The way Quincy'd been. Willie's mouth went as dry as if somebody'd stuffed it full of cotton.

His hands shook, but he stood the boots on the first two prints — the left one about a foot and a half higher and scooted over maybe six inches from the one on the right. The same way a man would take a step. Then he got out of the way and let her do the talking.

"I'd presumed, because the prints were identical, that someone had hopped across the cloth on one foot. But you can see from these boots that their matching soles fit the exact size of the stains on the silk." She walked alongside the fabric, pointing. "It appears he walked the full length of the cloth, turned around, and traveled it again in the opposite direction. Every print matches the soles of these boots, leading me to believe the same individual created all thirteen stains."

Mr. Felton pinched his chin between his thumb and fingers and stared down at the silk. With his lips downturned and his forehead scrunched, he looked good and mad. But mad at who? Turner for maybe messing up the Silk Room or Miss Warner and Willie for accusing him?

Mr. Felton crouched down and put his fingers on one of the stains. "Some local folks've been real loud about havin' the silkworm displayed here at the Cotton Exposition — say it's a slap in the face to the cotton growers. I've heard Turner talk that way, too. But I sure never thought . . ."

He stood. His knees popped the way Pa's did, and Willie got hit again with loneliness for his father. Mr. Felton put his hands on

426

his hips and glared at the cloth. "Lookin' at this makes somethin' else make more sense to me. I couldn't figure out how the night watchmen didn't see anything out o' the ordinary that night." He shifted his gaze to Willie. "But they'd met all you security guards. Did the same trainin' as you. So if they did see Turner on the grounds, they wouldn't think nothin' of it."

Willie licked his lips and took a hesitant step toward his boss. "If it does turn out that Turner's the one who tore up the Silk Room, you prob'ly won't need a guard in there anymore. Right?"

Mr. Felton aimed a scowl at Willie. "Wrong. A man who'd be low enough to make a mess like he did'll likely be one to hold a grudge. Turner's not stupid, an' he carries a heap o' anger toward any an' all who think different than him. He'll figure out who told on him, an' he'll want revenge. If I let him go, he won't be workin' durin' the day, an' that'll give 'im more time to find trouble. First place he'll look for it is in the Silk Room."

Miss Warner wrung her hands. "Do you believe he would attack either Mr. Sharp or me? Mr. Sharp is armed" — she glanced at Willie's gun, and her face went white — "but I'd rather he didn't have need to make use of his weapon."

Willie swallowed. He hoped the same thing.

"It's hard to say."

Willie didn't find his answer too comforting. By Miss Warner's frown, he figured she wasn't comforted, either.

His boss ushered both of them out of his office. "You two head on to the Silk Room. I don't want y'all in here when the others arrive. It'd be the same as hangin' a sign around your neck proclaimin', 'I accused Turner.' He ain't the only one with bad feelin's, an' I'd like to keep the whole lot of 'em from goin' after Sharp."

The door at the top of the stairs opened, and voices carried down the stairwell.

Mr. Felton grimaced. "C'mon." He hurried them to the set of steps leading to the inside of the Administration Building. He yanked the door open for them and whispered, "Go."

Miss Warner entered the stairway first, and Willie went in behind. Mr. Felton snapped the door closed after them, and full black encased them.

Fingers clutched at Willie's arm. "Willie?" Her raspy whisper was so soft he had to strain to hear. "I can't see a thing. I'm afraid to take a step."

He was, too, but they couldn't stay in there until the guards all cleared out. She needed to open up the Silk Room. They'd have to climb those stairs whether they could see them or not. He slid her hand down his arm and grabbed on to it. Then he put his other hand against the cool, rough wall. "I'll feel my way. You stay close an' step up when I do."

Shoulder brushing the wall, step by step he inched upward with Miss Warner's warm breath on the back of his neck. He knew he'd found the top when his nose bumped into a hard surface. He winced and pawed across the wood until he found the doorknob. He gave it a twist and pushed, and the door popped open. Light flooded over them, making Willie's eyes water, and both of them let out big sighs.

Miss Warner swished dust from her skirt. Willie pulled a few cobwebs from her hair. She did the same for him. Then she smiled the weakest, sorriest excuse for a smile he'd ever seen.

He gave her a smile he hoped was some brighter. "Ready to go?"

She nodded.

They didn't talk the whole way across the grounds to the Women's Building. Willie glanced over his shoulder a good dozen times, expecting to see Turner charging after him. But they made it inside safely. Miss Warner pulled a key ring from the little pouch that always dangled from her wrist and aimed one key at the lock. Then she jerked back and frowned at Willie.

"Did you not lock the door last night, as I instructed?"

Willie pushed his thoughts backward. Miss Millard had been with him, but he recalled turning the key before talking to her. "Yes, ma'am, I did."

"Well, this door isn't latched."

Chills attacked him. He put out his arm and moved in front of her. "Stay here." If the room was all tore up again, he didn't want her to see it. He eased the door open a few inches, his pulse thumping like the tom-toms in the Indian Village, and peeked inside. Nothing lying on the floor. He pushed it a little farther. None of the furniture'd been overturned. He flattened the door against the wall and stepped inside. All the curtains and tapestries still hung where they were supposed to. The room was as neat and tidy as the girls had left it last night.

Not until that moment did he realize he'd been holding his breath. The air whooshed out of him. He bent forward and put his hands on his knees, relief making his muscles weak. "It's fine. Come on in."

Miss Warner entered the room, looking all around. She put her palm on her throat and eased out a long sigh. "Thank goodness. Perhaps you didn't pull the door snugly enough into the frame and the latch simply didn't catch."

Shame hit him. He'd thought sure he'd closed that door, but he must've been distracted by Miss Millard. He wouldn't let that happen again. "I'm sure sorry, ma'am."

She patted his back. "Obviously there's no harm done, so you needn't worry. My Thaddeus used to say, 'All's well that ends well.' I suppose this is a good example of the statement." Her frame jerked, and her chin quivered. She grabbed one of Willie's hands. "I cannot tell you how wonderful it feels to say his name out loud. I've kept him hidden away in my heart, refusing to speak of him because it hurt so much to know he would never come back to me."

Willie squeezed her hand. "I am real sorry for what you lost, ma'am. An' I'm sorry I reminded you of it when I talked about Quincy."

She shook her head, holding up one palm. "No, it is I who should be sorry. I took my anger out on you and your friend, and

431

neither of you deserved it." Her lips curved up into a smile. One that even lit her hazel eyes. "I also need to thank you. Had you not spoken in defense of your friend, I wouldn't have spoken of my dear Thaddeus. A man like him, so honorable and faithful, should not be kept hidden away as if he never existed."

Her eyes got watery, and one tear found its way past her smile. "After you left yesterday evening, I took Thaddeus's tintype — the one in which he is wearing his uniform and looking so proud and handsome — from the bottom of my trunk and placed it on the mantel. I shall gaze upon his face each day and remember the love we shared."

Willie was glad he'd put a handkerchief in his pocket, because he needed it. He blew his nose and found his voice. "I'm happy for you, ma'am."

"As am I." She took a big breath and her tears dried up. She moved to her desk, talking as she went. "It's good to see that the girls carried out their responsibilities before retiring yesterday evening. They really are good girls, and I feel a bit guilty for neglecting to give them their —" She covered her mouth with her hand and stared at the desk.

Willie bolted to her, expecting to find a

dead rat or maybe a snake curled up. All he saw was the middle desk drawer slid out a few inches. Had whatever'd scared her gone to the back of the drawer? A mouse would do that. Or a scorpion.

"What's in there, ma'am? You step aside an' I'll take care of it."

She grabbed his arm. "There's nothing there. That's what is wrong. The girls' pay envelopes . . . They're missing."

Laurel

Over lunch, Laurel told Langdon about the stolen pay envelopes. He'd chosen the Hotel Aragon's restaurant on top of the Minerals and Forestry Building, and she ordered french onion soup because she'd so enjoyed it at his house, but she had a hard time eating. She couldn't even make herself appreciate the view, she felt so badly about Miss Warner's distress.

"She said she would do her utmost to replace our lost wages, even if it means taking some from her envelope each month and sharing it with us until every penny is repaid, but I don't want to take her money. It isn't her fault the envelopes were stolen."

Langdon dabbed his lips with his napkin. He flopped the linen square over his knee and dipped another spoonful of clam chowder. "Not to be unkind, but it is her fault."

Laurel's jaw dropped. "She couldn't know the envelopes weren't safe in her desk drawer."

He huffed and lowered his spoon to the table. "Laurel, while I find your spiritedness somewhat refreshing, you really must learn not to contradict me."

She tipped her head, repeating their last two comments in her memory. Hadn't he contradicted her? The rollicking polka being played by a band in the German Village just south of the restaurant vibrated the wooden building and made it hard to think clearly. "I only meant to express my opinion. I don't wish to be contradictory."

His smile returned. "Of course you don't, so you're forgiven." He patted the back of her hand and lifted his spoon again. "In answer to your question, it is her responsibility to secure the Silk Room each evening. She ignored that duty and left the room open to thieves."

"But she didn't."

He gave her a look of displeasure.

A nervous giggle built in the back of her throat. She swallowed a bit of broth to chase it down. "I meant to say, she asked Officer Sharp to lock the door. And he did. I know because I watched him do it."

Langdon's expression turned cunning. He took a spoonful, swallowed, applied his napkin, and dipped the spoon in the bowl, all without lifting his gaze from her face. "He has a key to the room?"

Had she not just said so? "Yes."

"Then he could reenter it."

Laurel slapped her spoon onto the table so hard her bowl bounced. "He wouldn't do such a thing."

"How do you know?"

Officer Sharp wouldn't steal. She knew he wouldn't, but she couldn't explain why she knew. She pressed her lips together and stared into her soup bowl.

He leaned forward and slipped his hand over hers. His thumb stroked her first knuckle back and forth. She lifted her gaze to him. His eyelids, with their thick fringe of lashes, lowered. "Dear Laurel . . . dear sweet, trusting, innocent Laurel . . . may I ask another question?"

His tender tone, the gentle caress of his thumb, and his contented-cat expression enticed her to offer a shaky nod.

"Did Officer Sharp know the envelopes were left in the drawer last night?"

Cold washed from her scalp to her toes, as if someone had dipped her upside down in an icy pond. Felicia's comment, *She left before she gave us our pay envelopes,"* whispered through her memory. Officer Sharp had surely heard her. He'd been standing less than two feet away. She jerked her hand free.

A knowing smile tipped up the corners of Langdon's lips. "So he did know."

"But that doesn't mean he took them." The band had stopped playing, and her comment blared as loudly as had the tuba's oompah-pah. Heat filled her face, awareness that she'd attracted the attention of every diner on the rooftop. Mama would be ashamed of her for shouting at a dining companion. She deserved the admonition in Langdon's stern expression.

She hung her head. "I'm sorry."

"Look at me." He cleared his throat. "Will you please look at me, Laurel?"

She met his ocean-blue eyes, which now seemed as stormy as a wind-stirred sea.

"You've been keeping company with me, have even visited my home, which I interpreted as interest in pursuing a relationship with me. Am I incorrect?"

She worked loose a strand of hair behind her ear and tangled it around her finger. "No. I . . ." Should she be so bold? "I'm interested."

"Then I find myself puzzled. I've told you

at least two times that I resent your friendship with Willie Sharp. Yet here you are, defending him." He tossed his napkin over his half-empty bowl and then stacked two silver dollars next to his water glass.

She stared at the coins. The soup was only thirty cents a bowl and the water free of charge. Yet he casually paid more than triple the amount owed.

Langdon linked his hands and rested his wrists on the edge of the table. "You really must make a decision. If you want to continue being in my company, then I expect you to honor my request and keep your distance from Sharp. But if you prefer his company over mine, despite his crass ways and limited means — I cannot fathom how he will ever be able to provide well for a family — then I shall gracefully retreat and leave you to your preference. Now . . ." He rounded the table and offered his arm. "It is nearly twelve thirty. I will escort you to the Silk Room. Come along."

She stood and slipped her fingers through the bend of his arm.

33

Langdon

Langdon escorted Laurel to the Women's Building. He'd said everything he believed needed saying before they left the restaurant. Father tended to reiterate a point until Langdon wanted to put his fingers in his ears, so he didn't speak a word the entire distance between the restaurant and her workplace. Besides, there were other ways of eliminating barriers between himself and what he wanted.

At the base of the concrete stairs, he stopped and gave her a stiff smile. "I'll leave you here. It is, after all, only a few more steps to the Silk Room, and you've made it clear there is adequate supervision inside the building."

She turned her face aside and bit the corner of her lip.

He lifted her limp hand and stopped just short of placing a kiss on its back. "Good day, Laurel." He headed in the direction of the Georgia Manufacturers Building.

"Wait."

He stopped but didn't turn around. The patter of footsteps met his ears, and then a small hand touched his arm. He looked into her repentant face. "Yes? What is it?"

"I'm very sorry we quarreled."

He feigned remorse. "As am I."

"But I wish you would understand. Officer Sharp is not in competition for my affection. He works in the Silk Room. I can't ignore him. It would be impolite."

Had he known she was such a stubborn little thing, he might have selected another girl. But the genuine penitence and the hint of desperation in her expression and tone proved too convenient to overlook. She was young and a bit hardheaded. He choked back a laugh. What was he thinking? More than a *bit*. But she could be taught to control her tongue.

He put his finger under her chin and tipped her face upward. "Miss Millard, you do what you believe is best, but I urge you to exercise caution. Do not place your faith in someone who might not be as trustworthy as you deem him to be."

"Y-yes, Langdon."

He grazed her jaw with his knuckle as he

lowered his hand. He started to slip his hand into his pocket, but then he pretended to remember something and snapped his fingers. "Ah, I'm glad you caught up to me. I meant to tell you that I won't be meeting you for breaks or lunch for the next several days."

"But why?"

Oh, how her disappointment pleased him. "Clyde Allday, one of the other gentlemen who works in the Rochester booth, is taking a week to visit his grandchildren. In Chattahoochee Hills." The improvised story flowed more easily than the truth would. "So I will be filling his responsibilities. Thus, I will see you only in passing until President's Day."

Her brown eyes widened. "But the exposition's President's Day isn't until the twenty-third. That's more than a week."

"Now, now, it isn't easy for me, either, to suffer so many days without gazing upon your sweet face. But think . . ." He caught the strand of hair falling in a little wave across her shoulder and twirled it around his finger the way she so often did when nervous or uncertain. "When we do see each other again, it will be a grand reunion. What did the poet Bayly write? 'Absence makes . . .'"

"'. . . the heart grow fonder.'"

He knew she'd be able to complete the phrase. He unwrapped the silky strand from his finger and brushed her cheek with his thumb. "I know it shall for me. Now hurry to the Silk Room. You're late." He remained in place and watched her scamper up the steps and across the porch. At the door, she sent a quick look over her shoulder. He waved and she went inside.

Langdon slid his hand into his pocket. Certainly there were times she vexed him, but it could prove enjoyable to spar with her from time to time. After a dispute came reconciliation. If given a full week to consider her foolishness, she'd certainly be ready for reconciliation. Ah, he would teach her so many pleasant means of reconciling . . .

Chuckling, he turned and took a step and nearly bumped into the black man who tended the rowboats. Langdon jerked to a stop. "Watch where you're going."

The man stopped, too. "I sorry, suh. I didn' know you was fixin' to move in front o' me."

Langdon raised his eyebrows. "Are you mocking me?"

"Not tryin' to, suh."

"And you're not trying to make amends, either." He appraised the man up and down, deliberately scornful. "Look at you, with mud on your knees and some kind of slime all over your hands. If you'd transferred any of that muck onto my clothes, you would have paid to have them cleaned. Or replaced."

"I be mo' careful from now on." His words seemed apologetic, but the sullen glimmer in his eyes stirred Langdon's ire.

Langdon leaned in close. So close he spotted his own reflection in the man's pupils. So close the odor of sweat and mildew and, of all the strange aromas, onions filled his nostrils. "See that you do." He glared into the man's dark eyes for several seconds before straightening, adjusting his lapels, and stepping around him.

Quincy
He'd meant to go to the maintenance building, wash up at the pump, and go buy himself a bowl of rice, shrimp, and stewed tomatoes at the Negro Building. How many times'd he breathed in the good smell coming from the brass kettle on the stove outside the building and swallowed the spit pooling under his tongue? He'd brung a extra nickel so he could buy lunch instead of carrying it from home, the way he'd done every day up until now. But Quincy wasn't

hungry no more. Langdon Rochester done stole the hungry right out of him. If he wasn't gonna eat, no sense in washing. He'd only get dirty again.

He hid his smeary hands in his pockets and plodded back to the lake. Why'd Rochester have to take a mind to move just when Quincy was passing by? Quincy'd been there first, but rich white men was always right in they own eyes, no matter if it was true or not. And that Rochester, he didn't never see hisself as wrong. Quincy bristled, remembering how the man had eyeballed him, all squinty, with disgust oozing outta him.

The rowboat he'd left bottom side up beside the lake still had a goodly amount of stringy green slime on it. Where'd that stuff come from, anyway? He'd scrub it off, and the very next week, it'd be there again. It sure was unsightly, so when it creeped up high enough to show, he flipped the rowboats and scrubbed 'em clean. That Rochester fellow rode the boats more'n any other one person on the whole grounds, but did he appreciate Quincy making the rowboats clean? No. All he do is fuss about getting his fancy clothes messy.

Bet Rochester woulda said "excuse me" if Quincy'd been wearing the blue-pinchecked suit instead of his ratty work clothes. He couldn't hardly wait for his suit and vest and bow tie to come from the catalog store. He'd wear it to the exposition and search out Langdon Rochester. He'd walk right across the man's path on purpose and hear his "excuse me." Then he'd go home and tell Mam, "See, what's on the outside do make things different."

Quincy smiled, thinking of it. But sitting here grinning wouldn't get the boat clean. He swished the grimy rag in the water until most of the green washed off. Then he put it to use again, rubbing so hard his arm muscles burned. Maybe he should forget about Rochester. Who cared what a high-and-mighty white man think, anyway? Mam'd scold again, probably louder this time, if she knew he'd come close to letting loose with his temper. Only thing stopped him was not wanting to be *owned* by something.

He paused and crinkled his brow. Mam'd declared she was still a slave. His stomach went trembly as he recalled how her face'd been all dreamy and somber at the same time. It sure didn't make sense to Quincy. Her and Pap, they'd been set free by the Emancipation Proclamation. That was the first thing Pap wanted to read when he

444

learned his letters and how to turn 'em into words. Pap could say whole parts of the proclamation from memory. It meant that much to know he wasn't *owned* no more by a white master.

Mam had told Quincy to think, and he'd thunk. A lot. Especially on what she said about being owned. He searched his memory and recalled her words.

"If you's owned, you a slave. Ever' body who's born got two choices — be owned by God or be owned by sin."

Seemed like there should oughta be a third choice — not be owned by nothing except hisself. That's the one he'd choose.

"Tate! You, Tate!"

He sat up straight and searched for the caller. The man who worked the leg part of the sock-shaped lake was hollering from the bridge. Quincy cupped his hands beside his mouth and bellowed, "What is it, Cass?"

"They got roasted turkey legs at the Negro Buildin' today. I's fixin' to git me one. Y' done et?"

If thinking about a roasted turkey leg didn't make him hungry, he was still powerful mad. Being mad enough to pass up a turkey leg made his mad grow stronger. "Go on. I's fine."

"All right, then. If you's sure you don't

need nothin'."

"You need to take hold o' God." Mam's voice went yammering in his head again.

Quincy gritted his teeth and told that voice inside him to hush. "I's sure."

Willie

Willie stayed behind at the end of the day and asked Mr. Felton if he had any word about who took the pay envelopes from the Silk Room. Mr. Felton said the police chief had told him not to talk about it and to let the authorities handle it. He advised Willie to do the same. The man wasn't very friendly — not like he'd been in the morning — but Willie didn't hold it against him. He'd had a rough day with discovering one of his guards likely broke into a building on the grounds he was supposed to protect and then having to deal with missing pay envelopes. Anybody would be grouchy after enduring a day like that.

He told his boss goodbye and to have a good evening. Then he climbed the stairs to the outside door. Out on the grass, he only made it two steps and something grabbed the back of his jacket and swung him around. His shoulder blades and noggin connected with the brick wall. For a few seconds black dots danced in front of his eyes. When his vision cleared, he found himself trapped by Turner and Briggs.

"Think you're real smart, don't you, boy?" Turner's hot, beer-scented breath hit Willie in the face.

Willie winced. "Not especially."

The man jabbed Willie hard on the shoulder. "Don't sass me."

Briggs caught Willie's jacket lapel and shook him. "You told Felton that my buddy Simon here tore up the Silk Room." He let go, shoving Willie against the wall again.

Willie couldn't deny it without lying, and he wouldn't lie. But coming out and confessing would be like throwing kerosene on a fire. Pa always told him the way to avoid a fight was to be calm and polite. A person couldn't stay mad at somebody who was calm and polite. The advice'd always worked before, so he'd use it again.

He shifted his jacket back into place. "Time to go home, fellows. Would you move out o' my way, please?"

" 'Would you move out o' my way, please?' " Turner made his voice high and squeaky. He jabbed Willie again, harder this time. "Not 'til I get my satisfaction."

Willie glanced at the basement door. When would Mr. Felton come up? Or did he use the other staircase, the one that opened inside the building? Willie sure hoped his boss would use this one. Until then, he'd have to keep these men too busy to batter him into the ground.

"Mr. Turner, I'm sorry things turned out the way they did. I was put in charge o' the Silk Room, told to keep watch over it. I was only doin' my job. I didn't set out to cause trouble for anybody."

"Well, you caused a heap o' trouble." Briggs planted one hand against the wall beside Willie's head. "Cost Simon his job even though he ain't been found guilty of any wrongdoin' in a court. Policeman who came said it was too circum . . . circum . . ." He grunted and looked at Turner.

"Circumspecial. Think that's what he called it." Turner puffed out his chest. "Said sure my boots matched the prints, but there's lots o' other men who could have boots like those. Says they can't prove I tromped that cloth." His face contorted into an ugly glower. "But it didn't matter to Felton. He told me take my things an' git."

Willie felt bad for Turner, but he was also a little angry. Quincy had got picked up and tossed in jail for doing nothing more than being on the fairgrounds. But the police hadn't bothered to arrest Turner, even though those prints matched up perfectly to his boots. But then, Quincy'd been innocent. Maybe Turner was innocent, too.

"If you didn't tear up the Silk Room, I don't want you losin' your job for somethin' you didn't do. I'll talk to Mr. Felton, tell him to let you keep your job, if you look me in the eye an' tell me you didn't make the mess in that room."

Both men stared at Willie like he'd just spit on them. Then they broke out laughing. They guffawed and slapped their knees and whacked Willie on the shoulders, the way he'd seen the other guards do to each other when they were horsing around in fun. So busy laughing, they weren't paying him any mind. Should he take off running? Turner'd been drinking, and Briggs was at least twice Willie's age. Willie could outrun them. But he didn't want to run if they were going to tell him the truth.

They finally stopped laughing. Turner sucked in a big breath and heaved out beer-stinky air. Then he took hold of Willie's jacket and pulled him up until they were nose to nose. "If you think I'm gonna ask some snot-nosed boy who's got no respect for his elders to talk to the boss for me, you're even dumber'n I thought you were." He shoved Willie against the wall, then held him there with both palms on his chest.

The rough bricks pulled Willie's hair. The spot where his head had hit earlier throbbed. Turner was going to beat him, and Briggs'd most likely help, and there wasn't anything he could do to stop them. He closed his eyes and braced himself for the first blows.

Please, God, don't let 'em hurt me too bad. I gotta keep workin' so I can pay for Pa's hospital.

"Them who grow cotton, they're facin' real hardship."

Willie opened his eyes and looked into Turner's face.

"They need folks buyin' their crop. We don't want some out-o'-staters as far away as Iowa stealin' sales from our own."

Briggs sneered at Willie over Turner's shoulder. "The silkworm folks didn't get the hint the first time."

Gooseflesh broke out over Willie's frame.

"So they're gonna need another one. It'll be worse the second time around." Briggs nodded, real solemn, like he was making a promise. "Not just stuff busted up, but maybe people."

"But the only ones workin' that room are women." Willie couldn't believe these two would be low enough to harm women.

"Oh, you're right about that, sonny boy." Turner thumped his palms on Willie's chest.

"Be pretty sad, wouldn't it, for them pretty ladies to suffer harm? You can keep it from happenin'."

Willie's jaw dropped open. "Me? How?"

"Tell that ol' lady who's runnin' the room to pack everything up an' send it back where it came from." Turner pulled Willie away from the wall and gave him a shove.

Willie stumbled several steps and regained his balance. He stiffened, waiting for their attack. But neither of them came at him.

"What about it, Sharp?" Turner jutted his jaw and glowered. "You gonna help the folks in your own home state or not?"

Willie rubbed the back of his head. A knot was growing back there. His thinking was all muddled. He didn't want to see anybody get hurt. But if they closed up the Silk Room, Laurel would lose her job. 'Course, if she didn't have a job at the exposition, maybe it would keep her from Langdon Rochester. Would his boss's spoiled son still pursue her if she wasn't so easy to get to?

"I'm waitin' for an answer."

Willie shook his head, wishing he could think straight. "I don't think I can get Miss Warner to pack up an' leave. She's real faithful to her employers. She won't go unless they tell her to."

The two men exchanged a look that made

Willie's stomach churn. Briggs shrugged. "Then whatever happens is on your shoulders."

34

Laurel

Wednesday and Thursday, Laurel gave a start every time she heard footsteps outside the Silk Room door. Every time, she paused in weaving and peeked over her shoulder, heart fluttering with hope, a smile ready to burst across her face if the arrival was Langdon. And every time, disappointment smote her.

To her bewilderment, Officer Sharp also reacted, yet he seemed anything but hopeful. She couldn't be certain whether worry or fear made him stiffen and jerk his gaze to the door, then slump his shoulders in relief, but he was watching for someone, too. She considered asking what had him so anxious, but what if she engaged Officer Sharp in conversation and then Langdon did come to the room to fetch her? She couldn't take the chance. Not without losing Langdon for good.

So she nodded greetings to Officer Sharp, and she just listened to his conversations with Miss Warner or Berta or Felicia. Sometimes she smiled secretly at the tales he recounted about a big orange cat named Rusty. She blinked back tears when he talked about missing his pa. Such a loving son he was, so determined to do what was best for his ailing father. He inspired her to put Mama first and do what was best for her.

Images of Langdon's big house, of the wondrous library, even of the two shining silver dollars on the table at the rooftop restaurant danced in her mind and reminded her why Langdon was the perfect one for her. He had the means to support Mama in grand style, giving her better things than even Papa had provided. As hard as it was — as awkward as it seemed to never speak a word to the friendly young man who spent the day in the Silk Room — she kept her promise.

By Friday she accepted that Langdon had meant what he said and wouldn't come see her until President's Day. She focused fully on weaving, celebrating every quarter inch added to the length of purple cloth shimmering on the loom. But Officer Sharp didn't relax. His jumpiness puzzled her but also worried her. Who did he expect to come through the door?

Now and then Langdon's intimation that Officer Sharp stole the pay envelopes from Miss Warner's desk echoed in her memory. She tried to push it far into the recesses of her mind, but the man's skittishness and the realization that his father would probably be in the hospital for months niggled at her. He wanted to do everything he could to care for his father. Could that possibly include taking money? If so, he would be on edge, always wondering if someone had found him out.

She hated thinking such a thing. Officer Sharp had never been anything but kind to her and the other Silk Room workers. She wished the police officers who had come to the Silk Room and questioned Miss Warner, Officer Sharp, and her and the other girls would discover the truth so she could put the unsettling thoughts aside for good.

Saturday dawned chilly and gray. Laurel shivered as she waited on the porch for Eugene's arrival. Saturdays were generally busier than weekdays at the exposition, with parents bringing their children to see the exhibits, but the dismal weather promised a slow day. Fewer visitors meant fewer distractions, and fewer distractions meant she wouldn't be able to prevent herself from thinking about Langdon. Her chest ached. She missed him. Did he miss her?

The carriage rattled around the corner, and Laurel darted to the edge of the street to meet it. Eugene set the brake and smiled down at her. "Do you mind getting into the carriage on your own this morning? I stubbed my toe on the bed frame last night trying to keep from stepping on Little Gene, and it's very swollen and purple. Ethel thinks I've broken it. Whether I have or not, it pains me to walk, and I'd rather not hop down unless I have to."

Laurel curled her fingers over the metal rail of the driver's seat. "I could get in on my own, but I think I'd rather sit with you. May I?"

He glanced skyward. "The air is damp. You might catch a chill."

"I need some advice. From someone who has courted and understands how it's done."

His eyebrows rose. "Ah. I see." He shrugged. "Well, then, climb up."

She handed him her lunch pail, then stepped on the wheel hub and hoisted herself up. Eugene took her hand and pulled, and she pushed on the footboard, and all at once she fell headlong into the driver's box. She sat up on her knees, laughing.

He grinned. "Here, clumsy, give me your hand."

She did so, and he helped her slide onto the seat. She swiped her forehead with her hand. "Whew! That's hard work. You make it seem so easy."

"I don't have to contend with two layers of skirts and a petticoat."

"Lucky you."

He laughed, and she couldn't resist smiling. He flicked the reins, and the horse broke into a gentle clip-clop.

She slipped her shawl back into place on her shoulders and settled more comfortably on the seat. "I think from now on I'll ride in the cab. It's easier to get in and out of it."

"You still have to get down by yourself when we reach the fairgrounds. So prepare yourself now for a mighty leap."

She pretended horror, and he laughed again. Eugene had always been so quiet and serious. She liked the lighthearted brother who had emerged over the past several weeks, and she told him so.

He angled a bashful look at her. "You have yourself to thank for that."

She pointed to herself. "Me?"

"Mmm-hmm. Your courage to step out into something new inspired me. I decided if you can be brave, so can I."

Tears made his image waver. "Oh, Eugene . . ."

He chuckled. "Now, don't start the waterworks. The sky might leak. We don't need your eyes leaking, too."

Laughter chased away the tears.

Eugene bumped her lightly with his elbow. "All right, you climbed up here to talk, so what did you want to ask me? I hope it isn't too complicated. I did my courting quite a while ago, you know."

Laurel shivered. The air was even more chilly up high than it had seemed on the ground. She crisscrossed the tails of her shawl over her chest, and then she explained Langdon's need to remain in the Rochester booth and admitted how much she missed seeing him each day. "Maybe it isn't decent for me to pine for him. He hasn't made any declarations of devotion, but he did call me his sweetheart and say we were keeping company. Doesn't that suggest he's interested in courting me?"

He chewed on his mustache, his brows low. "Yes, keeping company — especially taking you to his home to meet his parents — does seem as if he's leading up to a formal courtship."

She tightened her arms against her rib cage, stifling a cry of elation. "Then do you think it would be unseemly for me to visit him on one of my breaks?"

"Do you know where to find him?" The protectiveness she'd come to expect appeared in his frown. "You shouldn't wander the grounds searching for him. Mama would consider your behavior improper."

"No need for me to wander. I haven't been inside the Georgia Manufacturers Building, but I know where it is on the grounds. Berta and I passed it when we went to the tintype gallery and retrieved the photograph she'd had made beside the Liberty Bell. The building isn't very far from where we picnicked together, remember?"

He nodded. "Yes, I do recall seeing the name on the building. It's a fair distance from the Women's Building, but it isn't out of the way." He guided the horse into their final corner. The tops of buildings, flags, and rooftop statues came into view. They would reach the fairgrounds in only a few more minutes.

Laurel caught hold of her brother's elbow and peered into his face. "Since he isn't able to come to me, should I — could I — go to him? If we are approaching a courtship, is it acceptable for me to" — she swallowed a nervous giggle — "seek him out?"

Eugene didn't answer. The horse pulled the carriage up to the Administration Building, and he called, "Whoa." The animal stopped, snorting and tapping a hoof on the pavement. He set the brake and finally turned to her. "If you are interested in a courtship with this man and there will be others nearby to oversee your interactions, then I believe it would be all right for you to let him know you miss seeing him. But" — he pointed at her, his expression firm — "you tell him in words only."

Her face heated. In the brisk breeze, her skin seemed warmer than ever. She covered her cheeks with her hands. "Of course I would only use words. I haven't — He hasn't — We —" She lowered her hands and released a little huff. "I've only let him kiss my hand."

"Good girl." Without warning, he captured her in a hug. "Love is a wondrous thing." He spoke against her hair. "Marriage is a joy in spite of the challenges. You deserve the happiness that love and marriage can bring to you. If you love Langdon Rochester and you believe he is the partner God has chosen for you, then I'm very happy for you."

He gave her a squeeze and released her. He sniffed and rubbed his nose with his finger. "You'd better go."

Her chin wobbled, making it hard to speak. "Thank you, Eugene. I love you."

He grinned, his mustache twitching. "I love you, too. Now scat."

She laughed and climbed over the edge. He handed down her lunch pail, and she waved to him as he drove away. Then she scurried through the archway and across the square. The promise of time with Langdon made her want to skip and sing. She could hardly wait to see his face when she stepped into the Georgia Manufacturers Building at noon.

Gripping her lunch pail's handle in one hand and the tails of her shawl with the other, Laurel scurried across the bridge and followed the walkway beside the foot portion of Clara Meer. The wind had picked up during the morning, and a strand of hair blew across her face. She tossed her head, dislodging the strand, never slowing her pace. Only a half-hour break for lunch. So little time to spend with Langdon. She didn't want to waste a minute of it.

She reached the sprawling orange-colored building and trotted past the first of the twin towers that stood proudly at each end. The flags at the top flapped wildly in the breeze, creating offbeat claps. A wide arched doorway beckoned and she darted inside. She paused for a moment, sighing in relief to be out of the damp wind, and peeked first left and then right. A hippopotamus-shaped piece of machinery topped by a variety of items — from what resembled a train whistle to a pair of large wheels — caught her eye.

She glanced at the sign above the lurking hunk of gray iron, and her heart tripped into a double beat. Rochester Steam-Powered Engines — Langdon's booth. Smiling so broadly her chapped lips stung, she hurried to the large square of carpet upon which the engine stood.

Three men sat on a row of stools with their backs to the door. A fourth man, with thick hair and a mustache as gray as the engine behind him, looked up from a small table and nodded. "Good day, miss. Are you exploring the exhibits today?"

"No, sir. I'm seeking —"

"Miss Millard?"

Before she could turn in response to Langdon's voice, his hand was on her arm. She lifted a smile to him, but it faltered when she met his disapproving frown.

"What are you doing here?"

She'd anticipated a warm welcome, and his ire-laden question rendered her momentarily speechless. She licked her lips, gathering her wits, and braved an honest response. "I've come to see you."

He flicked a look over his shoulder at the other three men, presumably his coworkers, then guided her off the carpet square and several yards across the tile floor. He stopped in front of a window. The clouds hid the sun, bringing in very little light through the panes of glass, but electric lamps hanging from cords above their heads illuminated his unhappy face. "I thought you understood we wouldn't see each other until President's Day."

"You said you wouldn't be able to fetch me. But you didn't say I couldn't visit you." She peeked around him at the men in the Rochester booth. "Am I disturbing you? There aren't any visitors in your booth right now, and it seems to be well manned."

He stared out the window, his jaw muscles twitching, for several seconds. Then he faced her again, and the irritation she'd glimpsed earlier was gone. She risked another smile, and he returned it with a quick upturning of his lips. "I apologize for my less-than-friendly greeting. You caught me by surprise."

She'd intended to. Perhaps it wasn't such a wise plan after all. "I hoped we might find a place to sit" — she gestured with her lunch pail to a bench pressed against the wall between windows — "and visit while I ate my lunch. Mama packed three apple-sauce cookies with my sandwich. I'm willing to share." Would the prospect of a sweet treat erase the remainder of displeasure in his expression?

"That's kind of you, but I already ate." He patted his taut belly. "Allday and I had steaks at the Piedmont Driving Club. I couldn't eat another bite."

She frowned. "Did you say Allday? I thought he was away this week, visiting his grandchildren in Chattahoochee Hills."

Langdon laughed. He hooked his thumbs in his vest pockets and rocked slightly. "Yes, he'd intended to be gone, but one of the children developed croup, and his daughter sent a telegram advising him to delay his visit."

Something didn't make sense. "Then you weren't needed here in the booth after all. Why haven't you come to see me?"

"Laurel . . ." Hearing her name uttered in his low, smooth-as-warm-honey voice spun a web of longing around her. "I'd told you

464

the days of absence would make us all the more joyful to see each other again."

They'd been apart for four days. He hadn't appeared joyful at her arrival. She toyed with a wind-tossed strand of hair. "But —"

He pressed his finger to her lips. "Shh. Let's pretend we never made the agreement to have those days apart. Return to the Silk Room. Will your family attend on President's Day?"

Laurel nodded. None of them wanted to miss the opportunity to hear President Cleveland's speech.

"Then let's meet outside the Auditorium, beside the lion sculpture to the right of the doors." The finger he'd used to shush her glided to her cheek and along her jaw. "There's something important I want to address with your mother. Will you ascertain she is available to speak to me?"

Laurel's chest went light and fluttery. "Yes, Langdon. Of course."

35

Willie

The tower chimed six. Willie's shoulders slumped with relief. Another day done. A whole four days'd gone by, and nobody'd harmed any of the ladies who worked in the Silk Room. Maybe Briggs and Turner had only been spouting threats to scare Willie. They'd seemed awful serious when they had him against the wall, but he didn't know any man — rich, poor, or otherwise — who'd molest a woman. If they hadn't done anything by now, they likely wouldn't. He could relax.

Miss Hill and Miss Collinwood scooted out right away, jabbering like a pair of magpies. Miss Warner, as always, was at her desk, scratching notes on a page with her ink pen. Every day she recorded how many visitors came to the room and if anybody said anything she thought was important enough to write down for the folks who owned the silkworm farm. Such a faithful employee. No matter what happened, she'd stay until the end of the exposition.

Miss Millard could've been gone already, but she was moving slow, putting the loom away and getting it all covered up for the night. He leaned against the wall and waited for her and Miss Warner to finish up so he could walk them out. While he waited, he watched Miss Millard out of the corners of his eyes.

She'd been pretty quiet all week. And fidgety. He figured she was worrying about the lost pay. Or maybe sorrowing because Langdon Rochester had stopped coming around. But today, even though she'd still been mostly quiet and even a little fidgety, it hadn't seemed like nervous fidgets. When she came back from her lunch break, she wore a smile, and it'd stayed on her face all afternoon.

His lips twitched, wanting to smile, too. He'd been praying extra hard for the Silk Room ladies, for them to stay safe and not to worry. Seemed like his prayers were helping. Now if his prayers for Quincy and him to be friends again would do some good, and if Pa would get all better, and if Langdon Rochester would leave Miss Millard alone, then —

Miss Warner closed her desk drawer with a snap and stood. "Laurel, are you finished? I'd like to depart."

"Yes, ma'am." Miss Millard slung her shawl around her shoulders, picked up her lunch pail, and crossed the floor to her boss. "I'm sorry if I kept you. I'm a bit . . . distracted."

Miss Warner tipped her head. "Are you still troubled about the break-in? Mr. Felton assures me the night guards are keeping close watch on the building, and of course" — she aimed a warm smile at Willie — "Officer Sharp is an excellent deterrent to mischief during the day."

The two women moved toward the door. The strand of hair that never seemed to stay in Miss Millard's bun drifted across her cheek, and she pushed it behind her ear. "Oh, I'm not at all concerned about another break-in, ma'am. I have great confidence in Officer Sharp."

Willie's pulse gave a little leap. She did?

"Something wonderful happened." She hunched her shoulders and giggled. "I believe Mr. Rochester intends to request permission to court me."

"My, my, that is exciting news."

Miss Warner and Miss Millard entered the hallway, but Willie stopped inside the room and stared at Miss Millard's back. He'd been so sure Rochester was only toying with her, entertaining himself with the pretty young woman. Willie should be happy he was wrong, because she was so happy, but his stomach ached like he'd been mule kicked.

Miss Warner turned and frowned. "Willie, do you plan to stay all night? Please come out so I may lock the door."

"Sorry." He scuttled to the other end of the short hallway. He rubbed his jaw with his knuckles. "Um, Miss Millard?"

She aimed her secretive smile at him. It did something funny to his chest. "Yes?"

He swallowed. She was a sweet girl, kind and giving. He'd seen evidence of it. And what little Willie knew of Rochester didn't seem right for her. "I just wondered . . . are you sure?"

Her fine eyebrows pinched together. "Sure about what?"

His tongue felt swollen, making it hard to talk. "About courtin' with Langdon Rochester. It" — if his face blazed any hotter, his hair might catch fire — "doesn't seem like he matches you very good."

She shook her head real slow, the same smile she'd had all afternoon still giving her the rosy-cheeked look. "Officer Sharp, you sound like Mr. Rochester when he speaks of you. Would you believe he's jealous because you and I spend so much time together?"

Willie drew back. "But we don't hardly talk." Funny how much it bothered him to admit it.

"Oh, I know, and I've told him so. There's no reason at all for him to be jealous of you, and you needn't be jea—" Her eyes widened. She looked aside, licked her lips, then met his gaze again. "You needn't be concerned. Mr. Rochester's crossness will end once I've accepted his offer of courtship."

Miss Warner put her key in her little purse and stepped close to Miss Millard. "Are you very certain of that, Laurel? If Mr. Rochester is expressing jealousy over incorrect situations now, you could very well deal with such behavior — or worse — the entirety of your relationship. Please consider whether you could accept being questioned and treated with mistrust by your husband."

Miss Millard hung her head. Regret struck Willie. They'd stomped her happiness the same way Turner had stomped the silk. He didn't want to leave mars on her heart. He touched her arm. "Miss Millard, you must know him better than me or Miss Warner do, since you've spent time with him an' his family. You're a smart girl. You'll do what's right."

She looked up, first at him and then at Miss Warner. Her brown eyes were moist. "I know he's the right one for me. He's handsome, educated, well mannered, wealthy . . ."

Misery twined through Willie's gut. He wasn't any of those things. Maybe she and Rochester were evenly matched.

"The only concern I have rests more with myself than with him." She fixed her frown on Willie. "You see, his family has several servants . . . several black servants." She cringed, lifting her shoulders in a shrug. "I've never dealt with that situation. It would seem very awkward to live in a house and not be friendly with the others residing there. But not having any experience . . ." She shrugged again. "I had hoped you might advise me on how you and Mr. Tate developed your friendship, but —"

"Sharp?"

Miss Millard and Miss Warner looked past Willie, and the uncertainty on their faces made sweat break out over Willie's frame. Had Briggs and Turner come in? He turned around so fast he got dizzy. He grabbed the wall. The two troublemakers weren't there, only Mr. Felton with two police officers.

471

Relief buckled his knees, and he eased against the sturdy wall.

Mr. Felton quirked his fingers. "You ladies go on out. This don't concern you."

Anything to do with the Silk Room concerned Miss Warner. Worry exploded through Willie. He bolted upright. "Are you comin' about my pa? Did somethin' happen to him?"

"Ladies . . ." One of the policemen stepped forward. "We gotta talk privately to Sharp. Let me escort you out."

Miss Warner and Miss Millard moved past Willie. They both looked at him as they went, and the concern in their eyes made him want to assure them. But he couldn't.

As soon as the policeman closed the door on the ladies, he clomped back to Willie and the other men. "Let's get this done."

Mr. Felton stuck out his hand. "Lemme have your keys."

Fear gnawed at Willie's gut. His hands started to shake. He pawed in his pocket, his movements clumsy. "How come?" He put the keys in his boss's hand, and one of the policemen reached out and snagged his wrist. He snapped a handcuff on him.

Willie looked from man to man, confused and more scared than when Briggs and Turner had him cornered against the brick

472

Administration Building wall. "What're you doin'? What's goin' on?"

The officer hooked Willie's other hand in a metal cuff, locking his hands behind his back. The one next to Mr. Felton said, "You're bein' arrested for stealin'."

"Stealin' what?" Willie's voice came out like a frog trying to croak. His mouth was so dry his throat hurt. "What do you think I took?"

"The pay envelopes that turned up missin' from the desk drawer last Tuesday."

Was he hearing right? He shook his head, wishing he could wake himself up from a bad dream. "I guard this room. I guard Miss Warner. Why would I steal from her? Mr. Felton, tell 'em. Tell 'em I wouldn't steal."

Mr. Felton stared at the floor.

The police officer behind Willie grabbed one of his arms. The second officer took hold of his other arm. The two of them started marching Willie to the door. Willie dug in his heels and sent a frantic glance over his shoulder. "Mr. Felton!"

His boss looked up. "I'm sorry, Sharp, but they've got sound reason to suspect you. You're the only other person with a key to the Silk Room, an' you got a reason to need money."

"But I didn't take it. You gotta believe me.

473

I didn't take it."

The policeman on his left yanked hard, forcing Willie to take a stumbling step. "That'd be easier to believe if the empty envelopes hadn't turned up in your cubby."

Briggs and Turner . . . They had to've put those envelopes in his cubby to blame him. They needed him out of the way so they could —

He wriggled. "Mr. Felton, you gotta put another guard in the Silk Room. The ladies, they need somebody lookin' out for 'em. There's folks bent on runnin' Miss Warner out o' the exposition. Will you put somebody — Dunning or Elkins — in the room?"

Mr. Felton didn't look at Willie, but he nodded.

Assured the ladies would be safe, the fight went out of him. He staggered along between the two officers, handcuffs biting his wrists, humiliation bowing him forward. What would happen to Pa now? He'd worry something awful if Willie didn't come visit tomorrow. How would Pa be able to stay at the hospital if Willie couldn't pay the bill? The only good thing he could think of was at least Miss Warner and Laurel weren't watching him be led off in shame.

Langdon

Langdon plopped his bowler on his head, angling it slightly over his left eyebrow, and set off on the long walk around Clara Meer to the Administration Building's tunnel. The citrusy aroma of oranges filled his nostrils as he passed the California State Building. He wrinkled his nose. He'd enjoyed a glass of fresh-squeezed orange juice each morning until he started smelling oranges every day. He might never drink orange juice again.

Of course, oranges smelled a little better than the burnt-oil stink emanating from the Machinery Building. Perhaps he should have chosen a different route today. The damp wind blowing south to north seemed to assault him with unpleasant aromas. He angled his head sharply to the right in hopes of diminishing the stench, and he caught sight of some unique activity. Two policemen appeared to be dragging one of the exposition's security guards through the middle of the square.

His steps slowed, but when recognition dawned, Langdon broke into a trot. He jogged past the Mexican Village and the Agricultural Building and cut behind the Auditorium. He arrived at the Administration Building at the same time as the officers. As he'd suspected, they had Willie Sharp in handcuffs.

He stepped into their path. "Excuse me, why are you arresting this man?"

The policeman on Sharp's left tried to shoulder past Langdon. "Out o' the way. This don't concern you."

Langdon stood his ground. "I'm afraid it does. He is on a brief hiatus from his usual employment at my family's factory — Rochester Steam-Powered Engines." Ah, the satisfaction of seeing the two officers come to attention. "If he's involved in criminal activities, it could affect whether or not we keep him on the payroll."

The officer on Sharp's right harrumphed. "He's accused o' stealin' three pay envelopes."

"I see." When he'd mentioned Sharp's possible involvement in the theft, he'd been merely toying with Laurel, trying to determine how far she would go to defend the young security guard. But now . . . "Have you any proof?"

"We found all three packets wadded up in the back o' his cubby right here on the fairgrounds."

Then Sharp wasn't a very intelligent thief. He waited for the young man to react to anything that was said, but Sharp slumped between the two officers with his head low. Langdon stifled a snort. "Thank you for the information, gentlemen."

He moved out of their way and watched them escort Sharp through the tunnel to a waiting police wagon. The accused thief climbed into the fully enclosed black-painted cab as meekly as a lamb going to slaughter. Langdon shook his head. What a fool.

36

Laurel

The moment Laurel arrived home Saturday evening, she darted to the kitchen. If Langdon planned to ask Mama for permission to court Laurel, Mama needed fair warning. Mama also needed to be made to understand Laurel would not abandon her and leave her without companionship.

She found her mother at the stove, stirring a pot of something rich and savory — probably chicken stew. She captured Mama's elbow. "Please set the spoon aside and sit at the table with me. I have something important to tell you."

Mama gently disengaged her arm. "May we talk over dinner? I'm ready to drop the dumplings into the broth."

Laurel sighed, but she backed away and watched Mama portion spoonfuls of dough and flip them, one by one, into the burbling pot. Then she placed the lid on the pot and turned. She frowned. "Why have you not set the table?"

Laurel steepled her hands and pressed them beneath her chin. "Mama! Who can think about such simple things as making dumplings or setting a table when one's life is about to change?"

Mama's eyebrows shot up, disappearing beneath the steam-frizzed strands of silver hair falling across her forehead. "And how, pray tell, is your life about to change?"

Laurel dashed to her. "I have a beau. And he wants to speak with you. On President's Day. At the exposition. You'll say yes, won't you?"

Mama blinked several times, her expression blank. "Yes to what?"

"To his request to court me! Mama, aren't you listening?" Laurel drew her to the table and pressed her into a chair. She paced in circles around the table. "Langdon Rochester wishes to court me. Can you imagine living in his grand house? You'll never have to stand at the stove dropping dumplings into broth ever again, because the cook will make all the meals, and servants will see to the washing and mending, and you needn't worry about selling rugs, because you won't need to purchase a single thing for yourself. Alfred and the boys can keep all their pay, so they'll benefit, too."

She stopped and beamed at her mother.

Mama pinched her chin and stared at Laurel.

Laurel waited several seconds, but Mama didn't speak. Laurel rushed to the table and sat across from her mother. "Well? Aren't you pleased?"

"I'm not altogether certain." She rose, crossed to the stove, and lifted a corner of the lid. Steam poured out. When it cleared, she peeked inside, then closed the lid. She returned to the table. "I heard everything you said, but it doesn't make a great deal of sense to me. How does Langdon Rochester wanting to court you mean I will never make dumplings again?"

Laurel laughed. Of course Mama wouldn't understand, because she hadn't been privy to the conversation with Alfred, Nell, and the others. In her excitement, Laurel had forgotten. Now, with all the plans falling into place, she could explain. "Mama, I love you very much, and so do Alfred, Nell, Eugene, Raymond, and Mayme. We all love you."

"Yes, dear, I know. I love all of you, too."

"Because we love you, we want you to be cared for. So when I marry Langdon and move into his family's estate, you will come, too."

"No, I won't." Mama stood and went to the stove. Using her apron to protect her hands, she slid the pot to the corner of the stove, away from the heat source, and removed the lid. "Please fetch the bowls and I'll dish this up."

Laurel ignored the request for bowls and crossed to her mother. "What do you mean, no, you won't? You have to. You can't stay here by yourself. You'll wither up from loneliness."

Mama laughed.

Shocked, Laurel took a step backward.

At once, the laughter stilled. Mama drew near and cupped Laurel's cheek with her warm palm. "Dear one, forgive me. I know you mean well, and I love you for worrying over me. But have you not considered that I might enjoy having a little time to myself?"

Laurel tipped her head. "What do you mean?"

Mama fetched the bowls and dished servings of stew and dumplings, talking all the while. "I married your papa when I was very young, so I moved directly from my parents' house into one with your father. Less than two years later, Alfred was born, and then Nell, Eugene, Raymond, and Mayme followed." She carried the bowls to the table and gestured for Laurel to sit. "Of course you already know that I had other babies after Mayme, but they went straight from my womb to heaven."

Tears glistened in Mama's eyes, and Laurel automatically put her hand over Mama's.

Mama smiled and blinked several times. "Then, most unexpectedly, you came along, what your papa called a sweet spring rain after a long drought. And we had a baby in the house again." She turned her hand palm up and grasped Laurel's hand. "Raising you children has brought me much joy, and I love you more than words can express, but I've had children underfoot for nearly forty years — two-thirds of my life. Do I not deserve a few years of solitude?"

Laurel gaped at her mother. "You mean you want to be left alone?"

"Oh, not completely." Mama plucked two spoons from the small crock in the center of the table and handed one to Laurel. "I love having visits from my children and grandchildren. Seeing the whole family on Sunday at church is a special blessing. But — and it has nothing to do with wanting to get away from you, Laurel — I have enjoyed these quiet days to myself when you're at the exposition and I can see to my own needs, read or stitch or weave right through lunchtime if I take a mind to."

"And it hasn't been . . . lonely?" Laurel held her breath, half-afraid of the answer.

"It's been peaceful."

Laurel's breath escaped, making the steam rising from her bowl dance into little swirls. "But Alfred and Nell and . . . and the others said I should stay with you. Should take care of you. That it was my duty."

Mama pursed her lips. "Well, I shall address that with Alfred and Nell and the others, but let me assure you, Laurel, your duty is to follow the plan God has for your life. You can't haul me around with you like an old travel trunk because your siblings say you must. You have a mind and a heart of your own. Search them. Discover your God-ordained pathway, and then follow it. That's what I want for you."

Laurel's chest ached, but she couldn't determine if it was relief, sadness, or happiness causing the reaction. "But what of you, Mama? When you enter your dotage and you need someone and none of us are here, then what?"

"There's no sense in worrying about tomorrow. If and when the day comes that I'm unable to care for myself in my own home, we will make a plan then. All right?"

Laurel twirled her hair and bit her lip. "And you'll be the one to tell Alfred and Nell?"

Mama laughed again. "Didn't I already say so? Now, let's pray so we can eat before our dumplings grow cold."

Langdon

Every evening since the first day of the exposition, Father had requested a report of the day's events. Thanks to Clyde Allday's careful records, Langdon was able to recount the number of visitors, their state of origin, and how many requested purchasing information. He gave his account for Saturday over dessert. He saved the most interesting piece of information for last.

"Oh, and at day's end, Willie Sharp was taken into custody by a pair of police officers on a charge of theft."

"He was what?" Father dropped his fork. It hit the edge of the china dish and bounced onto the floor, scattering lemon cake crumbs.

Mother gasped. "Harrison, did it chip the plate?"

The dining room servant, Martha, hurried over. She peeked over Father's shoulder. "No, ma'am, plate's jus' fine."

Father shoved the plate and its half-eaten wedge of cake aside. "Take this."

Martha scooped the fork from the floor, grabbed the plate, and disappeared behind the swinging doors leading to the butler's pantry.

The moment the family was alone, Father thumped his fist on the table. "Repeat what you said."

Langdon repeated his statement.

Father shook his head. "I can't believe it."

Langdon took another bite of the tangy cake. "But it's true. The officers said they found the stolen money packets with his other property at the exposition."

Father glared at him. "I wasn't being facetious. I genuinely mean I will not believe Willie Sharp would do such a thing."

Would everyone defend that man? Langdon clanked his fork onto his plate, earning a second gasp from his mother. "Why is it so hard to believe? He's dirt poor. His father's in the hospital for who knows how long, and he needs money to pay the bill. He had easy access to the money. It seems very obvious to me."

"It seems obvious to you because you are looking at the circumstance instead of the individual."

Langdon's stomach tightened. "What do

you mean?"

"Willie's father, Otto, was the most honest, dependable employee I ever had."

Langdon released a little huff. "That doesn't mean the son is dependable. Some sons aren't anything like their fathers."

Father grimaced. "Yes, we know."

Fury rolled through Langdon's chest. "What are you insinuating?"

"Must I say it out loud?"

Mother lifted her teacup and held it to her lips. "Please, Harrison, do not engage in an argument at the table. It gives me indigestion."

Were it not for Mother's request, Langdon would start a ruckus the likes of which would keep the household servants' tongues wagging for weeks. He'd never measure up to his father's expectations. He'd known it for years. But to have Father put a common laborer's son above his own son went beyond anything Langdon had imagined.

He leaned toward his father, blinking against an intense sting in his eyes. "How can you be so sure Willie didn't take the money? Desperation can lead someone to do things they wouldn't ordinarily do." Like marry a girl he didn't love so he could give his mother the grandchild she longed to coddle.

"That's true of most men, but Otto and Willie Sharp aren't like most men. They are both God-fearing, honest men. There has to be a mistake." Father tossed his napkin aside and rose. "Langdon, ring the bell for the driver. I'm going to the courthouse jail."

Mother sat forward. "Oh, Harrison, you can't go tonight. It's already past eight. They won't let you in at this hour."

Father sank back into the chair. "You're right. And tomorrow is Sunday. I won't be able to check on the boy until Monday at the earliest." He put his head in his hand and moaned. "It pains me to think of him locked in a jail cell, alone and despondent."

Langdon slung his arm over the back of the chair. "I'm not sure you'd be this upset if it were I stuck in a jail cell over a weekend." Bitterness colored his tone.

Father reared up and pointed at Langdon. "I would go to your defense as well because I am your father, but I will be very honest with you. I have more faith in Willie's innocence than I would in yours if you were accused of a similar offense. He has never given me a reason to question his integrity."

Heat exploded in Langdon's face. He braced both palms against his chest. "And I have?"

Father's eyes spit fire. "Must I truly

answer that? You're intelligent, Langdon. Perhaps the most intelligent person I've ever known. You were reading — reading! — before you reached your fourth birthday. You could cipher two-digit sums in your head by the age of six. So bright. So full of potential. But so lazy." He pressed the heels of his hands to his forehead, as if struck by an intense pain. "I pushed and I prodded and I did everything I could conceive to force you to utilize the brain God gave you. And how did you use it?"

He lowered his hands to the table and fixed Langdon with such an expression of betrayal Langdon had to look away. "You used it to find ways to avoid study. You used it to manipulate people into giving in to your selfishness. Did you use it for good? Did you use it to benefit anyone other than yourself? No. No."

His voice broke, and Langdon shifted against his own will and met his father's gaze. The disappointment and sorrow etched into Father's features flayed Langdon worse than lashes from a strap. He swallowed. "Father, I —"

Father stood abruptly, nearly toppling his chair. He set his chin at a hard angle. "You, Langdon, could learn a great deal from Willie Sharp about what it means to be a man." He strode out.

Mother flicked a glance at Langdon, her forehead crinkled in worry, and hurried after Father. So she'd abandoned him, too.

Langdon sat gritting his teeth, more hurt than he could ever remember being. If he was, as Father proclaimed, the most intelligent person he knew, what could Langdon learn from an ill-bred, uneducated factory worker? How could Father compare him to Willie Sharp . . . and find him lacking?

The swinging door creaked open. Martha peeked in. "You min' I come in an' clear the table, Mistuh Langdon?"

He waved his hand. "Do what you need to do." He stormed to the parlor and stood at the front window, hands deep in his pockets, scowling at the lace curtain and the dark yard beyond it. He couldn't let someone like Willie Sharp get the upper hand. If Sharp was innocent, as Father believed, he'd be out of jail and back on the pedestal Father had erected.

Envy burned in Langdon's chest. If anyone should be elevated in Father's eyes, it should be his own son. But how to place himself above the factory worker? If Sharp were proved guilty, then Father would change his mind about him. And, by default, he would view his son with greater esteem.

A plan took shape. A plan so cunning it was destined to succeed.

Langdon bolted to the back door and rang the bell to signal for the carriage. He hadn't won his father's approval with good grades, athletic prowess, or business acumen, but he had one remaining ace up his sleeve. He would play it wisely.

37

Willie

Willie paced from one side of his cell to the other. Three slow strides east, turn, three slow strides west. Back and forth. Stirring dust. There wasn't anything else to do except lie on the lumpy cot and try not to breathe in the awful smells locked in the cot, blanket, and pillow. Quincy was right. This place did stink.

If they found him guilty of taking the money from Miss Warner's desk drawer, how long would he have to stay here? Two years? Three? Willie's stomach churned. Partly from the flavorless, greasy gravy over potatoes they'd given him for breakfast. Partly from fear. He'd only been in the jail two nights and he wanted to climb the walls and howl. How would he last for years?

Angry voices exploded from the other side of the iron door at the end of the hall. Willie took a step north and peeked as best he could to the door. He strained, trying to hear what the scuffle was about, and he thought he heard somebody blast his name. Were they already talking about taking him to court? He'd like to clean up some first. The baggy striped shirt and pants they'd given him when he came in hadn't looked too clean when he got them. After two nights of sleeping in them and wearing them the day in between, they were a wrinkled mess. He didn't have a razor, so his face was all scruffy. A judge would take one look at him and find him guilty based on appearance alone.

The door clanged open and Mr. Rochester charged up the hall. "Willie? Willie, where are you?" He paused at each cell and scowled at the bars. One of the other prisoners said, "I'll be Willie if it means you'll get me out," and Mr. Rochester ordered the man to shut up.

Willie was near the end — four cells down. He stuck his hand through the bars and waved. "Over here, Mr. Rochester."

The factory owner double-stepped to Willie, his arms swinging and his mustached face set in a mask of worry. He clasped Willie's dirty hand. "Are you all right?"

Willie was as far from all right as he'd been the day Pa suffered the attack of apoplexy, but he nodded. "Mr. Rochester, I want you to know — I didn't take the money."

"I believe you."

Nothing he could've said would have pleased Willie more. "Do you reckon you can make the officers who arrested me believe it? I'd sure like to get out o' here."

Mr. Rochester grimaced. "That won't be possible until your trial. According to the district judge, you'll face him one week from today."

Willie nearly groaned. A full week more in here?

"I will hire a lawyer for you, and I'll be in court as a character witness. We'll do everything we can to prove your innocence."

Willie gulped. "Thank you, sir. I don't know how to repay you."

"You'll repay me by returning to the factory and working hard, as you've always done."

"Yes, sir."

"Now, what can I provide to make your stay here more pleasant? Soap? Shaving items?" He glanced up and down Willie's length. "Clothing?"

Willie rubbed his scratchy jaw. "I don't wanna trouble you any more'n I already have."

"Nonsense. I'll put together a box and have it sent over this afternoon."

"Well, then . . ." Maybe he shouldn't take advantage.

"What do you need, Willie?"

Willie forced the request past the knot in his throat. "I'd sure like to have a Bible in here."

His boss reached through the bars and squeezed Willie's shoulder. "Of course." He poked his thumbs into his vest pockets. "Is there anything else I can do for you?"

There was one more thing. An important thing. Willie swallowed and curled his fingers around the bars. "Sir, could you talk to my preacher? Preacher Hines at Hillcrest Chapel. Let him know where I am. 'Cause I was stuck in here, I didn't get to church yesterday, an' I didn't go see my pa. They'll both be worried somethin' awful. It's not good for Pa to get upset. Maybe Preacher Hines can find a gentle way to tell him what happened."

"I will certainly send a message to your preacher." Mr. Rochester gripped Willie's wrist. "If need be, I'll visit the convalescent hospital and speak to Otto myself. Don't worry. We'll get this situation righted. You have my word."

Laurel

Miss Warner charged into the Silk Room, her face red and her breath puffing like a raging bull. She stormed to her desk, sat, slapped a sheet of paper in front of her, and uncapped her inkpot, muttering under her breath.

Laurel exchanged worried looks with Berta and Felicia. Their supervisor had gone to the Administration Building to inquire after Willie Sharp. All of them had been surprised when he didn't come to the Silk Room that morning. Seeing Miss Warner's fury, Laurel was afraid to ask what she'd discovered.

"Miss Warner?" Berta, always the boldest of the three girls, approached the woman's desk. "Is Officer Sharp ill?"

"No." She dipped her pen and scribbled on the page with a loud and angry *scritch-scritch.*

"Oh." Berta glanced over her shoulder, shrugged, and faced their supervisor again. "Then where is he?"

"In jail."

"What!" Felicia and Laurel squeaked the word at the same time. Laurel would have been less surprised if Miss Warner had declared he'd joined the circus. Laurel left the loom, Felicia abandoned the counter, and they joined Berta in front of Miss Warner's desk. Felicia said, "But why? What did he do?"

"Absolutely nothing. I'd bet Thaddeus's tintype on it." Miss Warner kept writing, not even glancing up. "It's a dreadful mistake, and I intend to fight it all the way to the Supreme Court if necessary."

Berta gasped. "Did he murder somebody?"

Miss Warner looked up with a withering glare. "Did I not say he's done nothing for which to be arrested? But that fool Felton claims Willie stole the pay envelopes from this room."

Laurel's knees went weak. She caught the edge of the desk to keep herself upright. "How . . . how did Mr. Felton come to that conclusion?"

"I have no idea." Miss Warner took up the pen again. "But it's absolutely ludicrous. I've never met a kinder, more honest young man than Willie Sharp. Girls, return to your duties so I may concentrate. I want this letter to make an impact." She bent over the page.

Laurel, Felicia, and Berta put their arms around one another's waists and moved as a unit to the loom. Laurel sank onto the stool, but she didn't pick up the shuttle or reach for the warp beam. Her mind whirled and she couldn't recall how to operate the loom. She sat with her hands in her lap, her gaze locked on the purple cloth.

Berta glanced at Miss Warner, then leaned in. "Who do you suppose" — she whispered so softly Laurel turned her ear closer to hear — "accused Officer Sharp? I bet whoever did it is the real thief. That's how it is in a lot of the mystery serials I've read."

Felicia's green eyes grew round. "Or the accuser might want revenge on Officer Sharp for something."

A sick feeling filled Laurel's stomach. Langdon had suggested Officer Sharp had the opportunity to take the pay envelopes. He'd often indicated resentment toward the officer. But Langdon wouldn't be malicious enough to place a formal complaint without proof, would he?

She stood and took two jerky steps sideways. "I . . . I need . . ." She clutched her stomach.

Berta pointed to the door. "Go!"

Laurel scurried out. She raced down the steps, skittered around a few stragglers on the walkway, and pounded across the bridge. She didn't slow her pace until she reached the Georgia Manufacturers Building. Outside the doors she paused long enough to catch her breath and smooth a few stray wisps of hair into place. Then, trembling from head to toe, she entered the building and went directly to the Rochester booth. Two of the men she'd seen in the booth last time were there, and one was speaking with a middle-aged couple.

She approached the second man. "Excuse me."

He smiled, showing off one gold tooth. "Yes, miss, what can I do for you?"

"I'm looking for Lang — for Mr. Rochester."

"He hasn't arrived yet today. May I deliver a message for you?" He pulled a small pad of paper from the breast pocket of his jacket and reached for a pencil on the table beside him.

She considered refusing. How embarrassing to leave word with a stranger. But she needed to know if Langdon had anything to do with Officer Sharp's arrest. "Yes, please. Ask him to come see Miss Millard."

The man applied the pencil to the pad. Then he looked at her, his expression bright. " 'See Miss Millard.' Anything else?"

"No, sir. He'll know where to find me." She would even take her lunch in the Silk Room so she'd be easily found.

"Very well, miss. Good day." He slid the

pad into his pocket and joined the little group at the engine.

Laurel made the return trip to the Women's Building, walking this time instead of running. As she crossed the bridge, she couldn't help noticing the rowboats on the water. She stopped and rested her hands on the wooden rail, watching a young man apply the oars and give a smiling young lady a ride.

The urge to cry struck with force. Was it possible that the man with whom she'd taken boat rides, who'd treated her to lunches at the rooftop restaurant, and to whom she'd surrendered her heart could be cruel enough to arrange someone's arrest? If he had, she knew his reason. Jealousy. Misplaced jealousy.

If she were responsible for Officer Sharp being wrongly accused and jailed, she would never forgive herself. She moaned, "It's not what I wanted . . ."

"What's that?"

She spun around, her hand over her thumping heart. Quincy Tate, Officer Sharp's friend, stood a few feet away, a boat oar over his shoulder like a fishing pole. She released a long breath. "Y-you startled me."

He flicked a wary look left and right; then seemed to focus somewhere behind her to her left. "Didn' mean to. Heard you say somethin'. Didn' know if you was talkin' to me."

"No, I wasn't, but I'm glad to see you." She sensed his discomfort in communicating with her, so she pretended to gaze across the water. "Did you know that Officer Sharp was arrested and taken to jail?"

The young man's gaze met Laurel's and then jerked away. "No. How's come he git took in?"

"He's been accused of stealing."

Quincy snorted. "That don't sound much like Willie. He learn bettuh a long time ago, when him an' me snitched a couple o' apples from a barrel at the market. His ma catched us eatin' 'em an' made us tell 'er where we got 'em. We both got our britches smoked. Never took nothin' that ain't mine since, an' neither has Willie."

Hope fluttered in Laurel's chest. "Would you be willing to tell Will — Officer Sharp's supervisor what you told me?"

" 'Bout us gettin' our britches smoked?"

"No, about how you know Officer Sharp wouldn't steal."

The man shifted the oar to his other shoulder. "Can't do that, miss."

Laurel stomped her foot. "Why not? You're his friend. You've known him since you were children. Your word could make all the difference."

Quincy puckered his lips and angled his face away from her. "Miss, ain't no white man gon' believe anythin' I tell him. I jus' be wastin' words." He trudged off, his heels scuffing on the bridge.

Langdon

Langdon leaned back in the springed chair and propped his feet on the edge of Father's massive desk. The first thing he'd done upon arrival to Father's office overlooking the factory floor was close the shutters to block as much noise as possible. For the first time, thanks to Willie Sharp's unfortunate — or was it fortunate? — incarceration, Langdon had control of the factory for the morning. Possibly the whole day, if Father chose to spend all of Monday at the courthouse.

Acid burned in the back of his throat every time he thought about Father roaring out of his chair in defense of that common laborer. But not even Father would believe in the man's innocence once he learned about the large sum of money placed on Otto Sharp's account at the convalescent hospital. Ninety dollars. The only way Willie Sharp could produce that amount would be to take it from someone. Or several someones.

He wasn't yet sure how he would bring this information to light without incriminating himself, but if he thought about it long and hard, he'd find a way. Father had instructed him to organize a stack of invoices, but Langdon passed it off to Father's assistant. He couldn't waste precious time shuffling through papers when his plan to elevate himself above Willie Sharp in his father's eyes was only half-completed.

Locking his hands behind his neck, he bounced the chair, stared at the painted ceiling, and waited for an idea to drop into his brain.

38

Quincy

Quincy paid his dime to a herdic driver and climbed into the back. He told the driver his address, then slumped low and rubbed his forehead. A pain throbbed behind his eyes. A worry pain. 'Cause of Willie.

He didn't wanna feel sorry for his old pal. Ever since Miss Millard told him about Willie, Quincy'd been trying not to think about him. But Willie stayed right there in Quincy's mind, pesky as a gnat. Why'd it bother him so much that Willie was sitting in jail? Hadn't he decided him and Willie couldn't be friends no more? That they was too different? He should be thinking serves him right, getting to find out how Quincy felt being locked up for no good reason. But no matter how hard he tried, he just couldn't be glad about Willie.

The cab bounced and jiggled side to side, scrambling the boiled egg he'd ate for his afternoon snack. He rubbed his belly and told that egg to stay put. The sick feeling in his gut maybe wasn't all because of the egg, though.

How many days now he been nursing his mad at Willie? Near three weeks. And that mad, it was festering inside him. *"Whatever control you, that what owns you."* Mam hadn't spoke one word about him being mad since the night she told him about being a slave to God or a slave to mammon, but it didn't matter. She'd been yammering inside his head most every day since. The only way he'd get her quiet was choose. God or mammon?

The herdic driver stopped the cab in the usual spot, four blocks away from Quincy's house. The drivers, they'd take his ten cents and give 'im a ride, but they wouldn't go clear to his neighborhood. Quincy tried to dredge up some indignation, but it refused to rise. With a sigh, he climbed out of the cab and started up the dirt street.

Should he oughta tell Mam and Pap about Willie? They'd be plenty upset. They'd likely want to pray for him. Maybe try to take him some of Mam's fried chicken and biscuits. The jail food, it was pretty bad. Part of him didn't want to get Mam all upset, and part of him wanted Mam to say some prayers for Willie and carry him some chicken. He huffed, kicking the toe of his scuffed boot against the ground and sending dust flying. What was the matter with him, anyway? His insides were all in a muddle.

He still hadn't made up his mind — tell or don't tell — when he got to the grassless yard of his folks' house. He took one step from the street and Bunson come running out of the house, all a-smiling and whooping like it was Christmas morning. He run right up to Quincy and grabbed on to his arms.

Quincy tried to shake him loose. "Lemme go, boy. What'sa matter with you? You actin' like you ain't got no sense."

Bunson laughed. "You gon' be actin' that-away in a minute. Guess what Pap brung home from the post office."

Something inside Quincy's chest made a jump. "It come?"

"It come!"

Quincy danced a circle in the yard with his brother, laughing at the sky. Then he broke loose and galloped to the house. He skidded to a stop on the wood floor, and right there on the settee, all laid out like somebody'd been raptured out of it, was his suit, vest, and bow tie. He hissed through his teeth and admired it all.

The little ones gathered around him, smiling like a host of jack-o'-lanterns. Sassy aimed a pudgy finger for one of the buttons.

Quincy grabbed her wrist. "Nuh-uh. Don't touch. It ain't yours." Sassy's lower lip poked out, and Quincy used one of her little braids to tap the end of her nose. She hunched her shoulders and giggled. Quincy sighed. "My oh my, ain't it a fine-lookin' suit?"

Bunson nudged Quincy. "Try it on. See how it looks."

Quincy grimaced. "I's too dirty. Don't wanna muck it up."

"If you'd transferred any of that muck onto my clothes, you would have paid to have them cleaned."

Langdon Rochester's voice blasted through Quincy's mind, and rage-burn stirred in his chest. "See if Mam'll lemme have a bath."

Port gaped up at him, showing the big gap where his two front teeth had fallen out. "You gon' take a bath on a Monday?"

Quincy grinned. "If Mam'll fill the tub, I am."

The three littlest ones stared at each other, then darted for the kitchen at once, their bare feet pounding the floorboards, all hollering for Mam.

Bunson sighed, shaking his head. "It's fine, Quince. It's the finest suit I ever did see."

Quincy nodded.

"You gon' look like a real gentleman when you got it all on."

And just like that, an idea hit Quincy square on the head. He grinned at Bunson and nodded hard. "A gentleman. Uh-huh." He better go convince Mam to let 'im have that bath on a Monday.

Laurel

The carriage came to a stop and Laurel reached for the door. Before she caught the handle, it opened. She gave a start. Eugene was still nursing his toe and hadn't climbed down from the seat to help her in, so she hadn't expected him to assist her out. She extended her hand and received the second surprise of the morning.

"Langdon?"

He smiled his disarming smile and bowed. "At your service, my dear."

A nervous giggle built in her throat. She clenched her teeth to control it and took his hand. She stepped from the carriage, waved to Eugene, then slipped her fingers into the bend of Langdon's arm. "I wasn't sure I would see you today." She hadn't seen him yesterday. She wanted to ask if he'd received her message and chose to ignore it, but she couldn't find the courage.

He placed his gloved hand over her fingers and guided her through the tunnel. "I wasn't sure I would have time to seek you out, either. Thus my decision to meet your carriage and at least steal a few minutes of your day." He gave her one of his lazy, crooked smiles. "I hope you were pleasantly surprised."

Surprised, most definitely. She had yet to determine whether it was pleasant. "Have you heard the news that Officer Sharp was taken into custody on a charge of theft?" She observed his face for hints of guilt or satisfaction. Either reaction would tell her a great deal.

His lips tipped downward into a moue of sympathy. "I actually witnessed the officers placing him in the police wagon. Such a distressing scene." His hand pressed more firmly against hers. "I hope you believe that I didn't want my suppositions proved true. I know you're . . . fond . . . of Willie Sharp."

He sounded sincere, but something in his eyes — a tiny glimmer of smugness — un-nerved her. "All of us in the Silk Room were quite distraught. Especially Miss Warner.

She holds a great deal of affection for Willie." His gaze narrowed. Heat attacked her face. "That is, Officer Sharp."

At once his expression cleared. "Yes, well, some people are adept at hiding their true character. But eventually it will be revealed. I'm sorry you had to experience the reality of Mr. Sharp's duplicity."

Laurel shook her head, examining his face. "Oh, none of us in the Silk Room are convinced he is guilty. As a matter of fact, Miss Warner believes he's been framed by an unscrupulous individual, and she's set on proving it."

"Is that so?" He met her gaze, seemingly mildly amused rather than indignant or worried. "I hope she won't be too badly crushed when it's proven he did take the money."

Laurel's feet refused to take another step.

He stopped, too, and frowned down at her. "What is it, dear?"

Did you arrange Willie's arrest? The query hovered on her tongue. She gazed into his handsome, concerned face, while a war took place under her skin. If she asked the question and Langdon said yes, she would be devastated. Eugene had told her she was brave, but at that moment she possessed not even a smidgen of bravery.

She sighed and hung her head. "I'd better go to the Silk Room. Miss Warner is already upset about Officer Sharp. I don't want to add to her concerns by arriving late."

"That's very considerate of you. Come along." He drew her forward. At the base of the stairs, he bent over her hand and gave her his customary kiss. He straightened and smiled. "Please don't spend your day brooding over Officer Sharp's situation. My father has hired one of the best lawyers in Atlanta to represent him." A hint of disapproval sharpened his tone, although his smile remained intact. "If he is indeed innocent, it will come out at the trial."

Laurel's pulse skipped a beat. "When is the trial?"

"Next Monday morning, at eight o'clock." He squeezed her hand. "Would you like to meet for lunch by Clara Meer today? Perhaps a picnic on a rowboat?"

Longing flooded her. How enticing he was when he spoke so sweetly and held her hand so tenderly. She nodded. "Yes. If you aren't too busy."

"I'll make the time for you, my dear." He gave her a gentle nudge. "Go on in, now."

Miss Warner was at her desk, pen in hand. Laurel hurried over to her. "Next Monday morning, Officer Sharp will face the judge."

Mama would be appalled at Laurel's lack of courtesy, but there wasn't time for manners.

The woman bolted upright. "Do you know the time for his trial?"

"Eight o'clock."

Miss Warner gave a firm nod. "We will close the Silk Room and attend the trial. If they allow character witnesses, I shall be the first to volunteer."

Laurel raised her chin. "And I shall be second."

Quincy

Quincy slid the bundle holding his new suit under the bench in the maintenance shack. Mam'd folded it just right and then wrapped it real careful with brown paper and tied it with string. It'd keep nice until he could put it on come lunchtime for his visit to Willie's supervisor. Trick now would be staying clean until then.

Pride puffed his chest as he recalled how his brothers and sisters had all oohed and aahed over him when he tried on the suit last night. Pap'd got watery eyed, and Mam'd told him he looked smart as a lawyer. He'd knowed that suit would make him different. When he talked to Mr. Felton about Willie being innocent, that man'd

511

surely listen 'cause he couldn't help but listen to a man dressed as fine as a lawyer.

Cass came in and headed for the corner where they kept their tools. "Mornin', Quincy. It's fixin' to be a sunshiny day. Clouds're rollin' off, an' I hear tell they finally got the fountain workin'. Exposition 'fficials gon' make it shoot up watuh at noontime. Ain't that gon' be a sight to behold?"

Quincy perked up. "Noontime, you say?"

"Uh-huh. Straight-up twelve. I heared it said to Mistuh Johnson with my own ears yestuhday aftuhnoon." He tapped his temple. "Held them words in my mind so's I could remembuh to watch the fountain today. Don't wanna miss seein' it."

Quincy didn't want to miss it, either. They'd been messing with that fountain since the very first day of the exposition. Likely every person on the grounds would gather around the lake to watch the show. A slow smile pulled at his cheeks. He'd give 'em more'n a fountain to gawk at.

39

Laurel

Laurel paused at the top of the rise leading to the lake. Why were so many people gathered around? She might never find Langdon in the crowd. She needed to find him. She'd finally mustered up her courage to ask if he'd had anything to do with Officer Sharp's arrest for the disappearance of the pay envelopes, and she wanted to verbalize the question before nervousness gave way to cowardice.

Someone's hand slid across her shoulders, a very deliberate touch, and she yelped in surprise. Soft chuckles met her ear, and then warm breath stirred her hair.

"It's only me, Laurel."

She looked into Langdon's teasing face. "Why didn't you say something first? You nearly frightened me senseless."

He chuckled again, shaking his head. "I spoke your name twice. You didn't hear

513

me." He bobbed his chin toward the milling throng along the lake. "What's all this about?"

"They's gon' start the fountain. Folks is wantin' to see it spout."

Laurel turned toward the voice and found a well-dressed young black man standing beside her with his hands in his trouser pockets. The pose pushed back the flaps of his suit jacket and exposed a vest the same color as Langdon's eyes. He seemed vaguely familiar. Recognition dawned, and at the same time Langdon blasted a laugh.

"Tate? Is that you?"

His head high, Quincy Tate angled his gaze in Langdon's direction. Pride shone in his dark eyes. "Yes, suh."

Langdon raised his eyebrows and scanned Quincy's length. "Did somebody hire you to drive their carriage? That's quite the getup."

Quincy's spine wilted. His bright countenance dimmed.

Laurel turned an astounded look on Langdon. "What an unkind thing to say."

Langdon shrugged. "I'm sorry" — he didn't sound sorry — "but I have to be honest. Anything else would mislead him into thinking he's something other than what he is."

Laurel put one fist on her hip. "And what is he?"

Langdon put on his low-lidded smile. "Come now, Miss Millard, you know as well as I what he is. One can put a fancy dress on a sow, but underneath you'll still have a sow."

Laurel gasped. She turned to Quincy, intending to compliment him on his stylish attire, but he was already stalking away, his shoulders stiff. She shifted her attention to Langdon.

He shook his head, watching after Quincy. "He'd do well to put a full-length mirror in his house so he could inspect his reflection and see the truth."

In that moment, Laurel saw the truth. She wanted to escape it. She whirled and headed for the Women's Building. The thud of footsteps came up behind her, and a hand caught her arm.

Langdon looked at her, confusion pinching his high brow. "Where are you going? We're to have a picnic."

A disbelieving laugh built in Laurel's chest and exploded. "A picnic? Is that all you can think about — having a picnic?"

His expression quickly darkened. "I don't care for your tone, Laurel."

"Nor I yours." She yanked her arm free.

515

"How could you treat Mr. Tate so rudely?"

His blue eyes — the ocean-blue eyes she'd thought so attractive — narrowed into slits. "Mr. Tate?"

"Yes. Mr. Tate." She stated the name with as much pomp as she would use if speaking of the president of the United States. "He did nothing to deserve your criticism, yet you were deliberately cruel. I cannot comprehend —"

"I cannot comprehend your defense of someone so far beneath your station." He folded his arms over his chest. "You will need to set aside your ridiculous notions before I am willing to request your hand in marriage. Your attitude will wreak havoc with the household staff, stirring them into a false sense of importance. I won't have rebellion under my own roof."

Laurel's chin quivered. He'd told her earlier that eventually a man's true character would show itself, and she saw his now in all its ugliness. Oh, how it pained her. She shook her head.

His eyebrows formed a stern V. "What does that" — he imitated her gesture — "mean?"

"I won't change how I feel."

A cheer went up from the crowd at the lake. Langdon looked over his shoulder, and

Laurel peered past him. Glistening water shot high into the air and fanned out like a peacock's tail. So very beautiful. So incongruous, given the shattered state of her heart.

Langdon pursed his lips. "It's about time they got that thing operational." He faced Laurel again. "My dear, if you don't agree to alter your attitude, I cannot speak to your mother tomorrow."

"Then don't."

Such anger blazed in his eyes that she drew back. He leaned in. "Are you telling me you would choose to throw away the opportunity to become my wife, to live in luxury, to elevate yourself to the highest status of society all because of . . . *them?*"

Dear God, please give me strength. From where had the prayer come? She hadn't taken time to pray in weeks. But the frantic, helpless utterance met God's ears, and He responded with such force that she felt as if she'd grown an inch taller.

She met Langdon's stormy gaze. "Yes. That's what I'm telling you."

In the space of one heartbeat, his entire demeanor changed. The anger melted. His tense frame relaxed. He unballed his fists and slipped one hand into his trouser pocket. With the other, he brushed her cheek with his fingertip. "Sweet Laurel, I'll give you an opportunity to rethink your hasty words. I'm sure when you've carefully considered the benefits of marriage to me, you'll have a change of heart. I will forgive you, and we can pretend this unpleasantness never occurred."

The fountain sent forth arches and fans of water. Langdon had once said they would float beneath the fountain's spray on a rowboat. Her chest ached. She blinked back tears and stared into his handsome face. "I've already had a change of heart."

He smiled and eased closer.

"I cannot marry you."

He stopped as suddenly as if a giant hand caught the back of his jacket and drew him up short. "Yes, you can. Furthermore, you will."

She tipped her head. Was he threatening her?

"I didn't spend this time wooing you only to be pushed aside. I've introduced you to my mother. She expects the announcement of an engagement. I will not disappoint her. My inheritance depends upon it."

Laurel considered his final statement. A picture took shape in her mind. She huffed out a mirthless laugh. "Are you saying you pursued me because a betrothal was required by your mother?"

He flipped his hand. "And I found you appealing. I couldn't possibly wed someone whose face I found repulsive."

"So you never really cared for me at all. You only wanted . . . someone pretty." Shame swept through her. How gullible she'd been.

"Marriage is a union, no different than a business merger. Yes, I want something from you, but you also want something from me — security for your mama, remember? How will you take care of her if you sever your ties with me?"

Her answer formed without a moment's hesitation. "The same way I always have. By trusting God for provision."

He laughed. "That's a very intrepid attitude, if not a little provincial. You realize you'll never have more than you have right now if you send me away. You've been in my home. You've seen what awaits the woman who will bear my name." He advanced again, assuming the adoring expression she now realized was only a mask. "Don't be foolish, Laurel. Think of what you're giving up."

She crossed her arms over her aching chest. "I know what I'm giving up. And I need to let it go. I've been reaching for the wrong thing. Instead of grasping for a relationship with you, I should have been holding to the One who truly cares for me." An image of the tattered fabric in the loom, caught in the frame by a single thread, filled her mind, and tears followed. She hadn't been holding to God, but He hadn't let go of her. He was clinging, as tenacious as that silken thread, and He would never let her go.

"Oh?" Langdon's derisive voice cut into her thoughts. "And who is that? Willie Sharp?"

Sadness struck her. How narrow minded Langdon was, how self-absorbed. How empty. "No, my Father God."

He gazed at her for several silent seconds, then gave a glib shrug. "Well, as with any potential merger, one must allow for last-minute jitters. I shall grant you a night to rethink your position. I'll be at the lion sculpture tomorrow as planned. If you change your mind, meet me at the sculpture. If you walk past, I'll seek a new partner."

If he had cared for her at all, he wouldn't so blithely release her. She wouldn't meet him at the sculpture. "Goodbye, Mr. Rochester."

He tipped his hat and sauntered toward the lake.

Sighing half in relief and half in remorse, she turned to the Women's Building. Out of the corner of her eye, she spotted Quincy Tate sitting on the wide rim around the large fountain's reservoir in the center of the square. His dejected pose — head low, hands flat on the concrete rim, toe grinding against the brick pavement — pierced her. Without conscious thought, she followed the sidewalk to the fountain and sat on the opposite side.

"Mr. Tate?" They faced away from each other with ten feet between them, so she spoke loudly and clearly. She wanted him to hear every word. "I'm very sorry for what Mr. Rochester said. He was wrong. Your suit is quite fetching. You look very distinguished in it."

A heavy sigh carried from the other side of the fountain. "It's real nice o' you to say so, miss, but it be best for me to accept the truth. I ain't nothin' much. An' this suit, it don't change that. My mam tried to tell me, but I's mule-headed. Hadda find it out on my own self."

Tears stung Laurel's eyes. "It sounds as if both of us were looking for something — wanting something — and neither of us got it."

"What you wantin' you didn' get?"

The genuine curiosity in his tone, as well as the safety of seemingly speaking to the air, enticed her to share her foolhardy search. "I wanted to love someone, and to be loved in return. I wanted" — she swallowed the knot of longing — "to matter to someone."

"Mmm-hmm." The huskiness in his voice told her that her words had affected him. "I reckon you ain't alone in that. Don't nobody not wanna be loved."

Laurel nodded, even though he couldn't see her. "I certainly made a fool of myself, trying to find what I was looking for in a courtship with Langdon Rochester." Embarrassment smote her, bringing a rush of heat to her face. "And what's sad is I know better. My mama taught me from the time I was a little girl to fully rely on God to meet all my needs."

A throaty chuckle sounded. "Yo' mama an' my mam, they sound a lot alike."

Laurel smiled. "Most mothers want what's best for their children. Mama told me to seek God's plan for my life." She sighed. "I'm awfully glad I realized I was running in the wrong direction before it was too late."

"How you find out?"

She twirled a strand of hair. Should she

tell him? She didn't want to remind him of Langdon's hurtful words. "Well, to be honest, Mr. Tate, you helped me see it."

"Me?" The word yelped out. "How I do that?"

She peeked over her shoulder and realized he'd turned sideways on the rim. He was staring straight at her, his wide dark eyes full of wonder. She shifted so she could face him more easily. "By being there in your fine suit. When Mr. Rochester spoke to you the way he did, it let me see his character. I don't like what I saw. I can't be courted by someone who treats another human being with such utter disregard and hatefulness. You gave me the courage to send him away."

He gawked at her for several seconds, unblinking, and then abruptly turned his back again. "Oh."

Laurel waited, but he remained facing away from her, so she resumed her previous pose. "Please forgive me if I offended you, Mr. Tate. That wasn't my intention."

"I kn-know."

Her heart caught. Had a sob broken the word?

"I ain't offended. I's . . . beholden to you."

She shifted sideways and looked at his back. "For what?"

"I was sittin' here callin' myself all kinds

o' names for spendin' money on somethin' that didn' make no diff'rence." He stood, slowly turned, and faced her. "My mam, she believes real strong that God don't waste nothin'. That all things is s'posed to work for good. But I ain't believed it 'til right now."

He gripped his lapels and struck a dignified pose. "If God c'n use me buyin' a suit I plumb didn' need so's you could be saved from a heap o' heartache, then I didn' waste that money after all."

A sheen of tears blurred his image, but she heard pride in his voice. She nodded. "It wasn't wasted. I'm beholden to you, Mr. Tate."

"An' somethin' else . . ." His hands slipped to his pockets. He lowered his head, hunched his shoulders, and dug one boot toe against the sidewalk. "Reckon you know you matter a whole bunch to God, but there's a fella — a real fine one — who looks favorable on you. Has for a long time." He peeked at her out of the corners of his eyes. "Maybe since you tol' Rochester to skedaddle, you might consider lookin' back."

40

Willie

The morning of his trial, Willie used the razor and soap from the box Mr. Rochester sent and stripped every whisker from his cheeks and chin. Then he changed into the suit his boss had given him. He smoothed his freshly washed hands down the lapels, and a shiver rattled his frame. The good kind of shiver. The tiny cracked mirror above the washbasin couldn't reflect his whole person, but if the suit looked as good as it felt, he ought to impress the judge.

When his lawyer, David Scott, had come in last Friday, he'd told Willie to be ready to move out of this cell when the trial was over. Willie hoped the man meant he'd get to go home instead of to the penitentiary. Either way, he needed to pack up his stuff, so he folded the security guard uniform he'd been wearing the day he got arrested and put it in the bottom of the crate. All the things Mr. Rochester sent over went in next and then, very last, the new Bible.

He owed a big thank-you to Mr. Rochester for the Bible. Reading it, especially passages from psalms written by King David, who'd been wrongfully accused and was running for his life, comforted him. He'd probably done more reading in the past week than in all the years before. He sure hadn't liked the reason he had so much time to read, but he liked knowing how God had protected King David. God would protect him, too. He held on to hope.

Preacher Hines had come in two different times, talked to him and prayed with him. It'd shamed him something awful for his preacher to see him behind these bars, but he'd needed those visits. Preacher Hines promised to be in the courtroom today. Mr. Rochester would be there, too. Having them on his side made it a lot easier to face the judge and jury.

The iron door clanged open, and a guard tromped all the way to Willie's cell. He jammed a skeleton key in the lock and turned it. That click was one sound Willie hoped he'd never have to hear again. Willie picked up the box and took a step toward the door.

"Leave that here."

Willie lowered the box to the bed, and his gaze landed on the Bible. He held it up. "Can I at least take this?"

The guard nodded. Willie tucked the book against his ribs and followed the guard up the dim hallway and out of the jail area. A feeling of relief hit him when the iron door closed behind him, making his head go fuzzy. He didn't want to go back in there. *Please, please, God . . .*

"This way." A second guard moved to Willie's other side, and the two of them escorted him all the way to the third floor and the courtroom. Mr. Scott was already there at the front, and a man dressed a lot like Mr. Scott was sorting papers on a second table. Some people were already sitting in what Mr. Scott had called the gallery on benches that looked like church pews — several on the far right-hand side and a few on the left. Seeing them there made everything very real. He was going on trial. Fear made his legs go trembly. Willie hugged the Bible tighter.

The guards walked him up the center aisle of the pews, and Willie glanced down the rows. Mr. Felton, a police officer, and a man Willie didn't know sat together on the left. On the right-hand side, Miss Warner and the three girls from the Silk Room sat three pews from the front. He hadn't expected them to come, but it sure lifted his spirits to see them. Preacher Hines was at the end of the pew in front of the ladies, and next to him —

Willie gasped. "Pa? An' Quincy?"

The guard on his right yanked his arm. "Hush."

Willie had to hush. His throat went so tight he could hardly breathe, let alone talk. He could hardly see, either. Tears blinded him. He blinked hard and fast and cleared his vision enough to recognize Mr. Rochester and Langdon on the first pew. The only one missing was Rusty. He tried to send them all a smile of thanks, but the guard moved in front of him and pushed him into a chair at the table with Mr. Scott.

The two guards strode to a door at the front of the room to the left of the judge's bench and stood on either side of it, their faces solemn and their hands on their sidearms. Willie gulped and hunkered low.

Mr. Scott put his arm around Willie. "Don't slouch. Sit up. Keep your head high. You've got nothing to fear because you're innocent."

Willie followed the lawyer's instructions, but he couldn't make his heart stop bouncing around in his chest. Sometimes innocent men got convicted. It had happened to Joseph, to Paul and Barnabas. It could happen to him, too. He clamped his fingers on the Bible and gripped hard.

One of the guards opened the door, and people filed in. They filled the jury box, and the last one in sat at the table between the lawyers' tables and the judge's bench. Then the guard said, "All rise. The Honorable Judge Josiah Stanwick presiding."

Everybody stood, and the noise of their shuffling seemed as loud as thunder to Willie's ears. The judge rounded the corner, his black robe flaring behind him, and stepped up behind the tall desk. He sat, and the guard said, still all solemn, "You may be seated."

The shuffles came again, just as loud, and Willie slid the Bible from the table and pressed it against his stomach. The judge called on Mr. Brownley, the lawyer from the other table, to talk first. Willie wanted to hide when the man told the jurors Willie had taken money from hardworking employees. But then Mr. Scott stood and told them Willie was a hardworking employee himself who would never steal. Willie looked at the jury members' faces. He couldn't tell which of the lawyers they believed, but he kept praying they'd believe Mr. Scott.

Then it was time for witnesses. Mr. Brownley called Mr. Felton to the witness box. The person from the table in between Willie and the judge asked Mr. Felton to put his hand on a Bible and vow to tell the truth, the whole truth, and nothing but the truth. Mr. Felton sat, and Mr. Brownley asked him to tell in his own words the events that led to Willie's arrest.

"Well, Miss Warner —"

"Who is Miss Warner?"

Mr. Felton pointed to the pews. "The one sitting there, wearing the black hat with feathers. She runs the Silk Room."

Mr. Brownley nodded. "Very well. Proceed."

"Miss Warner came into my office an' said —"

"When was this, sir?"

Mr. Felton scratched his head. "Uh . . . Tuesday, October fifteenth."

"Thank you. Continue."

Mr. Felton took a deep breath. "Miss Warner, who runs the Silk Room, came to my office on Tuesday the fifteenth an' said pay envelopes had come up missin' from her desk. There's only three people with keys to the Silk Room — me, Miss Warner, an' Officer Sharp."

"And who all knew the envelopes were in

Miss Warner's desk?"

Mr. Scott leaped to his feet. "Objection. Calls for speculation."

"Sustained," the judge said. "Rephrase, Mr. Brownley."

Mr. Brownley paced back and forth briefly, pinching his chin. Then he stopped and shook his head. "No more questions."

Judge Stanwick peered through his spectacles at Mr. Scott. "Your turn."

Mr. Scott rounded the table, adjusting his suit lapels as he went. Willie followed him with his gaze, somehow nervous sitting at the table all by himself. Mr. Scott rested his elbow on the edge of the judge's high table and smiled at Mr. Felton. "Mr. Felton, at the time of his arrest, how many days had Willie Sharp been under your supervision?"

The man rolled his eyes upward. His lips moved silently. He blurted, " 'Bout thirty in all. Mondays through Saturdays from September sixteenth to October nineteenth."

"During that time, what opinion did you form about Mr. Sharp's work ethic?"

Mr. Brownley waved his hand. "Objection. One man's opinion has little bearing on the evidence."

The judge scowled for a moment. "I'll allow it. You may answer, Mr. Felton."

Mr. Felton fidgeted on the chair. "I

thought he was a good worker. Always showed up on time, took his duties real serious. Tried real hard to figure out who made a big mess in the Silk Room. I'd say he had a good work ethic."

Mr. Scott nodded. "Thank you, Mr. Felton. You may step down."

Mr. Felton shot out of the box and past Willie's table without looking at him.

Mr. Scott returned to the table, and the judge said, "Your next witness, Mr. Brownley."

"I call Miss Felicia Hill to the stand."

Willie gulped. Was that why she'd come — to be a witness for the prosecution? Would Miss Millard and Miss Warner have to go up and talk against him, too?

Miss Hill gave the same vow as Mr. Felton, then sat. She seemed as nervous as a canary in a room full of cats. Willie understood the feeling.

"Miss Hill, on Monday, October fourteenth, were you in the presence of Willie Sharp?"

Miss Hill hunched her shoulders. "Yes, sir. In the Silk Room."

"Did you, on that day, in Mr. Sharp's presence, mention that your supervisor had not distributed pay envelopes at the end of the day?"

Her face glowed bright pink. She nodded. Willie wanted to groan. How had Mr. Brownley found out about their conversation?

Mr. Brownley headed for his desk. "No more questions."

Mr. Scott stood. "Miss Hill, when you mentioned that your supervisor had not distributed the pay envelopes, did you also mention where they were kept?"

"No, sir, 'cause I didn't know where they were kept."

Mr. Scott smiled. "Thank you, Miss Hill. No more questions."

The policeman sitting with Mr. Felton took the stand next and explained how the empty envelopes were found all crunched up in the back of Willie's cubby. Mr. Scott asked if anyone could testify they'd seen Willie with the envelopes, and the officer said not to his knowledge. He got to step down.

Willie held on to the Bible, his heart beating with hope. Things were sounding good. In his favor. Maybe Mr. Scott was right and he'd get to go home when this was done.

"Mr. Brownley, call your next witness, please," the judge said.

"I call Miss Eloise Warner."

Miss Warner swept past Willie's table and

placed her hand on the Bible. She recited the vow in a loud, clear voice, then seated herself and placed her hands in her lap. With her chin angled high, she reminded Willie of a queen on a throne.

Mr. Brownley linked his hands behind his back and approached the witness box. "Miss Warner, what capacity did Willie Sharp serve in the Silk Room?"

"He served as our security guard, and he did a very fine job."

The judge cleared his voice. "Miss Warner, please answer the questions and refrain from expounding."

Miss Warner gave him a tart look. "I swore to tell the whole truth, and that's exactly what I'll do."

The Silk Room girls tittered, and Willie bit back a smile.

The judge waved his hand. "Proceed."

Mr. Brownley unlinked his hands and slid them into his pockets. "Describe Mr. Sharp's duties."

"His first was helping me clean up the horrendous mess some troublemakers made. After that, he stood guard at the door, assuring none bent on mischief would enter the room. He kept careful watch over visitors and observed our daily happenings."

"Hmm . . ." Mr. Brownley paced a few

steps and aimed his gaze at the jury. "He was attentive to all the happenings in the room?"

"Yes." Miss Warner smiled at Willie. "He is a very diligent worker and takes his responsibilities quite seriously."

"Then he would have most likely noticed you putting the pay envelopes into the desk drawer."

Miss Warner quivered, the feathers on her cap fluttering like butterfly wings. "He most certainly did not."

"How can you be sure? You said he" — he peeked over the shoulder of the person at the desk in the middle of the courtroom — " 'observed our daily happenings.' " He faced Miss Warner. "So isn't it possible he observed where you placed the pay envelopes?"

She pulled in a breath. "It is possible, but —"

Mr. Brownley jammed his hand into the air. "No more questions."

Mr. Scott stood. "Miss Warner, please finish your sentence."

She blew out the air with a loud huff. "It is possible, but even if he did, he would not have helped himself to the envelopes. He has proven himself trustworthy through his every word and deed from the first minutes of our acquaintanceship. I do not believe that he is capable of thievery."

Mr. Brownley rose. "Objection. This is all opinion and can't be substantiated with facts."

"Oh, I believe it can, Your Honor." Mr. Scott gestured to the gallery. "I have several character witnesses ready to testify to Mr. Sharp's stellar reputation and trustworthiness."

The judge scowled into the gallery. "Who's here as a character witness?"

Mr. Rochester, Preacher Hines, and Miss Millard stood. Then Quincy bounced to his feet. He hardly looked like himself, his eyes shiny and head high, seeming so sure of himself. His suit was mighty nice, too — black with little blue dots and a vest to match.

"And you would stand behind Miss Warner's statements?"

"Yes, Your Honor," Mr. Rochester boomed, and the preacher, Quincy, and Miss Millard nodded.

Willie sniffed hard. He couldn't cry in front of all these people. Even if the jury found him guilty, he'd carry away happiness. They believed in him.

The judge drummed his fingers for a moment. He slapped the desk. "Well, then, let

Miss Warner's record stand, and for the sake of expediency, we'll allow her testimony to serve for all five character witnesses. Miss Warner, you may step down. Mr. Brownley, call your next witness."

Miss Warner returned to the pew, and Mr. Brownley stood. "This is my final witness, Your Honor. I call Mr. Benjamin Mealer."

The man Willie didn't recognize ambled to the front and promised his truthfulness. He slid into the seat and rested his elbows on his knees.

Mr. Brownley sat on the edge of his table. "Mr. Mealer, for the record, please state your occupation."

"I'm a resident aide at the Atlanta Hospital for Convalescents."

Mr. Scott leaned close to Willie. "Do you have any idea why he's here?"

Willie shrugged. "Maybe 'cause he helps my pa?"

The lawyer nodded and turned his attention to the witness.

"Were you working on the night of" — Mr. Brownley looked over his shoulder at his notes — "Saturday, October nineteenth?"

"Yes, sir."

"Did anything out of the ordinary occur that evening?"

The man chuckled and rubbed the side of his nose with his finger. "I guess you could say so."

"What was that event?"

"A fellow came in after hours an' left an envelope."

"What was in this envelope?"

"Ninety dollars."

A whisper went through the room. Willie's lawyer slid his arm across the back of Willie's chair and sat forward, tense.

Mr. Brownley folded his arms and crossed his ankles. The casual, cocky pose made the hair on the back of Willie's neck prickle. "Was there any kind of communication left with the ninety dollars?"

Mr. Mealer nodded. "Yes, sir. Right on the outside of the envelope, somebody'd written, 'For my pa, from Willie Sharp.' "

41

Laurel

Laurel sat forward and looked at Officer Sharp. His mouth hung open, making him appear as stunned as she felt. It was a mistake. It had to be a mistake.

His lawyer stood. "Objection. Hearsay."

The judge leaned toward the witness. "Young man, can you produce this envelope?"

Mr. Scott stepped to the side of his table. "Even if he can, there's no way to prove Willie Sharp wrote the note or that he sent the money."

The prosecuting attorney snorted. "Your Honor, who else would put money against an account for Mr. Sharp's father?"

The judge pointed at Officer Sharp. "Mr. Mealer, is this the person who came in and left the envelope?"

Mr. Mealer rubbed the side of his nose. "Well, sir, I don't know. The fellow who brought it in gave it to a janitor. Then the janitor gave it to me. I locked it up in the accountant's office."

"What is the janitor's name?"

"Ray Welch."

"Where would I find him?"

Mr. Mealer shrugged. "I reckon at the hospital. He works most every day."

"Thank you, Mr. Mealer. You may step down." The judge turned to the guards. "Send someone to the convalescent hospital and bring Mr. Welch here." He picked up his gavel. "Court is in recess until the witness appears." He banged the gavel on his desk and left the room.

The remaining guard escorted the jury members out, and the prosecuting attorney left with the hospital aide and the other three witnesses for the prosecution. Langdon and his father rose and filed out also.

Laurel watched them, waiting for Langdon to acknowledge her, but he strode past with his gaze straight ahead. She sighed. She and Mama had talked well past bedtime the night before President Cleveland visited the exposition, and they'd prayed together. Laurel was certain God had forgiven her for failing to seek His will, but it might be a while before she forgave herself.

Officer Sharp's attorney whispered something to him, and Office Sharp got up and stepped inside the gallery. He went straight to the slight gray-aired man sitting in front of Laurel and wrapped him in a hug. He pulled back, smiled into the man's face, then hugged him again.

The man tugged at him, and Officer Sharp slid onto the pew. The older man lifted his hand and curled it behind Officer Sharp's neck. "Wiii-eee, ah luuu you."

Tears rolled down the young man's cheeks. "I love you, too, Pa. It's sure good to see you. All of you, Quince . . ." The friends clasped hands — black and white, folded together — and smiled at each other for a long time. He swiped his face with his jacket sleeve. "Thanks for bein' here, for supportin' me."

He swept his smile across the man sitting with his pa, Miss Warner, Berta, and Felicia. When his gaze met hers, he seemed to pause for an additional second, and she took advantage of the moment to give him her biggest, brightest, most encouraging smile. He gave a quick nod in reply.

Felicia tapped his arm. "I'm sorry, Officer Sharp, about havin' to testify. That lawyer said I had to or I'd be in contempt."

Officer Sharp shrugged. "It's all right. You have to tell the truth. I don't hold that against you. An' by the way . . ." His grin turned sheepish. "Y'all should probably stop callin' me Officer Sharp. No matter how things end up here today, I likely won't have a job at the exposition anymore. So from now on, I'm just Willie."

Willie . . . A solid, simple, honest name. It seemed to float on a tune heard only in the center of her heart. Laurel nodded. It was just right.

Langdon

Langdon braced his hand on the window frame and stared out at the city. Father sat on a bench nearby, ankle on knee, bouncing his foot. For the third time, Langdon said, "Are you sure you don't want to leave? You aren't going to testify. The judge said so." If only Father would agree to go.

Father gave him the same impatient look he'd given the previous times he'd asked. "I will stay until the end. I've stood behind that young man, staunchly supported him. This latest piece of evidence presents a tiny flicker of doubt. I need to see it snuffed out."

Langdon pushed off the window and stomped to the bench. "Then may I leave? I don't really care about the outcome." He didn't dare be in the courtroom when Welch arrived.

Father pointed to the empty spot on the bench. "Sit. We'll leave together when the trial is done."

Langdon slumped onto the bench. Why had he thought his plan would make Father see Sharp — see his son — differently? For someone supposedly intelligent, he felt every bit a fool.

The courtroom door creaked open a few inches, and Sharp's minister peeked out. "The jury is coming in. The judge should be here soon."

Father grabbed Langdon's arm and they entered the courtroom. Father headed for the front pew again, but Langdon slipped into the rear one. Father sent him a frown but didn't insist he move. Everyone stood when the judge stepped into the courtroom. As soon as he sat, Langdon slid low on his pew, propped his elbow on the curved wooden back, and rested his forehead in his hand. He observed the proceedings from the corners of his eyes.

The clerk swore in the janitor from the convalescent hospital, and the man perched on the witness chair with an air of importance. The prosecuting attorney took the floor.

"Mr. Welch, I understand you were at work on the evening of October nineteenth when you had an encounter with a visitor to the hospital."

"Yup." The man nearly chirped, as cheerful as a spring robin. "I shore did, sonny."

A couple of the jury members snickered. Judge Stanwick shot them a glower. Things quieted quickly, but hope stirred in Langdon's chest. The man seemed as absent-minded as a squirrel that couldn't remember where it had buried its acorns. He probably wouldn't remember Langdon, either.

The lawyer linked his hands and rested them on the railing in front of the witness box. "Would you please tell the court what this visitor did?"

"He come in, handed me a fat envelope with some writin' on it, an' tol' me to give it over to whoever kept the books." He scratched his head, making his remaining wisps of white hair stand up. "Then he tol' me to make sure an' say he'd brung it sooner. He said" — he scratched some more — "he didn't want the one who give it to him to get upset 'cause he was late."

"Did he say who'd given it to him?"

"No, but he didn't hafta. It was writ right there on the envelope — Willie Sharp."

Mr. Scott put his hand in the air. "Objection, Judge. This is all hearsay and has little bearing on the case."

The janitor looked up at the judge. "What's 'at mean — hearsay?"

"Hearsay is information received from a secondary source that cannot be substantiated."

"Am I the seckuntdary source?"

"You are."

"An' what's sub-stanch-uh-ated?"

More titters from the jury box. The judge sighed. "*Substantiated* means 'proven.' We would need to hear from the original source to validate — er, prove — the statements are true."

The man perked up. "Well, that's easy enough, Judge. 'Cause the 'riginal source is here."

Chills attacked Langdon's scalp. He slunk lower.

The judge pointed to the defense table. "Are you referring to the young man sitting there?"

"Nuh-uh." Welch stretched up tall and looked to the back of the room. "He's sittin' there in the rear." He waved to Langdon. "Howdy." He grinned at the judge. "That's the fellow."

Every person in the room, Father included, turned and gaped at Langdon. His frame went hot, then cold, then hot again.

Everything within him screamed *Escape! Escape!* But his muscles had turned to stone. He couldn't move.

The judge dismissed the witness, then aimed his imperious finger at Langdon. "Come here, young man."

Langdon unfolded himself from the pew. He tipped his head sharply left and right, popping his neck, and then moved forward. His feet were so heavy he might have been dragging blocks of concrete. It seemed a thousand accusing eyes bored into him as he made his way to the front of the courtroom. He stopped in front of the judge's bench.

"Swear him in," the judge said.

The clerk held out a Bible, and Langdon placed his sweaty palm on the warm worn leather. "Do you swear to the tell the truth, the whole truth, and nothing but the truth, so help you God?"

Langdon swallowed. "Yes."

"Take the witness seat."

Langdon averted his gaze and sat stiffly on the wooden chair. He gripped his trembling knees.

Mr. Brownley leaned on the railing in front of the witness box. "For the record, please state your name."

"Rochester. Langdon Rochester."

"Mr. Rochester, we have heard testimony that you brought an envelope containing the amount of ninety dollars to the Atlanta Hospital for Convalescents and gave it to Mr. Welch" — Welch waved again from his seat next to Father — "with instructions to apply the money to Mr. Sharp's account. Is this correct?"

His knees hurt where his fingers dug in. He tried loosening his grip, but his fingers refused to cooperate. "Yes, sir."

"There was a message written on the envelope. Did you write the message?"

Langdon gritted his teeth. "Yes."

"Did you write the message at Willie Sharp's direction?"

Langdon closed his eyes.

"You're intelligent, Langdon. Perhaps the most intelligent person I've ever known."

If he said yes, Willie would go to jail. Father would believe he'd made a mistake in trusting the young man.

"Did you use it to benefit anyone other than yourself?"

If he said yes, he would discredit Willie in front of his pa, his supervisor, and Laurel. In front of Father.

"Mr. Rochester, did you write the message at Willie Sharp's direction?"

He opened his eyes and met Mr. Brownley's expectant gaze. "I . . . uh . . ."

"You, Langdon, could learn a great deal from Willie Sharp about what it means to be a man."

An image of Father's face at the dining room table — his disappointment, his disillusionment, his raw desire for his son to be a better man — flashed in Langdon's memory.

"You, Langdon, could learn a great deal from Willie Sharp about what it means to be a man."

Langdon knew what Willie would do. Willie would tell the truth. He gathered his courage and rasped out, "No."

The attorney stood upright. His brow furrowed. He glanced toward Willie's table and then pinned a frown on Langdon. "Was the money inside the envelope given to you by Willie Sharp?"

He shook his head. "No, sir."

"Where did you get the money?"

"From my own personal account."

Eyes wide, the lawyer gawked at him for several seconds. Then he shook his head the way a hound dislodged a burr. "Let me understand . . . You took money from your own account, placed it in an envelope, signed Willie Sharp's name to a note on the envelope, and handed it to the convalescent hospital's representative, all without Willie Sharp's knowledge?"

Langdon's hands went limp and slid from his knees. His spine went limp, too. He slumped low, completely defeated. "Yes."

Mr. Scott stood and turned a triumphant look on the judge. "Your Honor, on the basis of this new testimony, I suggest that there is insufficient evidence to find Willie Sharp guilty of stealing pay envelopes from exposition employees, and I ask that all charges be dropped."

The judge picked up his gavel. "In light of Mr. Rochester's admission, I agree. Jury, thank you for your service. You are excused." He banged the gavel. "Case dismissed."

Miss Warner, Laurel, and the other girls from the Silk Room released cries of joy. Willie's minister grabbed Willie in a hug, and then Willie darted to his father and crouched before him. The beaming smile, so full of love and pride, on the frail man's face brought a sting of tears to Langdon's eyes. The raucous celebration continued, rubbing salt in a wound.

Langdon rose wearily from the chair. He didn't want to look at his father. He didn't want to see disappointment, disillusionment. Disgust. But something inside him forced his gaze in his father's direction.

Their eyes met. Father left the gallery and slowly crossed the courtroom floor, his eyes never wavering from his son's face. Langdon stepped out of the witness box and onto the floor as Father reached him. Father stretched out his hand and placed it on Langdon's shoulder.

"Son, you set out to do wrong, but in the end you did the right thing by telling the truth. A man takes responsibility for his actions, and you did that today. I'm proud of you."

Langdon's chin quivered. Tears burned behind his nose. He clasped his Father's wrist. "Thanks, Pa."

42

Laurel

Laurel placed the last white linen napkin on the dining room table, then stepped back and admired her handiwork. Four silver candlesticks marched in a straight row down the center of the table, the candles' flames casting dots of light on the silver rims of the china plates and making the length of purple silk serving as a tablecloth shimmer. No cut flowers from a florist shop filled the vases between the candlesticks, but the dark-green sprigs with their tiny white flowers cut from Mama's Christmas box shrub added a lovely scent to the room.

She ran her finger along the rim of the closest plate, smiling. Only on special occasions — Christmas, Easter, birthdays, and anniversaries — did Mama take her wedding china from the cupboard. Allowing Laurel to use the set for this December Sunday evening told Laurel that she deemed the gathering special. It certainly was to Laurel.

Was it possible the exposition would come to a close in only another two weeks? In some ways, the months had flown, and at the same time, it seemed as though she'd lived years in the short span. She'd learned so much. About silkworms. About loyalty. About what really mattered. She slowly rounded the table, adjusting a piece of silverware at this setting, turning a glass at another.

When she was satisfied the table was as perfect as it could be, she entered the kitchen. The scents of ham, cloves, fresh-baked bread, and savory vegetables mingled together in the most heady aroma. Laurel's mouth watered. Mama was bent over in front of the open oven, reaching inside.

Laurel darted over. "Here, let me help."

Together they lifted the large roasting pan and set it on top of the stove. Mama wiped perspiration from her forehead. She surveyed the little table in the middle of the kitchen, seeming to take inventory. "That's everything. All we need now is" — a knock at the door interrupted, and Mama smiled — "the guests." She flicked her fingers at Laurel. "Go let them in. I'll bring the food to the table."

Laurel scampered through the dining room and parlor to the front door and swung it wide, a smile ready. "Welcome! Please come in."

Miss Warner entered first, followed by Berta and Felicia. Then Quincy Tate stepped over the threshold, slipping off his hat and pressing it against his blue vest. Last came Willie and his father, with the elder man holding on to his son's arm.

Laurel closed the door behind them and directed them to leave their cloaks and hats on the coat tree. She stood aside and listened to them banter with one another, vying for a hook on the rack. She couldn't stop smiling. In the past weeks she'd come to love these people — all of them — as a second family. Having them together around her dinner table was almost too good to be true.

Mama poked her head from the dining room. "Dinner is ready."

Quincy tossed his hat on the top of the tree. "Then le's eat."

Laughing, they filed past the loom and through the wide dining room doorway. Mama stood at the head of the table. She gestured to the foot. "Mr. Sharp, please take the end. Willie, I'm sure you'll want to sit next to your father. Quincy, would you like to sit across from Willie? Ladies, please choose an open chair."

Berta and Felicia took the two chairs next to Quincy. Miss Warner crossed to the chair next to Willie, but then she cast a knowing grin at Laurel and scooted over a seat, leaving the middle chair open. Her cheeks heating, Laurel scurried to the chair next to Willie. The place she'd hoped to be.

Mama looked to the opposite end of the table. "Gentlemen, would one of you like to ask the blessing?"

Quincy nodded. "I will, ma'am." They bowed their heads. "Lord, bless this food an' the hands that prepared it. Bless this comp'ny an' keep us on Yo' path. Amen."

Mama passed the platter of ham, the bowls of roasted carrots, mashed turnips, and applesauce, and the basket of bread. While they ate, conversation flowed, but Laurel contributed little. She'd had countless lunches with Willie and the others from the Silk Room and had even enjoyed a few private picnics near Clara Meer with Willie, but being in her home, at her own dinner table, with his elbow occasionally bumping hers, candles flickering, her mother and his father in attendance, lent an intimacy that left her a little flustered, a little giddy, and unexplainably tongue tied.

When they'd finished, Mama suggested everyone retire to the parlor for coffee and cookies.

Miss Warner laid her napkin on the table. "That sounds wonderful, Mrs. Millard, but please allow me to clear the table for you."

"We can help, too," Berta said.

Willie cleared his throat. "Why don't y'all go enjoy coffee an' cookies. Me an' Laurel can take care o' the dishes." He turned a shy yet hopeful look on her. "That is, if Laurel doesn't mind . . ."

Mama made a funny sound, like a giggle under water, and rose. "Thank you, Willie. I appreciate your offer. Miss Warner, Mr. Sharp, everyone, please make yourselves comfortable and I'll bring the tray to the parlor."

Quincy escorted Mr. Sharp, and the girls and Miss Warner followed them from the room. Moments later, Mama bustled through with the tray holding the coffeepot, cups, and plate of oatmeal-pecan cookies. Before Mama entered the parlor, she peeked back at Laurel and winked. Heat flared on Laurel's face, and she leaned over to blow out a candle, hoping no one noticed the blush surely staining her cheeks.

Since Willie had suggested they clear the table together, she expected him to speak to her, but he didn't. She circled the table, stacking the plates, and he followed her, gathering up the silverware. She glanced at him, and she caught him glancing at her, and although she was more aware of his presence than she'd ever been of anyone before, she didn't speak a word. Nor did he.

He trailed her to the kitchen and stood aside while she placed the stack of plates on the dry sink. She gestured to the washbasin, and he dropped the handfuls of cutlery. The heavy silverware clattered against the pan and they both jumped. A nervous giggle built in her throat. Why were they playing this cat-and-mouse game? They'd become so comfortable with each other over the past months that tiptoeing around each other in silence now seemed silly.

She turned to face him. "Willie, I —"

"Laurel," he said at the same time, and they both stopped.

The giggle escaped and he grinned. She tipped her head. "May I speak?"

He shook his head.

She offered a puzzled frown. "No?"

"No." He took a step closer. "I want you to listen. Because if I don't say what I wanna say, I might lose my nerve."

Her stomach fluttered like fingers playing

a trill. "A-all right."

His hands curled around her upper arms and slid downward until he caught her hands. He held them loosely and seemed to glue his gaze to their joined hands. "Laurel, what Quincy prayed — you know, the Lord keepin' us on His path — is what I've been prayin' for more'n a month now. An' every time I pray those words, I picture a path wide enough for two to walk side by side. I'm one o' the people walkin' on the path, an' I keep hopin' " — he raised his head and looked directly into her eyes — "that you're the other one."

The flutters lifted up into her chest, the tinkling notes creating a melody of joy.

" 'Cause I've grown to love you. But" — he glanced around the kitchen — "I can't offer you a nice house like this. I'll be goin' back to the factory once the exposition closes, an' that job doesn't pay enough for lots o' extras like fancy dresses or a fine carriage. The only thing I can give you is all my love . . . every day . . . for as long as I live." A sheen clouded his blue eyes. "If that's not enough for you, I'll understand."

The flutter of emotion whirling through her chest worked its way to her throat and emerged in a strangled sob.

His hands tightened on hers. "I'm sorry. I

know that wasn't a very good proposal. Not like you read about in books. I —"

She shook her head. Tears welled in her eyes, making his image swim, and she blinked hard so she wouldn't lose sight of his dear, honest, precious face. "What you said was better than any book. And what you offered is more than enough."

A smile quivered on his lips. "It is?"

"It is. And" — she inched closer, drawing up their joined hands beneath her chin — "I promise the same to you."

The smile became one of pure hosanna. He lifted her chin with their joined hands and leaned down. She closed her eyes in sweet anticipation, and then his warm lips met hers with a gentle pressure, a tender brush, an airy sigh, and he straightened.

He lowered their hands. "There's one other thing, though. My pa . . . He's doin' real good, gettin' stronger every day, but it'll be a while before I can leave 'im on his own. I'm all he's got, so I hafta be there for him. So even though I'd marry you tomorrow, I gotta wait. Are" — he gulped — "you willin'?"

She pressed her lips to his knuckles, then raised his hands to her cheek. "Willie, I will wait for however long it takes. Because being in your presence makes my heart sing.

You're the one God chose for me."

He wrapped his arms around her and held her close, her cheek on his shoulder, his chin on her hair. She could have remained there forever, trapped in the wonder of his embrace, but his father, her mother, and their friends were waiting.

She slipped free and captured his hand. She smiled. "Come on. Let's go tell our folks. Let them be happy for us, too."

He linked his fingers with hers, and they rounded the corner side by side while a sweet melody played through her heart.

READERS GUIDE

1. Laurel's siblings expected her to stay home and "take care of Mama." Why wasn't this a fair expectation? If you were Laurel, how would you have responded?

2. Willie lived a simple life and was content being "just" a factory worker. Should he have had higher aspirations? Why or why not? Laurel claimed that "those who strive for more and more seem to always be dissatisfied." Do you agree or disagree with her statement? Why? How can we know if we're meant to be content or to strive for more?

3. Langdon decided that if he couldn't please his father, he would live to please himself. Was this a good plan? Why or why not? How do you react to those with whom you never measure up?

4. Quincy struggled with controlling his temper. What was the true root of his anger — other people's opinions of him or his opinion of himself? What makes you think this?

5. Willie's partner told him, "Just 'cause you believe somethin' doesn't mean you have to tell everybody about it." Do you agree with Ted Dunning? Why or why not? If you were Willie, what would you have said in reply?

6. Miss Warner held a grudge against all African Americans after her fiancé was killed by a black man. Why was her reaction inappropriate? How would you have advised her?

7. Quincy's mam told him he had a choice — be a slave to God or a slave to sin. Do you agree with her? Why or why not? What does it mean to be a slave to sin? A slave to God?

8. When presented with the opportunity to tell a lie and discredit Willie, Langdon chose to tell the truth. Why do you think he changed his mind about lying? How would the story have gone differently if

Langdon had lied instead?

9. Where do you see evidence of racism in your community? What can you do to help end it?

ACKNOWLEDGMENTS

To *Mom* and *Daddy* — thank you for teaching me about Jesus's love by the way you live your lives.

To *Don, my daughters,* and *my grandkiddos* — I'm so glad you're mine.

To *Patti Jo* — every time I wrote a line of dialogue, I ran it past your voice in my head. Thank you for the guidance!

To *my Sunday school* and *Lit & Latte ladies* — your prayers avail much. Bless you!

To *Shannon, Julee, Kathy,* and *the entire team at WaterBrook* — your efforts and support are appreciated more than you know. Thank you for partnering with me.

Finally, and most importantly, to *God* — thank You for loving me in spite of my flaws and making good plans for me in spite of my failures. I don't deserve Your care and attention, but I'm so grateful You choose to give it anyway. May any praise or glory be reflected directly back to You.

ABOUT THE AUTHOR

Kim Vogel Sawyer is a highly acclaimed, best-selling author with more than one million books in print, in seven different languages. Her titles have earned numerous accolades including the ACFW Carol Award, the Inspirational Readers' Choice Award, and the Gayle Wilson Award of Excellence. Kim lives in central Kansas with her retired military husband, Don, where she continues to write gentle stories of hope. She enjoys spending time with her three daughters and grandchildren.